Christmas Kisses in the Snow

KATE HARDY

CARA COLTER

ROCHELLE ALERS

MILLS & BOON

First Published in Great Britain 2021
By Mills & Boon, an imprint of HarperCollins*Publishers* Ltd
1 London Bridge Street, London, SE1 9GF
www.harpercollins.co.uk

HarperCollins*Publishers*
1st Floor, Watermarque Building,
Ringsend Road, Dublin 4, Ireland

CHRISTMAS KISSES IN THE SNOW © 2021 Harlequin Books S.A.

A Diamond in the Snow © 2018 Pamela Brooks
Snowflakes and Silver Linings © 2013 Cara Colter
Sweet Silver Bells © 2014 Rochelle Alers

ISBN: 978-0-263-30267-7

A DIAMOND IN THE SNOW

KATE HARDY

For Jo Rendell-Dodd, with love and thanks for coming on my research trip, and Megan, with love and thanks for putting up with a recalcitrant author! Xxx

CHAPTER ONE

'VICTORIA?' FELICITY, THE textile conservation expert who was doing the annual survey of the displays at Chiverton Hall, stood awkwardly in the office doorway. 'Could I have a quick word?'

Victoria's heart sank. Felicity and her team were checking for anything that might need conservation work over the winter. The fact that she wanted a word must mean she'd found something. 'Bad news?'

'It's not *all* bad,' Felicity said brightly. 'There are a couple of rooms where you need to lower the light levels a bit more, to limit the fade damage, but those moth traps have worked brilliantly and there's no evidence of silverfish or death watch beetle—all the holes in the wood are the same as they were last time round and there's no evidence of frazz.'

Frazz, Victoria knew, were the little shavings of wood caused by beetles chomping through it. And that would've meant major structural repairs to whatever was affected, anything from a chair to floorboards to oak panelling. 'I'm glad to hear that.' Though she knew Felicity wouldn't have come to talk about something minor. 'But?'

Felicity sighed. 'I was checking the gilt on a mirror and I found mould behind it.'

'*Mould?*' Victoria looked at her in shock. 'But we keep

an eye on the humidity levels and we've installed conservation heating.' The type that switched on according to the relative humidity in a room, not the temperature. 'How can we have mould?' A nasty thought struck her. 'Oh, no. Is there a leak somewhere that's caused dampness in a wall?' Though Victoria walked through the rooms every day. Surely she should've spotted any signs of water damage?

Felicity shook her head. 'I think it probably started before you put in the heating, when the humidity wasn't quite right, and we didn't spot it at the last survey because it was behind the mirror and it's only just grown out to the edge. Unless we're doing a full clean of the wall coverings—' something that they only did every five years '—we don't take the mirrors and paintings down.'

'Sorry.' Victoria bit her lip. 'I didn't mean it to sound as if I was having a go at you.'

'I know. It's the sort of news that'd upset anyone.'

Victoria smiled, relieved that the conservation expert hadn't taken offence. 'Which room?'

'The ballroom.'

Victoria's favourite room in the house; she loved the way the silk damask wall hangings literally glowed in the light. As children, she and Lizzie had imagined Regency balls taking place there; they'd dressed up and pretended to be one of their ancestors. Well, Lizzie's ancestors, really, as Victoria was adopted; though Patrick and Diana Hamilton had never treated her as if she were anything other than their biological and much-loved daughter.

'I guess behind the mirror is the obvious place for mould to start,' Victoria said. 'We don't use the fireplaces, so there's cold, damp air in the chimney breast, and the dampness would be trapped between the wall and the mirror.'

'Exactly that,' Felicity said. 'You know, if you ever get bored running this place, I'd be more than happy to poach you as a senior member of my team.'

Victoria summoned a smile, though she felt like bawling her eyes out. Mould wasn't good in any building, but it was especially problematic when it came to heritage buildings. 'Thanks, but I'm never going to get bored here.' Though if Lizzie, the true heir to Chiverton Hall, had lived, she would've been the one taking over from their parents. Victoria probably would've ended up working in either food history or conservation but with books, rather than with textiles. 'How bad is it?'

'Bad enough that we'll need to take the hangings down to dry them out. We can't fix it in situ. Hopefully a thorough clean with the conservation vac and a soft brush will get out most of the damage, but if the material's been weakened too much we'll have to put a backing on it.'

'Worst-case?' Victoria asked.

'The silk will be too fragile to go back, and we'll need a specialist weaving company to produce a reproduction for us.'

Victoria dragged in a breath. 'The whole room?'

'Hopefully we can get away with one wall,' Felicity said.

Even one wall would be costly and time-consuming. 'I know the actual cost and time to fix it will depend on what the damage looks like on the reverse side, and the wall might need work as well,' Victoria said. 'I'm not going to hold you to an exact figure but, just so I can get a handle on this, can you give me a ballpark figure for the worst-case scenario?'

Felicity named a figure that made Victoria wince. It was way over the sum she'd allocated for maintenance in the annual budget. And she knew the insurance wouldn't cover it because mould counted as a gradually operating cause. She'd have to find the money for the restoration from somewhere. But where?

'Short of a lottery win or me marrying a millionaire—' which absolutely wasn't going to happen because, apart from the fact she didn't actually know any millionaires, she wasn't even dating anyone, and her exes had made it very clear that she wasn't desirable enough for marriage '—I'm going to have to work out how to fund this.'

'Start with heritage grants,' Felicity advised. 'You'll have a better case if you can show that whatever you're doing will help with education.'

'Like we did when we installed the conservation heating—putting up information boards for the visitors and a blog on the website giving regular updates, with photographs as well as text,' Victoria said promptly.

'And, if we pick the team carefully, we can have students learning conservation skills under our supervision,' Felicity said. 'The ballroom is a perfect example of a Regency interior, so it's important enough to merit conservation.'

Victoria lifted her chin. 'Right. I'd better face the damage.'

Felicity patted her shoulder. 'I know, love. I could've cried when I saw it, and it's not even mine.'

It wasn't really Victoria's, either. Even though her father had sorted out the entail years ago, so the house would pass to her rather than to some distant male relative, she wasn't a Hamilton by birth. Her parents loved her dearly, just as she loved them; but she was still very aware that their real daughter lay in the churchyard next door. And right now Victoria felt as if she'd let them all down. She was supposed to be taking care of her parents and the house, for Lizzie's sake, and she'd failed.

Actually seeing the damage made it feel worse.

Without the mirror over the mantelpiece to reflect light back from the windows opposite, the room seemed darker and smaller. And when Felicity turned off the over-head light and shone her UV torch on the wall, the mould growth glowed luminescent.

'The hangings from that whole wall are going to have to come down,' Felicity said. 'With polythene sheeting over it, to stop the spores spreading.'

'And everyone needs to be wearing protective equipment while they do it,' Victoria said. 'And we'll have to measure the mould spores in the air. If it's bad, then we'll have to keep visitors out of the room completely.'

Felicity patted her shoulder. 'Don't worry. We'll get this fixed so the ballroom shines again.'

Victoria was prepared to do whatever it took. Fill out endless forms, beg every institution going for a loan. Or find a millionaire and talk him into marrying her and saving the ballroom. After her ex had been so forthcoming about where she fell short, Victoria was under no il-lusions that she was attractive enough for an ordinary man, let alone a millionaire who could have his pick of women; but she knew from past experience that the house was a real draw for potential suitors. All she needed was a millionaire instead of a gold-digger to fall in love with it. Which kind of made her a gold-digger, but she'd live with that. She'd be the perfect wife, for the house's sake.

When Felicity and her team had left for the day, Victo-ria walked up and down the Long Gallery with her dog at her heels, just as countless Hamilton women had done over the centuries, not seeing the ancient oil paintings or the view over the formal knot gardens. All she could think about was what a mess she'd made. She wasn't a coward—she'd tell her parents the news today—but she wasn't going to tell them until she'd worked out a solution.

Pacing cleared her head enough for her to spend half an hour on the Internet, checking things. And finally she went to her parents' apartment.

'Hello, darling. You're late tonight. Are you eating with us? I've made chicken cacciatore—your favourite,' her mother said.

'You might not want to feed me when you hear the news,' Victoria said with a sigh. She wasn't sure she was up to eating, either. She still felt too sick. 'Felicity found a problem.'

'Bad?' Patrick Hamilton asked.

She nodded. 'Mould in the ballroom, behind the mirror. They found it when they were checking the gilt. Best-case scenario, they'll take the hangings down on that wall, dry them out, remove the mould and put backing on the weak areas of silk. Worst-case, we'll have to get reproduction hangings made for that whole wall. We won't know until the hangings come down.' She dragged in a breath. 'Hopefully we can get a heritage grant. If they turn us down because they've already allocated the funds for the year, then we'll have to raise the money ourselves. We'll have to raise a bit of it in any case.' And she had ideas about that. It'd be a lot of work, but she didn't mind.

'Firstly,' Patrick said, 'you can stop beating yourself up, darling.'

'But I should ha—' she began.

'It was behind the mirror, you said, so nobody would've known it was there until it reached the edge,' Patrick pointed out gently. 'If I'd still been running the house, the mould would still have been there.' He narrowed his eyes at her. 'You're too hard on yourself, Victoria. You're doing a brilliant job. This year has been our best ever for visitor numbers, and your mother and I are incredibly proud of you.' She could hear the worry and the warmth in her father's voice and she knew he meant what he said. But why couldn't she let herself believe it? Why couldn't she feel as if she was *enough*? 'Lizzie would be proud of you, too,' Patrick continued.

At the mention of her little sister, Victoria's throat felt thick and her eyes prickled with tears.

'It'll work out, darling,' Diana said, enveloping her in a hug. 'These things always do.'

'I've been thinking about how we can raise the money. I know we usually close from half-term so we have a chance to do the conservation work before the visitor season starts again, but maybe we could open the house at Christmas this year. Just some of the rooms,' Victoria said. 'We could trim them up for Christmas as it would've been in Regency times, and hold workshops teaching people how to make Christmas wreaths and stained-glass ornaments and old-fashioned confectionery. And we could hold a proper Regency ball, with everyone in Regency dress and supper served exactly as it would've been two hundred years ago.'

'Just like you and Lizzie used to pretend, when you were little and you'd just discovered Jane Austen.' Diana ruffled her hair. 'That's a splendid idea. But it'll be a lot of extra work, darling.'

'I don't mind.' It wasn't a job to her: she loved what she did. It was her *life*.

'We can hire in some help to support you,' Patrick said.

Victoria shook her head. 'We can't afford it, Dad. The cost of fixing the ballroom is going to be astronomical.'

'Then we can try and find a volunteer to help you,' Patrick said.

'Yes—I can ask around,' Diana added. 'There's bound

to be someone we know whose son or daughter is taking a gap year and would leap at the chance to get experience like this. We could offer bed and board here, if that would help.'

'Maybe this could be the start of a new Chiverton tradition,' Patrick said. 'The annual Christmas ball. In years to come, your grandchildren will still be talking about how you saved the ballroom.'

Grandchildren.

Victoria knew how much her parents wanted grandchildren—and she knew she was letting them down there, too.

The problem was, she'd never met the man who made her want to get married, much less have children. Her relationships had all fizzled out—mainly when she'd discovered that the men she'd dated hadn't wanted her, they'd wanted the house and the lifestyle they thought went with it. Once they'd discovered the lifestyle didn't match their dreams, she hadn't seen them for dust. And she'd been stupid enough to be fooled three times, now. Never again.

She'd fallen back on the excuse of being too busy to date, which meant her parents had taken to inviting eligible men over for dinner. Every couple of weeks they'd surprise her with someone who'd just dropped in to say hello. It drove her crazy; but how could she complain when she was so hopeless and couldn't seem to find someone for herself?

Maybe the one good thing about the ballroom restoration was that it might distract her parents from matchmaking. Just for a little while.

'A new tradition sounds lovely,' she said, and forced herself to smile.

'That's my girl,' Patrick said, and patted her on the shoulder. 'We'll find you some help. And we'll get that mould sorted. Together.'

* * *

Sam felt a twinge of guilt as he parked on the gravel outside his parents' house. He really ought to come home more often. It wasn't that far from London to Cambridge, and he was their only child. He really ought to make more of an effort.

His first inkling that something might be wrong was when he walked into the house with a large bouquet of flowers for his mother and a bottle of wine for his father, and his mother started crying.

He put everything he was carrying onto the kitchen table and hugged her. 'If I'd known you were allergic to lilies, Mum, I would've brought you chocolate instead.'

'It's not that. I love the flowers.' She sniffed.

He narrowed his eyes. 'What, then?' Please, not the unthinkable. Several of his friends had recently discovered that their parents were splitting up and were having a hard time dealing with it. But his parents' marriage was rock-solid, he was sure.

'It's your dad. He had a TIA on Wednesday night—a mini-stroke.'

'*What?*' Wednesday was three days ago. He stared at her in horror. 'Mum, why on earth didn't you call me? I would've come straight to the hospital. You know that.'

She didn't meet his eye. 'You're busy at work, sweetie.'

'Dad's more important than work, and so are you.' He blew out a breath. 'Is he still in hospital? Is he all right? And how are *you* doing?'

'He's recuperating at home, and I'm fine.'

The first bit might be true, but the second definitely wasn't. 'Mum, I hate that you went through this on your own.' On Wednesday night, he'd been out partying. Without a clue that his father was in the emergency department with a potentially life-changing illness. 'What did the doctors say?'

'That if he wants to avoid having another one, or even a full-blown stroke, he needs to take it easier. Maybe think about retiring.'

Which was Sam's cue to come back to Cambridge and take over Patrick's place as the head of the family firm of stockbrokers. Leave the fast-paced, high-octane job he loved in the buzzing, vibrant capital for a staid, quiet job in an equally staid, quiet city.

He pushed the thought aside. Of course he'd do the right thing by his family. He wasn't *that* shallow and self-ish, whatever his girlfriends liked to claim. There was a good reason why he kept all his relationships light. He'd learned the hard way that women saw him as a golden ticket to their future. Which wasn't what he wanted.

'And he needs to cut down on alcohol, stop smoking the cigars he thinks I don't know about, eat more healthily and take more exercise,' Denise added.

Sam glanced at the wine: his father's favourite. 'So this was the worst thing I could've brought him.'

'It's not your fault, love.'

'So, what—porridge rather than bacon for breakfast, no salt, and no butter on his vegetables?' Which meant his father wasn't going to be happy.

Denise nodded. 'But they've given him medication to thin his blood and stop another clot forming.' She bit her lip. 'Next time, it might be a full-blown stroke.'

Which might affect his father's speech, his mobility and his ability to think clearly. Sam's duty was very clear. 'I'll call my boss tonight and hand in my notice. I'm coming home to support you.'

'We can't ask you to do that, Sammy.'

'You're not asking. I'm offering,' he pointed out, and

hugged her again. 'Mum, I want you to promise me you'll never deal with anything like this on your own again. You call me. It doesn't matter what time of day or night. You and Dad come first.'

She blinked away tears. 'Oh, Sammy. I know you've got a busy life in London. I didn't want to bother you.'

'It bothers me a lot more that you didn't tell me,' he said grimly. 'Promise me.'

'I promise,' she said.

'Good. Put the wine in the rack, and I'll think of something else to give Dad. Where is he?'

'In the living room. He's, um, not in the best of moods.'

Sam could imagine. 'I'll get him smiling, Mum.'

Alan Weatherby was sitting in an armchair with a rug over his knees and a scowl on his face.

'Hey, Dad.' Sam patted his father's shoulder. 'On a scale of one to ten of boredom, you're at eleven, right?'

'Your mother fusses and won't let me do anything. She says I have to rest.'

But his father wasn't known for sitting still. Resting would be incredibly frustrating for him. 'Maybe we could go to the golf club and shoot a couple of holes,' Sam suggested.

Alan rolled his eyes. 'It's play, not shoot. Which just shows you're a complete rookie and you'll hack divots out of the green and embarrass me.'

Sam didn't take offence. He knew how he'd feel in his father's shoes: cooped up, miserable and at odds with the world. 'A walk, then,' he suggested. 'I could take you both to the university botanical gardens.' A place he knew his mother loved. 'And we could have a cup of tea in the café.' Though without the scones and clotted cream he knew his father would like. 'A change of scenery might help.'

'Hmm,' Alan said.

'In your shoes, I'd be bored and grumpy, too,' Sam said. 'But your health's important, Dad. You need to look after yourself, especially as you're—'

'I'm not old, before you say it,' Alan cut in. 'Sixty-three isn't old. There's plenty of life in me yet.'

'And I want it to stay that way,' Sam said. 'The medics told you to take things easier, eat well, take a bit of exercise and reduce your stress.'

'Your mother's trying to make me eat lentils. *Lentils.*' Alan looked disgusted.

Sam couldn't hide a grin. 'They're not as bad as you think.'

'Don't *you* start. I thought you'd bring me contraband.'

He had. But only because he hadn't known the situation. 'No chance. I want you about for a lot longer.'

'Is that why you're dragging your feet about settling down and having children?'

If only his father knew. But Sam hadn't told any of his family why he'd broken his engagement to Olivia, two years before. Or why he'd got engaged to her in the first place. Even now it left a nasty taste in his mouth. Nowadays he made sure his girlfriends knew that he was looking for fun and not for for ever. Olivia had broken his ability to trust, and he wasn't sure he wanted to take another risk with his heart.

'No,' he said. 'Dad, there's an easy solution to all this.'

Alan frowned. 'What?'

'Let me take over Weatherby's from you,' Sam said. 'You've more than earned some time off to play golf and have weekends away with Mum. And I've spent the last six years in the City, learning the ropes. You'll be leaving the business in safe hands.'

Alan shook his head. 'The fund you manage is high

risk. It's extreme. Half of our clients would look at your record, panic, and find themselves another stockbroker.'

'Apart from the fact that any strategy I recommended to a client would depend on the client's attitude towards risk,' Sam said dryly, 'I'm good at my job, Dad. That's why they promoted me.'

'You take risks,' Alan repeated.

'Calculated ones.'

'You're still young and reckless.'

'I'm twenty-seven,' Sam said, 'and I'm not reckless.'

'Prove it.'

Sam frowned. 'How?'

'Take an ordinary job for three months.'

'How's that going to prove anything?' Sam asked, mystified.

'It'll show me that you can connect to people in the real word. That you can see that actions have consequences.'

'Dad, I already do connect to people in the real world, and of course I know that actions have consequences,' Sam said, frowning.

'Take an ordinary job,' Alan repeated. 'Show me that you can take directions and listen to other people.'

Which had absolutely nothing to do with running a firm of stockbrokers, Sam thought.

Either he'd accidentally spoken aloud, or his doubts showed on his face, because Alan said softly, 'It's got everything to do with running the firm. It's about listening and relating to people—staff as well as clients. In London, you live in a bubble. You're insulated from your investors and everyone you mix with is like you—young, well-off and living in the fast lane.'

Most people would consider that Samuel Weatherby had made a success of his career. He'd got a job on his own merits after university rather than expecting to be a shoo-in at his father's business, he'd shown an aptitude for fund management and he'd been promoted quickly. But it sounded as if his father thought his job was worthless, and that hurt.

'Not all,' he said. 'There's Jude.' His best friend was an actor with a growing reputation on the stage, and people were talking about him in terms of being the Olivier of his generation.

'Right now,' Alan said, 'I don't think you're settled enough to work at Weatherby's. If I let you take over from me now, it'd be more stressful than running it myself.'

Sam reminded himself that his father had had a rough week—a mini-stroke that had brought him face to face with the idea of getting old or even dying, the prospect of having to change all the things he liked most about his lifestyle and feeling stuck at home when he wanted to be doing what he always did. Right now, Alan was simply lashing out at the nearest target—his son.

'Take an ordinary job for three months, and if you can do that then I'll be happy that I'm leaving the family business in safe hands,' Alan said.

Sam could tell his father to forget it and stomp off back to London in a huff. But the fear he'd seen in his mother's eyes stopped him. Alan was at risk of another mini-stroke or even a full-blown one. Sam couldn't stand by and watch his father drive himself into an early grave. 'So what sort of job do you have in mind, Dad?' he asked.

'Actually, now you mention it, there is one,' Alan said. 'Working for one of my clients. Nice chap. He owns a stately home. A building problem's cropped up in the last week or so and they need to raise some money. He was talking to me about cashing in some investments, but as the market's just dipped I think now's not a good time.'

Raising money. Sam was very, very good at turning

small funds into big ones. But he had a feeling that this particular client wouldn't be comfortable with the high-risk strategy he'd need to adopt to do that.

'The job would be voluntary,' Alan continued, 'because they can't afford to pay anyone. You'd be helping to organise the fundraising events.'

Sam couldn't help smiling.

'What's so funny?' Alan demanded.

'You wanted me to get an ordinary job. I thought you meant something in retail or a call centre. Ordinary people don't own stately homes, Dad.'

'No,' Alan said crisply, 'but their visitors and staff are ordinary and you'll be interacting with them.'

'A voluntary job.' Three months with no salary. But he'd be on garden leave; and even if that didn't work out, he'd managed his personal investments well enough that he could easily afford to take a sabbatical. Jude was coming back from a tour in rep to a three-month run in the West End and could stay at Sam's flat; it would save Jude having to find a landlady who was happy to have a theatrical lodger, and in return Sam would know that his flat was in safe hands. 'OK. I'll talk to him and see if I'll be a good fit.'

'Good.' Alan paused. 'The botanical gardens and afternoon tea, you said.'

'One scone, no cream, and no sugar in your tea,' Sam said.

Alan rolled his eyes. 'You're as bossy as your mother.'

Sam grinned. 'More like I'm as bossy as you, Dad.'

'You might have a point,' Alan allowed. 'Go and tell your mother to get ready. I'll have a word with Patrick and see if we can line up a chat for tomorrow.'

And Sam would have a quiet chat with his boss. This was time for payback. He wasn't thrilled with the idea of working in a stately home for three months, but if that was what it took to make sure his father stayed healthy and happy, he'd do it.

CHAPTER TWO

'So what do you actually know about this man who wants to come and help us, Dad?' Victoria asked.

'He's my stockbroker's son,' Patrick said.

'So is he taking a gap year? Is his degree going to be in history?'

'I don't know,' Patrick said, 'but Alan said he's very keen.'

He must be, Victoria thought, to arrange an interview for nine o'clock on a Sunday morning. 'Did you want to interview him, then, as you know his father?'

Patrick smiled and patted her shoulder. 'Absolutely not, darling. You're the one he's going to be working with. It needs to be your decision.'

'If you change your mind, we'll be in the office,' Victoria said.

It was a shame her father had been so vague about the details; he hadn't even asked for a rudimentary CV. Then again, her father came from the era of the gentleman's agreement and he didn't like paperwork. Hopefully the lad would bring his exam certificates with him and she'd be able to get an idea of his education so far and his interests, and whether he'd be the right one to help her.

Part of her thought there was something rude and arrogant about interviewing a volunteer for a job you weren't

actually paying them to do; on the other hand, if he was
hopeless, he'd be more of a hindrance than a help because
she'd have to double-check everything he did. Plus, even
though he wasn't being paid, he was getting valuable experience that might help him with applications for further
study or a job in the heritage sector.

'Come on, Humphrey,' she said to her fox-red Labrador, who was curled up on the chair where he knew he
wasn't supposed to be. 'Let's go for a walk.' It was more
to clear her head before the interview than anything else.
It felt as if she'd spent weeks wrestling with forms.

At the W-word, the Labrador sprang off the chair,
wagged his tail and followed her into the garden.

Growing up at Chiverton had been such a privilege.
Victoria loved everything about the place, from the mel-
low golden stone it was built from, through to the big sash
windows that surrounded the huge Venetian window at
the back of the house, through to the pedimented portico
at the front. She loved the gardens that sprawled around
the house and were full of daffodils and bluebells in the
spring, the way the sunrise was reflected in the lake, and
the formal knot garden at the side full of box and lavender. And most of all she loved the ballroom.

Her plans were going to require a lot of organisational
skills. But hopefully Samuel Weatherby would fall in love
with the place, too, and support her fundraising effort.

Humphrey headed straight for the lake as soon as they
were outside and was already swimming after the ducks
before she had a chance to call him back.

'I'm banishing you to the kitchen,' she said when he
finally came out of the lake and shook the water from his
coat. 'I don't want you scaring off our volunteer.' Unless
he was unsuitable—and then perhaps she could offer him

a coffee in the kitchen, and Humphrey would leap all over their volunteer and make him withdraw his offer of help.

She could imagine Lizzie's soft giggle and, 'But, Tori, that's so *naughty*!' Lizzie was one of the two people Victoria had ever allowed to shorten her name.

She shook herself. She didn't have time for sentiment right now. She needed to be businesslike and sort out her questions for her impending visitor to make sure he had the qualities she needed. Someone efficient and calm, who could use his initiative, drive a hard bargain, and not mind mucking in and getting his hands dirty. And definitely not someone clumsy.

In return, he'd get experience on his CV. She tried not to feel guilty about the lack of a salary. So many internships nowadays were unpaid. Besides, as her mother had suggested, they could offer him accommodation and meals; and Victoria could always buy him some books for his course. Textbooks cost an arm and a leg.

She changed into her business suit and had just finished dealing with an email when the landline in her office shrilled. She picked up the phone. 'Victoria Hamilton.'

'May I speak to Mr Hamilton, please? It's Samuel Weatherby. I believe he's expecting me.'

He sounded confident, which was probably a good thing. 'Actually,' she said, 'you're seeing me. I'm his daughter and I run the house.' She wasn't going to give him a hard time about asking for the wrong person. The message had probably become garbled between their fathers.

'My apologies, Ms Hamilton,' he said.

He was quick to recover, at any rate, she thought. 'I assume, as you're ringing me, you're at the gate?'

'Yes. I parked in the visitor car park. Is that OK, or do I need to move my car?'

'It's fine. I'll come and let you in,' she said.

Humphrey whined at the door as she walked past.

'You are not coming with me and jumping all over our poor student,' Victoria told him, but her tone was soft. 'I'll take you for another run later.'

The house was gorgeous, Samuel thought as he walked down the gravelled drive. The equal of any London townhouse, with those huge windows and perfect proportions. The house was clearly well cared for; there was no evidence of it being some mouldering pile with broken windows and damaged stonework, and what he could see of the gardens was neat and tidy.

He paused to read the visitor information board. So the Hamilton family had lived here for two hundred and fifty years. From the woodcut on the board, the place had barely changed in that time—at least, on the outside. Obviously running water, electricity and some form of heating had been installed.

Despite the fact that the house was in the middle of nowhere and he was used to living and working in the centre of London, a few minutes away from everything, there was something about the place that drew him. He could definitely work here for three months, if it would help keep his father happy and healthy.

All he had to do was to convince Patrick Hamilton that he was the man for the job. It would've been helpful if his father had given him a bit more information about what the job actually entailed, so he could've crafted a CV to suit. As it was, he'd have to make do with his current CV—and hope that Patrick didn't look too closely at it or panic about the hedge fund management stuff.

He glanced at his watch. Five minutes early. He could

either kick his heels out here, on the wrong side of a locked gate, or he could get this thing started.

He took his phone from his pocket. Despite this place being in the middle of nowhere, it had a decent signal, to his relief. He called the number his father had given him.

'Victoria Hamilton,' a crisp voice said.

Patrick's wife or daughter, Sam presumed. He couldn't quite gauge her age from her voice. 'May I speak to Mr Hamilton, please? It's Samuel Weatherby. I believe he's expecting me.'

'Actually,' she corrected, 'you're seeing me. I'm his daughter and I run the house.'

Something his father had definitely neglected to tell him. Alarm bells rang in Sam's head. Please don't let this be some elaborate ruse on his father's part to fix him up with someone he considered a suitable partner. Sam didn't *want* a partner. He was quite happy with his life just the way it was, thank you.

Then again, brooding over your own mortality probably meant you didn't pay as much attention to detail as usual. And Sam wanted this job. He'd give his father the benefit of the doubt. 'My apologies, Ms Hamilton.'

'I assume, as you're ringing me, you're at the gate?'

'Yes. I parked in the visitor car park. Is that OK, or do I need to move my car?'

'It's fine. I'll come and let you in,' she said.

He ended the call, and a couple of minutes later a woman came walking round the corner.

She was wearing a well-cut dark business suit and low-heeled shoes. Her dark hair was woven into a severe French pleat, and she wore the bare minimum of make-up. Sam couldn't quite sum her up: she dressed like a woman in her forties, but her skin was unlined enough for her to be around his own age.

'Sorry to keep you waiting, Mr Weatherby.' She tapped a code into the keypad, opened the gate and held out her hand to shake his.

Formal, too. OK. He'd let himself be guided by her.

Her handshake was completely businesslike, firm enough to warn him that she wasn't a pushover and yet she wasn't trying to prove that she was physically as strong as a man.

'Welcome to Chiverton Hall, Mr Weatherby.'

'Sam,' he said. Though he noticed that she didn't ask him to call her by her own first name.

'I'm afraid my father hasn't told me much about you, other than that you're interested in a voluntary job here for the next three months—so I assume that either you're a mature student, or you're changing career and you're looking for some experience to help with that.'

She thought he was a student? Then again, he'd been expecting to deal with her father. There had definitely been some crossed wires. 'I'm changing career,' he said. Which was true: just not the whole truth.

'Did you bring your CV with you?'

'No.' Which had been stupid of him. 'But I can access it on my phone and email it over to you.'

'Thank you. That would be useful.' Her smile was kind, and made it clear she thought he wasn't up to the job.

This was ridiculous. Why should he have to prove himself to a woman he'd never met before, for a temporary *and* voluntary post?

Though, according to his father, they needed help. Having someone clueless who'd need to take up lots of her time for training was the last thing she needed. In her shoes, he'd be the same—wanting someone capable.

'Let me show you round the house,' she said, 'and you

can tell me what you want to get out of a three-month placement.'

Proof for his father that he could take direction and deal with ordinary people. If he told her that, she'd run a mile. And he needed to get this job, so he could stay here to keep an eye on his parents. 'Experience,' he said instead.

'Of conservation work or management?'

'Possibly both.' He felt ridiculously underprepared. He'd expected a casual chat with a friend of his father's, and an immediate offer to start work there the next week. What an arrogant idiot he was. Maybe his father had a point. To give himself thinking time, he asked, 'What does the job actually entail?'

She blew out a breath. 'Background: we do an annual survey to check on the condition of our textiles and see what work we need to do over the winter.'

He assumed this was standard practice in the heritage sector.

'My surveyor found mould in the silk hangings in the ballroom. It's going to cost a lot to fix, so we're applying for heritage grants and we're also running some fundraising events.'

'So where do I come in?' he asked.

'That depends on your skill set.'

Good answer. Victoria Hamilton was definitely one of the sharper tools in the box.

'If you're good at website design, I need to update our website with information about the ballroom restoration and its progress. If you're good at figures, then budgeting and cost control would be a help. If you've managed events, then I'd want you to help to set up the programme and run them.'

Help to, he noticed. She clearly had no intention of giving up control. 'Who fills the gaps?' he asked.

'Me.'

'That's quite a wide range of skills.'

She shrugged. 'I started helping with the house as soon as I was old enough. And Dad's gradually been passing his responsibilities to me. I've been in charge of running the house for two years. You have to be adaptable so you can meet any challenge life throws up. In the heritage sector, every day is different.'

Her father believed in her, whereas his didn't trust him. Part of him envied her. But that wasn't why he was here.

'I'll give you the short version of the house tour,' she said.

Stately homes had never really been Sam's thing. He remembered being taken to them when he was young, but he'd been bored and restless until it was time to run around in the parkland or, even better, a children's play area. But he needed to look enthusiastic right now, if he was to stand any chance of getting this job. 'I'd love to see around,' he fibbed.

She led him round to the front. 'The entrance hall is the first room people would see when they visited, so it needed to look impressive.'

Hence the chandelier, the stunning black and white marble floor, the artwork and the huge curving double staircase. He could imagine women walking down the staircase, with the trains of their dresses sweeping down behind them; and he made a mental note to ask Victoria whether any of her events involved people in period dress—because that *was* something he could help with, through Jude.

There were plenty of portraits on the walls; he assumed most of them were of Hamilton ancestors.

'Once they'd been impressed by the entrance hall—and obviously they'd focus on the plasterwork on the ceiling, not the chandelier—visitors would go up the staircase and into the salon,' she said.

Again, the room was lavishly decorated, with rich carpets and gilt-framed paintings.

'If you were close to the family, you'd go into the withdrawing room,' she said.

Another sumptuous room.

'Closer still, and you'd be invited to the bedroom.'

He couldn't help raising his eyebrows at her.

She didn't even crack a smile, just earnestly explained to him, 'They didn't just dress and sleep here. A lot of business was conducted in the private rooms.'

'Uh-huh.' It was all about money, not sex, then.

'And if you were really, really close, you'd be invited into the closet. This one was remodelled as a dressing room in the mid-eighteen-hundreds, but originally it was the closet.' She indicated a small, plain room.

He managed to stop himself making a witty remark about closets. Mainly because he didn't think she'd find it funny. Victoria Hamilton was the most serious and earnest woman he'd ever met. 'Surely the more important your guest, the posher the room you'd use?'

'No. The public rooms meant everyone could hear what you were talking about. Nowadays it'd be the equivalent of, say, video-calling your bank manager about your overdraft on speakerphone in the middle of a crowded coffee shop. The more privacy you wanted, the smaller the room and the smaller the number of people who could overhear you and gossip. Even the servants couldn't overhear things in the closet.'

'Got you. So that's where you'd plot your business deals?'

'Or revolutions, or marriage-brokering.'

He followed her back to the salon.

'Then we have the Long Gallery—it runs the whole length of the house. When it was too cold and wet to walk in the gardens, they'd walk here. Mainly just promenading up and down, looking at the pictures or through the windows at the garden. It's a good place to think.'

She flushed slightly then, and Sam realised she'd accidentally told him something personal. When Victoria Hamilton needed to think, she paced. Here.

'Next door, in the ballroom, they'd hold musical soirées. Sometimes it was a piano recital, sometimes there would be singing, and sometimes they'd have a string quartet for a ball.'

'The room where you have the mould problem,' he remembered. Was she blinking away tears? Crying over a *room*?

'We've tested the air and it's safe for visitors—you don't need a mask or anything,' she said.

He wasn't going to pretend he knew much about mould, other than the black stuff that had crept across the ceiling of his friends' houses during his student days. So he simply followed her through.

'Oh.' It wasn't quite what he'd expected. The walls, curtains and upholstery were all cream and duck-egg-blue; there was a thick rug in the centre of the room, a grand piano, and chairs and chaises-longue laid out along the walls. There were mirrors on all the walls, reflecting the light from the windows and the chandelier.

'It's not a huge ballroom,' she said. 'Big enough for about fifty, and they'd have supper downstairs in the dining room or they'd lay out a standing supper in the Long Gallery.'

'Is it ever used as a ballroom now?' he asked, intrigued.

'Not for years, but I'm planning to use it as part of the fundraising. It'll be a Christmas ball, with everyone wearing Regency dress, and dinner will be a proper Regency ball supper.'

Her dark eyes were bright, and it was the first time Sam had seen her really animated. It shocked him to realise how gorgeous she was, when she wasn't being earnest. When she was talking about something she really loved, she *glowed*.

'That all sounds fun.'

'We'll attract fans of Austen and the Regency,' she said. 'And that'll be the theme for the week. Craft workshops and decking the house out for Christmas, so visitors can feel part of the past.'

Feel part of the past. Now Sam understood her. This was clearly her favourite room in the house, and she must be devastated by the fact that this was the room with the problem. Now he could see why she'd blinked away tears.

'Forgive me for being dense, but I can't see any signs of mould,' he said. 'Isn't it usually black and on the ceiling?'

'This is white and it's behind the mirror that usually goes over the mantelpiece, but it's just come to the edge. You can see it under ultraviolet light.' She sighed. 'We'll have to take the hangings down to dry them out and then make sure we get all the spores.'

He walked over to the mantelpiece and put his fingers to the wall, and she winced visibly.

'Don't touch because of the mould?' he asked.

'Don't touch because of the oils on your fingertips, which will damage the silk,' she corrected.

'So this isn't wallpaper?'

'It's silk,' she said, 'though it's hung as wallpaper.'

'Pasted to the wall?'

'Hung on wooden battens,' she said. 'I'm guessing you haven't covered the care of textiles or paper on your course, then.'

He was going to have to come clean about this—at least partially. 'Now you've shown me round, why don't we talk about the job?' he asked.

'OK.' She led him through the house without commenting, but he could tell that she didn't take her surroundings for granted, she loved the place. It was her passion—just as he'd thought that fund management was his, but meeting Victoria had shown him that his feelings didn't even come close. Otherwise why would he feel perfectly fine about dropping everything to take over from his father?

Stockbroking wasn't his passion, either. He was doing this to make sure his father had a lot less stress in his life.

Did he even have a passion? he wondered. His best friend, Jude, lit up whenever Shakespeare was mentioned. Whereas Sam... He enjoyed the fast pace of his life, but there wasn't anything that really moved him or drove him. Since Olivia, he'd shut off from everything, lived just for the moment. He'd thought he was happy. But now he was starting to wonder. Was his father right and he was living in a useless bubble?

He shook himself and followed Victoria through a door in the panelling, and then down a narrow staircase.

'Shortcut—the former servants' corridors,' she said, and ushered him into a room that was clearly her office.

Everything was neat and tidy. Obviously she had a clear desk policy, because the only things on the gleaming wood were a laptop computer, a photograph, and a pot of pens. The walls were lined with shelves, and the box files on them were all neatly labelled.

'May I offer you some coffee?' she asked.

Right now he could kill for coffee. It might help him get his brain back into some semblance of order. 'Yes, please.'

'Are you a dog person or a cat person?' she asked.

That was a bit out of left field. Would it affect a potential job offer? 'I didn't grow up with either,' he said carefully, 'so I'd say I'm neutral. Though I'd certainly never hurt an animal.'

'OK. Wait here and I'll bring the coffee back. My dog's a bit over-friendly and he's wet—which is why he's in the kitchen,' she explained. 'How do you take your coffee?'

'Black, no sugar, thanks.'

'Two minutes,' she said. 'And perhaps you can email me your CV while I'm sorting coffee.' She took a business card from the top drawer of her desk and handed it to him. 'My email address is here.'

'Sure,' he said.

Samuel Weatherby was nothing like Victoria had been expecting. He was older, for a start—about her own age, rather than being an undergraduate or just applying for his second degree—and much more polished. Urbane. Although she wasn't one for fashion, she could tell that his suit and shoes were both expensively cut. Way outside the budget of the nerdy young student she'd thought he'd be.

So who exactly was Samuel Weatherby, and why had he come for this job?

She put the kettle on, shook grounds into the cafetière and made a fuss over Humphrey, who was still wet and muddy from the lake. While the coffee was brewing, she slipped her phone from the pocket of her jacket and checked her email. Samuel had sent over his CV—and it was nothing like what she'd expected. She was right in that he was her own age, but there was nothing even vaguely historical or PR-based on his CV. His degree was in economics and he worked as a hedge fund manager. Why would someone who worked in high finance, with a huge salary, want to take three months' work as an unpaid intern in a country house? It didn't make sense.

Frowning, she poured two mugs of coffee, added milk to her own mug, and was in the process of juggling them while trying to close the kitchen door when Humphrey burst past her.

'No, Humph—' she began, but she was much too late.

Judging by the 'oof' from her office, thirty kilograms of muddy Labrador had just landed on Samuel Weatherby's lap. Wincing, she hurried to the office and put the mugs on her desk. There were muddy paw prints all over Samuel's trousers and hair all over his jacket, and Humphrey was wagging his tail, completely unrepentant and pleased with himself for making a new friend.

'I'm so sorry,' she said. 'He's young—fifteen months—and his manners aren't quite there yet. He didn't mean any harm, and I'll pay your dry-cleaning bill.'

'It's fine.' Though Samuel made no move towards the dog. Definitely not a dog person, then, she thought. 'Thank you for the coffee.'

'Pleasure. I'm going to put this monster back in the kitchen.' She held Humphrey's collar firmly and took him back down the corridor to the kitchen. 'You are *so* bad,' she whispered. 'But you might have done me a favour—put him off working here, so I won't have to ask difficult questions.'

But, when she got back to her office, Samuel was the picture of equanimity. He wasn't on his feet, ready to make an excuse to leave; he looked perfectly comfortable in his chair.

She was going to have to ask the difficult questions, then.

'I read your CV while I made the coffee,' she said. 'And I'm confused. You're a hedge fund manager. A successful one, judging by your career history.' There had been a series of rapid promotions. 'Why on earth would you want to give up a career like that to do voluntary work?'

'A change of heart from a greedy banker?' he suggested.

Victoria wasn't quite sure whether he was teasing or telling the truth. Everyone always told her she was too serious, but she just wasn't any good at working out when people were teasing. Just as she'd proved hopeless at telling who really liked her for herself and who had their eyes on the money.

She played it safe and went for serious. 'You're not into historical stuff. You were surprised by some of the things I told you, which anyone who'd studied social history would've taken for granted; and I took you past artwork and furniture in the public rooms that would've made anyone who worked in the heritage sector quiver, stop me and ask more.'

Busted. Sam had just seen them as pretty pictures and nice furnishings.

Which meant he had nothing left to lose, because she obviously thought he wouldn't be right for the job. The truth it was. 'Do you want to know why I really want this job?' he asked.

She just looked at him, her dark eyes wary.

'OK. My dad really is your dad's stockbroker, and he talked to your dad to set up an interview for me.'

'But why? Is it some kind of weird bet among your hedge fund manager friends?'

That stung, but he knew she had a point. People in his world didn't exactly have great PR among the rest of the population, who thought they were all spoiled and overpaid and had a warped sense of humour. 'No. They're all going to think I'm insane, and so is my boss.' He sighed. 'This whole interview is confidential, yes?'

'Of course.'

'Good. Bottom line—and I need to ask you not to tell anyone this.' He paused. At her nod, he continued, 'My dad's not in the best of health right now. I offered to re-sign and take over the family business, so he can retire and relax a bit.'

'That's more logical than working here. Fund manage-ment and stockbroking have a lot in common.' Her eyes narrowed. 'Obviously he said no, or you wouldn't be here. Why do you want to be my intern?'

He might as well tell her the truth. 'Because Dad thinks I live in a bubble and doing this job for three months will prove to him that I can relate to ordinary people.'

'I'd say you're switching one bubble for another.' And, to her credit, her mouth was twitching slightly. So maybe she did have a sense of humour under all that earnest-ness and could also see the funny side of the situation. 'I've never met your dad, because my dad still handles the investment side of things here.' She looked straight at him. 'Does your dad think you can't take directions from a woman?'

'Possibly. To be fair, neither can he. I think he'll be driving my mum insane,' he said. 'Which is the other reason I want to come back to Cambridge. Dad has a low boredom threshold and I think she'll need help to get him to be sensible and follow the doctor's orders.'

'That,' she said, 'does you a lot of credit. But I'm not sure this is the right job for you, Samuel. You're way over-qualified to be my intern, and frankly your salary is a lot more than mine. Even if you earn the average salary for your job—and from your CV I'm guessing you're at the higher end—your annual salary, pre-tax, would keep this house going for six months.'

It took him seconds to do the maths. It cost that much to run an estate? Staff, maintenance, insurance, taxes... Maybe he could help there and look at her budget, see if the income streams worked hard enough. 'Take my salary out of the equation. It's not relevant. What attributes do you need in your intern?'

'I want someone who can work on their own initiative but who's not too proud to ask questions.'

'I tick both boxes,' he said.

'Someone who understands figures, which obviously you do. Someone who's good with people.'

'I'm good with people,' he said. 'I have project management skills. I know how to work to a budget and a timeframe. I admit I know next to nothing about history or conservation, but I'm a fast learner.'

'I think,' she said, 'you'd be bored. You're used to living in the middle of London, with an insanely fast-paced job. Here, life's much slower. If I gave you the job, you'd be unhappy—and that's not fair on you, or on the rest of my team.'

'If you don't give me the job, I'll be unhappy,' he countered. 'I want to be able to keep an eye on my dad. He's not going to retire until I prove myself to him. The longer it takes me to find a job where I can do that—even though, frankly, it's insulting—the longer he'll keep pushing himself too hard, and the more likely it is he'll have a full-blown stroke. This is about damage limitation. I have most of the skills you need and I can learn the rest. And I have contacts in London who can help with other things— publicity, website design, that sort of thing.'

She shook her head. 'I don't have the budget for provincial consultancy fees, let alone London ones.'

'You won't need it. I can call in favours,' he said. 'Give me the job, Ms Hamilton. Please.'

CHAPTER THREE

IN THE HALF-HOUR since they'd first met, Victoria had worked out that she and Samuel had next to nothing in common. He was all about figures and she was about words. He lived in the fast lane and she was more than happy to spend her life here in the country house where she'd grown up, curating the past.

But she needed help to raise funds, and he needed a job to make his father believe in him. As long as they could work together, giving him this job could solve a problem for both of them.

'Let's say a week's trial,' she said. 'See if we can work together.'

'Thank you,' he said.

'If you hate it here, that still gives me enough time to find another intern before things get really hectic.'

He inclined his head. 'And if you can't stand me, then you only have to put up with me for a week.'

'I wasn't going to be rude enough to say that.' But she'd thought it, and she could feel the guilty colour bursting into her cheeks.

'Lighten up. I was teasing, Vicky.'

'Victoria,' she corrected. Not that she'd offered to be on first name terms with him.

As if he'd read her mind, he asked, 'Do your staff normally call you Ms Hamilton?'

'No,' she admitted.

'But you prefer formality.'

'Nobody shortens my name. Why are you making it a problem?'

'I'm not.' He looked at her. 'I need to make friends with your dog and meet the rest of your team. At work tomorrow, would you prefer me to wear a suit or casual clothes?'

'The house is open for visitors tomorrow afternoon,' she said. 'But if you're meeting Humphrey...' She winced, seeing the mud smeared over his expensive suit.

'How about,' he said, 'I wear jeans in the morning so it doesn't matter if the dog covers me with mud, but I bring a suit for when the house is open? Or do your house stewards wear period costume?'

'You'll need training before you can be a steward. And we don't usually wear period dress. But I was thinking about it for the events on the Christmas week,' she added.

'Good idea,' he said. 'It would be an additional visitor attraction.'

She had a sudden vision of him in Regency dress and went hot all over. Samuel Wetherby could *definitely* be a visitor attraction. He looked good enough in modern dress; in Regency dress, he'd be stunning. She shook herself. 'Yes,' she said, striving to keep her voice cool and calm. 'OK. I'll see you tomorrow at nine. If you can give me your registration number, I'll make the sure the stewards know you're staff so they won't ask you to pay for parking.'

'Sure. Do you have paper and a pen?'

She took a notepad from her drawer and passed it to him. He scribbled the number down for her. 'Nine o'clock, then.'

'Nine o'clock—and welcome to the team.' She held out her hand to shake his, and when his skin touched hers it felt almost like an electric shock.

How ridiculous. She never reacted to anyone like this. And it was completely inappropriate to have the hots for her intern. Even if he was really easy on the eye—tall, with neatly cut dark hair, green eyes and a killer smile. To give herself a tiny bit of breathing space and remind herself that she was his boss for the next week, at the bare minimum, so she had to keep this professional, she took a copy of the house guide book from the shelf behind her and handed it to him.

'Bedtime reading?' he asked.

Bedtime. There was a hint of sultriness in his tone. Was he doing this deliberately? A twinkle in his eye made her think that he might be teasing her. And now she felt tongue-tied and stupid. 'I thought it might be useful background,' she mumbled.

'It will be.' He smiled at her. 'Thank you for giving me a chance.'

Honestly. He could have charmed his way into any job, not just this one. Part of her wondered if it was some elaborate plot between her parents and his to set them up together; but of course not. A man as gorgeous as Samuel Weatherby had probably been snapped up years ago. Not that she was going to ask if accepting this job would cause a problem with his partner. She didn't want him to think she was fishing for information. 'See you tomorrow,' she said, hating that she didn't sound anywhere near as businesslike as she should.

From hedge fund manager to intern. This next bit of his life was going to be like the ancient Chinese curse, Sam thought: *interesting.* He sent a quick text to his mother to tell her he'd got the job and was just nipping back to London to sort out a few things but would be back later that evening. Then he hooked his phone up to the hands-free system in his car and headed back to London.

His first call was to his best friend.

'Bit early for you on a Sunday, isn't it, Sammy?' Jude asked.

'I'm in Cambridge, so I had an early Saturday night,' Sam explained.

'Is everything okay?'

'I'm not sure.' Sam filled him in on the situation.

'Oh, my God. I'm so sorry. How is your dad?'

'Grumpy. Worried sick and not admitting it. And I think Mum's patience with him is going to wear thin pretty quickly.' Sam paused. 'You'd do the same, wouldn't you?'

'Give up my career and move back home to keep an eye on my parents, you mean?' Jude asked.

'I was always going to come back to Cambridge and take over the firm from Dad,' Sam reminded him. 'It's just happening a bit sooner than I expected.'

'In your shoes, I'd do the same,' Jude said.

Which made Sam feel slightly better about his decision. 'I'm not putting the flat on the market until the spring, so I can rescue you from the dragon landladies and give you a key so you've got somewhere to stay for your West End run, if you like.'

'Are you sure?'

''Course I'm sure.'

'I can only afford to give you the going landlady rent towards the mortgage,' Jude warned.

Sam knew that theatre actors didn't have the massive salary everyone thought they did. 'That's not necessary. I'll know the flat is being looked after rather than being left empty, and that's worth more than any rent. But I'm very happy for you to dedicate your first award win to me.'

Jude laughed. 'You could be waiting a while. Thanks. I accept. And you've more than earned that dedication.'

'I'm heading to London now, to pack. Come and pick up the keys at lunchtime.'

'Will do. And thanks again.' Jude paused. 'Have you told your boss?'

'Not yet. That's the next call.'

'Good luck with that.'

'It'll be fine,' Sam said, with a confidence he didn't quite feel.

'Are you *insane*?' was his boss's reaction when Sam told him he was resigning.

'No.'

'You were supposed to be visiting your parents for the weekend. And I know you haven't been headhunted, because that kind of news never stays secret for long. Why the hell are you resigning?'

'Confidentially, Nigel?' Sam asked. 'And I mean it. Not a word to anyone.'

Nigel sighed. 'All right. Tell me.'

'Dad was rushed into hospital this week. Mum didn't tell me until I got home. It was a mini-stroke and he seems OK now, but if he doesn't slow down he could have a full-blown stroke. I need to be here to keep an eye on them both.'

'Fine—then take a sabbatical until your father's well again.'

'I can't do that. It's permanent. I'm not coming back,' Sam said. 'If I'd been headhunted, I'd be on three months of garden leave with immediate effect, according to my contract.' Which gave him the three months in which he needed to convince his father that he wasn't reckless.

Then it hit him. Of course, his father would know about the clause giving three months' garden leave; that was obviously why Alan had specified three months working in an 'ordinary' job.

'You haven't been headhunted,' Nigel pointed out.

'But I'm going to take over the family business from Dad,' Sam said, 'so that counts as working in the same area and it's the same thing. I'm pretty sure HR will have me locked out of the computer system at work as soon as you tell them.'

'What do you want—a pay rise or more responsibility?' Nigel asked.

'Neither. This isn't a ruse to get more money or a promotion. I really do want to keep an eye on my parents.' The way both of them seemed to have aged twenty years overnight had shocked Sam. As their only child, he knew it was his responsibility to look after them—and, more than that, he *wanted* to take care of them. They'd always supported him. Now it was his turn to be supportive.

'You're serious, aren't you?' Nigel asked.

'Completely.' Sam knew that people in his world had a reputation for being shallow, but any decent person would do what he was doing. Wouldn't they?

Nigel coughed. 'Well, if things change, you'll always be welcomed back. And I hope everything goes all right with your dad.'

'Thanks. Do you need me to do any paperwork?'

'I'll sort it out with HR. Email me the address where you're staying so I can get the paper copies to you.'

'I will do. And thanks, Nigel. I know I'm dropping you in it and I appreciate it.'

'I guess at least you're not going to a competitor. And, as you said, you'd be on garden leave anyway.'

'If whoever takes over from me needs any advice or information, I'll be available,' Sam said.

'That's fair. All right. Well, good luck.'

'Thanks, Nigel.'

All bridges fully burned, Sam thought. He'd agreed a week's trial with Victoria; now he'd officially resigned, he needed to make sure the trial worked out so she let him stay on at Chiverton until his dad was ready for him to take over.

He stopped off at a supermarket to buy a box of nice biscuits and some fruit as a welcome for his new colleagues. Then he browsed in the pet section and bought a squeaky toy, tennis balls, and a bag of dog treats.

Back at his flat, he packed a suitcase and his laptop. The rest of the contents, once Jude had finished his West End run and was back in rep, could either go with the flat or to charity. Funny how little sentiment Sam had for his belongings. Then again, he really only used his flat as a place to sleep. He didn't have the same connection to the building that Victoria Hamilton had to Chiverton Hall.

When Jude arrived to collect the key, he insisted on taking Sam for lunch. And then Sam drove back to Cambridge. To his new life. And hopefully he could help keep his father in good health.

The next morning, at exactly five minutes to nine, the phone on Victoria's desk shrilled.

'Victoria Hamilton.'

'Samuel Weatherby, reporting for duty, ma'am.'

'I'll come and let you in,' she said. Humphrey trotted along beside her to the gate, his nose just ahead of her knee; she'd given up trying to make him walk to heel. 'I want you on your best behaviour,' she warned. 'If Samuel's a good intern, I want to keep him until after the ball.'

Humphrey gave her a look as if to say, 'And if he's not?'

'If he's not, you can run off with all his things and make him chase you right to the end of the park—and then do some judicious chewing,' Victoria said.

And oh, Samuel *would* have to look good in jeans. Faded jeans that fitted him perfectly, teamed with a mustard-coloured sweater she suspected might be cashmere and brown suede boots. His coat was expensively cut, and he was carrying a battered leather satchel and a carrier bag from a high-end supermarket.

'I left my suit and shoes in the car,' he said with a smile.

'I can sort out a locker for you, if you like,' she said.

'It's fine.' He eyed the Labrador. 'Right. First off, dog, you and I need to make friends.'

'His name is Humphrey,' she supplied.

'As in Bogart?'

She nodded. 'When he was a tiny pup, he looked like Bogart, all droopy jowls.'

'Humphrey, I come bearing gifts,' Samuel said. 'May I?' He produced a tennis ball from the carrier bag. 'Sit, and I'll throw it for you.'

'Better go further back in the grounds before you throw it for him,' Victoria said. 'The garden team has enough to do without Humphrey running across the flower beds and squishing the new plants.'

'Oh.' Samuel gave her a sheepish grin, and it made her tingle all over. 'I didn't think of that.' He glanced in the bag. 'What about a squeaky toy?'

She wrinkled her nose. 'That's really kind of you, but it'll take him less than three minutes to unpick all the stitching, unstuff it, and get the squeaker out. Then he'll shred what's left and spread it over three rooms.'

He grimaced. 'You can tell I know nothing about dogs. I bought him some treats as well, but I guess you'd better check they're suitable. Though I did buy organic ones with no preservatives or gluten.'

He'd tried so hard. Victoria's heart melted. 'Thank you. I'm sure he'll love them.' She took pity on him. 'The way to make friends with him is to ignore him and let him come to you. No sudden movements, let him sniff you, and if he rolls over onto his back it means he likes you and he's expecting a tummy rub.'

Two minutes later, Humphrey was enjoying a thorough fuss. When Samuel stopped, Humphrey gave him an indignant look and waved his paw imperiously.

Sam grinned. 'You know what he's saying, don't you? "Play it again, Sam,"' he said in his best Bogart drawl.

Victoria didn't quite have the heart to correct him on the misquote. He was making such an effort. And his smile was so cute...

Not that she should be noticing how cute Samuel was. This was strictly business.

'OK. We've established you and Humphrey are going to get on.' Which was a big hurdle for her. If her dog didn't like her intern, it would make things really difficult. 'Just don't leave your lunchtime sandwich within his reach and unguarded, because Labradors are horribly greedy,' she warned. 'Coffee?'

'Yes, please. So what's the agenda for this morning?'

'I want to finalise what we're doing for Christmas week, then do a project plan for each event, costings and an overall critical path analysis.'

He looked at her as if she'd just grown two heads.

'What?' she asked.

'I wasn't expect—' He stopped himself.

'You weren't expecting me to be in the slightest bit businesslike?'

He winced. 'To be fair, when you showed me round

yesterday it was clear how much you love this place. And in my experience that kind of feeling tends to blind people to financial practicalities.'

'Sadly, you can't run a house like this on love. You have to learn to juggle things—and you need to keep an eye on costs, without making the sort of false economies that'll cause you problems in the future.'

'Noted,' he said. 'So, your timeline. Do you already have a list of events?'

'Yes and no. I brainstormed a few things with my parents.'

'It might,' he said, 'be worth brainstorming with a complete outsider. Someone who doesn't know the limitations and might come up with something totally impractical that will spark off a more practical idea.'

'Is that your way of telling me you want to brainstorm with me?'

He smiled. 'Why don't I make the coffee? By the way, I brought a box of biscuits and some fruit to say hello to the rest of the team. And I picked up some biscotti this morning from the bakery round the corner from my parents, as it's my first day working here and I need to make a good impression on the boss.'

She wasn't sure whether he was teasing her or not. 'Thank you,' she said warily.

'It's an intern's duty to make coffee, so point me in the direction of the kitchen and I'll make it. Milk and sugar?'

'Just a splash of milk, please.' She showed him the kitchen and where everything was kept, then headed back to her office with Humphrey by her side.

Samuel came back with coffee and a plate of biscotti and retrieved the dog treats from his satchel. 'Are these OK?' he asked, handing her the packet.

'They're his favourites. He'll be your friend for life.'

She looked at the dog, who was wagging his tail hopefully. 'Humphrey, sit.'

Humphrey sat.

'Paw,' she said.

Humphrey lifted one paw and gave Samuel a soulful look.

'Do I throw it to him?' Samuel asked.

'Yes, or you can leave it in your hand and he'll take it—though he might need reminding to be gentle.'

'I'm not scared of dogs. I know I sound stupid, asking, but none of my friends had dogs when I was growing up so I don't actually know how to act around them.'

The fact that he was admitting where he didn't have experience boded well for him working here and it reassured her. 'Would you say that to your dad?' she asked.

'If he asked me.'

She frowned. 'Then why does your dad think you're reckless?'

'Because my particular fund deals in high-risk investments.' He looked at her, his green eyes wide with sincerity. 'Which I wouldn't recommend to a client who wants a low-risk investment.' He shrugged. 'But I guess Dad's view of me might be a bit biased.'

'What did you do?' she asked, expecting him to say that he'd had a few speeding fines.

'I applied only to one university,' he said. 'Dad thought I was being stupid, not having a backup. But I didn't need a plan B because I knew I'd get my grades.'

She wasn't sure if she found his confidence more scary or sexy.

'And there's my car. Dad would prefer me to have a big four-by-four or a saloon car. Probably a grey one.'

'Don't tell me—yours is a red two-seater, low-slung and fast?'

'And convertible,' he said. 'And, yes, before you ask, I've had two speeding fines. But the last one was three years ago and it wasn't in this car. I've learned from my mistakes.'

Clever, capable, and charming. And the tiniest bit of a rogue, she thought. Women must fall for Samuel Weatherby in droves. She'd better make sure she wasn't one of them. Apart from the fact that her judgement in men was hopeless, she didn't have the time or the emotional space for it. She needed to concentrate on raising money for the ballroom restoration.

'Right. Brainstorm,' she said brusquely. 'We normally close the house to visitors from the middle of October through to February half-term, so we can clean properly and do any restoration work. But this year I want to open the house for the whole week before Christmas, maybe just the main rooms, and deck it out as it would've been in Regency times. I want to hold workshops for Christmas crafts, a dance class before the ball, and then a Regency costumed ball on the Saturday night with the kind of supper that would've been served during the Regency period.'

'Don't forget Santa for the little ones,' Samuel said.

She shook her head. 'If you mean Santa with his red suit and beard and ho-ho-ho, that's an American tradition and it didn't appear in England until the eighteen-fifties—which is way later than the Regency.'

'But if you're trying to attract family visitors, you know that the children will expect to see Santa,' he pointed out.

'This is a Regency Christmas,' she said, 'to go with the Regency ballroom.'

'So no Father Christmas.' He frowned. 'But you will at least have Christmas trees?'

She winced. 'In Regency times, Christmas trees were pretty much limited to the Royal family, after Queen

Charlotte introduced her yew tree decked with almonds, raisins and candles in eighteen hundred. They didn't become popular among ordinary people until after a magazine drawing of Victoria and Albert's tree in 1848.'

'No Father Christmas and no Christmas trees. It doesn't sound like much fun. What did they actually do to decorate the house in Regency times, then?' he asked.

'Greenery and garlands.'

'Dull,' Samuel said. 'People will look at it and see what they're missing from today—proper Christmas trees and Santa.'

'Which are anachronistic,' she protested.

'Who cares?'

'I do, actually.' She frowned at him. 'Attention to detail is important.'

'OK, I get that you're a history fiend, but normal people don't really care if you're a few years out on a tradition,' he said. 'Isn't Christmas meant to be about fun?'

'Ye-es,' she said warily.

'Then ignore the fact that they're a few years out and use Santa and the Christmas trees,' he said. 'You already have things in the house that are modern—electric light and running water, for starters. You don't light the house with candles any more, do you?'

'Only because the insurance company would have a hissy fit.'

'Well, then. What's the problem with having modern Christmas traditions as well?'

Because then it wouldn't be a Regency Christmas.

Her dismay must have shown in her face, because he said, 'Lighten up a bit, Vicky.'

'My name is Victoria.'

He raised an eyebrow. '"Plain Victoria, and bonny Vic, and sometimes Tori the curst..."'

It was so out of left field that she wasn't sure she was hearing him correctly. Was he quoting Petruchio's speech at her, but substituting every variety of her own name instead of Kate?

He continued, '"Queen of Plum Hall, my super-dainty Vicky…"'

He *was*. Her eyes narrowed. 'Are you calling me a shrew?'

'Just trying a few different names,' he said, though his expression said that he knew perfectly well what he was doing.

'*Shrew* was one of my A-level texts. You didn't do English A level—' according to his CV, she remembered, he'd studied maths, further maths, economics and law '—but you're the same age as me. Did your girlfriend take English and make you test her on quotes or something?'

'No. I tested my best friend on his lines when he was at RADA.'

She ignored the fact that his best friend was an actor. So he *had* been calling her a shrew. 'I'm not difficult.' Though there were parallels between herself and Katherine: she was the elder daughter, and Lizzie had been so beautiful. And she was unmarriageable without the house as a dowry.

'You can call me a stool, if it makes you feel better.'

He clearly understood all the nuances of the phrase. 'It doesn't. I'm trying to take things seriously.'

'Maybe too seriously,' he said.

That stung, because she knew it was true. But why couldn't he understand how important this was to her? 'It's not a game. Do you have any idea how serious mould is in heritage settings? Fabric is incredibly vulnerable to damage.'

'And it's being fixed.'

'We're taking the wall hangings down this week to dry them.' She was dreading what else they might find.

'Can't you leave them where they are and just put more heating in the room to dry it out?'

'No. If you just add heat, the mould will grow like mad and feed off the fabric. It's humidity that we need to deal with,' she explained.

'OK. I promise to take this seriously,' he said. 'But I still think you need Santa and Christmas trees. They might be anachronistically wrong, but not to have them would be commercially wrong—and this is about raising money.' He paused. 'What else?'

'In Regency times they'd have a kissing ball.'

His eyes gleamed slightly. 'Ball as in dance?'

'Ball as in greenery,' she said. 'It's made from holly, ivy, rosemary and mistletoe.'

'Hence the kissing.' The gleam intensified, making her feel hot all over.

'Hence the kissing.' And how bad was it that she found herself wondering what it would be like to kiss Samuel Weatherby? To cover how flustered she felt, she buried herself back in historical detail. 'It'd be decorated with spices, apples, oranges, ribbons and candles.'

'Spices?'

'Cinnamon sticks, most likely,' she said. 'Maybe nutmeg. And they'd keep a Yule log burning—which we obviously can't do, for insurance reasons. And there would be sprigs of holly in every jug and spread across every windowsill.'

'No tinsel, then.'

'Absolutely no tinsel. And no Christmas cards—the first ones were Victorian, they weren't in colour and they didn't really become popular until the Penny Post was introduced.'

'Victorian.' He looked thoughtful. 'Why don't you make it a Victorian Christmas week, then? It'd be easier.'

'Because Regency costume is nicer than Victorian,' she said, 'and the ballroom furnishings are Regency.'

'And you're going to get everyone to dress up in Regency costume for the ball?'

She nodded. 'I need to think about whether to do the food as standing tables—a buffet, in modern terms—or seated tables in the dining room. I think tables would be nice, and we can have them set out in the Regency way—though I'm not going quite as far as the Prince of Wales and having a stream of fish swimming down the room.'

'Fish?' He sounded mystified.

'The Prince wanted to be known as the grandest host of all time. When he became Prince Regent, he held a ball for two thousand guests; there was a table in the middle of the room, two hundred feet long, with a stream, banks lined with flowers, and real fish swimming in it. There were sixty waiters—one of them in a full suit of armour—and the banquet went on until dawn.' She spread her hands. 'And two years later he had another ball where they served more than nine hundred different dishes.'

'That,' he said, 'is showing off and disgustingly extravagant.'

'Exactly. So mine's going to be more sensible. I'll still serve it *à la française*, so all the dishes will be laid out on the table and you tell the servers what you'd like. Soup and fish for the first course, meats and vegetables and custards and jellies for the second, and then the wafers and sponge biscuits with dessert wine, fresh fruit and sweetmeats. Actually, the Victoria Hamilton who lived here in the Regency era kept a very detailed diary, and I was planning on using things from her menus.'

* * *

The woman she was named after, perhaps? Sam looked at her. When she was talking about historic food like this, she *glowed*. This was clearly her passion. And it drew him.

'Is that what you would have done if you hadn't taken over from your dad?' he asked. 'Food history?'

'That or book conservation,' she said.

He could definitely see her among rare old books, all quiet and serious.

'What's so different about historical food?' he asked.

'The taste,' she said. 'As a student, I did a seminar in food in history, and our tutor did a workshop where we made Tudor sweetmeats. We made candied roses, marchpane and these Portuguese oranges—basically filled with a kind of marmalade—and the flavours were so intense.'

'Could you run a workshop like that, as part of Christmas events?' he asked.

'It's on my list of possibles. I thought people might like to make Georgian stamped biscuits and sugar mice,' she said. 'And maybe violet and orange cachous.'

'Sounds good,' he said. 'What about outside? I know fairy lights aren't historical, but they'd mean you could open in the evenings, show people the garden as a kind of winter wonderland thing, and you could maybe have a kind of pop-up café offering mulled wine, hot chocolate, and hot snacks—say paninis and doughnuts. Oh, and definitely hot chestnuts as it's Christmas.'

'Cost it for me,' she said, 'and we'll discuss it.'

He blinked. 'Just like that?'

She shrugged. 'You're sensible. You know we're on a budget so it won't be all-singing, all-dancing and fireworks.'

'Fireworks?' He grinned. 'We *could*...'

'Cost it,' she said, rather than taking the bait and telling him they didn't have fireworks in Regency times. Or maybe they did. Not that he was going to ask her, right now.

She was clearly throwing him in at the deep end. That was fine by him. This was going to be a challenge—and he'd make sure it was also going to be fun. 'Do you have a list of approved suppliers, or can I just go wild?'

'I have a database,' she said. 'It's searchable by name, location and goods or service. And I've included ones we won't ever use again, with a note as to why.'

'Did you design the database yourself?' he asked, suddenly curious.

'Yes.' She shrugged off the achievement. 'It was a bit quicker than our old index cards.'

A woman not to underestimate, then. 'OK. Do you want me to work in here with you?'

'If you don't mind sharing my desk,' she said.

Her desk was an ancient table, easily big enough for them to share. 'That's fine.'

'I'll just move some of my stuff, to give you some room,' she said.

Given that he'd noticed her clear desk policy yesterday, she hardly had to move a thing. But she did move a photograph of herself as a teenager, standing with another teen; it looked as if the picture had been taken in the grounds here.

'Who's this?' he asked, picking it up from the mantelpiece where she'd put it and looking more closely. 'Your best friend?'

'My little sister, Lizzie,' she said.

But there didn't seem to be a more recent photograph of them in the room. They didn't look much alike, either; Lizzie was several inches taller than Victoria, with a mop of blonde curls and blue eyes rather than dark hair and dark eyes like her sister's. Yet the way they were posing together, their arms wrapped around each other and clearly laughing, made it obvious that they were close.

'So Lizzie doesn't help to run the house or the garden?' he asked. 'Or is she still a student, off somewhere working on her PhD?'

Victoria sucked in a breath. 'No. She died six months after this picture was taken. Leukaemia.'

Sam flinched. He'd had no idea. Why hadn't his father warned him? 'I'm sorry. That must've been hard for you.'

'For all of us, especially Mum and Dad. But you were sort of right. Lizzie was my best friend as well as my sister.'

And now he had an inkling why she was so serious. Losing your younger sibling would be hard at any age, but especially so in your teens. 'How old were you?' he asked.

'I was fifteen and she was thirteen. Twelve years ago, now.' She looked straight at him. 'Lizzie loved Jane Austen and the Regency. The ballroom was her favourite room, too.'

So Victoria wasn't just saving the room for the house's sake: it was in memory of her beloved little sister.

No wonder she was so serious about it.

'The restoration—and the ball—will be a nice testimonial to her, then,' he said.

She nodded. 'And it's why I can't just be frivolous and fluffy about it. It needs to be *right*.'

'I get that, now,' he said. 'Though Lizzie doesn't look the type who'd want you to be all doom and gloom.'

'No. Lizzie was one of these really sunny people who always saw the sparkle. She'd love the idea of planning a Regency ball and a historical supper, based on the diary of the Victoria Hamilton who lived here in Regency times.'

'Life's short,' he said. 'You learned that with your sis-

ter. I'm learning that with my dad. And maybe we need
to make the most of it and find the fun.'

'Gather ye rosebuds?' she asked dryly.

'Perhaps.' He looked at her. 'OK. I'll make a start on
the costings for the trees and Santa, if you can log me
into your database.'

'Thanks. Actually, I've already added you to the in-
tranet. Your password's valid for this week.' She wrote
it down for him. 'Let me know if you need any extra information.'

Even though he was busy making lists of what he
needed and companies that could quote for the work, Sam
found himself watching Victoria covertly. She absolutely
wasn't his type. The women he dated were glamorous
and high-maintenance, and they were all very clear that
he was looking for fun and not to settle down. Victoria
was reserved and didn't seem in the slightest bit bothered
that there was dog hair over her clothes, and she was definitely not the frivolous type. He had a feeling that it was
a long, long time since Victoria Hamilton had had fun.

And there was definitely something about her. Something that drew him, that intrigued him and made him
want to know more.

But he couldn't act on that attraction or on the urge to
get to know her better and teach her to lighten up. This
was only a temporary post and he was supposed to be her
intern. He needed to concentrate on that and on proving
himself to his father, he reminded himself sharply. OK,
she wasn't like Olivia—but he still couldn't let himself
get involved. For both their sakes.

CHAPTER FOUR

IT WAS WEIRD, sharing her office, Victoria thought. She was quite used to people popping in to see her or to make a fuss of Humphrey but having someone in her space all the time that morning felt odd.

She tried not to eavesdrop on Samuel's calls; she didn't want him to think she was a micromanager, and besides they both knew that he was way overqualified to be her intern. He'd spent years working in finance, so getting quotes and working out costings would be practically second nature to him. If he wanted her input, he'd ask for it.

She'd sent a note round to her team to let them know that Samuel was working with them for a week, possibly longer, to help with the ballroom fundraising. So of course everyone dropped in to her office to meet him and say hello.

Samuel charmed every single one of them, even the older and more guarded members of the team. 'I brought biscuits and fruit as a way of saying hello to everyone and I've put them in the kitchen, so please help yourself,' he said.

Watching him with everyone, Victoria had to admit that his people skills were excellent. He listened: he paid attention and he made everyone feel important.

He charmed her parents, too, when they dropped by

to say hello. Though she noticed that he didn't mention his father's health, so clearly her own father wasn't aware of the situation with his stockbroker. Maybe Samuel was worried that it would be bad for business if anyone knew about his father's mini-stroke, though she rather thought that her father would be more concerned about an old friend than panicking about the safety of his investments.

By the end of the morning, she still hadn't worked Samuel out. He was a mass of contradictions. His father thought him reckless; yet he was prepared to give up a high-profile job and a massive salary so he could come home to keep an eye on his parents. He was an only child, yet he'd empathised with the loss of her sister. His working life had been all about figures and predicting the future, yet he could quote obscure bits of Shakespeare.

He still hadn't mentioned a partner, so was he single? Was he a workaholic like herself, too busy to bother with dating? But she couldn't ask, because that would mean he could ask her personal questions, too—and she had a feeling that if she gave her stock answers he'd see right through them. She didn't want his pity. Didn't need it. She was quite happy with her life just the way it was.

All the same, she was glad when Nicola, the senior room manager in her team, offered to take him to work with the room stewards for the afternoon. Just so she could get her equilibrium back.

'See you tomorrow, boss,' Samuel said at the end of the day, after he'd helped the stewards to close up the house.

'Sure.' She smiled at him. 'Thanks for your help. And for the biscotti and Humphrey's treats.'

'Pleasure.' He raised an eyebrow. 'I'm beginning to get why this place is special.'

'Good.' If he fell in love with the house, then he'd go above and beyond to save the ballroom.

* * *

The tough day of the week was Tuesday: the day the hangings were coming down from the ballroom. Victoria was awake at stupid o'clock and walked through the ballroom, Humphrey at her side, before the sun rose. This was Lizzie's heritage, and she hadn't taken enough care of it. 'I'm sorry, Lizzie,' she whispered, feeling sick. 'I've let you down. And I've let Mum and Dad down.'

Humphrey whined and pushed his nose into her hand to comfort her.

'I'll fix it. Whatever it takes,' she said softly.

Felicity's team wore protective clothing and masks so they wouldn't breathe in the mould spores, and the ballroom was going to be out of bounds to everyone for a couple of days, to make sure there weren't mould spores in the air. On Friday morning, the room would get a thorough vacuuming—and she'd be the one to do it.

'You're going to need pictures of the hangings coming down for the website page,' Samuel said. 'Do you want me to take them for you?'

So she wouldn't have to face her favourite room being dismantled? 'Thank you,' she said, 'for being kind. But I need to face this. Humphrey, stay here, and don't chew anything,' she added to the dog.

'He'll be fine with me,' Samuel said.

The Labrador had taken a real shine to Samuel. Part of Victoria felt a bit miffed that her dog had seemed to switch his loyalties so fast; but then again it was good that Humphrey was behaving well and not chewing Samuel's laces or his car key.

'Thanks,' she said, and headed for the ballroom. Once in her protective clothing and mask, she went in to the ballroom.

Bereft of furniture, the carpet, the paintings and the

mirrors, the room looked forlorn. And the bare wall over the mantelpiece where the first strip of silk was coming down made her feel sick. It felt as if part of her childhood had been stripped away with the hangings—the part she'd loved so much with her sister. Misery flooded through her.

'OK, sweetie?' Felicity asked, patting her arm.

'Yes.' It was a big fat lie, and they both knew it.

'The good news is that you don't have a problem with the wall, so you're not going to have to get a builder in.'

Building work in heritage properties was always super-slow and super-costly, because there were so many regulations. She was glad that was one burden she didn't have to face.

'If we can't repair it well enough once it's properly dry and we've got rid of the mould, we've got the specialist weaving company on standby,' Felicity said. 'It's going to be fine.'

'Of course.' Victoria did her best to look and sound professional. And she took photographs of the wall as each strip came down, as well as photographing the silk itself, until the whole wall was bare.

When she got back down to her office, intending to make a start on the restoration project page for the website, Samuel stood up.

'You wanted an intern who uses his initiative, you said.'

She frowned. 'Yes.'

'Good. I'm taking you out to lunch,' he said.

She shook her head. 'That's kind, but I have a lot to do.' And burying herself in work had always helped in the past, when she was miserable.

'Delegate some of it to me,' he said, 'and let's get out of here. Just for an hour or so. Felicity's team has everything under control upstairs; the house isn't open this afternoon, so you can justify a lunch break.'

'I—'

'No arguments,' he said, not letting her even get the beginnings of an excuse out.

The fight went out of her. He was right. At this point, she could do with being away from here so she could get herself back under control.

'I'm driving,' he added. 'Get whatever you need. We're going out.'

There was no bossiness in his tone, just decisiveness. And a hint of sympathy. She picked up her handbag, put her phone in it, and grabbed her jacket. 'I'm guessing you're not planning on going somewhere dog-friendly?'

'No, but I'll scrounge some leftovers for Humphrey.'

'I'll go and leave him in my flat, then. Back in a tick.'

She settled the dog in his bed, then went back to the office and followed Samuel out to his car.

'Keep your coat on. It's cold, but the sun's shining. Roof down,' Samuel said.

Showing off?

But she had to admit that it was fun, driving with the cold air on her face while her feet were still warm. And he was a much more sensible driver than she'd expected.

'Lunch,' he said, parking at a country pub. 'I'm buying. No arguments.' He shepherded her inside, completely oblivious to the way every female head swivelled in his direction and then gave her a surprised look, as if wondering what someone as gorgeous as him was doing with someone as plain and ordinary as her.

Then he charmed the waitress into giving them a table near the open fire and perused the menu. 'Comfort food. Chicken Dijon with mashed potatoes and buttered kale sounds good to me. And don't tell me you don't feel like eating. Of course you don't. But this will help. Promise.'

She ordered the same as him. He didn't push her to

talk, but the food was fabulous and he was right about lunch making her feel better.

'Thank you,' she said.

He tipped his head slightly to one side. 'My pleasure. I know this ballroom thing's hard for you, but the silk's being looked after and today's going to be the worst day.'

'Unless I fail to get anything at all from the heritage fund,' she said, 'and the damage is worse than Felicity thinks it is, in which case we'll have to sell artwork. Which will break Dad's heart, because he loves every single painting in the house.'

'You've got costings for the worst-case scenario. And you're not the sort to give up. You're not going to have to sell any artwork. You'll get funding—plus there's the fundraising stuff we're working on.'

Strange how much it warmed her when he said 'we're'.

'I guess,' she said. 'I have a lot of memories of Lizzie in that room. We both loved it.'

'The memories will always be there,' he reminded her. 'And, OK, the room's going to look weird for a while, but in three months' time this will all be over and it'll look just as it always did. Plus you get to hold your costumed ball in there, just in time for Christmas.'

Without Lizzie. Every so often, something came out of left field to make Victoria miss her little sister dreadfully. This was just one of those moments. Lizzie would've loved all the dressing up and the music and the dancing. She would've enjoyed helping to choose the food, too. And Victoria would've enjoyed sharing it with her sister.

Her thoughts were clearly written over her face, because he said softly, 'Your sister will be there in spirit.'

'Yes. She will.'

Samuel made her eat pudding, too. Treacle sponge with custard. She was going to have to take Humphrey for a longer run than usual every day for the next week, to burn off all the extra calories—but Samuel was right. This helped.

'Better?' he asked when she'd finished her coffee.

She nodded. 'Thank you. Much. But I should pay for lunch. I mean, you're my intern.'

'Doesn't matter. My old salary—which I'm still being paid, by the way, as I'm officially on garden leave—is a lot more than yours. Plus this was my idea, so it's my bill.' His gaze met hers, and suddenly there was an odd feeling in the pit of her stomach.

'Tell you what—you can buy me lunch later in the week, if it makes you feel better.'

Which felt like planning a date, and it sent her into a spin. 'Won't your partner mind?' The words were out before she could stop them. How horrific. Now he'd think she was fishing—either for information about his private life, or for confirmation that this was an actual date, and she wasn't sure which one was the most embarrassing.

'No partner,' he said easily. 'And if yours minds, tell him it's a business lunch.'

Not a date.

Not that a man as stunningly beautiful as Samuel Weatherby would want to date her. He must have women falling at his feet every single day. A plain, over-serious woman like her—well, Paul had made it clear that the only reason a man would be attracted to her was Chiverton Hall.

Her tongue felt as if it was glued to the roof of her mouth. 'Uh-huh,' was about all she could manage to say.

Great. Now he'd think she had the hots for him.

Maybe she should invent a partner.

But then he might mention her 'boyfriend' to her parents, and things would get way too complicated. Better to keep it simple. 'No partner, and this is a business lunch.'

'Indeed,' he said.

And how bad was it that his smile made her knees go weak?

To her relief, he didn't push her to talk while he drove her back to Chiverton. Humphrey was thrilled to see them, and Felicity's team had left; but Felicity had left a note on Victoria's desk, together with a box file.

Found these behind the hangings. Thought you might enjoy them.

She opened the box file, glanced through the contents and exclaimed in delight. 'Look at this! We already know when the room was turned into a ballroom, because we have Victoria Hamilton's diary. But here's a dance card, and some sheet music. I wonder how they got behind the hangings?'

'No idea,' he said. 'But I'd say it's worth photographing for your restoration page.'

She nodded. 'And maybe a display case, later on.'

'What's a dance card?' he asked.

'A booklet, really, where ladies could record who they were dancing with for each dance. Before Regency times, dancing was super-formal and one couple had to go all the way down the set and back again, so it could take half an hour for just one dance. And there was a really strict hierarchy as well—but things became a bit more fluid in Regency times and the dances were shorter. People brought dance cards back from Vienna and they became really fashionable,' she explained. 'Some of them were really pretty—they looked like fans, and there might be a ribbon to attach it to your wrist.' She examined the sheet music again. 'This is in three-four time. Waltz.' She grinned. 'So our Victoria was a little bit fast, then.'

He blinked. 'Fast?'

'Not quite Lady Emma Hamilton,' she said. 'No relation, either. But the waltz was considered a bit indecorous. Even Byron wrote a poem against waltzing.' She shrugged. 'But it was super-fashionable.'

Victoria was glowing again and she'd lost that hunted look she'd had earlier, Sam thought.

He'd suggested getting away while the silk was being taken out of the house because he could see how much she hated the situation. He'd intended to be kind; but it had turned into something more than that. He'd been so aware of her—how her dark eyes had golden highlights in them when she was interested about something, and how her mouth had a perfect Cupid's bow.

Which was ridiculous.

Victoria Hamilton wasn't his type. She was way too earnest and serious. She was the sort of woman who'd expect for ever, not just for fun.

Yet she'd asked him about his partner.

Their relationship was strictly business, so if he *had* been dating someone he couldn't see how having lunch with Victoria would be a problem. And she'd looked surprised when she'd asked him. Had her question been inadvertent, then? And did that mean she was interested in him?

Though she'd neatly sidestepped his own question at first. It made him wonder why; but if he asked her then it might become an issue.

Instead, he made a fuss of the dog. 'Well, that all sounds good. Something to put in a press release, anyway.' He smiled at her. 'I'm going to talk to the garden team.' He wanted to find out their views about lighting up the grounds, what was practical and how he could organise the power supply. And also it would put enough distance between himself and Victoria so he could remind himself that she was absolutely out of bounds.

On Friday, Samuel presented Victoria with a folder. 'Costings and project outlines,' he said.

'OK. Talk me through them.'

'Christmas trees,' he said. 'We want a huge one in the courtyard and several in the house. I've got a deal with a local supplier. He gives us a very nice discount, and we allow him to mention that he's our official supplier this year in his promotional material.'

'Uh-huh.'

'Obviously we need lights, and I'm assuming you can't do traditional candles because of the fire risk. I did start researching Christmas decorations, but I thought that's more your thing so I haven't included costings or suggestions.'

'OK,' she said.

'Give me a list of what you want, and I'll sort out the sources and costings,' he said.

'I'll do that for this afternoon,' she said.

'Good. Next, staff,' he said. 'Obviously you have the house stewards, the ones with all the knowledge. But, if you want to make this real for people, you need staff in Regency dress. Tableaux. I was thinking six footmen and six maids should be enough, and they'll also be able to act as waiting staff at the ball.'

'It sounds wonderful,' she said, 'but I don't have the budget to hire actors. Even if we can talk volunteers into it, we'd still need costumes.'

'No budget needed,' he said. 'I'm calling in favours,

remember? They'll all bring their own costumes; in return, the people who make the costumes get photographs on their website and yours, with credit, and the actors can include this on their CVs and use photographs on their own social media.'

'You've talked actors into doing this for nothing?'

He nodded. 'They're all willing to learn any lines you might want, or to improvise.'

'How did you manage this?' she asked, astonished.

'It's a quid pro quo,' he said. 'They get experience of working in Regency costume, which they can use if they're auditioning for costume dramas or films. They're all people who trained with my best friend.'

She remembered him talking about his best friend learning lines from Shakespeare. 'So is your best friend well-known?'

'In theatrical circles, yes. He's going to be huge. Jude Lindsey.'

It wasn't a name she recognised, but she didn't get to the theatre in London very often nowadays. Though she was impressed by Samuel's clear loyalty towards his friend. 'OK.'

'Outside lights, I've talked to the garden team, and we've come up with a lighting plan. I can walk you through it outside, if you like. I've sourced lights we can hire at a very cheap rate for up to a fortnight, and it's the same deal as the Christmas trees—they get to mention that they're our official sponsors, and we name-check them on our website and on all publicity material.'

He had far more chutzpah than she did; it was hardly surprising that he'd done so well. She would've struggled. 'That's all great. Thank you.' She paused. 'Did you go for fireworks in the end?'

'Sadly, they're out of budget,' he said. 'But maybe you

could hold a concert in the grounds in the summer, with fireworks at the end—they'd look great reflected in the lake. And you could have pop-up food stalls.'

'It's a good thought,' she said. 'That's all really useful. And I owe you lunch and a quick chat.'

'An appraisal?' he asked.

'Something like that. Though it goes both ways. Do you like Italian food?'

'Yes.'

'Good. And I'm driving. Give me twenty minutes to assimilate this.'

'OK. I'll go and annoy the garden team,' he said. 'I'm scrounging cuttings and advice for my mum. I hope that's OK?'

'Of course,' she said with a smile.

His paperwork was impeccable. She didn't need him to walk her through the outdoor lighting scheme, because he'd mocked up photographs and marked up a copy of the visitor map. No wonder he'd been promoted so quickly as a hedge fund manager. He thought on his feet.

Once they were settled at their table in the Italian restaurant in the next village and they'd ordered lunch, she looked at him. 'First of all, your ideas are excellent. I have no idea how you sweet-talked everyone into offering you such amazing deals, but I'm very grateful. From my point of view, you've been a brilliant intern and frankly I think you're more than capable of doing *my* job, let alone the intern's.'

He inclined his head. 'Thank you.'

'I can't afford you as a consultant and I feel horrible about asking you to stay on until after the ball, without paying you anything.'

'So does that mean I don't get the job?'

'No. It means I feel guilty.'

He spread his hands. 'I knew the score when I accepted the week's trial.'

'So,' she said. 'The appraisal goes both ways. Your turn.'

'From my point of view, running events in a country house is nothing like what I do. It's like stepping into a different world. There are restrictions—which obviously there are in finance as well, but I'm surprised everything is so hidebound.'

Including the person who managed the house, who wanted everything to be as historically accurate as possible—except he was too polite to say so, she thought.

'But I'm enjoying it,' he said. 'We're talking until Christmas, right?'

'Three months' voluntary work,' she confirmed.

'I'm on three months' garden leave,' he said. 'Which means I can't take a job in any kind of financial services, including my dad's company. And I'm still being paid. So it's not as if I'm a starving student who has to rely on his parents' support. Working for you means I have a valid excuse for living with my parents and keeping an eye on them—but it also means I'm not with them twenty-four-seven, which I think would end up with all of us wanting to murder each other. And it also means I'm proving myself to my dad.'

'Carry on like this, and your reference will be glowing so much they'll see it from the space station,' she said.

'Thank you.' He smiled at her.

She had a feeling there was something more. 'But?'

'Can I be honest?'

He was going to turn her down. She ignored the sinking feeling of disappointment. 'Of course.'

'You need to lighten up,' he said. 'Worry less.'

She'd heard that before. 'It's who I am,' she said.

'Here's the deal. I work with you on the Christmas week events, and you let me teach you how to have fun.'

'That,' she said, 'sounds just a bit worrying. Especially when you told me that your own father thinks you're reckless.'

'Was I reckless when I drove you or when I put together the garden plan?'

'No.'

'Well, then. Those are my terms.'

'So that makes me your pet project?'

He shrugged. 'Take it or leave it.'

Even though she thought he was being a tiny bit patronising, she needed his help with the restoration funding. Without him on board, she might not get the deals he'd negotiated. She certainly wouldn't get the servants in Regency livery. She didn't really have a choice. And she wasn't going to admit to herself that she was rather enjoying having him around.

'I'll take it,' she said. 'Welcome to the team.'

'Thank you.' He raised his glass of water. 'So here's to having fun.'

'Here's to restoring the ballroom,' she said.

'And having fun.'

He'd left her no way out. 'And having fun.'

CHAPTER FIVE

'FUN,' VICTORIA SAID on Monday morning. 'That's what this week will be about.'

Samuel gave her a suspicious look. 'Define fun.'

'Christmas decorations,' she said.

'You've already told me about those,' he said with a sigh. 'They're not fun in the slightest. Greenery, holly and a mistletoe ball. No sparkle, no ho-ho-ho, no nothing.'

'As we're having semi-anachronistic Christmas trees,' she said, 'we need decorations for them.'

'Tinsel!'

She narrowed her eyes at him. 'You know perfectly well tinsel's ana—'

'—chronistic,' he finished with a grin.

She ignored him. 'I think they need to match the decor of the room they're in. So we'll have red baubles and taffeta ribbons in the dining room. The one by the staircase needs to be all gold—we can gather pine cones from the estate and dried allium heads, which we can spray-paint gold.'

'Because of course spray paint was available in Regency times,' he said dryly.

'You're the one who's all about anachronism,' she reminded him. 'Dried alliums and peacock feathers will make stunning centrepieces for the mantels or the table.'

'Aren't peacock feathers supposed to be unlucky?'

She shrugged. 'We have a late Victorian bedroom here with original wallpaper—the famous Liberty peacock one,' she said.

'Famous?'

'Sometimes I feel as if I'm fifty years older than you.' She sighed. 'Come with me and I'll show you. Humphrey, stay, because I don't want muddy paw prints on the counterpane. It's an original, which is way too fragile to go in the washing machine.' She showed Samuel up to the small bedroom with its glorious turquoise, gold and navy wallpaper. The same print was on the counterpane on the wrought iron bed, the drapes were plain blue to match the background of the wallpaper, and the wooden shutters were painted the same turquoise as the wallpaper.

'Wow,' he said. 'I wasn't expecting this. It looks almost modern.'

'Timeless elegance,' she said. The wrought iron bedframe had been painted ivory and gold, the lamps on the chests of drawers next to the bed had cream silk shades, and next to the fireplace was a wooden trolley containing a cream washstand set. The fireplace was black leaded and had a set of fire irons beside it.

'You can really imagine a guest at a house party staying here,' he said.

She nodded. 'It's my favourite room in the main house, after the ballroom and the library. I love the peacock feathers.'

'And that's why you're having them in the centrepieces.' He frowned. 'How do you even get peacock feathers? I haven't seen any peacocks in the ground.'

'Florist suppliers,' she said. 'The feathers are steam-cleaned. We have a rota of volunteers who do the floral arrangements in the house—in exchange, they get flowers from our garden to use at home. One of them's bound to know who to contact, and I'm hoping I can talk them into running a couple of workshops on Christmas wreaths and arrangements.'

'Sounds good,' he said. 'What other workshops are you planning?'

'There's a local artist who sells her stained glass in our shop,' she said. 'I'm hoping she'll run a couple of workshops on making a stained-glass tree ornament. Plus the Regency Christmas sweetmeats—the local sweet maker who supplies our shop will hopefully agree to do that. Then there's the Regency dance class and the ball.'

'If you're recreating the ball from Victoria's diary, maybe you should publish a transcription of the diary,' he said thoughtfully.

'I'd love to do an edition,' she admitted. 'But I don't have the time right now.'

'Delegate more to me to give you some time,' he suggested.

She smiled. 'That's nice of you to offer, but I think Victoria's diary could be my research rabbit hole. Once I start, you might not see me again for months.'

What did it feel like to be so passionate about something? Sam wondered. Part of him envied her. Keeping everything light meant he never really connected with anything.

'OK. So this week we're planning Christmas decorations,' he said.

'And a couple of trial runs, so we can see how long it takes to make them. We need to dry orange slices and either source or make snowflakes, plus dry the alliums and spray-paint them and the pine cones.' She gave him a wry look. 'You're the one who was on about fun. Don't back out on me now.'

'I'm not backing out. Though I probably haven't done anything artistic since infant school,' he warned.

'That's OK. And it might impress your dad.'

Sam wasn't convinced. 'Uh-huh. What else?'

'The ball. We need to book someone to run a Regency dance class—the steps aren't the same as modern ballroom dancing—and call the dances in the evening,' she said. 'Plus a string quartet. As you have contacts in the acting world, do you have musician friends as well?'

He shook his head. 'The dance teacher will probably know someone. Or it might be worth talking to the university.'

She looked thoughtful. 'That's a good idea. My old college had a really strong music department. I could call them.'

'You were at Cambridge?' Though he didn't know why he was so surprised. He already knew she was bright. 'What made you choose Cambridge over Oxford?'

She shrugged. 'It meant I could live here and keep an eye on Mum and Dad.'

So she hadn't had the full student experience, the way he had, living away from home and having the space to find out who you were. He didn't have to ask why she'd felt she needed to look after her parents; it had been only a few years after her sister's death. Now he knew why she'd been so understanding about why he wanted to keep an eye on his own parents. She'd already been there. 'Call them,' he said. 'What else?'

'Food. I've been working on the menu, based on Victoria's diary. My best friend, Jaz, is a food historian, so I'm hoping to get her students involved.'

'You could get a lot of interest from magazines if you wrote an article about a Regency Christmas dinner. They'll be planning the Christmas issue about now,' he said.

'Planned them already and putting them to bed, more like,' she said. 'Anyway, it's not a Christmas dinner. It's a ball supper.'

'Even so. You'll need to do a trial run on the food, so you could set up a table here. If we're careful with the angle, it won't matter if there isn't a Christmas tree in shot.'

'Do you have any magazine contacts?' she asked.

'No.' He shrugged. 'OK. So that's decorations, workshops, food and the ball itself. What about costume? Do you have a Regency dress?'

'I do, but it's a day dress rather than a ball gown. Meaning it's lawn rather than silk,' she explained.

He grinned. 'I would say, Cinderella, that you shall go to the ball—except obviously you're organising it so of course you'll be there, plus you're the daughter of the house rather than the one who'd been forced to be a skivvy.'

'Watch who you're calling an ugly sister,' she said. Her tone was light, but Sam had noticed her flinch.

'What did I say?' he asked.

'Nothing.'

'Victoria.' He took her hand. 'I was teasing. In my hamfisted way, I was trying to say I thought it might be nice to sort out our costumes together. If you don't mind me going to the ball with you, and obviously I'll buy a ticket.'

'Uh-huh.'

He sighed. 'Tell me. Please. So I don't put my foot in it again.'

The thing that gnawed away at her, the thing that pushed her to try harder and harder.

'Tell me,' he said softly.

He was still holding her hand.

Her voice felt cracked as she whispered, 'I kind of am Cinderella. I'm adopted.'

He looked at her. 'You're still the daughter of the house. From what I can see, you parents adore you. Your dad spent ages in the garden with me last week, singing your praises.'

'It's not...' She dragged in a breath. 'Mum and Dad didn't think they could have children. They tried IVF, but it didn't work out. So they adopted me—and then Mum fell pregnant with Lizzie. They've never, ever made me feel less than theirs or less important than Lizzie; but I've always thought that if they had to lose a daughter, it should've been me, not her, because she was their real daughter.'

'That's survivor guilt talking,' he said. 'And you're not being fair to yourself.'

'I promised Lizzie when she was dying that I'd look after them. Look after the house. Be the Hamilton daughter.' She swallowed hard. 'The house would've gone to Lizzie, because she was Mum and Dad's biological daughter, and I was fine with that. But then...' She closed her eyes for a moment and looked away, unable to bear the pity in his face. 'Lizzie died. Which left us all in limbo. Dad unpicked all the legal stuff so the house would go to me rather than to the nearest male relative, but it's not really mine. I'm the custodian.'

'Listen to me.' His voice was very soft. 'You are most definitely the heir to the house and it definitely belongs to you. You're the heart of this place. It doesn't matter about biology. You love this place and this family, and that's what's important.'

'Uh-huh.' She blew out a breath. 'But that's why...'

'Why you're so serious and earnest all the time, because you feel you owe your parents a debt and you have to work three times as hard as anyone else, to prove you're worthy of the Hamilton name.'

She stared at him, shocked that he'd understood without her having to explain. 'Yes.'

'Newsflash,' he said. 'You *are* worthy. And if your little sister loved you even ten per cent as much as you clearly loved her, she would've hated to see you beating yourself up like this.'

Humphrey chose that moment to bark.

'Even your dog agrees with me,' he said. 'You're more than good enough to do this.'

And he was still holding her hand.

This time, she met his gaze head-on. His green eyes were filled with sincerity—and something else she couldn't quite put her finger on. Shockingly, she found herself leaning towards him and her lips parting slightly. He was leaning towards her, too. For a second, she thought he was actually going to kiss her. And oh, how much she wanted this.

But then Humphrey barked. Samuel dropped her hand as if he'd just been scalded and took a backward step.

Two seconds later, there was a rap on her open door. 'Victoria?'

She forced a smile. She liked the senior room manager very much, but right now she felt as if she'd just made a fool of herself. And she was grateful that Nicola hadn't witnessed it. 'Hi, Nicola. What can I do for you?' she asked rather more brightly than she felt.

'Just checking that you're happy with the steward rota for this week.' Nicola smiled at her.

She hadn't had time to look at it. But Nicola knew what she was doing. 'It's fine.'

'Good. Sam, are you joining us at all this week? I

haven't put you in the rota, but I can fit you in anywhere you like.'

Samuel gave her his most charming smile. 'Although I'd love to, I think the boss has plans for me, this week—something to do with alliums, pine cones and spray paint.'

'Shame. You had all the ladies eating out of your hand—he hand-sold a dozen cream teas the other day, you know,' Nicola added to Victoria.

'Good for the café, then,' Victoria said, making an effort to recover her equilibrium.

'One thing, though. I didn't like to correct you in front of visitors, Sam, but I'm not sure our scone recipe really is originally from Chiverton,' Nicola confided.

'Maybe,' Victoria said, 'I should take a look at Victoria's diary and see if there's anything there. I was planning on using some of her recipes for the ball, anyway.'

'On behalf of the stewards,' Nicola said, 'we'd be very happy to be guinea pigs for anything you want to try making beforehand.'

'Sounds like fun,' Samuel said. 'We could have a Georgian lunch party, maybe. Or an early dinner after the garden closes, so the garden team can be part of it, too.'

'What a good idea,' Nicola said.

The idea was gathering momentum; although Victoria could say no, she didn't want to sour the atmosphere. 'Thursday next week, then,' she said. 'Though I need a sous-chef.' She gave Samuel a pointed look.

'My cooking skills aren't advanced enough.' He held up both hands in a gesture of surrender. 'When I hold dinner parties, it's either out at a restaurant or I get caterers in.'

'Time you broadened your skill set, then, young man,' Nicola said with a grin. 'Anything we need to know about, Victoria?'

'The information boards for the ballroom should be arriving at some point today. And I've checked the mould levels in the room—it's all fine.'

'Grand. I'll see you later,' Nicola said with a smile, and disappeared.

'I really don't cook,' Samuel said. 'Unless you count shoving something into the microwave.'

'You're the one who suggested holding a trial run of the supper,' she reminded him. 'And didn't you tell me to delegate stuff to you?'

'Not cooking. Unless you want to go down with food-poisoning,' he retorted.

'Microwave meals,' she said, rolling her eyes.

'There's nothing wrong with them. Anyway, you still live with your parents. Does your mum cook for you?'

'Sometimes; and sometimes I cook for my parents. Technically, right now you're living with yours,' she pointed out, 'so you're not in a position to criticise.'

'I'm not criticising.' He looked at her. 'Really. I don't cook.'

'We'll do it Regency style,' she said. 'Though I'll use a modern oven, the rest of it will be by hand.'

His eyes glittered. 'You said this week's going to be about fun.'

'It is.'

'Hmm. I bet Mr Darcy never had to cook anything.'

'You,' she said, 'are not Mr Darcy.' Though she had a feeling that he'd look absolutely stunning in Regency costume. To get her wayward thoughts under control, she resorted to briskness. 'Right. Jaz gave me the name of a woman who makes period costumes—Mrs Prinks—and the costumes on her website look really good, so I'd like to make an appointment with her to organise a dress.'

'Does she do men's costumes as well?'

'Yes.'

'Then we should go together,' he suggested. 'Is Mrs Prinks her real name?'

'I'd guess it was her business name,' Victoria said. 'If you can organise an appointment with her, I'll contact the man who teaches Regency dance in Cambridge and see if Jaz can fit us in this week. And, after we've organised all that, we're going to make Georgian biscuits.'

'Right.' His eyes narrowed. 'And I get decent coffee for being a kitchen serf?'

'Decent coffee,' she promised. 'And you also get to charm the stewards this afternoon by offering them something to have with their cup of tea that you made with your own fair hands.'

It didn't take long to sort out all the meetings. 'It's a pity that we couldn't have done both London trips on the same day,' she said.

'We could stay in London on the night between,' he said. 'At my flat.'

'Your flat.' She thought of that almost-kiss and went hot all over.

'I have a spare bedroom,' he said, 'so that wasn't a proposition.'

And how embarrassing that she'd thought that—albeit only for a nanosecond. 'It's a sensible suggestion. Thank you. I accept,' she said briskly. 'Right. I'll divert the office phone to my mobile. My kitchen awaits.'

'How do you know you've got the ingredients?' he asked.

'Shortbread biscuits and the like have been around for more than a thousand years,' she said. 'The recipes haven't changed that much over the years.'

'Are you telling me you've got a recipe for biscuits made a thousand years ago?'

'Not exactly, but I can make you fourteenth-century gingerbread from *The Forme of Cury.*'

'Curry?' He looked mystified.

'*Cury.* From the French *cuire*, to cook,' she said. 'Though it's not quite like the cakey gingerbread you get today.' She was glad of the safety of historical research. Where she wouldn't have to think about Samuel Weatherby and what it would be like if he kissed her. 'Think yourself lucky I'm not suggesting you make Roman honey cakes with a hand whisk. Jaz and I did that as undergraduates and you wouldn't believe how long it took to get the honey and eggs to the right texture.'

Sam was intrigued. What would Victoria's flat be like? He was guessing it would be as neat and tidy as she kept the office, but would it be as impersonal? Or would it give him more of a clue to the woman who'd surprised him earlier by her lack of confidence?

She led him through one of the servants' corridors—clearly this was a shortcut she'd been using for a long time—and then into her flat. Like the rest of the house, the rooms had high ceilings and large sash windows. The living room was almost entirely given over to books, though there was a comfortable-looking sofa and a small television in the corner. 'My room,' she said, indicating a closed door. 'Bathroom, if you need it. And the kitchen.'

The layout was incredibly old-fashioned—a butler's sink, which overlooked the lake, open shelving full of Kilner jars, a dresser with what he guessed were antique china plates, a scrubbed pine table with four chairs—but with a very modern oven. He blinked at it. 'Shouldn't you have an Aga or something?'

'Nope. Mum doesn't, either. I like the open, old-fashioned kitchen layout, like the nineteenth-century one we have on show downstairs, but I also love my modern oven.' She opened a drawer, took out an apron and handed it to him.

'You seriously expect me to wear a floral pinny?'

'If you're as much of a novice in the kitchen as you claim to be, you'll end up covered in flour without it.'

'As long as you don't take photographs and stick them on your website,' he grumbled.

She looked thoughtful. 'Experiments in Georgian cooking... Actually, you're pretty enough to get us a lot of hits.'

'Pretty?' This was outrageous.

And then he realised that the most earnest and serious woman he'd ever met was teasing him. And that he was more than tempted to extract a forfeit in the form of a kiss.

Which wasn't a good idea.

He needed to focus.

'Right.' He put the apron on.

'If you dressed as Mr Darcy, we could pose this in the kitchen downstairs,' she said. 'And then it could go on the website. Floral pinny being optional.'

'No,' he said.

'Fine.' She took some old-fashioned scales from the dresser, a large earthenware bowl from the cupboard, and grabbed a wooden spoon and rolling pin. Then she took her phone from her pocket and flicked into the Internet. 'Here we go. One historical biscuit recipe.'

It appeared to be a photograph of a page in a book. A very old printed page. 'Is that an F?' he asked, squinting at it.

'It's a long S,' she said.

'China oranges—does that say "rasp"?'

'Yes. Meaning you grate the rind,' she explained.

'OK.' He peered at the page. 'I don't know a lot about cooking, but six pounds of flour sounds a lot.'

'We'll divide the recipe by four, just to make it manageable. A pound and a half of flour, half a pound of butter, four ounces of granulated sugar—and you're lucky I'm not making you prepare loaf sugar—and enough milk to make it into a dough.'

'What's volatile?' he asked as he rolled up his sleeves.

'Ammonium bicarbonate. We'll use baking powder instead,' she said.

'OK.' He washed his hands while she took the ingredients from her store cupboards, then read the recipe again. 'Rub the butter into the flour.' He didn't have a clue what that meant, and it must've been obvious because she smiled and demonstrated. 'It needs to look like sand. Quite fine.'

Once he'd done that to her satisfaction, he grated orange rind and added it to the mixture, stirred in the sugar and baking powder, then poured in the milk and stirred it until a dough formed.

She'd already floured a marble pastry board for him.

'Is this an antique?' he asked.

'No. You get to play with the antique in a minute.'

'Seriously? I'm actually cooking with something antique? But shouldn't it be in a display case or something?'

'No. It was made to be used,' she said. 'I'd use a quarter of the dough at a time. Roll it once, turn it, and roll again.' She showed him.

'How thin?'

'Half a centimetre—or, in Regency terms, a quarter of an inch.'

He did so.

'And then you cut the dough into strips, using the rolling pin as a guide.'

'Lay the strips on top of each other in a pile to prevent the face drying,' he read.

'Don't worry too much about that. They won't dry out in the quantities we're making,' she said.

He cut the strips.

'And now for the fun bit.' She gave him a wooden block with a handle. 'This is an antique biscuit stamp, made of boxwood so it's durable and it won't taint the food.'

'Regency?'

'Regency,' she confirmed. 'Two hundred years old, so if we say each generation is twenty-five years, your five-times great-grandmother would've been a baby when this was first used.'

He handled the block reverently. The knob acting as the handle was worn smooth, but he could make out the pattern on the bottom of the block: a crown and a border of leaves. And six nails. 'What are the nails for?' he asked.

'Docking,' she said. 'The nails prick the biscuits to make sure the dough doesn't bubble up in the oven. It's old tech, but it works beautifully.'

'Like the old nursery rhyme. "Pat it and prick it and mark it with B,"' he said.

'Exactly.'

He pressed the stamp on to one of the strips of dough.

'Cut alongside the edge of the stamp, and that's your biscuit made,' she said.

It was amazing how quickly the pile of biscuits grew. And how much fun it was. Victoria transferred them to a baking tray lined with paper, and Sam realised she must have preheated the oven.

'Ten minutes,' she said. 'They would've used wire racks, possibly lining them with paper, but we'll do it the modern way.'

Within a few moments, the kitchen was filled with a faint scent of orange.

'We dunk our biscuits in tea,' she said, 'but in Regency times you'd dip them in dessert wine at the end of a meal.'

'I can't believe you just made me bake cookies. Or that you actually use an antique in your kitchen.'

She smiled. 'I like the connection to the kitchen here from centuries ago.'

He had the strongest feeling that she used history as a protective layer. Just as he used his fast lifestyle to protect him from getting involved.

What if...?

He shook himself. OK, she wasn't like Olivia, but how did he know he could trust her?

Once the biscuits were out of the oven and cooling, she looked at him. 'So do you want me to get you a coffee of your choice from the café?'

'No. I'm happy with whatever you have here,' he said. 'As you have a modern oven, do I assume you have a modern coffee machine hidden away?'

'Using pods that will take quite a few decades to disintegrate in a landfill site?' She shook her head. 'I use a cafetière. In Regency times they would've boiled the coffee in a pot, added isinglass to clarify it, then set it by the fire until the grounds had sunk to the bottom of the pot.'

Trust her to know that.

'Have you thought about running regular workshops here about Regency cookery? I think you'd get a lot of takers,' he said. 'You know your stuff. Although I'm not a cook or a history buff, I've really enjoyed doing this.'

She went pink. 'Thanks. Maybe I should think about it.'

'You'd be really good.'

She looked away, not quite able to accept the compliment. From what she'd let slip earlier, he understood why;

but at the same time surely she could see how much her parents valued her? The only person who didn't value Victoria Hamilton, he thought, was herself.

'I'll make coffee,' she said.

By the time she'd made the coffee, the biscuits were ready and cool enough to handle. He tried one. 'Wow. You can actually taste the orange. This is nicer than I thought it'd be.'

'I've always liked that recipe. You can tweak it a bit to suit the circumstances—add lemon rind instead of orange, or other spices. Cinnamon's nice at Christmas.' She fed Humphrey a corner of a biscuit. 'You've done well.'

He'd risen to her challenge. Now it was his turn to challenge her. 'So do I get to see these ancient recipes of yours?'

Her eyes narrowed for a moment, as if she was making a decision. 'OK. But unless your hands are scrupulously clean, I'd ask you not to touch pages of the older books—and don't touch the print. The oils on your fingers will damage it.'

'Right.' He'd put up with her being super-serious about that. This was what mattered to her—and she was sharing it with him. Trusting him. Funny how it made him feel so warm inside.

She showed him the modern edition of the medieval cookbook she'd talked about earlier. And then he discovered that some of her collection really was old. No wonder she'd been a bit wary about letting him handle it. It must be worth a fortune. He blinked at the frontispiece of one. 'That's getting on for two hundred and fifty years old. Is it from the library here?'

'No. It was my twenty-first present from Mum and Dad.'

'Most women would've asked for jewellery.'

He realised he'd spoken aloud when she shrugged. 'So I'm weird.'

'No... Just different.' And, the more time he spent with her, the more she intrigued him. Even though he'd told himself she wasn't his type, he was beginning to think that maybe she was. Victoria Hamilton was like no other woman he'd ever met. And, if her senior room manager hadn't knocked on the door this morning, he would've kissed her.

He still wanted to kiss her. Very much. Although it also scared the hell out of him, he had a nasty feeling that, if he let her, Victoria Hamilton could really matter to him.

He distracted himself by looking at the photographs on her mantelpiece. Pictures of herself and Lizzie and their parents, as she'd expected. Her graduation. And one on graduation day, with another woman. 'Who's this?' he asked.

'Jaz. My best friend.'

The food historian, he remembered. In the photograph, Victoria was smiling and relaxed. And, for once, her hair was down. 'Are you going to wear your hair like that for the ball?'

'Regency women always had their hair up for formal occasions—usually in a bun at the back, sometimes with flowers or jewellery wound in it, and with little ringlets in the front. Which is probably how I'll do mine for the ball, though I'll use modern curling tongs rather than Regency ones.'

Trust her to know that. And she'd look beautiful.

'Right. Have you finished your coffee? The house will be open for visitors soon, and it'd be nice to give the biscuits to the stewards before we open,' she said brightly.

In other words, she wasn't comfortable with him being in her space. She was putting distance between them. Which was probably a very good idea.

CHAPTER SIX

PREDICTABLY, ALL THE stewards were thrilled by the biscuits. So were Victoria's parents. And Samuel insisted on taking samples to everyone they spoke to connected with the ball during the week, basking in all the praise.

'I could be your official biscuit-maker for the ball,' he said. 'They should go on the menu as Weatherby's Wonders.'

She groaned. 'I've created a monster.'

'Call me Frankenstein,' he said with a grin; then, before she could protest, he added, 'And yes, I know Frankenstein's the doctor, not the creature.'

'You've read it?' she asked, slightly surprised.

'No, but Jude acted in a performance,' he said. 'And he's determined that I shouldn't ever become a boring financier with no culture, so he made sure I knew the important bits.'

She couldn't help smiling at that. 'Indeed.'

'My dad,' Samuel said, breathing on his nails and polishing them ostentatiously on his cashmere sweater, 'was so impressed with the biscuits last night that he would like to know who I am and what you've done with his son.'

She laughed. 'You're incorrigible.'

When they went to London on the following Tuesday, Jaz adored Samuel from the second he offered her a biscuit. 'It's made from a two-hundred-year-old recipe and stamped with a block that was used when my five-times great-grandmother was a baby. *And* they're my first ever attempt at baking,' he said, fluttering his eyelashes at her.

'I'll make coffee to go with them,' Jaz said, and tried a biscuit. 'Well, now. It looks as if we might have another sous-chef to add to my third-year tutorial group,' she said with a smile. 'My second years want to know if you'll do another ball next year, Tori, so they get the same experience. My third years don't care that it's the week before Christmas and technically it's out of term-time, because they're all thrilled at having the chance to cook a historical banquet for fifty people—and even more thrilled that you're letting them stay at Chiverton.'

'I can't afford to pay them,' Victoria said, 'so the least I can do is give them a bed and their food.'

'The experience is going to be so good for them. They've all been sketching layouts and suggesting menus—even though I warned them you're probably going to use recipes from the house rather than ones from Hannah Glasse or Frederick Nutt.'

'I'm very happy to have their input,' Victoria said. 'It can be a joint thing.'

'Here you go. Six lots of suggestions,' Jaz said, handing her a file, 'and I'm pleased to say they're all original and nothing's copied from source material.'

Samuel pored over the layouts with Victoria. 'I'm assuming that's a separate layout for each course, but... I don't quite get it. They've got puddings on the table at the same time as roast meat and vegetables.'

'It's how things were served at the time. Nowadays we serve *à la russe*,' Jaz said, 'which means one course after the other. In Regency times it was *à la française*, so all the dishes were set out at the same time and you served yourself and the people round you with the dishes you wanted. Or, if what you really wanted was at the other side of the table, a footman would bring it round.'

'Right.' He still looked confused.

'Presentation was really important,' Victoria said. 'Everything needs to be symmetrical.'

'But no stream in the middle of the table with fish swimming in it, right?' he asked.

'You've obviously been talking about *that* ball,' Jaz said with a smile. 'It also has to be practical. So, right, no fish. And we're going to do this as a buffet.'

'So if you've got blancmange and jelly on the table at the same time as a game pie and vegetables,' Samuel said, 'then do people go up for a second time to make it two courses?'

'No. We start with soup and fish on a white tablecloth,' Victoria said, 'and then the table's cleared away and the next course is laid out. The tablecloths are layered over each other, so the servants can clear things away quickly.'

'A lot of the ball-goers will be Austen fans,' Jaz said. 'So you absolutely have to include white soup.'

'What's that?' Samuel asked.

'It's a sort of cream of chicken soup, made with almonds,' Victoria explained. 'Agreed, Jaz. And artichoke soup for a vegetarian option.'

'Were people vegetarian in Regency times?' Samuel looked surprised,

'Yes. They called it the Pythagorean system,' Victoria said. 'Mary Shelley was a veggie. As was her husband— and even a barbarian like you must've heard of Percy Bysshe Shelley.'

'*Ozymandias*,' he said. 'Jude used to declaim it a lot in sixth form.'

'Jude?' Jaz asked.

'Jude Lindsey. My best friend,' Samuel said.

'As in the actor?' At Samuel's nod, she said, 'I saw him in *Twelfth Night* last year and he was amazing. Usually I think Sebastian's a selfish opportunist, but your friend actually made me sympathise with him.'

'I'll tell him,' Samuel said. 'He'll be pleased.' He looked at the table plan again. 'So how much of this is vegetarian? You can't just feed them side dishes.'

'Absolutely,' Victoria said.

'What about something with tofu?' he asked. Then he wrinkled his nose. 'No, they wouldn't have had tofu in Regency England.'

'Actually, Benjamin Franklin wrote a letter from London to a friend in Philadelphia in 1770, talking about tofu,' Jaz said. 'So we could mould tofu into a fish shape, colour it with paprika, and carve cucumber scales. Call it mock salmon. We could make two smaller ones to flank the salmon centrepiece. Are we doing notes with the menu, Tori?'

'To give the historical perspective? I think we should,' Victoria said. 'And maybe include some of Victoria's recipes from her diary.'

'Two soups, salmon, mock salmon, and salads,' Jaz said.

'When everyone had finished the first course, the dishes would go back to the kitchen and the footmen would take off the white tablecloth to reveal a green one,' Victoria said to Samuel. 'What's the consensus for the second course, Jaz?'

'My students think two roast meats—chicken and beef—plus a raised game pie, with a vegetable fricassee and maccheroni for the vegetarian options,' Jaz said promptly.

'Macaroni?' Samuel blinked. 'It's not just a nineteen-fifties thing?'

'It's been about since at least the fourteenth century,' Jaz said.

'Though the Regency version would've had a béchamel sauce with lemon and nutmeg rather than cheese,' Victoria said. 'They ate cauliflower cheese, too—they called it cauliflower *à la Flamand.*'

'We can have that as a side,' Jaz said. 'My students also suggest celery stewed in broth, haricot beans *lyonnaise*, and carrots.'

'Perfect,' Victoria said. 'Maybe lentil cutlets or a mushroom pudding as another vegetarian option.'

'Done,' Jaz said, adding it to her list.

'Puddings?'

'And they're really going to be served at the same time as the mains?' Samuel asked. 'Won't they get cold?'

'Yes and yes,' Victoria said. 'We're going to cheat and use cold puddings, so it won't matter.' She looked at the file the students had put together. 'Blancmange, apple tart, lemon jelly—plus raspberry cream, because we can use one of Victoria's recipes. I'll photograph that one for you and send it over with a transcription.'

'Fantastic. So that leaves us with the sweetmeats,' Jaz said.

Samuel coughed. 'Weatherby's Wonders.'

Jaz patted his arm. 'Yes, sweetie. You can show off your biscuits. Though my students have been studying Nutt and they're dying to try out his orange, ground almond and egg white biscuits.'

'Sounds good to me,' Victoria said. 'So at this point, Samuel, the footmen take away the cloth to reveal bare wood, and dessert is laid out. Wafers, biscuits and fresh fruit.'

'Definitely including a pineapple—that would impress the guests in Regency times. You needed a hothouse to grow pineapples, meaning you'd spent a lot of money on your garden,' Jaz explained. 'And I think prawlongs.'

'That's pralines, to you,' Victoria added in a stage whisper to Samuel. 'Almonds and pistachios browned in a sugar syrup.'

'Chocolates?' he asked hopefully.

'Anachronistic,' Victoria said. 'It'd be another forty years before dipped chocolates were produced.'

'But your modern audience will expect them.'

'No, they won't. The ball audience will be mainly history buffs. They'll *know*,' Victoria countered.

Jaz raised an eyebrow. 'This sounds like an ongoing fight.'

'It is. He wants Christmas trees and *Santa*,' Victoria said, rolling her eyes.

'You try telling a four-year-old why the mean lady in the house won't let her see Santa,' Samuel retorted.

Jaz laughed. 'You have a point. Probably with the Christmas trees as well, even though the Hamiltons weren't close to George III. But I agree with Tori over the chocolates. Best stick to fruit, wafers and sweetmeats.'

'You're ganging up on me,' Samuel complained, but he was smiling. And it was hard to take her eyes off him.

'I think that's it,' Victoria said. 'I'll make sure we have rooms ready for the students, and I'll give them a personal tour of the house. We don't usually have stuff that people can handle in the kitchen, but I'll make an exception for your students, plus I'll let them play with my collection. And I'll pick up the transport bill.'

'That'll be a minibus with me driving,' Jaz said.

'Perfect. Thanks.'

Jaz smiled at her. 'I know technically we could've done all this over the phone.'

'But it was a good excuse to come and see you,' Victoria said.

'I've managed to move a meeting so we can do lunch, if you have time?'

'Definitely.' Victoria looked at Samuel. 'Would you like to join us, or would you prefer some time to yourself?'

'How could I refuse two such charming companions?' he asked. 'Plus, as your intern, I'm supposed to be shadowing you.'

'Overqualified intern,' she corrected.

'Still your intern,' he said with a grin, nudging her. 'You don't get rid of me that easily.'

Jaz found them a table at a nearby Greek restaurant which she said served amazing *meze,* and they spent the next hour talking. When Victoria excused herself to go to the Ladies, Jaz said, 'I'll come with you.'

Victoria knew she was in for a grilling.

'Just imagine him dressed as Darcy,' Jaz said. 'You've got to do that for the promotional material for the ball. You'll sell out in *seconds.*'

'Don't say that in front of him,' Victoria begged. 'His head's big enough already. All the stewards are eating out of his hand—and even Bob the gardener has taken to dropping in to my office every morning to say hello to "his boy". Normally I have to go and find Bob for an update.'

Jaz whistled. 'Impressive. Seriously, though, Sam's adorable. I know you said you're doing each other a favour with this intern thing, but are you an item?'

Victoria felt a wave of heat spread through her. 'No. He's my intern.'

'You don't look at each other as if he's just your intern,' Jaz said thoughtfully. 'So what's the problem? He's already seeing someone?'

'No. Don't read anything into it. He's just a born flirt and a charmer, and I'm responding to that.'

'On the surface, maybe. I think there's more to him than that. Otherwise he'd be too selfish to come home and keep an eye on his parents,' Jaz pointed out.

'He's nice,' Victoria admitted. 'His dad doesn't give him enough credit. But...' She wrinkled her nose. 'I don't think he's the settling type. Plus he's already told me he thinks I'm too serious.'

'Well, you know you are,' Jaz said, giving her a hug. 'Though he's definitely a good influence on you. It's great to see you laughing.'

Victoria ignored the compliment. 'And he's way out of my league.'

Jaz scoffed. 'Of course he isn't.'

'Come on, Jaz. The last three men who dated me saw me as the heir to Chiverton, not as me. And I was too stupid to see that they were all gold-diggers who wanted what they thought was the big stately home and tons of money.' Whereas the reality was that stately homes were massive money-pits.

'They were the stupid ones, not you,' Jaz said loyally. 'I love Chiverton, but you're worth way more than the house.'

'That's because you're my best friend. Paul made it very clear that nobody would want to date me for my own sake.' And Victoria hadn't let herself get involved since.

'Paul,' Jaz said firmly, 'was a liar and a slimeball. He wasn't good enough for you. And I think Samuel likes you.'

'As a colleague.'

'No, I mean *like* likes.'

'He doesn't.' Victoria was really glad that she hadn't confessed to her best friend about that almost-kiss. 'Nothing's going to happen. He's negotiated some brilliant deals for me with suppliers and I won't do anything to jeopardise that. I need the fundraising to work, Jaz.'

'I know.' Jaz hugged her again. 'Make a move on him after the ball, then.'

'Maybe,' Victoria said, to stop her friend arguing. Nothing was going to happen between her and a man as gorgeous—and as unserious—as Samuel Weatherby. They absolutely weren't suitable. Chalk and cheese. She'd be stupid to let herself hope for anything more than their business arrangement.

Jaz had a tutorial after lunch, so Samuel looked at Victoria. 'Your choice. Exhibition, museum, art gallery, or back to my flat? Jude's in rehearsal today but he'll be around this evening so you'll get to meet him then.'

'Your flat sounds good,' she said. And then, while his heart was halfway through skipping a beat, she added, 'Would you mind if I did a bit of work?'

'Sure,' he said easily. He'd pretty much expected that to be her reaction. She'd clearly enjoyed seeing Jaz, but even then she'd been focused on the task in hand, finalising the menu for the ball.

Though he'd also noticed something else. 'You said nobody ever shortened your first name,' he said. 'Jaz did.'

'I've known her for nearly ten years.'

'So she's the only one allowed to call you Tori?'

'And Lizzie.'

He frowned, remembering that she'd told him about being adopted. Had her parents been more formal and reserved with her than with their biological daughter? 'Did your parents call her Lizzie?'

'No. They called her Elizabeth,' she said. 'Which isn't to say they weren't close. Just they grew up in a more formal family atmosphere.'

'Dad only calls me Samuel when he's angry.' He looked at her. 'You always call me Samuel.'

'Not because I'm angry with you. Because I guess I'm like my parents,' she said. 'More formal.'

Except with her sister and her best friend, he thought. 'And Jaz?'

'Nobody ever calls her Jasmine. She says it's too much like "jazz hands".'

He couldn't help laughing. 'I liked her.'

'Good. Because you'll be making Weatherby's Wonders under her supervision.'

'Can't I make them under yours?'

She shook her head. 'I'm going to be running around with a clipboard and a pile of lists, making sure everything's been done.'

At his flat, he opened the front door. Funny, he'd been away for less than a month, but he could barely remember how the place felt.

Jude had thankfully left the place tidy.

'Right. Grand tour. Bathroom—there are clean towels in the linen cupboard, so help yourself to whatever you need.' He opened the next door. 'Bedroom. Make yourself comfortable.'

'Thank you.' She placed her bag neatly in the room.

'Jude's room.' He gestured to another door. 'I think I told you he's looking after the place for me for the next couple of months.'

'So where are you sleeping?' she asked.

'The sofa.'

'But—'

'But nothing. You're my guest and my sofa's comfortable enough for me,' he cut in. 'Kitchen.'

She peered in. 'Either Jude is even tidier than I am, or this room never gets used.'

'Apart from making cups of tea and toast,' he admitted, 'it probably doesn't. Jude normally sweet-talks other people into making him dinner and he'll either pay his share of dinner or bring the wine.'

'Got you.' She tipped her head to one side. 'Though, now you know how to make Weatherby's Wonders...'

He laughed. 'I don't possess a set of scales and I'm pretty sure Jude doesn't. If it doesn't come out of a tin to serve on toast or out of a supermarket chiller cabinet to go in the microwave, it won't be in this room.'

'Shame,' she said, wandering over to the dining table by the window. 'You've got an amazing view here. Right over the river.'

He had a sudden vision of her in his kitchen, pottering around and creating historical dishes. A dinner party where her academic friends mingled with his City friends, where the wine was good and the conversation was even better...

He shook himself. That was *so* not happening. He didn't live here any more and he couldn't imagine anything that would make her move from Chiverton. Plus they weren't an item. He wasn't looking for a girlfriend.

'It's the same as the view from the living room,' he said, ushering her into the next room and trying to get that weird image out of his head. If he ever did settle down, it would be with someone much less earnest than Victoria Hamilton.

And he wasn't going to let himself think about what it might be like to kiss her.

She was off limits.

'This is a lovely room,' she said, walking over to the French doors in the living room. 'And you've got a balcony.'

'It's nice in the summer, sitting with a glass of wine and watching the river,' he said. Though he was aware of how different his living room was from hers. No walls lined with books. No dog asleep on a chair. A much, much larger television with a state-of-the-art games console.

'It's lovely,' she said.

But he'd seen her apartment at Chiverton. A place that was much smaller than his but was definitely home. A living room that was practically a library, but also was a place where friends would squash up together on the sofa, or where she'd sprawl out on the sofa with a book, and Humphrey would be curled up next to her. A kitchen that was used every day, where she'd cook for friends or for her parents.

And he absolutely wasn't going to wonder if her bedroom was anything like that old-fashioned room she'd shown him in the main part of the house, with a cast-iron Victorian bedstead; or how she'd look with her hair loose and spread over her pillow...

'Do you mind if I do some work?' she asked, clearly oblivious to what was going on in his head.

'Sure. When I brought work home, I'd work on the table in the kitchen. Is that OK for you?'

'It'll be lovely, thanks.'

He didn't want her to be polite and businesslike. He wanted those barriers down.

But that wasn't fair. He wasn't offering a future, and Victoria Hamilton wasn't the sort who'd live in the moment or have a fling just for fun.

'I'll make coffee,' he said. 'I'll check with Jude to see

if he's going to be home for dinner. Would you rather I ordered a takeaway or would you like to go out for dinner?'

'Provided I pay, I don't mind which,' she said.

Weird how he couldn't settle to anything. Once he'd made coffee and Victoria had thanked him politely, she busied herself on her laptop. He went into the living room to give her a quiet space to work in. Flicking channels used up some time, but there wasn't anything he wanted to watch. He was bored within ten minutes of switching on the games console. Even sitting watching the river had lost its appeal.

He texted Jude, who replied that he'd be back for dinner. And then Sam lasted for as long as it took to finish his coffee before he went back to where Victoria was sitting. 'More coffee?' he asked.

'No, thanks.'

Why did he have to notice how cute her smile was?

He realised he must've been staring at her, because she tipped her head to one side. 'Sorry. Am I in your way?'

'No, of course not.'

'Something you wanted?'

Yes, but he couldn't ask. 'No.'

'Bored?'

He wrinkled his nose. 'I never used to spend enough time here to get bored.'

'In work at the crack of dawn so you were ready for the opening of trading, then out partying afterwards until late?'

Why did that suddenly sound so shallow—and, worse still, uninviting? 'Yes.'

Was that pity he saw in her eyes? 'You probably work longer hours than I do,' he said. Well, *did*. Since he'd been working at Chiverton, she'd sent him home dead on five o'clock. He'd spent more time with his parents in the last two weeks than he had in the whole of the previous year. The strain on both their faces was easing, convincing him that he was doing the right thing by moving back to Cambridge.

Today offered more proof, because he didn't feel as if he belonged here any more. He'd lived in London since his first term at university, when he was eighteen, and had loved every second of it. But he hadn't thought about the city once since being back in Cambridge. He hadn't missed it at all.

'If you're really bored and none of your friends are available,' she said, 'you could make a start on drafting the programme for our Christmas week.'

'OK,' he said. 'Mind if I sit with you?'

There was a glint of amusement in her eyes. 'We've been here before. Except your table is a bit newer than mine.'

'I guess.' Sharing his space instead of hers.

And her smile warmed him all the way through.

Predictably, Jude swept in later and charmed Victoria by wanting to know all about the house and quoting Shakespeare and Austen at her. She absolutely bloomed under his attention, still her usual earnest self but there was a sparkle about her. Sam was shocked to realise that the weird, unsettling feeling in his stomach was jealousy.

For pity's sake.

He'd never been jealous before, and he had no grounds to be jealous now. He wasn't in the market for a relationship, he had absolutely no claims on Victoria, and Jude was his best friend. Why the hell should he be jealous?

But he was.

And he didn't trust himself not to snap, particularly when Victoria—who'd refused to let him buy her dinner—accepted Jude's offer of buying them all the best pizza in London.

'Pizza's hardly Regency food,' Sam said.

'Ah, but the lady's off duty right now, so she can eat modern stuff,' Jude said with a smile.

'Plus, I hate to tell you this, but Neapolitan pizza's been around since the eighteenth century, and a kind of version of it—basically flatbread—has been around since Roman times,' Victoria added.

'Know-all,' Sam muttered, annoyed by Jude and frustrated that Victoria seemed to be blossoming so much under his best friend's attentions.

Jude and Victoria shared a glance. '"Why, he is the Prince's jester, a very dull fool; only his gift is in devising impossible slanders,"' Jude said.

'Yeah, yeah. I know. *Shakespeare*,' Sam said and scowled, even more irritated.

Jude clapped his shoulder. 'Cheer up, mate.'

'Mmm,' Sam said, knowing he was being an idiot and not having a clue how to stop himself.

'Worrying about your dad?' Victoria asked.

And now he had guilt to add to the jealousy. He hadn't even called his parents today.

This was stupid. He'd met Victoria's best friend and liked her; and he'd wanted Victoria to like Jude. The fact that she did ought to make him happy, not foul-tempered. 'I'll go and call home,' he said. 'Excuse me.'

Jude topped up Victoria's wine. 'He's not usually grumpy like this. He must be really worried about his dad.' He looked at her. 'So he's really going to stay in Cambridge?'

'You know the situation. He's doing an excellent job—obviously he's way overqualified to be my intern—and I think his dad's completely out of order with all this stuff about Samuel being reckless, because he isn't.'

'Sam parties hard,' Jude said. 'But he works harder.'

'So you've known him since university?' Victoria asked.

'Since we were toddlers,' Jude said. 'And it didn't matter that he was this maths genius and I always had my nose in Shakespeare. We understood each other.'

'He said he used to help you learn your lines.' She gave him a rueful smile. 'I'm assuming you played Petruchio at some point.'

'He quoted Petruchio at you?' Jude winced. 'I know we've only just met, but you're no Katherine. I'd say you were Beatrice, if anything.'

'Thank you for the compliment. But he might have a point.'

'So you're a Shakespeare fan?'

'*Shrew* was my A-level text. But, yes, Jaz and I used to go to all the student productions. She saw you in *Twelfth Night*, by the way, and loved you.'

He rolled his eyes. 'Sebastian's a selfish idiot. I tried to make him decent.'

'She noticed,' Victoria said. And it occurred to her how well Jude and Jaz would get on together. Maybe she could introduce them. 'So you always wanted to act?'

Jude nodded. 'Sam bought me champagne when I got a place at RADA. Just as I bought him champagne when he got his first job—and his first promotion. Not that there was ever any doubt he'd do well.'

It was pretty clear that Jude and Sam loved each other like brothers.

'He's one of the good guys,' Victoria said. 'And he's been amazing with the restoration project. He's called in all kinds of favours I wouldn't have been able to do.'

'I think it's good for him to be out of London for a bit,' Jude said. 'And I can't believe you've got him baking.' He smiled. 'Sadly, I'm performing in the matinee and the evening show that day, or I'd so buy a ticket to the ball.'

'You're welcome at Chiverton any time,' she said. 'If you have a day off, come down and we'll cook you a trial run of some of the dishes.'

'So I get to see Sam in a pinny?' Jude grinned. 'I'll definitely give you a donation for the restoration, for that.'

'I heard that,' Sam said, walking into the room. 'If the pinny makes an appearance, there are strict rules. Very, very *strict* rules. No photographs and no video calls.'

'Spoilsport.' Jude laughed.

'How was your dad?' Victoria asked.

'Fine.'

'Good.'

Whatever dark mood he'd been in seemed to have lifted, and the conversation for the rest of the evening was much lighter. Victoria excused herself to go to bed relatively early, presuming that Sam and Jude would want some time together to catch up. But when she went to get herself a glass of water from the kitchen, half an hour later, she could hear them talking in the living room. And then she heard her name.

'I like her,' Jude said. 'And I think you do, too.'

'Don't try to matchmake,' Sam warned. 'You know I'm not looking for a relationship.'

Exactly as she'd guessed. There was no way she'd consider making a move now. She was done with making a fool of herself.

'Yes, and I know why.' Jude sighed. 'Does she know about Olivia?'

Olivia? He'd never mentioned the name before. Victoria felt sick. He'd said he didn't have a partner. Had he been lying to her?

'I haven't told her. I don't want her to know what a gullible idiot I was.'

Gullible idiot? The words were spiked with hurt. It sounded as if Olivia was his ex and she'd hurt him. Badly. Victoria knew how that felt. She'd made that mistake herself, falling for someone who had a different agenda from her own. Worse still, it had been more than once. But now she knew that her judgement in men couldn't be trusted. It sounded as if Sam felt the same way about his judgement in women. That he, too, had huge trust issues.

'Anyway, we're not dating. I'm her intern. End of.'

'That's not the way you look at her,' Jude said. 'Or the way she looks at you.'

'Still not happening,' Sam said. 'Don't interfere.'

'It's been two years,' Jude said. 'Maybe—'

'No. I don't do serious. I'm looking for fun, not for for ever.'

And then it sounded as if one of them was getting up—maybe heading for the kitchen to replenish their glasses or something. Not wanting to be caught eavesdropping, Victoria fled.

Back in her bedroom—Sam's bedroom—her mind was whirling. Who was Olivia, and what had she done to hurt Sam so much that he didn't want to get involved with anyone?

Not that she could ask him. And it was none of her business.

But it was clear to her that he didn't want to act on any attraction he might feel towards her. So she was going to have to squash any feelings she had, too, and keep things strictly business between them.

CHAPTER SEVEN

THE NEXT MORNING, Sam noticed that Victoria was very quiet over breakfast.

'Everything OK?' he asked.

'Fine, thanks.' But her smile didn't quite reach her eyes. She was quiet on the way to Mrs Prinks the costume-maker, too, whereas Sam had expected her to be lit up, talking about patterns and fabrics and design.

'So what do I need for a Regency ball outfit?' he asked.

'Breeches, shirt, cravat, waistcoat, tailcoat, white stockings, and pumps,' she said.

Nothing about colours or materials. Weird. The Victoria he knew was all about details. He tried another tack. 'I'd like to buy your dress.'

'There's no need.'

'I know, but I'd like to.' He paused. 'And then I can choose the material.'

'OK.'

What? Now he knew there was definitely something wrong. 'The Victoria Hamilton I've got to know would've given me a lecture about authentic styles, colours and fabrics. You just told me I could deck you out in lime-green polyester with purple spots if I wanted to.'

'Sorry,' she said. 'Just a bit of a headache.'

He wasn't sure she was telling the truth. It felt as if

she'd gone back into her shell. The woman who'd taught him how to make Regency biscuits and shyly tried to tease him was nowhere in evidence. And he missed her.

It wasn't until they were actually in the costume workshop and she was discussing bias cut with Mrs Prinks that the bright, sparkling academic he knew made an appearance.

'Red,' he said. 'You need a red ball gown. Bright scarlet.'

She shook her head. 'Something a bit plainer.'

'Beige?' He scoffed. 'It's your ball, Victoria. Your ballroom. And you've put a lot of work in. You should be the belle of the ball.'

'I'd rather be in the background. Red's too bright.'

'Actually he's got a point. With your colouring, it would look stunning.' Mrs Prinks took a bolt of silk from her shelf, unwrapped a few turns and held the silk up against Victoria.

The colour definitely suited her. For a moment, their gazes met, and his heart actually skipped a beat. Not good. He'd been frank with Jude last night after Victoria had gone to bed. He liked her. A lot. But he couldn't offer her for ever, he had his parents to think about, and she had Chiverton Hall to think about. He knew she was nothing like Olivia, but his ex had destroyed his trust in love.

He couldn't see how they could get over the obstacles.

There was the slightest, slightest wash of colour in her face.

'I'll take it,' she said.

Within half an hour, everything was wrapped up. They'd come back for a final fitting in a few weeks, and their costumes would be ready before the ball.

They headed back to Cambridge, grabbing a sandwich from a deli on the way to the station to eat on the train.

As Sam had half expected, Victoria worked on the train. He wasn't sure if it was just her work ethic kicking in, or if she was trying to avoid him.

Just before they reached Cambridge, he sent her a text.

Have I done something to upset you? If so, I apologise, and please tell me what I've done so I don't repeat it.

She looked up from her phone. 'You're sitting opposite me, Samuel. You could've just spoken to me.'

Not when she was this remote. 'That doesn't answer my question.'

She shook her head. 'You haven't done anything. I'm just tired.'

He was still pretty sure she wasn't telling the whole truth, but he'd also worked out that Victoria Hamilton was stubborn. Pushing her now would end up with her backing further away.

He'd let it drop for today, and maybe tomorrow would be better.

'You can go straight to your parents', if you like,' Victoria said when their train pulled into the station.

'I need a quick word with Bob about the outdoor stuff,' Samuel said. 'So if you don't mind me sharing a taxi with you, I'll come back to Chiverton.'

What she really wanted was time on her own so she could get it through her thick skull once and for all that Samuel Weatherby was off limits. But he already thought he'd upset her, so she also needed to play nice—because she definitely didn't want to tell him what was going on in her head. 'Sure,' she said.

But when they got back to Chiverton, they didn't even make it to her office before her parents intercepted them.

'Darling, did you have a nice time? How's Jaz?' Diana asked.

'Yes, thanks,' Victoria fibbed slightly, 'and Jaz is fine. She sends her love.'

'Good, good.'

Why were her parents looking so shifty? she wondered.

'You remember Donald Freeman, don't you, darling?' Patrick asked genially. 'He just popped over to say hello, so we've asked him to stay for dinner.'

Oh, no. Now she recognised that shifty look for what it was. Her parents had just found her yet another suitable man to date. They'd invited him to dinner, so then he'd feel obliged to ask Victoria out to dinner.

Maybe she really was tired, or maybe she'd gone temporarily insane, because she found herself saying, 'Well, it'll be nice for him to meet my fiancé.'

'Fiancé?' Diana stared at her in shock. 'You're engaged?'

Oh, no. Saying she was dating would've been enough. She really shouldn't have panicked and made up an engagement, of all things, but when she opened her mouth to backtrack, the lie decided to make itself that little bit more tangled. 'Yes, I know it's ridiculously fast, but you know when you meet The One, don't you, Mum?' She gave Samuel a sidelong glance.

'You mean, you and Samuel?' Patrick asked, his jaw dropping.

'Yes.' She took Samuel's hand and squeezed it, sending him a silent plea to run with this for now and she'd explain and fix things later.

'Oh, my dear boy. I'm so pleased.' Patrick took Samuel's free hand and shook it warmly.

'One thing,' Samuel said. 'This isn't common knowledge, and I need it to remain that way, but Dad's not in the best of health right now. So we weren't planning to announce anything officially until he's better.'

He was thinking on his feet faster than she was, Victoria thought. And she was so grateful that he wasn't exposing her for the liar she was.

'Of course we'll keep it to ourselves—about your father's health and about the engagement.' Diana hugged him warmly. 'I'm so sorry to hear your father's poorly, Samuel, but how lovely about you and Victoria. You know, the news might well cheer him up.'

'To be on the safe side,' Samuel said, 'I'd rather keep this between us.'

'Of course, of course,' Patrick said.

'A whirlwind romance.' Diana's face was wreathed in smiles. 'Every cloud *does* have a silver lining. If we hadn't had that problem in the ballroom, you wouldn't have needed an intern, Victoria, and you would never have met Samuel.'

'No. Just let us put our things in the office,' Victoria said brightly, not daring to look at Samuel's face. He'd sounded neutral rather than furious at the stunt she'd just pulled, and she hoped he'd hear her out and let her explain. 'We'll come up and see Donald in a moment.'

'Of course, darling.' Patrick hugged her. 'We're so pleased.'

She'd think of a way to 'break' the engagement nicely, with the minimum of hurt to her parents. But in the meantime she really needed to concentrate on the fundraising. Having to deal with her parents' matchmaking was just too much right now.

Samuel didn't say anything until they got to the office. Then he closed the door behind them. 'Right,' he said, his voice still neutral and his face completely unreadable. 'Care to tell me what that was all about?'

'Firstly, thank you for going along with it—at least for now. And I'm sorry I've dragged you into this.' She took a deep breath. 'Basically, my parents are desperate for me to find Mr Right, settle down and produce grandchildren.'

'Uh-huh.'

'Because I haven't met anyone, they've taken to parading suitable men in front of me—the sons of family friends, mainly. Donald's just one more in a long, long line. And right now I could do with not having to deal with men who don't really fancy me and are trying to be polite to my parents for their own parents' sake. I want to concentrate on the fundraising. I guess I panicked and said the first thing that came into my head to put them off—that I was already seeing someone.'

'Engaged, you said,' he corrected. 'The One.'

She squirmed. 'Again, I apologise. I panicked and they were the first words out of my mouth. I know I shouldn't have said it and I hope I haven't done any harm. You did say you weren't seeing anyone.'

'As long as your parents don't take out an ad in *The Times* or something.'

'They're not going to make any announcements without our permission,' she said. 'You heard my mum. They'll keep the news to themselves.'

'So why,' he asked, 'don't you date?'

She definitely wasn't telling him the real reason. She didn't want him to know how stupid and hopeless and worthless she was—or see any pity in his eyes when he looked at her. 'I just haven't met anyone I really want to date.' Except Samuel himself, and he didn't count. She looked at him. 'And you don't date, either. Why not?' She held her breath. Would he tell her about the mysterious Olivia?

'I want to concentrate on supporting my parents.'

In a situation he'd only known about for a couple of weeks. What about before then? Not that she wanted to risk alienating him by asking awkward questions. She needed him to support her. Just for a little while. 'I know it's a bit of a cheek,' she said, 'but would you mind going along with this, just until after the ball?'

'Let me get this straight,' Sam said. 'You want me to pretend to be your fiancé for the next couple of months—and then you're going to break it off with me at Christmas?'

She winced. 'We might have to finesse the timing a little bit, but basically yes. It'll stop my parents trying to find me a suitable husband and give me the space to concentrate on the fundraising.'

'My parents do that every so often, too,' he said. 'They invite suitable women over for dinner parties.' It was one of the reasons he hadn't come home often enough.

'So, as you know exactly what it's like, maybe we can be each other's dating decoys?' she said.

'Lying doesn't sit well with me.' He blew out a breath. 'Going along with this means lying to your parents.'

'I know, and I feel bad about that, but it's for a good cause. And it's not a lie that will hurt them.'

'What about when we break up?' he pointed out.

'I'll think up a good reason. And I'll take the blame—I'm not going to paint you as a heartless cad or anything,' she said.

Her fake fiancé.

Then again, his last engagement had been even more fake. At least Victoria was being honest and not pretending to be in love with him, the way Olivia had. Maybe there were degrees of lying. 'What about an engagement ring?' he asked.

'We don't need one. We can say we're waiting until your dad's better.'

'And you're absolutely sure my parents aren't going to hear anything about this?'

'If we let people here know that it's a big secret, they'll all be thrilled that they've been taken into our confidence,' she said. 'And we can get them to promise to keep it secret.'

'If we're engaged, people are going to expect us to kiss.' A wave of heat spread through him at the idea. The thing he'd wanted to do almost since he'd first met her—the thing he'd almost done recently—except his common sense had held him back.

Kiss the girl.

'No, they're not. They know I'm—well, a bit formal and not demonstrative.'

'But I am,' he said. 'Maybe meeting me is what changed you. Because I'm The One.'

Her eyes narrowed. 'Are you saying you're expecting benefits?'

'I'm saying,' he said, 'that people are going to expect to catch us holding hands and kissing. Otherwise, they're not going to believe that we've had a whirlwind romance and we're engaged within a couple of weeks of first meeting.'

Her eyes widened again. 'I…'

'So,' he said. 'If I go along with this pretend fiancé thing, what's in it for me?'

'Not a reference for your dad,' she said promptly. 'I wouldn't insult you like that. You'll earn your reference.'

She might be lying about their relationship, but otherwise he knew she was scrupulously honest. 'Noted. And thank you.'

'You could,' she said, 'have a sense of doing something kind and helpful. That's what's in it for you.'

'Uh-huh.'

She sighed, as if realising that it wasn't enough. 'Or I could owe you a favour.'

'Of my choice, to be taken at a time of my choosing.'

She looked at him for a long, long while. Then she nodded. 'I forgot you're a hotshot negotiator. And I'm not in a place to argue with you right now. OK. A favour, to be taken at the time of your choosing.'

'And now we seal the deal,' he said. 'As an engaged couple would.'

Her eyes were huge and full of panic.

'It's not going to hurt, I promise,' he said, and brushed his mouth very lightly against hers. Once, twice.

'Oh! Sorry,' a voice said behind them.

'Mum!' Victoria flushed to the roots of her hair.

'I was just coming to see… Well. Come up when you're ready,' Diana said, and backed out of the office.

'Your mum's just caught me kissing you. Mission accomplished, I think,' Sam said.

'Uh-huh.' Victoria looked slightly dazed.

'Last thing. I need a pet name for you,' he said. 'I can't call you Ms Hamilton. And I'm not calling you Victoria.'

'You've only known me for a couple of weeks,' she said.

'But I'm your fiancé. Which means I get to call you a pet name.'

She shook her head. 'All my boyfriends called me Victoria.'

'A fiancé is one step closer than a boyfriend.'

'Don't push it,' she warned.

'Victoria. Vicky. Vickster. The V-woman.'

Her eyes narrowed. 'I'm no Katherine, but you could definitely be Petruchio right now.'

'Kiss me, Vicky,' he said with a grin. At her rolled eyes, he said, 'You *so* set that up.'

'Not funny.'

Just to show her that it was, he stole a kiss.

But then it suddenly wasn't funny any more, because his mouth was tingling where it touched hers.

He hadn't reacted to anyone like that since Olivia— or even with her, if he was honest. He'd asked Olivia to marry him out of a sense of duty, knowing it wasn't what he wanted but knowing he had to do the right thing.

He pulled back. Victoria's face was flushed and there was a glitter in her eyes that told him she felt this weird sensation, too.

This was *dangerous*.

'We'd better go and see your parents,' he said.

Donald Freeman turned out to be a nice enough man, but he definitely wasn't right for Victoria, Samuel thought. Thankfully, after he'd congratulated them on their engagement, he excused himself from dinner, having suddenly remembered a previous appointment. And that meant Samuel could excuse himself, too, on the grounds of wanting to check on his dad.

Victoria drove him back to his parents' place. 'Thank you,' she said.

'OK. I'll see you tomorrow. And thanks for the lift.'

'I'm doing the meal for the stewards tomorrow,' she said. 'You could ask your parents if they'd like to come.'

He sucked in a breath. 'And then yours will think they know about the engagement, and things will start to get *really* complicated. No.'

'OK. Perhaps you can take some dishes home for them, then.' She gave him a smile. 'In anachronistic plastic tubs.'

'They'll appreciate that. And I'll take some photographs for the website,' he said. 'Without any anachronistic plastic tubs in sight.'

Part of him wanted to kiss her goodnight. He'd liked the feel of her mouth against his. But that wasn't part of the rules of their fake engagement.

'See you tomorrow,' he said.

Victoria told her parents another white lie, that night: that she was tired, and could do with an early night. She sat up to make her lists of what she was going to cook tomorrow, the prep plan and the timings; but she was still wide awake at stupid o'clock, guilt weighing heavily on her. Samuel was right. When she broke the engagement, her parents would be so hurt. She should've just steeled herself and told them gently that she didn't want them to keep trying to fix her up with suitable men. It would've upset them, yes, but not nearly as much as learning the truth was going to upset them.

What an idiot she was.

She couldn't even talk this over with Jaz, because she knew what her best friend would say: that Victoria was attracted to Samuel, and her subconscious had seen this as a chance to get together with him, which was why she'd said they were engaged rather than dating.

She was horribly aware that was very near the truth. And she just hoped that Samuel hadn't worked that out for himself.

She was up at the crack of dawn and headed for the supermarket, armed with a list of groceries she needed for the trial run of the ball supper. At least she'd be so busy cooking this morning that she wouldn't have time to think. She'd left a note for Samuel, saying that she'd switched the office phone through to her mobile and was working in the café kitchen this morning; but what she hadn't expected was for him to come over to the kitchen before anyone had even started in the café that morning.

'Good morning.' She eyed him warily.

'Sous-chef reporting for duty,' he said. 'What do you need me to do? Even if it's just washing up or keeping an eye on a pot for you—you can't cook for twenty people single-handed. And I assume you're cooking with modern equipment, as you're in the kitchens here.'

'I need more oven space than I have in my flat,' she said. 'I'm sure the kitchen team won't mind giving me some help.'

'But I'm your intern. I'm meant to be helping you.'

She looked at him. 'OK. If you don't mind topping-and-tailing the French beans and peeling the carrots, that would be great.'

'Good.' He smiled at her. 'Where's Humphrey?'

'With Mum and Dad. He loves roast chicken so he's on a promise of leftovers.'

He smiled. 'And a good run, after the meal.'

'Absolutely.'

'So are we cooking the meal that you planned out with Jaz?'

'Not the whole thing,' she said. 'I'm just doing the white soup and the artichoke soup for the first course, roast chicken with roast beef, fricassee, maccheroni and vegetables for the main course, and apple tart and blanc-mange for pudding. I'm going to plate it up as it would've been served in Regency times, though.'

'No Weatherby's Wonders?'

She smiled. 'Everyone's already tried them and given them the seal of approval.'

'Oh.' He looked faintly disappointed, and she relented. 'OK. Make them. You're right: they'll be nice with coffee.'

'I'll make the biscuits,' he said. 'If I get stuck at any point, I'll ask you. Just tell me what else you need and I'll do it.'

'Thank you. Apart from anything else, would you mind nipping up to my kitchen and bringing the biscuit stamper down? Plus I could do with little menus being printed for everyone.'

'Sure. Talk me through what you want and I'll sort it out.'

Why did his smile make her feel weak at the knees?

Probably, she admitted to herself, because it made her think of that kiss yesterday. She'd never reacted to anyone so strongly before.

But this was just a fake engagement and she knew that Samuel wasn't really interested in her. So they'd concentrate on work. She scribbled down the recipe for him and set to work on the soup.

Samuel reappeared with the biscuit stamper and prepared the biscuits and then the vegetables. He helped her with the apple tart and the blancmange, and she found herself relaxing with him as the day went on, to the point where she even managed to sneak in enough time to check her emails as well as answering one important call.

She'd earmarked tables in the back room of the café, putting 'reserved' signs on them, and while the vegetables were cooking and the chicken and beef were roasting she and Samuel set the table for twenty people—the house stewards, the gardening team and the café team, plus her parents.

'This isn't quite the full menu—I'm doing more dishes with each course at the ball—but I hope you'll all enjoy this,' Victoria said when everyone was seated. 'Although I'm using period recipes, I used our kitchen here.'

'It's really nice of you to do this for us all,' Nicola said.

'Samuel helped,' Victoria said, not wanting to take all the credit. 'Even though he doesn't usually set foot in a kitchen, he did lots of the prep, and he made the biscuits to go with coffee.'

'Weatherby's Wonders,' Samuel corrected her with a smile.

She rolled her eyes at him. 'Before I bring the soup through, I have good news and bad,' she said. 'The good news is that we've got the heritage funding. Not quite as much as I asked for, but it's going to pay for three-quarters of the work.'

There was a general cheer.

'The bad news,' she said, 'is that the mould damage can't be repaired. The silk's just too fragile. We need to get modern reproductions of the hangings made, and Felicity recommends we do the whole wall. The good news is that, although the timing's tight, it should all be ready just before the ball so we'll be completely up and running.' She smiled. 'And I'd like to thank all of you in advance for your support in the Christmas week fundraising. I've got a running list of who's offered to help with what and it's really, really appreciated. Anyway. Samuel and I are bringing the soup through. We'll be serving from the table behind us. I apologise in advance for not doing this proper Regency style, with the different tablecloths and everything, but it's a trial run. There's enough for everyone to have a taste of everything, and I'd welcome any feedback because I'm using recipes from the time and they might not be to modern tastes.'

'And anything that goes down really well,' said Prue, the head of the kitchen team, 'maybe we can add to the café specials board. Maybe we can produce an historical dish once a week. I reckon the visitors would love it.'

'That,' said Victoria, 'is a brilliant idea, Prue. Let's do it.'

Samuel took photographs of the two soup tureens in situ, and then of everyone sitting at the table with their soup; and he handled the photography again when he and Victoria had set out the second course.

The food went down really well, to Victoria's relief.

And then, after coffee, Patrick stood up. 'I'd like to thank my daughter for being such a trouper,' he said. 'The amount of work she's put in is amazing. And I'd like to thank Samuel, too.'

For a nasty moment, Victoria thought that her father was going to blurt out that they were engaged. She caught her father's eye and gave the tiniest, tiniest shake of her head, enough to remind him that it was meant to be a secret. For a second, he looked crestfallen, but he recovered himself quickly. 'And thank you, all of you, for your support. We couldn't do what we do here without you.'

'Hear, hear,' Diana said, standing up to join him. 'Here's to Chiverton and the ballroom restoration.'

'Chiverton and the ballroom restoration,' everyone said, and raised their coffee cups.

Afterwards, Prue and the kitchen team insisted on helping clear away, and Victoria sent Sam back to his parents' with a pile of plastic tubs, so they, too, could taste the Regency dinner.

'He's all right, our Sam,' Prue said to Victoria. 'You picked a good one there.'

'Dad knows his father, so actually I didn't pick him as my intern. He applied, and it was convenient to give him the job,' Victoria said.

Prue smiled and patted her arm. 'That isn't what I meant. Your last young man thought he was a toff and much better than everyone else. Sam doesn't. He mucks in with all of us.'

'Sam's not my—' Victoria began, panicking.

'It's all right. I won't say anything,' Prue cut in gently. 'But I think all of us see the way you look at each other.'

Oh, no. This was starting to get out of hand. The only good thing was that her father hadn't spilled the beans about the 'engagement'. 'That was a really good idea you had about using historic dishes in the café here,' she said, hoping to distract Prue.

Prue smiled at her as if to say that she knew exactly what Victoria was doing, but to Victoria's relief Prue went along with it and talked about which recipes would work where.

When everyone had gone home, although it was dark, Victoria took Humphrey for a good run in the gardens; she practically knew the layout blindfolded but took a torch with her for safety's sake.

'I'm going to have to be really careful,' she told the dog. 'Because Samuel doesn't feel the same way about me that I'm starting to feel about him. And Dad nearly slipped up about the engagement. I'm beginning to wish I'd kept my mouth shut up and just dated Donald a couple of times to keep Mum and Dad happy.'

And in a few short weeks Sam would be out of her life and he wouldn't be back.

She couldn't let herself lose her heart to him.

This whole thing was about Chiverton and the ballroom. And that would have to be enough.

The following week saw a day that made Victoria happy and sad in equal measures: Lizzie's birthday. She tried hard to concentrate on her little sister's sweetness and

how lucky she'd been to have Lizzie for thirteen years.
But at the same time she was sad for all they'd missed out
on. Lizzie would've been twenty-five, now. Graduated,
maybe married to the love of her life.

'I miss you,' she said, arranging the paper-white
scented narcissi she'd always bought Lizzie for her birthday on the grave. 'What I'd give for you to be here now.
You'd love all the ball stuff. And I can just see you in
a sky-blue silk gown to match your eyes. You'd be the
beauty of the ball.' She blinked hard. 'I know you'll be
there with me in spirit. I just wish we'd had more time
together.'

Humphrey nudged her and licked away the tears that
slipped down her cheeks.

'You'd love Humphrey,' Victoria said. 'And I think
you'd like Samuel. I'm making such a mess of this, Lizzie.
He's been kind enough to agree to keep up the fake engagement until after the ball, but I...' She blew out a
breath. 'I wish I was different. That I didn't keep letting
Mum and Dad down, time and time again.' She grimaced.
'Sorry. It's your birthday. I shouldn't be whinging. I love
you. And I so, so wish you were here.' She stood up and
patted the headstone. 'Happy birthday, darling. I'm going
to make Mum and Dad our special meal tonight and we'll
toast you.'

When she headed back to her office, Samuel was already there.

'Are you OK?' he asked.

Obviously her eyes must still be a bit red. 'Of course,'
she fibbed.

He didn't look convinced, and disappeared, returning with two mugs of coffee and two brownies. 'In my
department,' he said, 'this used to fix most things. Or

at least put people in a place where the tough stuff was more manageable.'

The kindness was too much for her, and the tears spilled over.

'Sorry,' she said, wiping her eyes with the back of her hand. 'Lizzie would've been twenty-five today.'

'Ah.' He took her hand, drew her to her feet, and gave her a hug.

Part of her wanted to howl even more; part of her was really grateful for the kindness; and part of her felt an inappropriate longing to hold him back, to take comfort in holding him.

But that wasn't fair.

He was her fake fiancé, not her real one.

Too late, she realised they weren't alone. Diana was standing in the doorway,

'I take it Samuel knows what today is?' Diana asked gently.

'I do now,' Samuel said. 'A tough day for all of you.'

Tears glinted in Diana's eyes. 'Almost half her lifetime ago, the last birthday we shared.' She rested her hand on Victoria's shoulder. 'But I still have my Victoria, so I know I'm lucky.'

Victoria couldn't say a word.

'Samuel, we always have a special dinner on Elizabeth's birthday. You're very welcome to join us,' Diana offered.

'Roast chicken followed by rice pudding—her favourites,' Victoria added.

'And champagne. The last of the first case Patrick laid down, the day she was born.' There was a noticeable wobble in Diana's voice. 'We celebrate having her for those thirteen years.' She stroked Victoria's hair. 'Just as we celebrate your day, darling.'

'I know, Mum.'

'I'll be there,' Samuel said. 'Thank you for inviting me. It's an honour.'

When Diana had left, Victoria said, 'You don't have to come. I'll make an excuse for you.'

'No, I'd like to be there,' Sam said. What he wanted was to be there for Victoria and support her.

'Thanks.' She dragged in a breath. 'We don't get maudlin.'

No, they'd hide their sadness to protect each other, Sam thought.

'I'm cooking, so dinner's at my flat,' Victoria said.

'Can I bring anything? Do anything?'

'It's fine. All organised,' she said.

All the same, Sam nipped out to buy seriously good chocolates and ground coffee that had been roasted locally. He knew he'd done the right thing when Victoria hugged him spontaneously.

Weirdly, even though she was his fake fiancée, having her in his arms felt more real than when he'd held Olivia. He was going to have to be really careful not to let his feelings run away with him. She was only doing this to distract her parents until after the ball.

He discovered that Victoria had been speaking the truth. It wasn't a maudlin evening, The Hamiltons smiled and remembered the good times, and Diana had photographs on her phone. Victoria was still in the shy teenage stage, but she looked happy. And Sam found himself drawn to her that little bit more.

At the end of the evening, Victoria walked him to the gate.

'Lizzie seemed lovely,' he said.

'She was.'

He rested his hand against her cheek, just for a moment. 'I know you have survivor guilt, but you don't have to make up for her. Your parents love you just as you are.'

She swallowed hard. 'I know.'

'I don't get why you don't think you're enough,' he said softly. 'Unless it's something to do with being adopted?'

She shook her head. 'I don't have abandonment issues. My biological mother was very young when she had me. She wasn't a wild child—she'd given in to pressure from her boyfriend and she was just unlucky. Her parents were taking her away for her eighteenth birthday and I was being looked after by family friends, but the three of them were killed in a car accident. There wasn't anyone else in the family who could take me on, and my mum hadn't named my dad, so I was put up for adoption. Mum and Dad chose me.'

'And I can see how much they love you.'

She nodded. 'I've been so lucky. I've always felt loved.' She lifted a shoulder. 'As you say, survivor guilt. I think I'll always feel this way.'

'Don't. Because you're loved,' he said, 'for exactly who you are. Never forget that.'

CHAPTER EIGHT

THREE WEEKS LATER, nearly everything was organised: the plan for the outdoor lights and a special menu for the café; Father Christmas; the workshops for stained-glass ornaments, wreath-making and Christmas confectionery; and the ball itself.

The only things left to put in place were the dance music and the teacher who'd hold the workshop in the afternoon before the ball and call the dances at the ball in the evening. Michael Fillion had an appointment to come and see the ballroom that morning and discuss the ball with Victoria and Samuel.

'So have you actually done Regency dancing before?' Samuel asked her.

'Yes, when I was a student. There was a group of us who loved all the Regency stuff, Jaz included. Our dance teacher died a couple of years ago, but her daughter gave me Michael's name—he apparently took over Lily's classes.' She looked at him. 'So I'm assuming you've never done any kind of formal dancing?'

'No.'

'Maybe Michael can take you through some steps today, if he has time.'

'Or you could teach me,' Samuel suggested.

Oh, help. She could just imagine teaching him to dance—and seeking a payment for her lessons in kisses...

She shook herself. 'I'm a bit rusty.'

When Michael arrived, she made coffee and showed him around the house, ending up at the ballroom.

'The room has perfect proportions,' Michael said. 'Did Lily ever come here?'

'Not for dancing,' Victoria said.

'Pity,' Michael said. 'She would've loved this. I like how you've got the room set up as it would've been in Regency times, with the seating by the wall. So you have a mirror over the mantelpiece, usually?'

Victoria swallowed hard. 'Yes. That's where we found the edge of the mould. The silk hangings—or at least the reproductions—will be back in place just before the ball. We've got a heritage grant to cover some of the costs, and the ball and other fundraising events that week will raise the rest.'

'It's a beautiful room. I'm glad it's being used for its proper purpose,' Michael said. 'We can have the quartet seated next to the piano—you did say your college has a quartet who'll play on the night?'

'Yes, so if you can let me know what music you want, they can rehearse.'

'Excellent. Will everyone be in Regency dress?' Michael asked.

'I think so,' Victoria said. 'If people prefer to stay in modern dress, that's fine, but I've asked that people don't wear stilettos, so the floor doesn't get damaged.'

'Very sensible. I have pumps in a selection of sizes, so my students can try out the classes in comfort and decide whether dancing's for them. I'll bring some along just in case anyone needs them on the night,' Michael said. 'And you mentioned you'd like a quick lesson now?'

'Is that a horrible cheek?' Victoria asked.

Michael laughed. 'In a room like this, it'll be a privilege and a pleasure.'

'I haven't danced for a long while, so I'm rusty,' she warned.

'It'll come back. How about you, Sam?'

'Never,' Sam said. 'I'm a total novice.'

'That's fine. I can lend you shoes. Victoria, do you have shoes?'

'In my office. I'll get them,' she said.

'Tell me your shoe size, Sam, and I'll get you a pair.'

Sam knew how much Victoria hated being in the ballroom right now, with the bare wall symbolising what she saw as her failure. 'Would you rather do this in another room?' he asked quietly when Michael had gone to fetch the shoes.

'It's fine,' she said.

He had a feeling that she was being brave about it; but if he made a fuss about it he knew it'd make her feel awkward.

Michael returned with shoes and a small portable speaker, which he connected to his phone. 'Obviously we'll have live music on the night,' he said, 'but this will do for now.'

Once Samuel had changed his shoes and the three of them had rolled the carpet back to give them a decent space for dancing, Michael talked them through the first steps. Everything was very measured and mannered, Samuel thought.

'It's a cotillion and reel,' Michael explained, 'and it's danced in sets. There might be four, eight, or sixteen of you, and you repeat the moves until each of you has danced with all the other partners in the set.'

'It's not quite what I was expecting,' Samuel said. 'I

thought it was going to be more like the ballroom stuff you see nowadays. But you don't seem to get close to each other. Even the one where we're crossing arms, my left arm's behind my back and my right arm's behind Victoria's, just as her left arm's behind my back and her right arm's behind hers. It's as much as we do to hold hands. There's no real touching. We're even standing beside each other rather than properly opposite each other.'

'It's the propriety of the day,' Victoria said. 'And don't forget the women would all be wearing gloves, so there'd be no skin involved at all.'

'Jude was saying something about the waltz being considered very fast,' Samuel said thoughtfully.

'In both senses of the word—it's very energetic as well as being considered very daring for the times,' Michael said. 'Victoria, have you ever done Regency waltzing?'

'Yes, though I'm a bit rusty,' she said.

Michael smiled. 'That's fine. Let's give Sam a demo.' He put on some music that sounded like a harp, or at the very least like the musical jewellery box Sam remembered from his childhood.

Sam watched, fascinated, as Michael and Victoria marched together, then turned to face each other, one arm above their heads like an old-fashioned ballerina pose and the other arm clasped round each other's waists, and turned in a circle. Then they lowered their arms so they were much closer and added in little hops as they spun round in faster and faster circles.

'I think,' Sam said, 'that would make people dizzy.'

'Fun, though. It's a bit like the modern quickstep in places,' Michael said. 'Come and have a go. I'll talk you through it.'

Having Victoria in his arms was dangerous, Sam thought. He was aware of how close they were; enough though by modern standards there was a lot of space be-tween them, he could see a massive difference between the formal group dances where partners changed after every few steps and this, where you'd be dancing with the same person for the whole dance. How you were close enough to have a whispered conversation without every-one else hearing. How you could really flirt with your partner and break all the conventions.

Michael slowed the steps right down until Sam was confident, and then he grinned. 'Time to do it at full speed.'

The music only lasted for about three minutes, but Sam could definitely feel his pulse racing and felt very slightly dizzy when it stopped.

'Do you get it, now?' Michael asked.

'I think so. That was very different,' Sam said.

'It'll be even better in Regency dress,' Victoria said.

Apart from the fact that she'd be wearing gloves, put-ting another barrier between them. He'd enjoyed holding her hand through the dance and feeling the warmth of her skin against his.

Though this was crazy. She was his fake fiancée, not his real one—and the pretend engagement was purely to help her out and stop her parents matchmaking.

He really needed to get a grip.

The lesson was over all too soon. They rolled the car-pet back to its usual position, and Michael promised to send an invoice and formal confirmation of the booking later that day. 'This is going to be a joy,' he said, shak-ing their hands.

Sam and Victoria went back to her office.

'Let's see where we are right now,' she said. 'OK. The workshops are sold out—I have a waiting list for people who want a place on the next ones. So maybe I should look at running the workshops once a month in future.'

'Good idea,' he said. 'How are the ball tickets doing?'

'Halfway,' she said.

'Looks as if we have a success on our hands, then.'

'Don't count your chickens just yet,' she said. 'There are a lot of things that could still go wrong.'

'Not with you in charge,' he said.

Three days later, Sam and Victoria headed for London, for their final costume fitting with Mrs Prinks. Victoria had agreed to do a guest lecture at Jaz's university on what it was like to run a stately home; Sam sat at the back of the lecture theatre and watched, spellbound, as she went through the presentation without a single note in front of her, and then encouraged questions from the students. She paid attention to what they were asking and didn't brush a single thing aside.

She was absolutely in her element, and she shone.

It would be so, so easy to fall in love with her. She was sweet, she was bright, she was enchanting. And he could even forgive the lying about the engagement, because he understood why she was doing it.

She was nothing like Olivia.

But he still couldn't quite trust anyone with his heart.

He was going to have to be really, really careful.

At Mrs Prinks's workshop, after Victoria's lecture, Sam stared at himself in the mirror when he was dressed up. He'd never been one for fancy dress, even as a child. And it felt weird to be wearing knee breeches, stockings, a frock coat and a fancy shirt and cravat. Not to mention the shoes; with their suede soles they'd be ruined as soon as they were worn outdoors in the rain. He looked like himself—but also not like himself. It was as if the centuries had just blurred.

Feeling slightly awkward, he pulled aside the curtain of the cubicle where he'd changed into his costume and walked out. At almost exactly the same time, Victoria did the same.

Sam had no idea how she'd managed to put her hair up so quickly, but she looked stunning in her red silk ball gown. Like a woman in a costume drama; and yet at the same time he could imagine her walking through Chiverton Hall, centuries ago.

'Wow,' he said. 'You look amazing.'

She blushed. 'So do you.'

'Fitzwilliam Darcy and Elizabeth Bennet, eat your hearts out,' Jaz said.

Sam swept into a deep bow. 'I hope you're going to save me a waltz on your dance card, Miss Hamilton.'

Jaz scoffed. 'Are you seriously telling me you can do a proper Regency waltz?'

He laughed. 'I've been doing homework, I'll have you know. And in these shoes, yes, I can waltz. Miss Hamilton, if I may presume?'

Samuel gave another courtly bow, and Victoria's knees went weak.

'We don't have any music,' she mumbled, flustered.

'That's easily fixed,' Jaz said, and flicked into the Internet on her phone. 'Here we go.'

Victoria had danced a Regency waltz with Samuel before in the ballroom at Chiverton: but here, in the middle of a historical seamstress's workshop, with both of them wearing reproduction Regency clothing, it felt different. Last time, her fingers had been bare against his. Oddly, now she was wearing gloves, the dance felt more intimate. Forbidden, almost.

For a second, the workshop and Jaz and Mrs Prinks were forgotten. It was just the two of them and the music. And it would be oh, so easy to...

His pupils were huge, his green eyes almost black. So he felt it, too, that weird pull? And at the end of the dance they were only a breath away from a kiss. She felt herself leaning towards him and could see him leaning towards her; and then she was aware of the sound of applause, shocking her into pulling back.

'Very impressive. You're a quick learner, Sam,' Jaz said.

Sam bowed first to Victoria and then to Jaz. 'Save me a dance at the ball, Jaz,' he said.

She shook her head. 'I can't. I'm supervising my students.'

'Then dance with me in your serving outfit and pretend you're Cinderella,' he suggested.

'Yeah, yeah,' Jaz said, laughing.

But then she caught Victoria's gaze, and her expression said, *I'll be grilling you later.*

'You both look fabulous,' Mrs Prinks said. 'I want to take up your hem by about two centimetres, Victoria. Sam, your outfit's fine so you can take it away now.'

Sam went back into the cubicle to change out of his costume, and Victoria waited while Mrs Prinks expertly pinned the hem.

'Right. When are you going back to Cambridge?' Mrs Prinks asked.

'Our train's in an hour,' Victoria said.

'That doesn't give me enough time to do the alterations.' Mrs Prinks looked thoughtful. 'Either I can courier the dress to you, or you can come back for another fitting.'

'Or,' Samuel said, 'we can play hooky, stay overnight, come and see you first thing tomorrow for a fitting and then get the train. If that's giving you enough time to do the hem, Mrs Prinks?'

'Absolutely,' the seamstress said with a smile.

'That's settled, then,' Samuel said. 'Are you free for dinner tonight, Jaz? And maybe we can go and watch Jude treading the boards afterwards, if I can get tickets. My treat,' he said quickly, before Victoria could say a word. 'You can't argue with Mr Darcy.'

'You're not in costume any more, so you're not Darcy,' she pointed out.

He spread his hands. 'Too late.'

'Actually, that'd be really nice,' Jaz said. 'Thank you. And do I get to meet Jude?'

'I'll see what I can do. Give me a few minutes and I'll get Victoria to text you with all the details.' He smiled at Mrs Prinks. 'You've done a fantastic job. Thank you so much. I'm almost tempted to wear this tonight, except I don't want to spill anything on it or wreck the shoes—which I assume can only be worn indoors.'

'Indeed,' she said.

And, in that outfit, he'd turn every female head in the theatre, Victoria thought.

After they'd left Jaz and Mrs Prinks, Victoria said, 'We'd originally planned to go back to Cambridge, so I haven't got any spare clothes or toiletries with me.'

'My flat has a washing machine and a dryer. We can borrow everything else from Jude; or we can go shopping now, if you'd rather.' He shrugged. 'I don't think you need any make-up.'

Because she was too plain for it to make much difference, according to her ex, Paul. 'Uh-huh,' she said.

'Because you're lovely as you are,' he said softly. He

stole a kiss—and then looked at her in utter shock. 'Um. Sorry.'

'It's OK. It's what a fiancé would do—even though we don't actually need to keep up the pretence right now, as my parents are nowhere around,' she said lightly, even though her heart rate had just sped up several notches and her mouth was tingling where his had brushed hers.

'Does Jaz know about the fake engagement?' he asked.

'No. Does Jude?'

'No.'

'Then we don't have to keep up the act.' Particularly as she couldn't trust herself not to fall for him. That moment in the dressmaker's had shaken her. She'd nearly kissed him in front of a very small audience that included her best friend. How crazy was that?

'OK. But staying overnight might also help to keep your parents convinced about our "engagement",' he said.

She nodded. 'I need to let them know where we are, so they don't worry.'

'Ditto,' Sam said.

Not wanting to hear the hope and happiness in her mother's voice at the idea of her staying at her fiancé's flat, when Victoria knew she was going to let all those dreams down so very shortly afterwards, she chickened out and sent a text.

Second dress fitting tomorrow, so it makes sense to stay over. Do you mind having Humphrey tonight as well? Having dinner with Jaz—she sends her love.

And of course her mother would expect a message from Victoria's fiancé.

So does Samuel. Love you xxx

The reply came back almost immediate.

H fine with us. Dying to see the dress. Have fun! LU xxx

'Everything OK?' Samuel asked.

She nodded. 'Just feeling guilty about lying to Mum.'

'The whole thing was your idea,' he reminded her.

'And not one of my better ones,' she admitted glumly.

'It's done now. Let's make the best of it.'

'Mmm,' she said awkwardly. 'I do need to buy stuff, Samuel. I can't just…' She grimaced and shook her head.

'Jude won't mind you using his shower gel or shampoo, or lending you a T-shirt for tonight. And I'll do the laundry when we get in tonight.'

'It still feels a cheek.'

He tipped his head on one side. 'Is that Victoria-speak for you want to go shopping? Because I would've guessed that unless it involved a book, something to do with Chiverton or a present for someone, you're not a shopper.'

She wrinkled her nose. No wonder Paul had called her boring. He'd even spitefully called her Vic-*bore*-ia, and the name had stuck in her head. 'That's a horribly accurate summary.'

For a nasty moment she thought she'd spoken her thoughts aloud, when Samuel said, 'Actually, that's so refreshing.'

She looked blankly at him. 'What is?'

'Being with someone who sees life as more than just buying stuff.'

'That sounds as if you've dated too many Miss Wrongs,' she said before she could stop the words.

A shadow passed across his face, and she wondered if he was thinking about Olivia. Then again, he didn't know that she sort of knew about Olivia. Not the details, just that the woman had hurt him. The more she was getting to know Samuel, the more she liked him; there was depth beneath his charm. She didn't understand why anyone would want to hurt him.

'Coffee, then. Or if you need to go and get girly face stuff, I'll stay outside the shop and try and get tickets for tonight.'

'Thanks, but I'm paying for the tickets,' she said.

'Nope. My idea, my bill,' he said firmly. 'I might let you buy me dinner, though.'

'Deal.'

By the time she'd bought toiletries and underwear, Samuel had booked tickets for Jude's play and a table for three in a nearby Italian restaurant. 'I hope you don't mind me being presumptuous,' he said.

'I'm not difficult about food, and neither's Jaz,' she said with a smile. 'What's more difficult is actually getting a table, so thank you for sorting it out.'

'Pleasure.'

She texted the details to Jaz, and they headed back to Samuel's flat.

Jude welcomed them warmly and seemed thrilled that they were going to see him perform that evening.

Dinner before the show was good, and they spent more time laughing than talking. Jaz gave Victoria a couple of pointed looks, as if to say that Samuel was perfect for her and she really ought to act on that; but Victoria knew that this whole thing between them was fake. OK, so there had been that kiss this afternoon, and it looked as though it had shocked him as much as it had shocked her; but this was all a business arrangement. And, after her last three disastrous relationships, she knew better than to hope that this could turn into something more.

Jude was amazing and, when they went backstage to meet him and the rest of the cast, Jaz was noticeably star-struck.

'I'm so sorry that I've already got unbreakable arrangements for tonight,' Jude said, 'or I would've suggested going out. But I might see you at breakfast—and I want to see you dressed as Darcy, Sammy.'

'He looks pretty good,' Jaz said.

But Victoria knew her best friend well and her body language said, *I think you'd look even better.*

Maybe...

Back at Samuel's flat, she asked, 'Is Jude dating anyone?'

'No.' Samuel's eyes narrowed. 'Why?'

'He and Jaz seemed to hit it off. And I was thinking...'

He gave her a wry smile. 'You and I have both been victims of matchmaking.'

'This isn't the same,' she pointed out. 'We're not our parents. Plus they've actually met and liked each other. This would be a little nudge.'

'True.' He made hot chocolate and handed her a mug. 'We could pass on their mobile phone numbers and leave it to them. But you're right—they did seem to like each other.' He smiled. 'Ironic that a real relationship might come out of our fake one.'

Her heart skipped a beat. Was he talking about them?

No, of course not. He meant their best friends.

They curled up on opposite ends of his sofa, watching the river by night—the reflection of the lights and the bridges on the water—in companionable silence.

When Victoria went to bed that night, she lay awake, thinking of Samuel. The more time she spent with him, the more she liked him. But he'd made it clear to Jude that he didn't feel the same way about her, so it was pointless wishing or hoping or even dreaming that they could make their fake engagement a real relationship. It wasn't going to happen.

Sam sat watching the lights on the river, snuggled up under his spare duvet and wishing that Victoria were still there next to him. Preferably in his arms.

He liked her. A lot. The more she came out of her shell with him, the more he was starting to wonder if maybe he could talk her into trying to make their fake engagement a real relationship. OK, so they came from different worlds, but they weren't so far apart.

Once the ball was over and the stress was off her, he'd ask.

But he was definitely looking forward to the ball. To dancing with her and seeing her shine.

Mrs Prinks was satisfied with the dress, the next day, and boxed it up for their train journey.

Outside the workshop, Victoria said quietly to Sam, 'I'm giving you the money for my dress.'

'No. I said I'd buy it for you.'

'I don't expect you to do that.'

'I'd like to,' he said. 'We're friends, aren't we?'

Her dark eyes were huge. 'I guess.'

'Well, then. Think of it as a friend doing something nice for you. An un-birthday present.'

'It feels mean and greedy, taking things from you. I'm taking advantage of you.'

How different she was from Olivia—who would've expected jewellery, shoes, and a handbag to go with the dress, and sulked if anything hadn't been expensive enough. 'Humour me,' he said. 'There aren't any strings.

Or, if you really want to do something for me, you can teach me to cook something healthy but tasty for my dad.'

'I'll do that with pleasure,' she said. 'And thank you. The dress is perfect.'

Funny how her smile warmed him all the way through.

Part of Sam wished that they were at Chiverton right now, so he'd have an excuse to hold her hand. Which was crazy.

When they did get back to Chiverton, Patrick and Diana greeted them warmly—as did Humphrey, who was ecstatic at seeing Victoria again.

'I know, I know. I've neglected you for a gazillion years.' Victoria dropped to her knees and made a huge fuss of her dog.

'So do we get to see you both in your finery?' Diana asked.

'Fine by me,' Sam said. Then he had an idea. 'Meet us in the ballroom in ten minutes? We'll get changed and come straight up.'

'The ballroom,' Victoria said, grimacing, when her parents had gone.

'It's appropriate,' Sam said.

She sighed. 'I guess. OK. We'll change in my flat.'

He followed her up to her apartment. 'Where do you want me to change?'

'The living room?' she suggested. 'Knock on my bedroom door when you're ready.'

'OK.' He paused. 'Do you need a hand with the z— the fastening of your dress?'

She grinned. 'You were going to say "zip", weren't you?'

'Then I thought it might be...'

'Anachronistic. Just a tiny bit. Good call,' she finished. He loved it when she relaxed enough to tease him.

It didn't take him long to change. Then he knocked on the door. 'Ready when you are,' he called.

She emerged, fully dressed.

'You look amazing,' he said.

'Thank you. So do you.'

He smiled at her as they walked through the house together. 'I feel as if I've just stepped back two hundred years.'

'Dressed like this, so do I.'

'Let's do what your parents expect,' he said quietly, and took her hand.

'Oh, darling,' Diana said when they entered the ballroom. 'You look...' Her voice cracked with emotion.

'You look amazing. Both of you.' Patrick said. 'I'd like to take a photograph of you both together like this.'

'Yes—for the website,' Diana agreed. 'The rest of the tickets will sell like hot cakes when people see you.'

'And we should send it with a press release to the local paper,' Sam suggested.

'I'm glad I brought my proper camera,' Patrick said. 'And if you sit at the piano, darling, and you stand this side, Samuel, I can take the shot at an angle that won't show the bare wall.'

Victoria looked totally at ease behind the piano stool. 'Do you play?' Sam asked, suddenly curious.

'She does—and very well,' Diana answered.

'Would you play something for me?' Sam asked.

'Sure. What do you want?'

'Anything.'

He'd been half expecting her to play something obscure; but he recognised the *Moonlight Sonata* instantly. 'Beethoven?'

She nodded. 'Victoria's diary talks about hearing someone play it in London.'

'It's beautiful,' he said. 'Play me some more.'

He recognised Chopin and Bach, then was totally lost when she played an incredibly fast piece.

'You're Grade Eight standard, aren't you?' he asked when she'd finished.

She gave another of those half-shrugs. 'This is a nice piano to practise on.'

Diana patted her daughter's shoulder. 'She got distinctions in all her piano exams up to Grade Eight. Our Victoria will insist on hiding her light under a bushel. And she really shouldn't.'

'Agreed,' Sam said. He took his phone out of his pocket and flicked into the piece of music he'd downloaded earlier, while Victoria was changing. 'May I have this dance, Miss Hamilton?' He pressed 'play' and bowed to her.

She went very slightly pink. 'I guess we can use that bit of the floor alongside the carpet.'

Just as they had in the dressmaker's, they waltzed together. With her in his arms, it felt as if the whole world had faded away, and there was just the two of them and the music. And it didn't matter that she'd put her gloves back on again after playing the piano; he could still feel the warmth of her skin through the silk.

When the music came to an end, it really was a wrench to stop.

'Amazing,' he said, keeping his voice low so that only she could hear him. 'You're amazing.'

Her eyes looked absolutely enormous. All he had to do was lower his mouth to hers...

He just about stopped himself kissing her stupid, the way he wanted to do. It would be inappropriate in front of her parents. And, if he embarrassed her, he knew she'd back away from him. He wanted her closer, not further away.

'Thank you for the dance, Miss Hamilton.' He gave her a formal bow, then turned to Diana. 'Mrs Hamilton, I hope you'll save me a dance at the ball.'

'It's Diana, and it will be my pleasure,' she said. 'You both look wonderful. You'll do Chiverton proud.'

'We will,' Sam promised. 'If you can let me have those photographs, I'll update the website and talk to my contacts at the local paper.'

'Perfect,' Patrick said, clapping him on the shoulder.

'I'll go and change back into my normal clothes,' Sam said. 'I need to keep these ones looking nice for the ball.'

'Me, too,' Victoria said.

Her parents watched them leave, smiling indulgently.

'OK?' Sam asked when they were back in her flat.

'Yes.'

She didn't sound OK. 'Hey. It's going to be fine,' he said. 'Everyone's rooting for you and for Chiverton.'

'Uh-huh.'

There was a sadness in her eyes, and he couldn't stop himself putting his arms round her and giving her a hug. 'I believe in you,' he said. 'You're amazing. And don't let anyone tell you otherwise.'

Oh, but they had. And it had fed into the guilt Victoria felt about being the surviving child. That she wasn't enough. That she would never be enough.

'I know you're sad about not being able to share this with Lizzie,' Samuel said. 'But maybe it's time to let the sadness go and focus on all the good memories. Maybe you can dedicate the ball and the restoration to her.'

She thought about it. 'That's a lovely idea. I'll talk to Dad.'

'You do that. I'll grab you some coffee.'

Could she let go of the sadness? Of the guilt?

It would be hard, but maybe he was right and it was time she tried.

Later that evening, Diana came to Victoria's flat.

'Everything OK, Mum?' Victoria asked.

'No,' Diana said, and enveloped her in a hug. 'Because I had no idea.'

'No idea about what?'

'That you thought it should've been you who died and not Elizabeth. That she's the real daughter, not you.'

Victoria flinched. 'How did you...?' Then she realised. 'Samuel told you.'

'Don't be angry with him. He was just worried about you. We had a little chat.'

'And he told you.' Victoria's throat thickened.

'We *chose* you, Victoria,' Diana said gently. 'You were the light of our life. You still are. And I could never, ever choose between either of my daughters. I don't care about biology. You were ours from the second we first saw you. And we both love you so much. So very much.'

'Oh, Mum.' Victoria hugged her. 'I love you, too. And it's not anything to do with biology.'

'No. It's those dreadful men you picked. I know we should let you make your own choices and your own mistakes—you've never told me what happened and I've tried very hard not to pry—but you always seemed to pick men who didn't really see you for yourself and who didn't treat your properly. Men your father wanted to horsewhip.' She grimaced. 'That Paul—I could've horsewhipped him myself.'

'So that's why you and Dad always try to fix me up with the perfect man?'

'Not perfect, but they all had good hearts. We want you to find someone who loves you as much as we do.'

'Oh, Mum.' Guilt flooded through Victoria, and she

almost told Diana the truth about Samuel, but she couldn't find the right words.

'Samuel, though—you've definitely made the right choice there. He's a keeper. I really appreciate that he told me how you'd been feeling.' Diana stroked Victoria's hair. 'Don't ever feel you're second-best. You're not. You're my eldest daughter, and I love you more than I can say. So does your father.'

'You're the best parents anyone could've wished for,' Victoria said. 'I was thinking, maybe we can dedicate the ball to Lizzie.'

'No,' Diana said. 'The ball should be dedicated to the hard-working, clever, wonderful woman who put it all together. To *you*.'

'But I...'

'You hide your light under a bushel, darling, when your father and I are desperate for you to let it shine. You have that same brightness as the woman you're named after—the Victoria Hamilton who lived here two hundred years ago,' Diana said firmly. 'Now, I want you to promise me that you won't undervalue yourself again. You're my daughter and I'm very, very proud of you. I don't just love you, I *like* the woman you've become. And every day I'm glad you're ours.'

'I love you, too, Mum,' Victoria said, wrapping her arms round Diana.

When her mother had left, she video-called Samuel.

'When did you have a chat with my mother?'

'Ah.' He looked slightly guilty. 'Interfering, I know.'

'Yes,' she said. 'But Mum and I talked about things we should've talked about a long time ago. So thank you.'

'You're not furious with me?'

'I was horrified when I realised,' she said. 'But now I'm grateful.'

'I can work with grateful.' He gave her a grin that made her feel weak at the knees, and as if this thing between them were real rather than a pretence. 'See you tomorrow.'

'Tomorrow,' she echoed.

CHAPTER NINE

THE PHOTOGRAPH MADE a whole spread in the local newspaper, along with photographs of the house.

'So are you and Victoria…?' Denise asked, looking at the photograph of Sam and Victoria together at the piano.

'We're strictly colleagues,' Sam said with a smile. That wasn't the whole truth, but he wasn't prepared to talk about it just yet. He definitely didn't want to tell his mother about the fake engagement. 'Hopefully that picture will sell the rest of the tickets to the ball.'

His mother looked faintly disappointed. 'I worry about you, Sammy. I wish—'

He cut her off by giving her a hug. 'I know, Mum, and I'm fine. Right now my priority is you and Dad—and doing a good job to help the Hamiltons.'

'I know. And I'm sure they appreciate you as much as we do,' Denise said.

Sam realised he'd definitely have to make sure that Patrick didn't bump into Alan socially for the next couple of weeks. Just in case he accidentally mentioned the 'engagement'.

'Your father and I ought to buy tickets,' Denise said ruminatively.

'Mum, that's lovely of you, but you know how much Dad would loathe dressing up in a costume and doing formal dancing,' Sam said with a smile. 'Though if you want to donate the cost of a ticket, I'm sure that would be really appreciated. And I will make cookies for you.'

'Good idea. We'll do that,' Denise said.

'Thanks. I need to go or I'll be late,' he said, and gave her another hug.

Towards the end of November, it snowed. Big, fat, fluffy flakes that settled swiftly and covered the garden in a blanket of white.

'I love this place in the snow,' Victoria said. 'It looks perfect. And it's amazing at night—with everything blanketed in snow, when you look outside it feels as bright as daylight.'

Sam looked up from the file he'd been working on. Snow. Irresistible. Would this make Victoria be less serious? 'Would the garden team mind us going out in this?'

'Provided we stay off the flowerbeds, it'll be fine,' Victoria said. 'And you can do no wrong in Bob's eyes.'

'Then I challenge you to a snowball fight,' he said. He ruffled the fur on the top of the dog's head. 'You and me versus her, right, Humph?'

Humphrey woofed, and Sam laughed. 'That's a yes. Right. Last one out gets a forfeit.'

She grabbed her coat and they tumbled outside in a rush of laughter, pelting each other with snowballs. Humphrey bounded about between them, his tail a blur, chasing snowballs that Sam threw for him.

Sam couldn't remember the last time he'd had this much fun. 'It's years since I had a decent snowball fight. This is probably the first one since I was a student,' he said.

'It's been a while for me, too. Lizzie and I used to have snowball fights—but obviously, because she was younger

than me, I always made sure I didn't throw them too hard,'
Victoria said. 'And we used to make snowmen.'

'I'm up for that,' Sam said. 'And we need to make a
snow dog in honour of Humphrey.'

Between them, they made a massive snowman and a
rather less than perfect snow dog.

'Selfie,' Sam said, and took a snap of them together
in front of the snowman, and a second snap where they'd
crouched down with Humphrey. Both of them had red
faces from the cold, but their eyes were sparkling.

'That was fun,' he said. 'Thanks for sharing this with
me. It must've been amazing growing up here as a child,
with all those trees to climb.'

'We didn't really climb trees. We used to act out being
knights and ladies, with pretend sword-fights and dancing across the lawn,' Victoria said.

'Did you make snow angels?'

She smiled. 'I haven't done that in years.'

Unable to resist, Sam pulled her down into the snow.
She landed on top of him, and automatically his arms
closed round her to steady her.

Her face was full of panic. 'I'm too heavy.'

'No, you're not.' He brushed his mouth against hers.
'Cold snow, warm you. It's a very nice contrast.' Just to
prove his point, he did it again.

This time, she kissed him back. Her mouth was sweet,
and the cold and wetness seeping through his clothes
didn't matter. Nothing mattered apart from the way she
felt, leaning into him and kissing him.

When she broke the kiss he was shocked to realise he
was shaking—and not from the cold.

'Victoria.' His voice sounded cracked and hoarse to
his own ears.

Panic skittered across her expression. 'You'll be soaked. Freezing. We'd better go in.'

He didn't want to move, not when she was in his arms. 'I'm fine.' He stroked her hair.

'You're cold. And wet. I don't have anything that would fit you, but I'm sure Dad can lend you some dry clothes.'

She was babbling, and they both knew it.

If he pushed her now, she'd really panic. Whoever she'd last dated had obviously really hurt her—and Sam, who'd never thought of himself as the violent type, found his fists actually clenching with the urge to punch the guy.

He let her climb off him and lead the way back to the house.

'Go up to my flat and have a hot shower,' she said. 'I'll bring you something of Dad's, and if you leave your wet stuff outside the bathroom door I'll put it in the tumble dryer.'

'Thanks.' He looked at her. 'You're as wet as I am. You have a shower and change first, and I'll make us both a coffee—if you don't mind me using your kitchen.'

'OK. Thanks.'

What had she been thinking?

Well, obviously she *hadn't* been thinking. She'd lost herself in old memories of snowball fights and making snowmen, enjoying herself with Samuel.

That kiss... It had been propinquity, that was all. Victoria knew Samuel didn't want a proper relationship. They were becoming friends, but the kiss hadn't meant anything to him, and she would be stupid to let it mean anything to her.

She showered and changed. 'Back in a tick. I've left you clean towels,' she said, not meeting his eyes.

'Thanks. I've left your mug of coffee by the kettle.'

'Great. I appreciate that.' She borrowed some dry clothes from her dad, then rapped on the bathroom door. 'The dry clothes are outside the door,' she called. 'See you back in the office.' And she fled before she could make more of a fool of herself.

When Samuel came down to her office, a few minutes later, Victoria's vision blurred for a second. She could imagine him leaning against their shared desk in forty years' time, laughing and with a mug of coffee in his hand. Just like her father had shared this office with her mother. And it put a lump in her throat.

But it was pointless wishing for something she couldn't have. Samuel had broken down some of her own barriers, but his were still in place. Whatever he'd said about her being enough, he'd meant enough for her parents— not for him.

'I put your clothes in my dryer,' she said. 'Give it half an hour and I'll go and check if they're ready.'

'Thanks. And it's kind of your dad to lend me stuff.'

'No problem,' she said lightly.

'I guess our snow break's officially over.'

He looked slightly wistful. Was it the snow he was thinking about—or when he'd kissed her?

She shook herself. Not appropriate. 'It is. And I have a pile of stuff to do.'

'We'll divvy it up between us,' he said.

Sam stuck to being professional with Victoria for the next couple of weeks. But, the week before the Christmas events, he sat on the edge of their shared desk. 'Engaged couples go out to dinner. Or dancing.'

She frowned. 'We've done dancing.'

'Regency dancing,' he said. 'Not modern.'

She spread her hands. 'Can you imagine me in a night-club?'

'Well—no,' he admitted. 'But your parents are going to start wondering why we're not going out anywhere on dates.'

'They can see we're really busy with the Christmas week preparations,' she pointed out. 'The house opens on Sunday.'

'We could,' he said, 'have a night out in London. There's a performance I thought it'd be fun to go to.'

Her eyes widened. 'Are you asking me out on a date?'

'A fake one,' he said quickly, not wanting to spook her.

'OK.'

'Friday night?' And maybe he could talk Jude into staying at a friend's for that night. 'Everything's on track and we'll be back for Saturday afternoon to deal with any last-minute trouble-shooting. Plus I think it'll do you good to take an evening off—before you burn out.'

For a moment, he thought he'd pushed her too far; but then she nodded.

'You're right. And thank you—that'd be nice to go to a show.'

On Friday, they dropped their things at Samuel's flat and went for an early dinner. When they walked to the theatre, the show name was in lights outside: *The Taming of the Shrew*.

'Really?' she asked. Did he still think she was a shrew?

'Sorry, I just couldn't resist it,' he said with a grin. 'But we do have good seats.'

'It's a while since I've seen it. And Shakespeare's always a treat.'

'"Why, there's a wench. Come on and kiss me—Vicky."'

He pronounced the 'ky' as 'Kate' and she groaned. 'That's terrible.' But she couldn't help smiling.

They walked into the foyer, and suddenly he grabbed her hand.

'What?' she asked.

'That favour? I'm calling it in, right here and right now,' he said. 'Can you please just go with whatever I say next?'

She'd done that to him without any prior warning, and he'd gone along with her; the least she could do was agree now. 'Sure.'

'You can start by kissing me. Not full-on snogging, just kind of stealing a kiss. Like a fiancée would.'

She had absolutely no idea what had spooked him like this, but she could see the wariness in his eyes. Something was definitely wrong. 'Well, sweetie,' she said softly, resting her palm lightly against his cheek. 'Let's do this.'

She reached up and brushed her mouth against his and he wrapped his arms round her, holding her tightly as if she were the only thing stopping him from drowning.

'Thank you,' he whispered against her mouth.

'Sam? Sam Weatherby? I *thought* it was you!' a voice cooed behind them.

'Olivia,' he said coolly.

Olivia? *The* Olivia? Victoria wondered.

The woman who was sashaying over to them with a man in tow was tall and willowy, with immaculate blonde hair and the kind of high-maintenance barely-there make-up that took an hour to do. Her clothes were all clearly designer labels, Victoria would bet that her shoes cost a fortune, and Olivia was wearing enough jewellery to dazzle the entire theatre.

'Good to see you, Sam.'

From the look in his eyes, Samuel didn't think it was

good to see her—or maybe it was her companion that he objected to. But he said politely, 'And you.' Though Victoria noticed that his eyes didn't crinkle at the corners when he smiled.

'This is Geoff, my fiancé,' she said. 'Darling, Sam and I are old friends.'

That wasn't quite how Victoria would describe it. That snippet of conversation she'd overheard between Samuel and Jude had told her that Olivia and Samuel had been a lot more than friends. And that it had gone badly wrong.

'Good to meet you, Geoff,' Samuel said, shaking the other man's hand. 'And may I present my fiancée, the Hon Victoria Hamilton of Chiverton Hall.'

Now Victoria realised what his favour was: the same as she'd asked of him. Except she was distracting his ex rather than his parents.

Though she didn't have time to wonder if it meant that he was still in love with Olivia, because she'd promised to go along with what he asked.

'Goodness! I didn't realise you'd got engaged.' Olivia's expression was very put out for a moment; then she looked Victoria up and down. Her gaze settled on Victoria's bare left hand, and then she made very sure to clutch her own left hand—which had the most massive diamond on her ring finger—to her chest, to accentuate the difference between them. She gave Victoria a slightly triumphant smile, as if to say that in no way could she imagine someone as attractive as her ex-fiancé wanting to settle down with someone who just wasn't pretty enough or scrubbed up well enough to compete with Olivia herself. 'Well, I do wish you the best. I take it your ring's being resized at the moment? Or is he making you wait, Vicky?'

'My name is Victoria, not Vicky,' Victoria corrected coolly. 'And, actually, we're not bothering with a ring,

Lily.' She deliberately got the other woman's name wrong, and she could see that the barb had hit home. 'Real love doesn't need the trappings and suits.' Before the other woman could make a spiteful comment, she linked her fingers through Sam's. '"My bounty is as boundless as the sea, My love as deep; the more I give to thee, The more I have, for both are infinite."' She drew Sam's hand up to her mouth and kissed the backs of his fingers. 'Which obviously is Juliet rather than Katherine, but what's a play between people who love each other?'

Olivia's expression was like thunder.

'So nice to meet you, Lily,' Victoria said, letting just a hint of patronisation into her tone. 'But I think we're being called to our seats right now. Enjoy the play.' She tugged at Sam's hand, and headed towards one of the doors. 'If this is the wrong way to our seat, it doesn't matter. We'll find another way round,' she said out of the side of her mouth.

Sam took their tickets out of his pocket. 'This is the right door, and hopefully they're not sitting anywhere near us.'

She hoped so, too. 'Are you OK?' she asked, seeing the tension in his eyes.

'Yes.' That was a lie, she knew. 'And thank you for coming to my rescue.'

'No problem.' She squeezed his hand, letting him know she was firmly on his side. If that woman thought she was going to get a second chance to hurt Samuel, she had another think coming. 'She's a festering lily.'

Samuel looked at her. 'That's Shakespeare, right?'

'Sonnet Ninety-four.' In the looks department, Victoria might be a base weed, but Olivia was most definitely a festering lily, and Victoria knew which of the two she'd rather be. 'Ask Jude.'

'Is that why you called her Lily instead of Olivia?'

'I was being petty,' she admitted. 'But it turned out to be appropriate.'

'Yeah.'

To Victoria's surprise, Samuel didn't let her hand go. He held it throughout the whole play, and all the way back to his flat. She didn't comment on it or push him to talk until they had arrived.

'Coffee, wine, or something stronger?' she asked.

'I'm fine.'

'No, you're not.' She gave him a hug. 'Look, I know it's not really any of my business, but seeing Olivia clearly threw you. I'm assuming she's your ex.' She knew that for sure but didn't want to admit to eavesdropping. And he'd helped her overcome feeling as if she was worthless. The least she could do was to be there for him. 'I'm here if you want to talk.'

'I don't really want to talk,' he said, 'but I owe you an explanation.'

'You don't have to tell me anything if you don't want to,' she said.

She thought he was going to close up on her, but then he sighed. 'Olivia was my fiancée.'

Now she understood why Samuel had wanted her to pose as his fiancée tonight. She had a feeling that the whole flashing-my-massive-diamond thing had been Olivia's way of telling him that she'd met someone who suited her better.

'We met at a party, a friend of a friend kind of thing, and...' He grimaced. 'Let's just say I wasn't very nice when I was in my early twenties. I dated a lot. I never, ever cheated on any of my girlfriends, but I never really gave any of them a chance to get close to me, either. I didn't let the relationship develop into anything deeper because I thought the world was my oyster and I had all the time in the world—or maybe my dad was right in that I was selfish and reckless and thoughtless. But somehow Olivia stuck. We'd been dating for six months when she told me she was pregnant.'

Victoria waited.

'So I did the right thing. I didn't think I was really ready to settle down—but she was my girlfriend and she was pregnant with my baby, so of course I wasn't going to abandon her. I asked her to marry me. She said yes.' He closed his eyes for a moment. 'It was only when I accidentally saw a text on her phone—it was on the lock screen,' he added quickly. 'I wasn't snooping. I just glanced casually at the screen when the light came on, as most people do, and I saw the words. It was from one of her friends. She seemed to be laughing at the fact that Olivia had pulled it off.'

Victoria frowned. 'Pulled what off?'

'The trap she'd set for me,' Samuel said. 'The massive rock on her finger, moving into a flat overlooking the river—not this one, I moved here later—and the fact she was never going to have to work again. Because that's what it was, a trap. She wasn't actually pregnant. She just knew that was what it would take for me to marry her—and, once she was married to me, that would mean either sticking with it or handing over an expensive divorce settlement.'

Victoria blinked, not quite taking it in. Olivia had pretended she was pregnant, just to make sure Samuel married her and financed her lifestyle? 'That's a horrible thing to do. What about love?'

'That's when I realised Olivia loved only herself,' he said dryly. 'And she made sure we both saw tonight how massive her new engagement ring is. Bigger than the last one. I feel sorry for the guy, because I don't think she's capable of loving anyone.'

Now Victoria understood that conversation she'd overheard. Why Samuel felt he'd been naive and gullible. But he hadn't. He'd been *decent*. 'So what happened? Did you confront her with the text?'

'I lied. I said I'd overheard her talking to her friend Hermione about the baby that didn't exist and suggested that she might like to tell me the truth. I thought she was going to tough it out, but then she crumpled and admitted it. And I ended the engagement right there and then. I gave her a month to find somewhere else to live and I moved in with Jude. I followed up with a letter from my solicitor, and I think she realised she wasn't going to get anything else out of me—so, thankfully, she left. She stripped the flat, but she left.'

No wonder he had trust issues. Olivia had treated him even more badly than Paul had treated her. 'I'm sorry. That's a horrible thing to happen.' She frowned. 'Though, as she was supposed to be pregnant, um, didn't you notice?'

'That she was still having periods? No. Hers were never regular, and her boss sent her on a couple of courses. I realised later the timing of the "courses" must've coincided with her periods. I wouldn't be surprised if she'd just taken time off and was staying with Hermione rather than going away somewhere on a real course.' He lifted a shoulder. 'I was a gullible, naive fool.'

'No, you weren't. You did your best by her,' she said. 'And we all want to be loved. It's easy to convince yourself someone loves you; it's really not very nice to realise that actually they're looking at your assets instead.'

'That,' he said, 'sounds personal.'

She inclined her head. 'Stately homes are worth a lot of

money. But, unless you've grown up with one or worked in one, you might not realise that owning a stately home means you're asset-rich and cash-poor. Or that stately homes cost an awful lot of money to run.'

'You had a guy like Olivia?' he asked.

'Yes, but we didn't get as far as an engagement, and unlike you it took me three attempts before I finally twigged why any of them wanted to date me.' She grimaced. 'I'm a slow learner. The last guy made it very clear to me that the house is the only attractive thing about me.'

'You,' he said, 'are far from being a slow learner. Your mind's first-class. And words fail me about your ex. That's a vile thing to say, and it's not true.'

She shrugged. 'I saw the way Olivia looked at me tonight. With pity. I'm not like the women in her world— well, in your real world. I don't have an expensive hairdo, expensive shoes, expensive clothes, expensive make-up or expensive jewellery.' She didn't want them, either. They weren't important.

'You don't need them.'

'Thank you for being gallant, but I'm not fishing for compliments. I'm aware of what I am.'

'I don't think you are,' he said. 'When you're talking about history, you light up. And that's *my* Victoria. The one who pays attention to detail, the one who knows obscure stuff and delights in it.' He smiled. 'The one who doesn't bat an eyelid when her muddy dog puts a paw on her knee. Yes, you can be horribly earnest and overserious, but there's a warmth about you and you've got a huge, huge heart: and that's what I see. It's like that thing you were saying to Olivia about trappings and suits—you don't need them. You're enough as you are. Not just for your parents. For *anyone*.'

Tears pricked at her eyelids and she blinked them back. 'That's such a nice thing to say.'

'I'm not being nice. I'm being honest.' He wrapped his arms round her. 'I happen to *like* you.'

Her throat felt thick. 'I like you, too.'

'I mean I really, *really* like you.' He stole a kiss. 'And this is nothing to do with Olivia and everything to do with you.'

This time, when he bent his head to kiss her, she kissed him back. And she made no protest when he picked her up and carried her to his bed.

The next morning, Victoria woke in Samuel's arms. She was pretty sure he was awake—his breathing wasn't deep or regular—and she didn't have a clue what to say to him. This was so far outside the way she usually behaved. She had no idea of the protocols. Had this been a one-night stand, or was it the start of something else?

She still didn't have her thoughts clearly together when Samuel said softly, 'Good morning.'

'Um. Good morning.' She wanted to bury her head rather than face him, but the way she was lying meant that would mean burying her head in his bare chest. And she didn't want him thinking she was needy or would make any kinds of demands on him.

'Are you OK?' he asked.

This time, she met his gaze. 'Yes.' She wasn't—she was all over the place—but no way was she admitting that. 'Are you?'

'Yes and no.' He shifted to kiss the tip of her nose. 'I'm better for waking up with you in my arms.'

'Uh-huh,' she said, not knowing what he wanted to hear.

'Last night probably shouldn't have happened—but I'm glad it did.'

So was she. Though part of her felt antsy. She was used to everything being under control and ticked off a list. This was stepping so far away from that, it sent waves of panic through her. 'So where do we go from here?' she asked.

'I don't know,' he said. 'Maybe see how things go. Though obviously we have next week to get through, first.'

And then his internship would officially be over. 'Then you'll be busy taking over from your dad.'

'But,' he said, 'at least we'll be living near each other. And maybe we can...' He blew out a breath. 'I'm not very good at proper relationships.'

'Neither am I,' she admitted.

'Then maybe we can learn together,' he said. 'Learn to trust each other, learn to make it work.'

Was she hearing things?

'If you'd like to, that is,' he added.

He meant it. He really meant it. And her heart felt as if it would burst with joy. 'I'd like that. A lot,' she said.

He kissed her again, and by the time they got up it was way too late for breakfast. Especially as they had a train to catch.

'Maybe we should have brunch on the train while we go through our lists?' he suggested.

'Good idea.'

Even though they were officially going through all the things they needed to troubleshoot before the house opened to visitors the following afternoon, Sam found himself distracted by Victoria on the train. There was a new softness to her expression when she looked at him.

And the way she made him feel… It was a long time since he could remember being this happy. This thing between them was new and fragile, but he knew she was Olivia's opposite—she was honest and fair and *nice*.

When they reached Cambridge, he took his phone from his pocket to call them a taxi. Then he realised that he must've left his phone switched on silent from the theatre, the previous night, because there were five missed calls from his mother, and a text.

Please call me urgently, Sammy.

He felt sick. Had something happened to his dad? 'I need to call my mum,' he said to Victoria.

'Anything I can do?' she asked.

He shook his head and called his mother.

'Sammy, we're at the hospital. Your father had a stroke this morning,' Denise said.

'I'm on my way,' he said. 'I'm at the station. I'll get a taxi straight to the hospital. Text me the ward name and I'll text you when I'm nearly there.'

'Samuel? What's happened?' Victoria asked when he ended the call.

'Dad's had a stroke. I need to get to the hospital.'

'I'll come with you.'

To the hospital?

Given that she'd lost her sister to leukaemia, Sam was pretty sure that Victoria would find hospitals difficult. In her shoes, he would. OK, so she'd offered to go with him—but it wouldn't be fair to take her up on that offer.

Right now he had no idea what the situation was with his dad. The stroke might've been mild, it might've been severe, or it might've been the first of a series that would end in Alan's death. He couldn't hurt Victoria by making her face that.

He shook his head. 'You have things to do at the house.'

'They can wait.'

He dragged in a breath. 'I need to do this on my own.'

'Anything you need, just call me. *Anything*,' she said. 'It doesn't matter how big or small, or what time it is. Call me.'

Right now what he really wanted was to turn the clock back and for his dad to be OK. But that wasn't possible. 'Thanks,' he said. 'I'll call you later.'

'Give my best to your parents.'

'Thanks. I will.'

The drive in the taxi felt as if it were taking for ever. Seeing his father in a hospital bed, with Alan's mouth twisted and one eye half shut, was a shock.

'Mum. I'm so sorry.' He hugged his mother, and sat on the edge of his father's bed, taking Alan's hand. When had his father's skin become this papery—this *old*? 'Dad, I'm here. I'm sorry.'

The sounds that came out of his father's mouth didn't bear much resemblance to words.

'Don't try to talk. Just rest. I'm here now,' Sam said.

Time, at the hospital, was different. Like treacle. And, although the medical staff were kind, nobody could give any real answers about when—or if—Alan would recover his powers of speech or walk again. Sam was used to organising things, making things happen; the seven words he kept hearing drove him insane. *We'll just have to wait and see.*

How long would they have to wait?

And actually having to feed his father because Alan couldn't hold cutlery or a cup or a sandwich. Sam knew how much his father was hating this. The loss of control. The loss of his dignity.

All Sam could do was to grit his teeth and hold both his parents' hands. 'We'll get through this,' he said. 'We'll get you back on your feet and back to your normal self, Dad.'

His phone beeped several times but he ignored it, until Denise pushed him to go and get himself a mug of coffee. Then he checked his messages.

There were a couple from Victoria. Not demanding, needy, look-at-me messages like the ones Olivia had been fond of sending. Just a quiet, At Chiverton. Hope your dad's doing OK. Thinking of you all.

There wasn't much he could say to that. Because right now nobody knew how his dad was doing.

Thanks, he typed back.

He wished he hadn't pushed her away and told her to go back to Chiverton. Right now he could really do with her arms round him, His steady, quiet, *safe* Victoria.

But that wasn't fair.

Hadn't his father said he was selfish and reckless?

There was a second text, sent two hours later.

Let me know if there's anything I can do. Any time.

She was so kind and supportive: and, at the same time, it was clear she was trying to give him space and not pressure him. That she understood what it was like to be at the bedside of someone you loved, worried sick, and she wouldn't be huffy if he didn't reply within a couple of hours, let alone within seconds.

And because he knew what she'd been through, he knew he had to do the right thing. Distance himself. Protect her from having to face this nightmare all over again. So, later that evening, he sent her a text.

Sorry to let you down. I need to support my parents right now. Book a temp to help you next week and I'll pick up the bill. Hope all goes well with the ball.

Victoria stared at the text.

He'd said nothing about how his dad was. How *he* was. He'd ignored the supportive texts she'd sent him—and she hadn't flooded his phone with needy messages, either. She'd simply told him when she got back to Chiverton and asked him to let her know if there was anything she could do. She'd tried to be supportive and give him space at the same time.

She blew out a breath and tried to unpick his message.

Sorry to let you down.

Of course he wasn't letting her down. This was an emergency.

I need to support my parents right now.

Again, in his shoes, she'd feel the same. It wasn't a problem.

Book a temp to help you next week and I'll pick up the bill.

Meaning that he wasn't coming back as her intern. It would be a bit of a headache for her, but over the weeks she'd worked with him she'd discovered that they had the same attitude towards project management and she knew his files would contain all the information she'd need to keep everything ticking over. As for getting in someone to help her—she'd just pick up the slack herself. She didn't expect him to pay for a temp to replace his unpaid position.

Hope all goes well with the ball.

And that was the bit that stuck in her throat. He wasn't coming to the ball. She'd so been looking forward to it. To dancing with him in the restored room, dressed up in her Regency finery.

OK. She'd have to stop being selfish and suck it up. Samuel's dad was seriously ill. Of course he wouldn't want to come and do something so frivolous.

She had no idea whether his phone was even on, so a text was the easiest way to reach him. He'd pick it up whenever.

You're not letting me down and of course I understand your parents need you. Let me know if there's anything I can do.

She didn't quite dare add a kiss. Because now she was starting to think that what he'd said to her in London had been in the heat of the moment.

You're enough as you are. Not just for your parents. For anyone.

Maybe he'd meant it at the time. But now all her old fears came flooding back. She hadn't been enough for Paul, and Samuel was ten times the man Paul was. Whatever made her think she'd be enough for him?

And how selfish was she, putting her own feelings first when she knew how ill his father was?

She'd do what he wanted and keep her distance.

Victoria was nothing like Olivia. Of course she'd be understanding and wouldn't put pressure on him, Sam thought. She was kind. She offered help because she genuinely cared and wanted to help, not because she thought it would score points.

But everything was muddled in his head. Right now he couldn't get over the fact that his father was seriously ill.

Alan Weatherby had definitely got the measure of his son. Reckless and selfish.

So maybe it was time to be unselfish and not keep Victoria dangling on the hook. She had enough on her plate without worrying about him.

He'd do what he always did with relationships. Distance himself.

Thanks, but no need. Good luck with the future.

CHAPTER TEN

GOOD LUCK WITH the future.

That sounded pretty final, Victoria thought.

Obviously Samuel didn't plan to be part of that future.

What an idiot she was. So much for thinking she'd learned her lesson. Yet again she'd fallen in love with a charmer who didn't feel the same way about her. Though at least Samuel hadn't had his eye on the house.

She'd just have to suck it up and deal with it. The only thing she could do was to visit Alan Weatherby in hospital when he was a little better and give Samuel the glowing reference he deserved. Just because things hadn't worked out between them, she wasn't petty enough to deny the hard work he'd put in.

In the meantime, she had enough to keep her super-busy, with the house due to open for visitors, the work-shops and the ball.

She spent the day putting the finishing touches to the Christmas trees and trying not to think about how she and Samuel had collected the pine cones and the giant allium heads together and spray-painted them gold. She made a couple of kissing balls, binding the hoops together with string and covering them with greenery, adding dried orange slices and ribbons and mistletoe; and all the while she tried not to think about kissing Samuel. She made pomanders, pressing cloves into oranges and tying them with ribbons. Having something to do that required her attention so she didn't have time to think was really, really good.

The team who always did her flowers had gathered greenery to be spread along the windowsills and mantelpieces, and they'd done her proud with the table centrepieces.

And the one good thing about working ridiculous hours was that it meant she was physically so tired that she actually slept instead of lying awake, brooding.

The next day, Samuel's team of footmen and servants turned up—thankfully in exactly the kind of clothes they would've worn in Regency times. She set them to work with Nicola, sorted out a room for her anachronistic Santa, and made sure she was around in case any of the visitors had any questions.

Despite the fact that all their visitors seemed delighted to have the chance to talk about Regency Christmas customs and she was rushed off her feet, she still missed Samuel. Every so often she found herself turning to say something to him—and of course he wasn't there.

Stupid, stupid, stupid.

Once the house had closed, she cut some flowers from the garden, then headed for the hospital.

'Sorry, we don't allow flowers at the moment,' the receptionist on the ward told her. 'We have strict rules for controlling the spread of infection.'

'Of course. Sorry.' She bit her lip.

But at least they allowed her to visit Samuel's father. And, thankfully, Samuel wasn't there.

'Mr Weatherby? I'm Victoria Hamilton—Patrick and Diana's daughter,' she said. 'I did bring you some flowers from Chiverton, but unfortunately I'm not allowed to give them to you.'

'Thank you anyway.' Alan squinted at her.

'I'm so sorry you're ill.'

'Getting better. Words aren't...' He grimaced. 'Can't get the right ones.'

'They'll come back,' she said, wanting to reassure him.

'Got some words today, though. Getting better. You work with Sammy.'

She nodded. 'Your son is a good man. He's way over-qualified to be my intern, but he did the job anyway, with a good heart. He's easy to work with.'

Alan frowned. 'Reckless.'

'A little bit headstrong at times,' she said, 'but Samuel listens to people. He thinks about things. He's impulsive, yes, but that's not a bad thing because he has great ideas.'

'You taught him to bake.' Alan smiled. 'His mum nearly fell over.'

She smiled back. 'He was very pleased with himself about that. And he insisted on making everyone in the house try the biscuits. He's—*was*,' she corrected herself, 'going to make them for the ball. They're on the menu as Weatherby's Wonders.'

'Weatherby's Wonders.' Alan gave a wheezy chuckle.

'Mr Weatherby? Are you all right? Can I get you a glass of water, or would you like me to call a nurse?'

'I'm all right, love.' He patted her hand. 'Tell me. Sammy.'

There was a lot she could say about Samuel, but it wasn't appropriate. Instead, she said, 'He's kind to my dog, he makes time for everyone on the team and makes them feel valued, and our head gardener Bob—who's no-torious for being grumpy—has taken a real shine to him and comes into the office for a daily cuppa with him. I miss him. We *all* miss him,' she added swiftly.

'You think he could take over?'

'From you? Yes. No hesitation. Samuel would make an excellent job of anything he decided to do.'

'You'll give him a…?' Alan frowned, clearly unable to find the right word.

'Reference?' She nodded. 'He's more than earned it. He's done everything from spray-painting pine cones, to organising a Santa and negotiating an amazing deal on Christmas trees. He learned to bake from a recipe that's centuries old, and he learned the steps to the Regency dances when he'd never done anything like that before. He never complained once. Argued with me, yes, but he had valid points.' And he'd stolen her heart in the process.

Samuel recognised that voice.

He stopped dead, not wanting Victoria to see him. What was she doing here?

Knowing that he shouldn't be eavesdropping, he listened.

She was talking to his father. And she was really giving him a glowing report.

Guilt flooded through him. He'd pushed her away—and she'd still come to give support, in a place that had to be difficult for her. She could've just ignored all this or sent a formal letter with a reference, especially as she was right in the middle of the fundraising and she was horrendously busy.

But she hadn't. She was here in person. Not to score points, but because Victoria Hamilton was a really, really good woman. Dependable. Trustworthy. Brave.

I miss him.

Yeah. He missed her, too. So much that it actually

hurt. But he didn't know what to say to her; and all the things that were in his head definitely weren't appropriate to say in front of his father. Plus he didn't want to do anything that might make his father have a relapse or a second stroke.

This was a conversation he needed to have with Victoria, on his own—and not right now. For his father's sake, he'd go and have a cup of coffee and come back in half an hour.

As for Victoria herself... He was going to have to sort that out, too. He'd let her down. Hurt her. He wasn't entirely sure how to fix it, but he'd find a way to make a start. Because hearing her voice again had crystallised everything for him. He finally knew what he wanted for the rest of his life. The question was whether she wanted that, too. But the way she spoke to his father gave him hope.

The workshops went brilliantly, including the pre-ball dance workshop. Victoria had to nip out to the supermarket and get emergency supplies for the café, because they had even more visitors than she was expecting. The reproduction silk hangings for the ballroom were so perfect that when they were up even she couldn't spot the difference; and Jaz's third years were all thoroughly enjoying the preparations for the ball supper.

And today, on the day of the ball, it was snowing. Not enough to cause problems, but a light dusting—enough to make the house look really, really pretty.

Victoria loved the house in the snow. For her, Chiverton glowed brighter than any diamond.

Her professional life was perfect, right now. The house was looking better than ever. The fundraising week had put everyone on a real high. Today ought to be one of the happiest days of her life.

Except it wasn't.

She really, really missed Samuel. So did Humphrey; he looked up hopefully every time someone walked down the corridor to her office, and every time it wasn't Samuel he put his head back dejectedly between his paws. Right now, that was what Victoria wanted to do, too. Curl up in a ball and huddle in misery.

But tonight was the high point of the fundraising week. She was expecting guests and the press any second now, and she needed to pin that smile on her face and be dazzling.

It was a week since his father's stroke. In that time Sam had done a lot of thinking. A lot of talking. A bit of persuading.

Tonight, he was hoping that the whole lot would come together. That he could fix the mess he'd made. His mother had given him wise advice; the Hamiltons had been shocked at first when he'd told them the truth about the 'engagement', but then they'd been understanding. Given him their blessing.

And now it was time to face Victoria.

He'd waited until the press had gone and the ball was in full swing. Just before supper, by his reckoning.

'Sam! I didn't think you were coming,' Jenny, the house steward stationed in the reception area, said. 'How's your dad?'

Obviously Victoria had explained his absence to everyone in terms of his father's illness, rather than pointing out that he'd let everyone down. 'He's on the mend, thanks.' He smiled at her. 'Everyone's upstairs?'

'They are. And you don't need anyone to show you the way to the ballroom, do you?'

'No. It's fine. But thanks.'

He strode up the massive curved staircase and through the Long Gallery. He could hear the music playing, and he looked through the doorway into the ballroom.

He'd seen the pictures on the website, but it hadn't prepared him for the real thing. Instead of that bare wall that made Victoria flinch, the silk hangings were back. The mirrors on the walls reflected the chandeliers, candelabra and each other, spreading the light further. And the walls actually glowed in the light.

It was stunning.

No wonder she loved this room.

The carpet had been removed temporarily; people were on the dance floor, following Michael the dancing master's instructions, and others were sitting on the *chaises longues* and chairs at the side of the room, watching them.

Victoria was dancing. In her red silk dress, she looked amazing, and his heart skipped a beat.

Please let her talk to him. Let her give him a chance.

He waited until the music had finished, then walked over to her. 'Good evening, Miss Hamilton.'

She stared at him, looking shocked. 'I thought you weren't coming tonight.'

'The night when the ballroom was back to its former glory? Wild horses wouldn't have kept me away.' Though it wasn't the room he wanted. It was her.

'Is your dad all right?' she asked.

'He's home and grumbling at my mum about not being allowed a bacon sandwich. He's got all his words back, and the physio's having to tell him not to overdo things because he's so determined he wants to be back in the swing of things. Though he's agreed to let me take over the business.'

'Is that what you want?'

'It's part of what I want.' He looked at her. 'And that's why I'm here.'

She looked him up and down. 'But—your boots!'

'I know, I know, Regency men aren't supposed to wear boots to a ball. Mrs P told me. My dancing shoes are in a bag. I can't wear them outside or they'll be ruined—especially in the snow.' He smiled at her. 'Come with me?'

She shook her head. 'I can't. It's the middle of the ball.'

'Which looks as if it's going like clockwork. Jaz and the students have the food covered, Michael and the quartet have the dancing covered, and your dad will do whatever needs to be done.'

Her eyes narrowed at him. 'How do you know that?'

'Because I've spoken to your dad.'

Her frown deepened. 'He didn't tell me.'

Because Sam had asked him not to tell.

'What did you talk about?' she asked.

'By and by,' he said. 'Come with me, Victoria. Please.'

'Outside, you mean?' She frowned. 'But I'm...' She gestured to her dress.

'That's OK—I have an anachronistic blanket.' He smiled at her. 'I was going to get you a coat, but Mrs P said even she can't make a Regency woman's coat in an afternoon.'

'Pelisse,' she corrected.

He grinned, loving the fact she was being pernickety. 'And she also said that traditionally it was trimmed with fur, and I thought you might have a problem with that.'

'I do.'

'Hence the anachronistic blanket. It's downstairs by the front door.'

She gave in and let him shepherd her downstairs, where he wrapped the blanket round her.

'I need to get some shoes.'

'No, you don't.' He swept her up into his arms.

'Samuel! You can't—'

'Yes, I can,' he said, and marched her out of the house to the waiting carriage.

'Oh, my God,' she said, seeing the horses and carriage.

He grinned. 'To me they look white, but I've been told this is a pair of matched greys. I don't care if the carriage is anachronistic, I don't want you being frozen, and an open-topped carriage on a December night in England is impossible.' He deposited her in the carriage, made sure she was settled, and then sat opposite her.

'I...' She shook her head, as if unable to think of what to say.

He grinned. 'I've got you lost for words. That's good. This is my chance to talk.' He took a deep breath. 'First off, I owe you a huge apology.'

She looked at him, her dark eyes wide.

'When Dad had his stroke, I was really unfair to you. I pushed you away—even though I know I can trust you and you're not like Olivia. I didn't know how ill Dad would get, or if he'd die, and I didn't want to put you through that. And that's why I went all cold on you and basically—' He raked a hand through his hair. 'Yeah. Stupid, I should've talked to you and told you how I feel, but I'm a bloke and I'm not very good at that sort of thing.'

'Right. So you've kidnapped me in the middle of the fundraiser ball to tell me that.'

'No, I've kidnapped you for another reason,' he said. 'By and by. Firstly, I overheard what you said to Dad in the hospital.'

'Eavesdroppers,' she said primly, 'never hear any good about themselves.'

'Oh, but I did,' he said. 'That I would make an excellent job of anything I decided to do. Which is why—'

He gestured round them. 'Technically, we don't need the suits and trappings. But I thought they'd be nice today. On a day when you've taken the house back two hundred years, it seemed appropriate to take my transport back two hundred years.'

'Only you would turn up in a landau with a pair of matched greys.'

He laughed. 'Trust you to know what the carriage is.'

She simply raised her eyebrows at him.

'Victoria. The reason I brought you out here is because I want to tell you that I love you. I've never felt like this about anyone. On paper, this shouldn't work. You're this massive history nerd and I work with figures. You live in the middle of nowhere with your parents and my house is a total bachelor pad in a very trendy bit of London.' He took a deep breath. 'But.'

'But?'

'It's you,' he said. 'Everything about you. I love that you're so serious and you pay attention to detail. I love that you pour your heart and soul into what you do. I love that you're the centre of your family—your parents adore you and your dog adores you and everyone who works in the house just lights up when you walk by because you pay attention and you listen to them and they know it.' He reached over to her and took her hand. 'But most of all I love you for you.'

'Uh-huh.'

'Which is Victoria-speak for the fact you don't know what to say.' He removed the glove from her left hand. 'I have actually done this the right way, this time. I talked to your parents about our fake engagement.'

'You did what?' She looked horrified.

'Actually, they understood. But we need to stop with the fake engagement business.'

'Agreed.'

'And the reason we need to stop with the fake one,' he said, 'is because I want it to be a real one. Let's be clear: it's *you* I want, not the house.'

'So you don't want to live here?'

'I want to live with you, whether it's here or in a—' He cast about for the most unlikely thing he could think of. 'In a yurt.'

She laughed, then. 'A yurt?'

'A yurt pitched in the middle of a swamp,' he said. 'I don't care where I live, as long as it's with you. And that's why I talked to your parents. Asking permission and stuff.' He dropped to one knee and took a velvet-covered box from his pocket. 'So this is why I kidnapped you from the ball. I love you—and, even though I haven't given you the chance to say it, I think you feel the same way about me, or you wouldn't have woken up in my arms that morning and you wouldn't have said what you did to Dad. And if Dad hadn't had that stroke, we would still have been having this conversation. Maybe not in the middle of the ball and maybe not in a carriage in the snow, but we would still definitely have been having this conversation. I've wanted to have this conversation with you for weeks.' He took a deep breath and opened the box. 'Will you marry me, Victoria?'

The ring nestled among the velvet was very simple, a single diamond set in platinum, and Victoria loved it.

And she loved the effort he'd put into this, too. That he'd clearly visited Mrs Prinks to get the right kind of boots, that he'd hired a carriage and horses, that he knew her tastes well enough to buy the perfect engagement ring—and he'd asked her parents, too, so he had their blessing before he proposed and obviously her mother had told him her ring size.

But most of all he'd said the important things.

That he loved her. Loved her for *herself*. Loved the things about her that her exes had all found annoying.

She swallowed hard. Time for her to say it. And it was different, saying it when you knew the other person felt the same way. 'I love you, too, Sammy.'

He blinked. 'Did you just call me Sammy?'

She nodded. 'And I guess you can…call me Tori.' The pet name he'd wanted to call her before, but she'd refused.

He kissed her and slid the ring onto her finger. 'I love you, Tori,' he said softly. 'And now we're going back to the ball before you freeze. How the hell did they do all this stuff in Regency times?'

'You must be freezing, too, in that frock coat.'

'Come and dance with me and we'll warm up,' he said. 'You were supposed to keep a waltz free for me.'

'I would've done, but you weren't there when they played the waltz.'

He laughed and kissed her again. 'Michael will get them to play another one for us. Especially as I have champagne on ice.'

She frowned. 'How did you manage that?'

'I had it delivered to your dad.'

'What if I'd said no?' she asked, suddenly curious.

'Then I would've written you really bad poetry and worn you down until you agreed.'

'Bad poetry.' She grinned. 'If I'd known that, I might've said no. Just to see how bad your poetry is.'

'Too late. You're wearing my ring now.' He drew her hand up to his mouth and kissed the inside of her wrist. 'Seriously, if you'd said no, then I asked your dad to give everyone champagne on my behalf to celebrate the ballroom restoration. And then I would've found myself a yurt and started writing bad poetry.' He raised an eyebrow. 'Actually, as you seem interested, I might do the poetry anyway. And I'll grow my hair out like Byron's. Be "mad and bad and dangerous to know".'

'Oh, please,' she said, laughing.

'Wait, wait. I have good, proper Regency poetry. Which I admit Jude found for me.' He coughed. '"She walks in beauty, like the night…" And you do. I love you.' He kissed her again. 'And you've just made me the happiest person in the world. Thank you.'

She felt her eyes fill with tears. 'I love you, too, Sammy.'

He carried her back to the house, then changed his boots for the dancing shoes.

'I can't believe you bought Regency boots just for tonight,' she said as they walked up the staircase together.

'Oh, I have plans for those boots.' He raised an eyebrow. 'They're the perfect footwear for whenever I want to carry my wife off somewhere and play Darcy to her Miss Bennet.'

She laughed.

'But keep your hands behind your back for now,' he said. 'Our parents need to be the first to know.'

Back in the ballroom, they went over to her parents. 'Can I borrow you both for a quick word?' Samuel asked.

Patrick and Diana looked thrilled and led them out to the Long Gallery.

'Anachronistic but necessary,' he said, taking his phone from his pocket. 'Excuse me a second. My parents need to be in this conversation as well.' He put the phone on speaker, waited while the line connected, and the call was picked up within two rings.

'Sammy?' Denise asked. 'What did she say?'

Her parents looked as if they were desperate to know the answer, too.

Victoria brought her hands from behind her back to show the engagement ring and smiled. 'I said yes.'

EPILOGUE

A year later

PATRICK STOOD BY the piano and the string quartet. 'I'm delighted to welcome you all to the second annual Chiverton Christmas ball—a tradition started by my wonderful daughter Victoria. And it's time for our first dance.'

'Well, the Hon Mrs Hamilton-Weatherby, it's all looking very festive. And oh, look, we're under the kissing ball.' Samuel stole a kiss. 'I still think we should have tinsel.'

Victoria knew he was teasing her. 'Not on your life.'

'Anachronistic,' he said with a grin. 'Come and waltz with me.'

They were in the middle of the ballroom when she said to him, 'The thing about Regency waltzes is that you were close enough to whisper secrets.'

'Oh, yes?'

'I would say that I love you, but that's not a secret.'

He laughed. 'I love it when your eyes are full of mischief. So what are you going to tell me, then?'

Demurely, she turned in a circle with him. 'Our honeymoon.' He'd taken her on a mini version of the Grand Tour, and she'd loved every second of it, sharing the museums and art galleries with him. He'd even talked the orchestra outside Florian's in Venice into playing a Regency waltz so he could dance with her through St Mark's Square.

'What about it?'

'It seems,' she said, 'it had consequences.'

'Consequences?'

'That's the thing about Regency dress,' she said, enjoying herself. 'The Empire neckline is very flattering. It hides bumps.'

'Bumps?' He sucked in a breath. 'Are you telling me we're…?'

She nodded. 'Two months. I thought I just missed a period because we were so busy. But I did a test this morning. I've been waiting for the right moment to tell you.'

'I didn't think I could be any happier, but…' He beamed at her. 'That's amazing. I really hope you're ready for this baby to be utterly spoiled by two sets of grandparents.'

'Not to mention the baby's doting papa,' she said with a smile.

'If it's a girl,' he said softly, 'maybe we can call her Lizzie.'

'I'd like that.'

'Just think,' he said. 'Last year the ball was our engagement. This year, it's our news. Next year…'

She grinned. 'Next year I'm sure the Weatherby Wonder will think of something.'

He laughed back. 'Just you wait…'

* * * * *

SNOWFLAKES AND SILVER LININGS

CARA COLTER

With thanks to Shirley and Rebecca

I am in awe of your creative genius, amazing discipline, and unflagging professionalism.

PROLOGUE

CHRISTMAS.

Turner Kennedy was a man who took pride in his ability not just to cope with fear, but to shape it into a different force entirely.

He had jumped from airplanes at 8,200 meters into pitch blackness and an unknown welcome.

He had raised all kinds of havoc "outside the fence" in hostile territory.

He had experienced nature's mercurial and killing moods without the benefit of shelter, sweltering heat to excruciating cold, sometimes in the same twenty-four-hour period.

He had been hungry. And lost. He had been pushed to the outer perimeters of his physical limits, and then a mile or two beyond.

He had been the hunted, stranded in the shadows of deeply inhospitable places, listening for footfalls, smelling the wind, squinting against impenetrable darkness.

It was not that he had not been afraid, but rather that he had learned he had a rare ability to transform fear into adrenaline, power, energy.

And so the irony of his current situation was not lost on him. After a long period away, he was back in the United States, a country where safety was a given, taken for granted.

And he was afraid.

He was afraid of three things.

He was afraid of sleeping. In his dreams, he was haunted by all the things he had refused to back down from, haunted by a failure that more fear, on his part, might have changed a devastating outcome.

And maybe it was exhaustion caused by that first fear that had led to the second one.

Turner Kennedy was afraid of Christmas.

Maybe not the coming Christmas, specifically, but of his memories of ones gone by. Those memories were lingering at the edges of his mind, waiting to leap to the forefront. Today, it had been seeing an angel Christmas tree topper in a store window.

Without warning, Turner had been transported back more than two decades.

They came down the stairs, early morning light just beginning to touch the decorated living room. The tree was eight feet tall. His mother had done it all in white that year. White lights, white Christmas ornaments, a white angel on top of the tree. The house smelled of the cookies she had baked for Santa while he and his brothers had spent Christmas Eve on the backyard skating rink their dad had made for them.

It had been past ten when his mother had finally insisted they come in. Even then, Turner hadn't wanted to. He could not get enough of the rink, of the feeling of the ice beneath his blades, of the cold on his cheeks, the wind in his hair, the power in his legs as he propelled himself forward. The whole world had seemed infused with magic....

But now the magic seemed compromised. Though the cookies were gone, nothing but crumbs remaining, Santa hadn't been there. The gifts from Santa were always left, unwrapped, right there on the hearth. This morning, that place yawned empty.

He and his younger brothers, Mitchell and David, shot each other worried looks.

Had they been bad? What had they done to fall out of Santa's favor?

His parents followed them down the steps, groggy, but seemingly unaware that anything was amiss.

"Let's open some gifts," his father said. "I've been wanting to see what's in this one."

His dad seemed so pleased with the new camera they had gone together to buy him. His mother opened perfume from Mitchell, a collectible ornament from David. She'd looked perplexed at Turner's way more practical gift of a baseball mitt, and then laughed out loud.

And just as her laughter faded, Turner had heard something else.

A tiny whimper. Followed by a sharp, demanding yelp.

It was coming from the laundry room, and he bolted toward the sound before his younger brothers even heard it. In a wicker basket with a huge red bow on it was a puppy. Its fur was black and curly, its eyes such a deep shade of brown a boy could get lost in them. When Turner picked it up, it placed already huge paws on his shoulders, and leaned in, frantic with love, to lick his cheeks. Much to the chagrin of his brothers, Chaos had always loved Turner best of all....

Turner snapped himself out of it, wiped at cheeks that felt suddenly wet, as if that dog, the companion who had walked him faithfully through all the days of his childhood and teens, had licked him just now. The last time Chaos had kissed him had been over a dozen years ago, with the same unconditional love in his goodbye as had been in his hello....

To Turner's relief, his cheeks were not wet, but dry.

For the third thing he was afraid of, perhaps even

more than going to sleep and the coming of Christmas, was tears.

He got up, restless, annoyed with himself. This was the fear, exactly. That something about Christmas would weasel inside him and unleash a torrent of weakness.

He went to the barracks window. It was temporary housing, between missions. Would there be another mission? He wasn't sure if he had it in him anymore. Maybe it was time to call it quits.

But for what? It had been a long time since he had called anyplace home.

He could not stay here, at the military base, for Christmas. He hated it that emotion seemed to be breaking through his guard. It was too *empty*. There was too much room here for his own thoughts.

There was too much space for that thing he feared the most.

A yearning for the way things had once been.

David and Mitchell hadn't told him not to come for Christmas, but hadn't asked him, either. Of course, they probably assumed he was out-of-country, and he hadn't corrected that assumption.

It was better this way. He had nothing to bring to their lives. Or anyone's.

There were lots of places a single guy could go at Christmas to avoid the festivities. Palm trees had a way of dispelling that Christmassy feeling for him. A tropical resort would have the added benefit of providing all kinds of distractions. The kind of distractions that wore bikinis.

Turner was aware he wasn't getting enough sleep. Not even the thought of women in bikinis could shake the feeling of ennui, mixed with the restless, seething energy that wouldn't let him drift off.

Just then his cell phone rang.

He must have another mission in him, after all, because

he found himself hoping it was the commanding officer of his top secret Tango Force unit. That Christmas would be superseded by some world crisis.

But it wasn't his CO's number on display. Turner answered the call. Listened. And was shocked to hear himself say, "Yeah, I'll be there."

It had been a voice from that thing he most wanted to avoid: the past. A time he remembered with the helpless yearning of a man who could not return to simpler things, simpler times, his simpler self.

But Cole Watson, his best friend from *before* Turner had ever known he had a gift for dealing with fear, had been trying to track him down for weeks. Said he needed him.

And Turner came from a world where one rule rose above all the others: when a buddy needed you, you were there.

Okay. So it wasn't a life-or-death request. No one's survival was on the line.

Cole was putting his life back in order. He'd lost nearly everything that mattered to him. He said he'd been given a second chance, and he planned to take it.

Was that the irresistible pull, then—second chances? It certainly wasn't a place in the backwoods of New England called the Gingerbread Inn, though the fact that Turner had never been there was a plus, as it held no memories.

No, Cole had casually mentioned that the inn sat on the shores of Barrow's Lake, where a man could put on his skates and go just about forever. That sounded like as good a way as any to spend the holiday season.

As good a way as any to deal with the energy that sang along Turner's nerve endings, begging for release. It sounded nearly irresistible.

CHAPTER ONE

CASEY CARAVETTA SIGHED with contentment.

"Being at the Gingerbread Inn with the two of you feels like being home," she said. She didn't add, *"in a way that home had never felt like."*

"Even with it being in such a state?" Emily asked, sliding a disapproving look around the front parlor. It was true the furniture was shabby, the paint was peeling, the rugs had seen better days.

"Don't you worry," Andrea said, "You are not going to recognize this place by the time I'm done with it. On Christmas Eve, Emily, for your vow renewal, the Gingerbread Inn will be transformed into the most amazing winter wonderland."

"I am so humbled that all the people Cole and I are closest to are going to give up their Christmas plans to be with us," Emily said.

"Nobody is giving up their Christmas plans," Andrea answered. "We're spending a magical Christmas Eve together, and then scattering to the four corners, to be wherever we need to be for Christmas."

Except Casey, who didn't need to be anywhere. And the inn, despite its slightly gone-to-seed appearance, would be the perfect place to spend a quiet day by herself.

The thought might have been depressing except for the gift Casey had decided to give herself....

Outside, snow had begun to fall, but the parlor's stone hearth held a fire that crackled merrily and threw a steady stream of glowing red sparks up the chimney.

Until she'd received Andrea's plea to take a little extra time off work and come to the Gingerbread Inn to make magic happen for Emily and Cole's renewal of vows, Casey had been looking forward to Christmas with about the same amount of anticipation she might have for a root canal.

In other words, the same as always.

Except, of course, for the gift, her secret plan to get her life back on track.

Now, here with her friends, cuddling her secret to her, Casey actually felt as if she might start humming, "It's beginning to feel a lot like Christmas...."

"That sense of home doesn't have a thing to do with looks," she said, wanting to share what she was feeling with her friends.

Belonging.

She had never felt it with her own family. At school, she had been the outsider, the too-smart geek. Her work was engrossing, but largely solitary.

But being here with Emily and Andrea, the Gingerbread Girls all together again, Casey felt hope.

Even though, sadly, Melissa was not here. Why did it take a tragedy for people to understand that friendship was a gift to be cherished, and not taken for granted?

Casey and Andrea had spent two days together here early in December, Casey seeking the refuge of friendship to try and outrun her latest family fiasco. Really, any given year she might as well block out all of December on her calendar and write "crisis" on it.

But before her meeting with Andrea it had been far too long since she and her friends, who'd always called themselves "the Gingerbread Girls," had been together.

After seeing Andrea, Casey had made her decision.

Now, she was loving the fact that they were as comfortable as if they had been together only yesterday. Sentences began with "Remember when…" and were followed by gales of laughter. The conversation flowed easily as they caught up on the details of one another's lives.

"Speaking of looks, I can't believe the way *you* look," Emily told Casey for about the hundredth time. "I just can't get over it."

"You should be modeling," Andrea agreed.

"Modeling?" Casey laughed. "I think models are usually a little taller than five foot five."

"The world's loss," Andrea said with a giggle, and took a sip of her wine.

Casey sipped hers, as well. Emily, pregnant, her baby bump barely noticeable beneath her sweater, was glowing with happiness and was sipping sparkling fruit juice instead of wine.

Next year at this time, that could very well be me, Casey mused, and the thought made her giddy.

"How do you get your hair so straight?" Andrea asked. "You didn't have it like that when I saw you earlier this month. Remember how those locks of yours were the bane of your existence? All those wild curls. No matter what you did, that head of hair refused to be tamed. Remember the time we tried ironing it? With a clothes iron?"

Would her baby have wild curls? Casey hoped not.

"I always loved it," Emily said. "I was jealous."

"Of *my* hair?" she asked, incredulous. She touched it self-consciously. She had a flat iron that was state-of-the-art, a world away from what they had tried that humid summer day.

Still, her curls surrendered to the highest setting with the utmost reluctance, and were held at bay with enough gel to slide a 747 off a runway. And yet as she touched her hair, it felt coiled, ready to spring.

"I thought you were quite exotic, compared to Andrea and me."

"Really?"

"Why so surprised?"

Maybe it was her second glass of wine that made her admit it. "I always felt like the odd woman out. Here was this wonderful inn, out of an American dream, filled with all these wholesome families, like yours and Andrea's. And then there was the Caravetta clan. A boisterous Italian family, always yelling and fighting and singing and crying and laughing, and whatever we were doing, we were doing it loudly. Next to you and Andrea, I felt like I was a little too much of everything."

"But you weren't like that," Emily said. "You were always so quiet and contained. If you were too much of anything it was way too smart, Doc. Thinking all the time."

Casey dismissed the comment with a wave of her hand. "I didn't mean that. You were both tall, reed thin and fair, while I was short and plump, and had skin that came straight from the olive grove. You had well-behaved blond ponytails. I had dark tangles and coils that did whatever they wanted. You both have that all-American look, Emily, with your eyes like jade, and Andrea's like sapphires."

"There is nothing wrong with your eyes!" Andrea declared.

"Ha! My grandmother used to look at my eyes and say they were so dark she could see the devil in them. And then she'd cross herself."

Would Casey's baby have her eyes? Did she get to choose the eye color of the father? So much to learn!

"The devil? That's ridiculous, especially given how studious you were. But still, I always thought you were unusually striking, and faintly mysterious," Emily insisted.

"A model," Andrea reiterated. "I think you should be a model."

"A model," Casey snorted. "Believe me, I'm quite happy doing research at the lab."

"As noble as medical research is, Casey, isn't that a tad dull?" Emily asked.

"I love it," she said honestly. "I have such a sense of purpose to my days, a feeling I could make the world a better place."

"Isn't it a little, well, depressing? Childhood cancers?" Andrea pressed.

"My twin brother died of nasopharyngeal cancer when he was six," Casey said. *And so a family unravels.*

"I'd forgotten," Andrea said. "I'm so sorry."

"It was long before I met you," Casey said. "Don't worry about it." Out of the corner of her eye, she saw Emily give her little baby bump a protective pat. "And don't you worry about it, either. Childhood cancers are extremely rare," she assured her pregnant friend.

Casey was aware she might have chosen her work in some effort to make right all that had gone wrong in her family. But regardless of her motives, the order of science, after the unfolding chaos in her family, appealed to her. The wine hadn't, thankfully, loosened her tongue enough to tell them why she'd chosen the vow renewal over spending Christmas with her widowed mother.

"Maybe you could model on the side," Andrea said hopefully.

"Why would I want to?" Casey asked. "Talk about dull. Good grief. Hours on hair—" well, okay, her hair took nearly that long, anyway "—and makeup? I'd expire of pure boredom."

"Men," Andrea said knowingly. "You'd meet a zillion guys. How many do you meet in your dusty old lab?"

No sense pointing out there was not a speck of dust anywhere in her lab!

"And then," Andrea continued dreamily, "you could meet the right one. Look at how much Emily loves being married. Renewing her vows! And Rick and I will probably have a spring wedding. If you could find the perfect guy, all our kids could grow up together here in the summers, the same as we did."

How quickly things could change! Just a few weeks ago Andrea had been as determined not to fall in love as Casey herself was. Her friend was no weakling, so Casey inadvertently shivered at how love could overpower the most sensible of plans.

Emily shot Andrea a warning look that clearly said, *Careful, Casey is recovering from a broken heart*—last year's Christmas crisis. Then she tactfully tried to guide the conversation in a different direction. "Anyway, the inn is for sale."

Andrea appeared pained for a minute, but then shrugged it off. "I don't know. I've seen how Martin Johnson, the electrician, looks at Carol. I think he's a man capable of restoring the Gingerbread Inn to its former glory. And it seems it would be a labor of love."

"Carol is resisting him," Emily said. "I'm afraid I overheard a bit of a shouting match between them."

"Well, I'm going to help things along. I've already asked him to come and help with the lighting for the vow renewal, and he seemed very eager to say yes!"

"Good for you," Emily said, but doubtfully. "Honestly, while Cole and I were working things out we bonded over a few cosmetic repairs around the place, but every single thing we did has made us so aware of what else has to be done. Poor Carol, on her own, could not keep up. It may have deteriorated too badly to be saved."

They all sadly contemplated that.

The Gingerbread Inn was special. It always had been, and there could never be a replacement in Casey's heart. The walls held memories: laughter and love, families coming together. The ghosts of their younger selves played out there on the waters of Barrow's Lake, swimming, canoeing, sunning themselves on the dock, playing volleyball on the beach.

There would never be another place like the Gingerbread Inn. It was a refuge of simplicity in a complicated world.

"We could find a different place to spend family summers together," Andrea suggested tentatively. "Wherever it is, or whatever it is, the three of us will be there with our soul mates. I think that's what Melissa would have wanted us to learn. That this is what is important. Love. And I hope someday it will include all our babies. Babies who will grow into toddlers as love deepens all around us. Rick and I plan to adopt someday. Tessa would love a little brother or sister."

Tessa was the six-year-old who would become Andrea's stepdaughter. She was hands down the most adorable little girl on the planet.

"It's what I want for this baby, too," Emily said tenderly.

That old feeling of being the odd one out whispered along her spine, but Casey reminded herself she was not going to be that for long! But she was going to do things her way.

For as happy as both Emily and Andrea were now, Casey had been a bridesmaid at both their weddings. How those beautiful days had fuelled her longing for romance! But Andrea's dreams had ended in a terrible tragedy on her honeymoon. And Casey had seen the cracks appear in Emily's relationship almost before Emily had seen them herself.

Oh, sure, Emily and Cole were like lovers again *now*,

and Andrea was still in the over-the-moon stage with her new love, Rick, but it was too late for Casey to believe in love.

The pain interwoven with the love in those relationships had just helped cement Casey's resolve to wrestle her weakest point to the ground. And that wasn't her hair, either!

"Well, you girls can believe in fairy tales if you want. I'm done with that," she announced.

"I've been there," Emily said sympathetically.

"Me, too," Andrea said. "But the old saying is true—it's darkest just before the dawn." Catching Emily's warning look, she added, "Okay. Casey doesn't have to be with someone. She could come by herself."

"Actually," Casey said slowly, her heart beating hard, "I may not be by myself."

If she told them it was like committing. Like carving it in stone. And yet who better to share this gloriously happy decision with than her best friends?

"What?" Andrea squealed. "Have you met someone new? Why did you let me prattle on about your dusty lab if you have? I'm so happy for you! Really, a year is quite long enough to recover from a rascal like Sebastian. I told you when I saw you earlier this month that eventually you would see your breakup as a blessing. And I am a testament to the fact that things can turn around in an absolute blink."

It had been a year, almost exactly, since the rather humiliating disintegration of her relationship. Only these two women knew all the details: how a coworker had tipped her off that her fiancé, Sebastian, was seeing another woman, only days before they were going to make a Christmas announcement of their engagement!

"I haven't exactly met someone," Casey said cautiously, suddenly feeling vulnerable about saying it out loud.

"What is going on, Casey?" Andrea asked. "You asked

me to join you here earlier in the month because you were down, but now you look great. So who is he?"

"It's not a he. I've made a decision to give myself the most amazing gift."

"What?" her friends asked in unison.

"I'm going to have a baby. I'm going to start investigating third-party reproduction and cryobanks right after the holidays are over."

Her friends looked stunned. "Cryo what?" Emily asked weakly.

"You mean you're going to raise a child by yourself?" Andrea finally asked.

"Why not? I'm well established. I'm financially able to afford the procedures. I'm ready. I think, on my own, I could provide as stable a family as most I've seen."

"That seems very scientific," Emily ventured. "Procedure as a way to make a baby?"

"I am a scientist!" And really, science had given her far more than her family ever had. "I'm done with romantic love. I'm saving all my love for my baby."

Her friends were very quiet.

"Hey," Casey said, trying for humor, when she was really disappointed they weren't more supportive of her decision. "You're both so serious. I said I was done with love, and that there could be a baby in my future, not that I was going to burn the Gingerbread Inn down!"

"You couldn't," Andrea said with dreamy satisfaction. "Rick would rescue it."

Rick, the adorable Tessa's father, was a fireman.

"I'm curing myself of romantic notions. I'm tackling my fatal flaw," Casey surprised herself by announcing.

"Your fatal flaw?" Andrea said, frowning.

"I believed in romantic love," Casey said. "Worse, I believed in love at first sight. It's done nothing but cause me grief, and I'm done with it."

"Love at first sight?" Emily said, puzzled. "I thought you and Sebastian worked together for some time before you agreed to go out with him."

But her secret, even from Em and Andrea, was that Sebastian had not been her first love. Her first love she had loved at first sight. He was the one who had made her so foolishly long for love that she had been willing to overlook her own family's history with passion, and imbue her former fiancé with characteristics he did not have.

"I'm done with love," Casey repeated, even more firmly than before.

"You are not!" Emily said, dismayed. "How can anybody just be done with love?"

"We buried Melissa," Casey said. "That's enough all by itself."

"I understand how you feel," Andrea said softly. "After Gunter died I wanted to give up on love, too. But I'm so glad I didn't."

Though Casey could not say it, the death of Andrea's husband—on their honeymoon, no less—felt like part of her disillusionment. Giving your heart was a risky business.

"No one would be more appalled than Melissa if you made fear of love her legacy!"

The Gingerbread Girls had always bowed to Emily's leadership, and Casey conceded slightly now. "Okay. This kind of love I'm fine with. The bonds between friends. The love between a mother and a child. Romantic love I'm done with. *Finis.*"

"I always love it when you speak Italian," Andrea said, deciding in the face of Casey's intensity it was time to lighten up.

"It's Latin," she said. "Not Italian."

Andrea rolled her eyes at the correction and went on as if she had not been interrupted. "You aren't done with it. You're hurting right now. But it has been a year, and I think you have healed more than you think you have. You are planning on having a baby, after all. Though I do wish you'd wait for the right guy to come along, and spadoodle, life as you know it, over."

"Spadoodle?" Casey laughed in spite of herself.

"I thought it sounded Italian," Andrea offered with an impish grin.

"Sort of," Emily said, as if she was considering. "Like *spaghetti* and *noodle* mixed." And then they were all laughing, like the carefree girls they had once been. It felt again like a homecoming, it was so good to be with them.

"I agree with Andrea, though. The right guy will come along and you'll see that every single thing about your life, including the parts that seem bad, were getting you ready for that moment," Emily said. "Should you put off having a baby until that happens? Really, I know that's not for me to say."

Casey felt her friend was not entirely approving and had decided to keep it light, and she was grateful for that.

"From spadoodle to deep philosophy in the blink of an eye?" Casey said, lightly. "It's enough to make my head spin."

Emily grinned. "Way too deep, eh, Doc?"

"Way," Casey said with an answering smile, and it all seemed okay again. Her decision to come here had been a good one. The sisterhood between them that allowed them to squabble and exchange confidences and well-meaning advice, and then just rest in pure love and laughter again, was balm to her soul.

"I wish you'd give love a chance," Andrea insisted.

"I have given love a chance," Casey said firmly. "What's that old saying? If you always do what you've always done, you'll always get what you always got. Falling in love, for me, equals heartbreak. And I'm not doing it anymore."

"You sound sure of yourself," Emily mused.

"I am."

"Maybe Andrea's right. Maybe you've spent too much time in the lab and it has given you this illusion about what you can control. Maybe before you fully commit to the idea of having a baby on your own, you should try getting out a bit."

"I'm getting out. I've joined yoga! And I'm taking a calligraphy class. My life is exceedingly full."

She inwardly begged Andrea not to mention that desperate call a few weeks ago when she had been so unbearably down.

Andrea, blessedly, didn't.

But Emily said, "Full does not mean fulfilling."

"That's why I want a family of my own. Besides, when did you become such a philosopher? Now you two quit picking on me."

"I'm sorry," Emily said, "I didn't mean to pick on you. If this decision makes you happy, I'm happy for you."

Casey just wanted to change the subject. "Andrea, tell me what I should get the adorable little Tessa for Christmas. I was thinking a nice chemistry set."

They all laughed, and it didn't take much of a shove to get Andrea talking about her new life and her new family. "I've already tucked away the giant gingerbread man Tessa fell in love with at the shop."

Andrea went on to talk about what she was getting Rick. She was glowing with passion, that thing that Casey was most suspicious of.

Both her friends knew what a philanderer her father had been. He'd no doubt made moves on both their mothers at some time over the summers here! And when her own mom had found out? Shrieking and pot throwing and breaking glass.

And then passion clouding the poor woman's judgment all over again.

"How is your mother since your father passed?" Andrea asked suddenly, as if she had picked it up telepathically. Such was the way between old friends.

You don't want to know. "Fine," Casey said briefly.

"I wish she would come for the vow renewal," Emily said. "She's not going to be alone because you've come here, is she?"

"Oh, no," Casey managed to squeak. "She's not going to be alone."

She could feel her throat tightening suspiciously, and she swallowed hard and focused quickly on the inn's dog, a gorgeous golden retriever mix named Harper. The female dog came up with her happy grin and put her head in Casey's lap.

"This kind of love I can live with," Casey said lightly, scratching the dog's ears and smiling at the tail thumping on the floor. "Oh, look! It's snowing."

She gently maneuvered free of the affectionate pet, then got up and went to the window. She shouldn't have told her friends she had given up on love. Maybe she shouldn't have told them she was thinking of alternative ways to have a family, either. She had left herself wide-open to a Christmas campaign to make her change her mind.

But she'd had enough proof of the folly of love to last her a lifetime, and it should be easy enough to change the subject when it came up.

As she looked out the window, headlights illuminated the thickly falling snow. A cab emerged from the night and pulled up in front of the inn, sliding a little when it tried to stop on the icy driveway.

A man got out of the back, dressed casually in a parka with a fur-lined hood, jeans tucked into laced snow boots. He strode around to the rear and waited for the driver to retrieve his bags from the trunk. Then, with his luggage at his feet in the snow, he paid the cabbie, clapping him on the shoulder at his effusive thanks for what must have been a great Christmas tip.

It was dark and it was snowing hard, but there was something about the way the new arrival carried himself that penetrated both the storm and the night.

Something shivered along Casey's spine.

She had the alarming feeling it might be recognition, but she shook it off.

It simply was not possible that, following so quickly on her announcement to her friends that she had sworn off love, Turner Kennedy—the first man who had ever stolen her heart—would show up here.

CHAPTER TWO

"Did somebody just arrive?" Andrea asked. "Another member of my little work party?"

"I thought *we* were your little work party," Casey said, trying not to panic. "Emily and me."

"Well, you were, but Cole pointed out to me he doesn't want Emily to do any heavy lifting, and he didn't really think you would want to be up on the roof replacing strings of Christmas lights. He wanted another guy, even though I asked Martin to help with the electrical. He said he'd be happy to do it for nothing. Isn't that nice?"

Casey was having trouble focusing on Martin's niceness.

"Who is it?" Emily asked. "He wouldn't tell me who he invited. He just said it would be a surprise. I'm guessing Joe."

"I'm not sure who it is," Casey said, though she was guessing it was not Joe! She was amazed at how normal her voice sounded, considering she was forcing words out past constricted vocal chords. Because if it was who she suspected, it was a surprise, all right. Of the worst possible sort!

And why wouldn't Turner Kennedy be just the surprise Cole would bring to the inn? the scientist in Casey insisted on asking. It was certainly one of the available options!

Turner had been the best man at Emily and Cole's wedding. Why wouldn't he be here as they assembled as much of the original wedding party as was possible for their renewal of vows? Why wouldn't he jump at the chance to help get the old inn ready for their magical day, just as she had?

Because he disappeared, Casey wailed to herself.

Still, at one time, he and Cole had been best friends. Casey had assumed the friendship had been left behind, because when she had asked—not nearly as frequently as she wanted to, and with only the most casual interest— Emily had been vague.

"Oh. I'll have to ask Cole. I think he said Turner is overseas. He's some kind of government contractor."

She'd thought, in those three magical days they had spent together following the wedding, that they had known everything about each other. Government contractor? Casey had felt the first shiver of betrayal at that. He hadn't mentioned anything about being a government contractor. But in retrospect, he *had* headed her off every single time she had tried to delve into his life.

Just pretend I'm a prince who found a glass slipper. And that it fits you.

"If Turner is somewhere amazing, like France or Italy," Emily had said, thankfully not reading her friend's distress, "Cole and I should go visit!"

And when, after waiting an appropriate amount of time, Casey had screwed up the nerve to ask if Emily had asked Cole about Turner, her friend had replied, "Cole said he's lost touch. Men! Relationships are a low priority."

That was actually the first time Casey had heard bitterness in Emily's voice in reference to her busy husband. But not the last.

Why would Turner be here now? Well, why not?

Why wouldn't he come and help celebrate Christmas with his best friend's newly reunited and rejoicing family?

It went with everything Emily had been saying about the changes Cole was making. Her husband was giving a new priority to building and keeping relationships.

That's what Casey was doing, too, wasn't it? Making a vow to realize the importance of friendships before it was too late? Celebrating Christmas and the spirit of love with her best friends instead of that crazy, unpredictable, painful conglomeration of people sometimes known as a family?

Even her decision to create the kind of family she had always wanted for herself seemed to be wavering, perhaps due to some combination of her friends' lack of enthusiasm and his arrival.

Stop it, Casey ordered herself. She didn't even know if it was Turner. But all the ordering in the world would not slow her heart as the cab pulled away, and the man bent, effortlessly picked up a duffel bag and looped the strap over his shoulder, before turning to the steps that led to the front porch.

Casey was aware she was holding her breath as he stepped toward the faint light being thrown by a string of Christmas lights with too many burned out bulbs.

The light may have been weak, but it washed the familiar contours of his face, and turned the snowflakes caught in the glossy darkness of his hair to gold.

Her gasp was audible, and she covered it with quick desperation by clearing her throat. Casey's wineglass trembled in her hand. She set it down. She told herself to move, to get out of here *fast*.

Instead, she was glued to the spot, her feet frozen, her eyes locked on his face.

It was him.

It was Turner. It was Turner Kennedy in the flesh.

Not unchanged, though the changes were subtle. Something in the way he held himself made a shiver go up and down her spine. As he arrived at the bottom of the step, he paused.

He had broadened in the years since she had last seen him, youthful litheness giving way to the pure power of a man completely in his prime. What hadn't changed was that he was exuding an almost sizzling sense of himself, who he was in the world, and what he could take on.

Anything.

If the door of the inn had suddenly crashed open and a horde of bandits had fallen upon him, she had the sense he would be ready for it. He might even enjoy it!

Casey shook the picture off, annoyed that she could be so susceptible to the whisper of imagination. She knew nothing about him. She had once convinced herself otherwise, and she had been wrong.

The faint light illuminated his face, and she shivered again, despite herself. There seemed to be a certain remoteness in his expression that was different, but what did she know? She'd been a naive young bridesmaid when Turner Kennedy had been Cole Watson's best man.

She had been the geeky girl, the science nerd, the brain, who had been noticed by the most popular boy in the school, the captain of the football team, the boy whose picture in every girl's yearbook was marked with inked hearts.

Despite his closed expression, Turner was still the most astonishingly handsome man she had ever seen, so good-looking that a girl could fall for him.

At first sight.

So much so that when he had taken her chin in his hands as dawn broke, the morning after Cole and Emily's wedding, and said, "Run away with me," she hadn't even hesitated.

Casey had tossed years and years of absolute control right out the window.

"Three days," he'd said. "Spend the next three days with me."

She should have known better than to share her new resolve about love with her girlfriends. It seemed she had thrown a gauntlet before the gods and they had responded with terrifying swiftness.

"Casey?"

She turned to her friends and saw the instant concern register on both their faces.

"What's wrong?" they asked together.

What's wrong? She was a scientist. Andrea had been right; she spent too much time in the lab. And nothing in that carefully controlled environment had prepared her for this encounter.

She was amazed when her voice didn't shake when she said, "It looks like Turner Kennedy is here."

"Turner?" Emily said. "I can't believe it! We haven't seen him since our wedding. I thought Cole had lost touch completely."

Emily got up, raced to the front door and flung it open. "Turner Kennedy! What a wonderful surprise!"

Casey was experiencing that trapped feeling, a sensation of fight or flight. When Andrea went into the front hallway to greet the newcomer, too, Casey quietly set down her unfinished wineglass, left the parlor by the back door and slipped up the rear staircase to her room.

She went in and softly closed the door, leaning against it as if she had escaped a twisting, foggy London street with the Ripper on her heels.

Her heart was beating hard and unreasonably fast, not entirely the result of her mad dash up the stairs.

She turned and looked at her suitcase.

Good. Not completely unpacked yet. She could throw the few things she had unpacked back in it. She could wait in here, quiet as a mouse, until the old inn grew silent, and then slink out that door and never come back.

She could spend a quiet Christmas in her apartment. Never mind that she had yearned for the company of loving friends. Never mind that she had longed for holiday traditions, for bonfires and impromptu snowball fights, hanging stockings on the hearth and making gingerbread cookies with the Gingerbread Girls. Never mind that she had longed for a little taste of the kind of Christmas she would create for her own child someday soon!

Never mind all that. She would go to her little apartment, where it was safe and everything was in her control. She could look up everything she needed to know about third-party reproductive procedures.

Maybe she'd even go to the lab for part of Christmas Day. Why not?

Her research there could be her greatest gift to the world. Ask any parent whose child had been diagnosed with cancer!

Another option would be to accept her mother's invitation.

To join her at the Sacred Heart Mission House, where the Sisters of Mercy would be serving Christmas dinner to the poor. Where her mother, glowing with a soft joy she had never had while Casey was growing up, would remind her, ever so gently, not to call her Mom.

It's Sister Maria Celeste.

There. Both the Caravettas—except her mother did not consider herself a Caravetta any longer—selflessly saving the world at Christmas.

Her crazy family, the reason Casey had sought refuge with her friends at the inn.

But she couldn't stay here now.

It was one thing to say you were sworn off romantic love. It was another to be tested.

And Turner Kennedy had that indefinable *something* that would test any woman's resolve, never mind one who had been locked away in a lab nursing a broken heart for nearly a year.

Or had it been longer? Had it really been ever since that three days together in a fairy-tale kingdom he had created? Just for her. A Cinderella experience. The little scrub-a-muffin noticed by the prince. The prince enchanted with her.

Only in the end, the fairy tale had been reversed. He had been the one with secrets. The one who had resisted her every effort to find out why only three days, where he was going, what he would be doing next. He had been the one who had disappeared into the night, only unlike the fairy tale, Turner had not left a single clue.

She had been left holding a memory as fragile as a glass slipper, only she had never again found the person who fit it.

But now he was here. Yes, Turner had a raw masculine potency combined with a roguish, boyish charm that had completely bowled her over on their first encounter.

Casey turned off the lights in her room and lay on her bed, staring at the glow of the mostly burned out string of Christmas lights outside her window. They were making a really ugly pattern on her waterstained ceiling. She contemplated how the hurt Turner had caused her felt recent, more recent than the hurt of her broken engagement!

In a different part of the house, she could hear everyone's voices, Cole's and Turner's, raised in greeting, followed by laughter and conversation. She could, after all these years, pick out the tone of Turner's voice. It was deep, a masculine melody touching the harp her spine had become.

It was obvious the men were now in the front room where the Gingerbread Girls had been earlier.

No chance of sneaking down the staircase without being seen. Casey fervently wished they would shut up and go to bed, so she could get out of here.

Instead, Turner's voice triggered powerful memories of a presidential suite at the Waldorf Astoria. Jumping on the beds. Sitting in front of the fireplace wrapped in a luxurious, pure white robe, while he painted her toenails red. Walking to the theater. Taking a carriage ride through Central Park.

Three days of barely sleeping, of living with an intensity that was exhilarating and exhausting, of being on fire with life and love… Strip away all the luxury, and it was his hand in hers that had caused her to feel so exquisitely alive, his eyes on her face that made her feel as if she had never felt before.

Enough! Casey shook her head clear of the memories. Finally, after experiencing what she had once seen described in a poem as the "interminable night," she felt it was safe to creep out of her room, jacket on against the cold, suitcase in hand.

She checked the hallway. Nothing. Not a sound beyond the wheezing of an exceptionally cranky old furnace. She was pretty sure Harper slept with her owner, the innkeeper, Carol.

Casey tiptoed through the house and out the front, where the screen door shrieked like a cat whose tail had been stepped on.

She froze, listened, waited for lights to come on. It was really dark out here. Even the Christmas lights had been turned off, no doubt part of the Gingerbread Inn's austerity program.

Stumbling through the inky darkness found only in the country, Casey finally made it to her car, where she opted to use the key so there would be no blink of headlights or short blast of the horn when she unlocked it. She actually had her key in the door when it hit her.

She could not let Emily and Andrea down like this. It wasn't about her. It was about making Emily's day the most incredible experience of her life.

Besides, what explanation could she offer to her friends for her sudden defection? As close as she was to them, she had never let on about those three days she and Turner had spent together. Had never breathed out loud that she harbored a crush on the man, that she had waited and hoped and prayed that he would contact her again.

The memory of that—of waiting—made her cheeks turn crimson with anger.

She was acting like a thief! Acting as if *she* had done something wrong.

It was Turner who had breathed fire into her soul in those three days that had followed Cole and Emily's wedding. And then he had walked away, and never, ever called. Or written. Had disappeared as if they had not shared the most intense of all experiences.

As if they had not fallen in love at first sight.

Slowly, she pulled her key out of the car door.

Casey was a scientist. She didn't believe in the phenomena of coincidence, certainly did not believe in the universe conspiring to help people out. But really, in terms of her vow never to love again, could there be a more perfect test than this?

Could there be a better conclusion than coming face-to-face with the man who had made her aware of her fatal flaw?

It was perfect, really.

The perfect ending.

Not the one Andrea and Emily wanted her to believe in. No, in this story, the princess was not kissed awake by a prince. In this ending, the princess came awake all by herself. In her new happily-ever-after, Casey would walk away, sure of herself, entirely certain of her ability to be completely independent, to live with purpose and joy without being encumbered by a belief in the fairy-tale ending of love.

Love, even love that worked, was an uphill battle with heartache. Look at Em. Look at Andrea, having to bury her husband before her honeymoon had even ended!

Casey decided—right then and there, in the parking lot of the Gingerbread Inn, with fresh snow drifting down around her—to be on a quest, not for love, but for emotional freedom. She would rid herself once and for all of the lifelong myths and fantasies and hopes and dreams that had bound and imprisoned her.

Her life would be about her baby. Who better than a scientist to conduct the search for a donor with the perfect qualities to give her child?

She could make that decision about creating her own family in the way all the best choices were made. She would be measured and rational. She hadn't got far in her research about how to choose a donor, but she hoped she would get to review photos. She would make sure the father of her child was nothing like her own devastatingly handsome father had been, or her immensely charming, but ultimately fickle fiancé.

The man would, especially, be nothing like Turner.

Who could turn those silvery eyes on a woman and enchant her entirely.

No, better to look for brilliance and gentleness, physical health and even features.

Really, she was surprised she hadn't thought of it sooner—that science could provide her with a perfect father for her children!

When she thought back on it, she was a totally differ-

ent woman than she had been in those few long-ago days
with Turner.

She'd experienced nothing but heartache at the caprice
of love. She'd buried her father, lost her fiancé to another
woman and her mother to the church, attended the heart-
breaking funeral of one of her best friends. She'd seen Andrea devastated by the death of her husband, and Emily
by a struggling marriage. It was enough! Casey's heart
was in armor.

She was glad that Emily and Andrea had found love.
She really was. But she was concluding her mission. The
rejection of romantic love would make her a better mother
to her future child, devoted and not distracted. Their lives
wouldn't be in a constant jumble of men moving in and out.

If the gods were throwing down a gauntlet in the face
of her decision, she was accepting the challenge!

And with that firmly in mind, Casey grasped the handle of her suitcase and turned back to the inn with a certain grim determination. She plowed through the growing
mounds of snow and marched up the steps onto the covered porch.

Something wet and cold brushed the hand that held her
car keys. Casey dropped them with a little shriek of surprise, then looked down to see Harper thrust a wet snout
into her palm.

"What are you doing out here?" she asked the dog.

A deep voice, as sensual as the snow-filled night, came
out of a darkened corner of the porch.

"Keeping me company."

CHAPTER THREE

CASEY SHRIEKED EVEN more loudly than she had when the dog had thrust its wet, cold snout into her hand.

She dropped her suitcase from nerveless fingers, and it landed with a thump beside her keys. The suitcase was an old one with a hard shell, and to her horror, the latch popped and the lid flew open, displaying her neatly packed underthings.

Right on top were embarrassingly lacy garments she would no longer be needing now that she had decided to move procreation into the controllable field of science, rather than the uncontrollable one of attraction.

The dog shoved her head forward as if about to follow her instincts and retrieve.

Casey squatted down and slammed the lid, nearly catching Harper's snout. The dog whined, perplexed at being thwarted, then while Casey struggled with the sticky latch, she noticed the keys.

"Harper," Casey pleaded, "don't—"

With a happy thump of her tail, the dog scooped up the keys. Holding them in her mouth as gently as she would have a downed bird, she delivered them to the shadowy figure in the darkness of the porch, forcing Casey, finally, to look at him.

Harper sat down, tail thumping, offering him the prize.

"Keys," he said, in the voice that played music on Casey's harp.

He took them, examined them, jingling them with a certain satisfaction.

"To the chambers of a lovely maiden? What a good dog. So much better than a newspaper or slippers."

It was said with the ease of a man comfortable with his attraction, confident in how women reacted to him. Luckily for Casey, her guard was up. Way up. And luckily for her, she was intensely wary of men who were so smoothly sure of themselves!

Gathering her composure—it was a test of the gods, after all—she straightened, turned and glared in his direction.

His voice was deep and faintly sardonic. She tried to ignore the fact it felt as if his words had vibrated along the nape of her neck, as sensual as the scrape of fingertips.

Turner Kennedy was sitting on the railing that surrounded the covered porch, one foot resting on the floor, the other up, swinging ever so slightly as he watched her.

He had a cigarette in his hand, but it wasn't lit.

She detested men who smoked. Which was a good thing. Coupled with his flirtatious remark, and the fact he had scared her nearly to death, Turner was at strike three already, and she had shared the porch with him for barely fifteen seconds.

Still, a part of her insisted on remembering he had not smoked back then.

Good grief! It had been years ago. He hadn't smoked then, but they were both different people by now! She had been tried, tested and spit out by life since then. Plus she wasn't a callow, stars-in-her-eyes girl any longer. She was a respected member of an important research team.

How long had he been there? Had he seen her exit the inn with determination, stumble through the darkness, put her key in the car door, only to come back with just as much determination?

Casey wanted to escape, dash in the front door of the Gingerbread Inn without another word. Over her shoulder she could give instructions for him to leave her keys on the table on the front entryway.

But that was childish. And that was not why she had come back. Her responses to him seemed very primal—flight or fight.

She was going to have to see him sometime. She was rattled, but she was not letting that show! She was ready to fight!

She had run from him once tonight, and she was not doing it again. Casey ignored the hammering of her heart and forced down her clamoring insecurities. She crossed the distance between them with all the confidence of the successful, purposeful woman she had become since their last meeting.

This was an opportunity to face her demons head-on. To rid herself of the pull of such men, so that she could be a better mother. Her own mother would say that such a coincidence was heaven sent, though as a scientist Casey didn't believe in such things.

Smiling faintly, Turner watched her come.

He had been exceptional looking all those years ago: dark-chocolate hair, eyes the color of pewter, high proud cheekbones, straight nose, strong chin, sensual full lips. Now, he had matured into something even finer.

Though the night was frosty, his jacket was hanging over the railing beside him. Underneath a beautifully tailored dress shirt—a deep shade of walnut that set off the silver of his eyes—his shoulders were unbelievably broad, his chest deep. Casey could tell there was not an ounce of superfluous flesh on him. The shirt was open at the throat and he had rolled up the sleeves to just below his elbows. His forearms were corded with strength.

She could actually feel some masculine power heat the cool air around him as he gazed at her, that smile lifting one corner of his sexy mouth. He was a man who was way too sure of himself.

"Just keys," she said, "to an ordinary room. Not a suite at the Waldorf." She held out her hand for them.

The Waldorf Astoria with Casey Caravetta. When Turner had been lured here by the promise of endless ice, he hadn't really thought of that.

Of who else might be here. He certainly had not thought *she* would be.

Casey had been a bridesmaid at Emily and Cole's wedding. Turner had been the best man. Unknown to anyone, even his best friend, he had been on countdown.

The newly formed and top secret Tango unit had been shipping out on their first mission four days after the wedding.

Maybe it had been that heightened awareness that had made him see Casey in an entirely different light than he usually would have.

They had spent the night of the wedding together—and not in the way he was used to spending nights with young women. She wasn't, after all, his regular kind of girl.

She had been almost comically uptight at first. Geeky and sweet. With just the tiniest nudge, she had poured out her heart to him. Her walls had come down and revealed a young woman who was brilliant and funny and deep. And damaged by life.

He'd found himself unable to say good-night, and feeling compelled to give her something. A break from herself—from the rigid control she exercised over herself. He wanted her to have some carefree, no-strings-attached fun, a taste of the life-lit-from-within intensity that predeployment was making him feel.

He'd had the means to do it. Settlements from his father's death had left him with a whole pile of money that he wanted to get rid of. What if he used it to do something good?

He'd had four days before he flew off to an uncertain future. Everyone who signed up for Tango knew they were in for highly dangerous work. With no guarantee they were ever coming back.

It had been like adopting a little sister.

Except, before the days had come to an end, he had not been feeling very brotherly toward her. Looking at her now, he could remember jumping on the bed at the Waldorf, and painting her toenails, and laughing until his stomach hurt. He could remember the feel of her hand in his, the light that had shone, wondrous, in her eyes, the break from a self-imposed discipline that had made him crush the fullness of her lips beneath his own on the final night....

As Casey watched recognition darken Turner's eyes, his smile faded. But not before she had noted teeth that were as white as the snow that fell around them. They drew Casey's gaze, unwillingly, to the sinful sexiness of that mouth.

But it was not the smile she remembered. The one she recalled had been boyish and open. Now, despite his flirtatious tone, and the faint smile, she could see something ever so subtly guarded in him.

She met his eyes, and again noted a change. The once clear gray held shadows, like frozen water reflecting storm clouds.

She frowned. Her memory, from those days together after Cole and Emily's wedding, was of eyes that sparked with carefree mischief.

Turner's eyebrows edged up. He threw the cigarette away and got down off the railing.

He reached out with his right hand and touched, ever so lightly, the hollow of her throat.

"I did scare you," he said apologetically. "Your heart is beating like that of a doe trapped against a fence by wolves."

More like a deer in the headlights, because though she ordered herself to slap his hand away, she stood absolutely paralyzed by his touch. His fingers radiated a stunningly sensual warmth on the cold of her neck.

Still, by sheer force of will, she managed to keep her expression neutral. Better he think her heart was pounding like that from being startled, rather than from seeing him again.

Unfortunately, she wasn't sure which it was, especially with his merest touch causing a riot of sensation within her. Which it was best he not know about, as well!

So, telling herself it was completely her choice, Casey didn't move, not even when his hand drifted briefly to her hair and rested there for a deliciously suspended moment in time.

"Casey Caravetta," he said, his voice gruff, his hand dropping away. "No, wait. I'm sure I heard it was Dr. Caravetta now. Congratulations."

How was it that he had heard things about her when she had heard nothing about him? Not even a whisper.

She felt just like that young bridesmaid again. The geeky girl who had been noticed by the most amazingly attractive man she had ever laid eyes on.

His touch on the pulse at her throat had been soft, hardly a touch at all. Why did it feel as if a mark were burned into her skin?

This was what she was fighting, Casey reminded herself. And really, she was armed with the knowledge now that it was nothing but chemistry: serotonin, oxytocin, adrenaline, dopamine, a system flooded with intoxication. Attraction was the pure and simple science of a brain wired to recreate the human race, but of course, it was way more palpable to people if it disguised itself as romance. She was a scientist; she should know better. She was a scientist and science had provided more convenient ways to have children.

But somehow it was not a scientist that watched as Turner ran his hand through his thick, glossy hair. Snow had melted in it, and little drops flew off as he did so.

She never looked away from him, and was astounded again at the stern lines that bracketed a mouth she remembered quirking upward with good humor and boyish charm.

She had to gain control of herself! She had to remind herself—and him—about the painful past between them.

"Are you just going to pretend you didn't ditch me at the Waldorf Astoria?" she asked. She hoped for a cool note, but could hear her own fury.

"I didn't ditch you," he said, genuinely perplexed. "You always knew I was going. I told you right from the beginning—three days."

"And on the morning of the fourth day, I woke up in that huge suite by myself! You didn't even have the decency to say goodbye."

His eyes rested on her lips. "I said it the night before." His voice was like gravel. Was it remembrance of that final kiss—the leashed passion in it—causing that slightly hoarse note?

"Humph." Did she have to sound like a disgruntled schoolmarm?

"It's not as if we were parting lovers, Casey. You were innocent then, and despite the showy underwear—"

He *had* seen! Casey could only pray the darkness of the

porch would hide the fact her cheeks probably matched the underwear at the moment!

"—I bet not much has changed. I take back the remark about keys and chambers. Sheesh. I feel like I've propositioned a nun."

She flinched, and he jammed his hands in the pockets of his jeans.

"Sorry," he muttered. "I didn't mean that I don't find you—"

"Stop!" she said. She did not want to hear all the reasons why she was not the girl for him. He'd already made that more than plain.

"I wasn't offended," she said quickly, her tone deliberately icy. Well, maybe she was. A little. But he certainly didn't have to know that. "I'm just a little sensitive on the topic of nuns right now."

His lips twitched. "That hasn't changed. You have this way of saying things that is refreshing and funny."

"I wasn't trying to be funny," she said, annoyed.

Her annoyance had the unfortunate effect of deepening his amusement.

"I know you weren't trying to be funny, but that's part of what makes it so. I mean, who is sensitive on the topic of nuns? Right now? It would be like me saying, 'I'm sensitive to the topic of Attila the Hun. Right now.'"

"The comparison only works if I mentioned Attila the Hun in reference to you. Which I didn't."

Rather than getting her point, he deepened his smile.

"Dr. Caravetta," he said, "you are funny, even if unintentionally. And brilliant. So, what makes you sensitive to the topic of nuns? Right now?"

His lips were twitching, but his own amusement seemed to catch him off guard, as if he was not easily amused by much anymore. Was that why he contained it before it fully bloomed, or was it because he caught on she was not sharing his amusement?

"It's a long story, and one I am not prepared to go into in the middle of the night." *Or ever.*

"Okay," he said. "Just to set the record straight, I wouldn't have made that crack about the key to your chambers if I'd known it was you. Really. It feels as if you're my best friend's little sister."

"Which I am not! I'm not even remotely related to Cole."

"Logically, I know that. At a different level, you have this quality of innocence that makes me feel protective of you. Even after a glimpse of the flashy underwear. I mean you are, by your own admission, the kind of girl who is sensitive to nuns."

Flashy underwear? Protective of her? Little sister? Casey was being flooded with fight-or-flight chemistry again, because she had a very uncharacteristic desire to smack that smirk right off his face!

Her memories of those days together were of electricity, of feeling like a woman for the first time in her life. Of acknowledging a deep and primal hunger within her that only one thing would fill. Her memories of those days were of being on fire with wanting.

For him. For this man.

Who probably set off that very same chemical reaction in every single female he came in contact with!

But for the entire three days they had spent together, he had stopped short, way short, of anything that would have fulfilled that wanting. Yes, they had kissed on that final night—the memory made it feel as if that pulse in her throat was hammering harder—but he, not she, had put on the brakes. It was Turner who had sent her into the other bedroom, on those rare occasions when they had given in and slept.

She felt they had connected so deeply on so many levels. She had been convinced at a soul level.

While he'd been thinking it felt as if she was his best friend's little sister!

No wonder, with the dawn of the fourth day, he had disappeared, never to be seen or heard from again.

Now, as well as seeing her as his best friend's little sister, he was going to think of nuns when he saw her? Which, of course, was better than him thinking of flashy underwear. Wasn't it?

"Don't act as if you know anything about me on the basis of three days of acquaintance," Casey said tightly, "because you don't."

If he mentioned the underwear, she was going to die.

Of course he mentioned the underwear.

"But I do," he said softly. "I know that, despite the undies, the only thing wild about you is your hair. Or at least it used to be." He lifted his hand as if he was going to touch her again, and then drove it into his pocket instead. "Now it's not even that."

"I'll repeat," she said, with a coolness she was far from feeling, "you don't know anything about me."

"I know I liked your hair better the way it used to be."

"That's about you," she pointed out. "What *you* like."

"You're right," he said, cocking his head, considering her. "I am an accurate representative of the colossal self-centeredness of the male beast."

It seemed to her that her underwear should have intrigued a healthy male beast, at the very least, not been dismissed out of hand!

"But those curls," he added, mournfully. "It was as if a gypsy dancer was trapped inside of you, champing to get out."

It was still faintly dismissive, as if he found her funny

rather than sexy. He, the one who had touched his lips to hers, and very nearly set that gypsy free!

But, thank goodness, he hadn't unleashed that family legacy of passion in her. Still, the silly girl in her who wanted to preen at his admiration of her hair had to be quashed. Immediately.

So did the gypsy inside her who had, after all, chosen that underwear, and who knew *exactly* how to erase little sisters and nuns from his mind in association with her.

An insane image materialized in her brain. Of her shocking him. Of her being the kind of woman who could pull off sexy red lace. Of her taking one step forward, capturing his lips, kissing him until he was begging her not to stop, but to go on.

Casey wrestled her multiple personalities into submission and held out her hand. "My keys?"

He dangled them above her waiting palm, but didn't let go. When he looked at her, his gaze steady and stripping, she was shocked that she felt astoundingly the same as she had felt all those years ago.

As if he truly saw her. As if he saw things about her no one else ever had. As if he knew everything and anything there was to know about her that was of any interest at all! But she'd been so much more naive back then than she was now.

Now she knew some men just had a gift—an intensity, a power of focus—that could make a woman feel as if she was the only one in his world.

"Is Christmas still the hardest thing for you?" he asked, softly.

Oh, no. There was seeing underthings, and then there was seeing under things.

"W-w-what would make you say that?"

"You told me. You told me that your twin brother died on Christmas Day. Angelo," Turner said softly.

Her best friends had not remembered this. Did Emily and Andrea even know her brother's name?

"I remember," he continued softly, "that you told me how you so wanted a Christmas miracle, and prayed for one. How you bargained with God. And Santa Claus. *'Just let my brother live.'* That stuck with me.

"And when I heard you'd gone into medical research, it was, like, *you go, girl.* You *make* your miracle happen. If any such thing exists, I hope you are the one who gets it."

He looked hard at her, and she had a feeling she was not hiding the tears that pressed from behind her eyes.

"I'm sorry," he said. "I probably shouldn't have mentioned that. I'm turned around. I'm somewhere between exhausted and delirious."

"How could I get a miracle?" she demanded softly. "No matter how my research goes, I can't bring back my brother."

"Not that I consider myself anything of an expert on miracles—" he laughed slightly, a deeply cynical sound "—but it seems to me it's something of one that you are determined to turn your own loss into something good for someone else."

Casey realized it was this exact thing she had run from when she had headed for her car in the deep, dark night instead of wanting to chance an encounter with him.

It felt as if Turner *saw* her, went straight past the red lace to the core of her, and went to it with alarming swiftness.

This was the same way she had felt during those three days together.

As if, for the first time in her life, someone had seen her. As if, for the first time in her life, she was not completely alone.

But that was why she was at the beginning stages of making her plan to create her own family, to have a baby.

So that she would not be so alone anymore. And so she did not have to rely on someone who had proved himself as unreliable as Turner Kennedy, to make that happen.

She was not letting Turner disrupt her carefully planned world!

CHAPTER FOUR

"ARE YOU HAPPY, Casey?" Turner asked softly.

The question was a disruption of her carefully planned world. And it was what she least expected. Not suave. Not teasing. Not flirtatious. She hated that he had asked that, because even if she didn't answer him—and she certainly did not intend to—she had to answer it to herself.

She had to get her guard back up!

"Of course I'm happy," she said, in a tone with so much bite she sounded anything but.

Happy? She was suddenly and achingly aware she was the furthest thing from happy. She was a woman who had experienced way too many losses in much too quick a succession.

Was it fair to have a baby to make herself happy?

Ridiculous to ask herself that! The point would be to make the baby happy. To give it the joyous, stable, wonderful family she had always craved.

Her life would finally be on track. She would have someone to live for, and to love!

This was just what he had done that night of Cole and Emily's wedding. Sitting with Casey on a darkened stretch of grass under a star-studded sky, wrapped in a blanket, Turner Kennedy had pulled her secret longings from her one by one, leaving her vulnerable and exposed.

Making her do something crazy. *Run away with me. Just pretend I'm a prince....*

And then, she reminded herself, leaving her. Period.

"And I'll be even happier when you hand over my keys," she said.

The keys dropped into her hand with a cold jingle. "I liked your hair better the way it was before."

"Thank you. You said that already. I'll take your opinion under careful consideration."

"You do that."

That was better. A certain awkwardness between them, as if they had never shared anything at all.

And then it all changed in a split second.

Bang.

The noise, a huge boom above their heads, was deafening in the quiet night. Before she knew what had happened, she was on the floor of the porch, Turner's hard body on top of her, shielding her, crushing the breath out of her.

A logical mind, which Casey's usually was, would have screamed *Danger!*

And she felt danger, all right, but not the kind that came from some unknown threat on the roof!

Silence settled again, and then was broken by the hiss of something sliding through the snow across the roof.

Turner's arms tightened around Casey, even as he peered upward. And while he was totally focused on the dangers above them, she was totally focused on the danger within her.

Casey could feel an intense sensation of heightened awareness. She could feel the crush of his chest against her breast, could count the ridges of his ribs where they were pressed into hers.

She could feel the coiled tension in arm muscles folded around her, and where the hard line of his thigh met the softer line of hers. She could feel the steady, elevated tattoo of his heart and the ragged beat of her own.

He was so close she could see the shadow of whiskers darkening the exquisite cut of his cheekbones, his jaw. She could see the perfect texture of his skin.

His scent—pine trees and cool mountain lakes—enveloped her.

Her scientific mind insisted on posing a question: Why was it that she felt so safe, when it was obvious he felt anything but?

She stared up into his face and knew, suddenly, that it had worked both ways during those long-ago few days.

Turner Kennedy had seen her as no one else ever had. But she had seen him, too, felt she had known things about him. Now, studying his face as he squinted up toward the porch ceiling, she put her finger on what was different about him.

During those playful days, Turner Kennedy had seemed hopeful and filled with confidence. He had told her about losing his dad under very hard circumstances, but she had been struck by a certain faith in himself to change all that was bad about the world.

Now, Casey was aware she was looking into the face of a warrior—calm, strong, watchful. Ready.

And also, deeply weary. There was a hard-edged cynicism about him that went deeper than cynical. It went to his soul.

Casey knew that just as she had known things about him all those years ago. It was as if, with him, she arrived at a different level of knowing with almost terrifying swiftness.

And the other thing she knew?

Turner Kennedy was ready to protect her with his life.

A second passed and then two, but they were long, drawn-out seconds, as if time had come to an amazing standstill.

This was what chemicals did, she told herself dreamily. He thought, apparently, they were in mortal danger.

She was bathing in the intoxicating closeness of him.

Casey could feel the strong beat of his heart through the thin fabric of his shirt. He was radiating a silky, sensual warmth, and she could feel the exact moment that his muscles began to uncoil. She observed the watchfulness drain from his expression, felt the thud of his heart quieting.

Finally, he looked away from the roof and gazed intently down at her.

Now that his mind had sounded some kind of all-clear, he, too, seemed to be feeling the pure chemistry of their closeness. His breath caressed her face like the touch of a summer breeze. She could feel her own heart picking up tempo as his began to slow. His mouth dropped closer to hers.

The new her, the one that was going to be impervious to the chemistry of pure attraction, seemed to be sitting passively in the backseat instead of the driver's seat. Because instead of giving Turner a much deserved shove—fight— or scooting out from under him—flight—she licked her lips, and watched his eyes darken and his lips drop even closer to hers.

But then the dog whined, did her best to insert her furry self between them, and licked Casey's face.

"Ugh!" She spat in pure disappointment. A dog's kiss instead of his!

But at least it had brought Casey to her senses. She managed to get her hands up in between them, and pushed.

Turner reared back off her, got his legs under him, leaped up with ease. But when she went to rise, too, he glanced at her, his expression once again remote. Stern, even. She didn't question her obedience when he held up his hand, stilling her while he scanned the darkness.

He went and leaned out over the porch railing, glanced

up, and she could see whatever tension that remained in him dissipate completely.

He turned back to her, looking faintly sheepish. When he stretched out his hand to her, she took it, felt the chemical reaction again to his touch, his easy strength as he pulled her to her feet. He made an awkward attempt to brush off her jacket, then gave up.

"Sorry," he said. "I overreacted."

She thought of his lips nearly claiming hers, but apparently that wasn't what he felt he had overreacted to.

"A branch from this oak tree broke under the weight of the snow and landed on the roof."

She glanced where he was looking, and saw a huge limb had broken off, hit the porch roof and slid down it. Part of the broken branch was visible where it hung off the edge.

"What did you think it was?" she asked him softly.

He shrugged. "Who knows?"

Something made her push, but she wasn't sure what. Certainly it wasn't the self-preservation of fight or flight. "What did you think it was?" she asked again.

This time he rolled his shoulders, looked away, then back at her, obviously pained by her persistence.

"What?"

"I thought it was an explosion," he said quietly.

She took in again the expression on his face, registered the warrior way that he carried himself and had reacted.

"Where have you been, Turner?" she murmured. "Where have you been that your first thought would be it was an explosion?"

He looked away, gazed out into the darkness of the night. When he turned back, a small smile toyed with the edges of his mouth. But she could see it hid more than it revealed, and that was the way he wanted it.

"Why?" he asked. "Were you waiting for a postcard?"

Something dangerously close to sympathy for him had been rising in her. Now, his sardonic tone erased that.

As if her hair loved all the fuss it was causing tonight, a strand, loosened from gel hell by the humidity of the wetly falling snow, sprang free and curled wildly. She blew it out of her eyes. "You know, it wouldn't take much for you to succeed at making me angry."

"Now, *that* is something I would really like to see," he said, unperturbed. "Though if knocking you to the floor didn't do it, I'm probably safe from your temper for to-night."

"Don't be so sure. Maybe I wasn't expecting a post-card, but would it have been so hard? To wake me up before you left that morning? To call just once to let me know what you were doing? To write a little note saying you enjoyed the days we spent together? To let me know you were all right?"

He didn't say anything, just looked at her steadily. She ordered herself to shut up, but she didn't.

"Nothing," she said, hoping it was anger and not pain he heard. "Not a single, solitary word. I'm surprised you even remembered my name, let alone my hair. And my brother. And my brother's name. And the way I feel at Christmas."

"I've never forgotten anything about you."

Some horrible weakness uncurled within her, but she saw it as completely forgivable since her defenses had been weakened by being pinned under him on the floor.

"That surprises me," she said coolly. She ordered herself to leave it there, but then reconsidered. They were going to be spending time here under the same roof, working toward the same goal of creating a perfect day for Emily and Cole.

Maybe there were some things they needed to get out of the way, that should be addressed so the tension between them didn't spoil things for others.

"I thought I would hear from you again," she said.

"I made it clear from the outset. I had three days. *We* had three days. That was all."

But she had thought those three days would change everything. She had nursed the hope that whatever mysterious thing was taking him away, the pull of what existed between them would prove irresistible! She had thought she would be able to wheedle his secret out of him, but she hadn't been able to, and in truth, hadn't that been part of the excitement? His mystery?

"Yes, you made that abundantly clear," she said coolly. "But you never said why."

"It's a long time ago," he said wearily.

"You're the one who brought up the postcard you never sent."

He sighed.

She could feel color rising in her cheeks. The last thing she would ever want him to know was how she had waited. And believed. That he would call. That he would come back. That he had felt it, too.

An intensity of connection that had left her bereft as she had accepted he wasn't going to call. He wasn't coming back.

"It didn't have anything to do with you," he said, as if he could see suddenly in her eyes, despite the fact she was trying to guard her thoughts from him, all those desperate nights of waiting for him. The unexpected gentleness in his tone nearly undid her.

He raised his hand, as if to touch her throat or her hair again, but she stepped back. She was not sure what she would do if he touched her.

What she would want to do, that crazy gypsy dancer inside her, drenched in the chemical reaction to having his body over hers moments ago, would be to turn her head and catch his fingertips with her lips.

So she pulled her coat tighter around her, dropped her keys in one of the deep side pockets, and let her hand follow them. Suddenly, she realized how easily he had deflected her when she had asked him where he was. He had turned the question, making it about her instead. Was it possible he had even irritated her on purpose?

"You never did say where you went, why you had only three days." Did she sound as if she was begging for an explanation? She hated that! She had begged for an explanation then, to no avail.

At the time she had taken his "let's just live for the moment" as a sign of how wonderful everything was, not a warning that there would be only those moments.

He hesitated, looked away from her and then looked back, frowning.

"That night of Em and Cole's wedding, those crazy days in New York with you, that was the last time I was in *that* world. I left it behind completely," he admitted softly. "I left it behind completely because that is what I had trained to do. Immerse myself in a new reality. If I even glanced back, I would not have been able to perform."

"Emily thought you were in France! Or Italy."

He snorted.

"Perform what?" Casey whispered.

But he looked closed now, even annoyed with himself, and equally annoyed with her, as if she had dragged state secrets out of him.

And suddenly she wondered how close that was to the truth. A shadowy job no one seemed to know that much about, even his closest friends. A contractor for the government. And now, reacting to a snapping branch as if a gun had gone off. Or an explosion.

She absorbed it, along with the new air about him. "You're a spy," she guessed.

But his expression was closed now, completely unforth-coming.

"Bond," he said drily. "James Bond."

It was sarcastic, and it was a deflection. But it was not a denial.

"Are you?"

"A spy?" he said, and laughed, but it was a sound without humor. "That would imply a certain level of glamor, and I'm afraid nothing could be further from the truth. I've held some contracts that were sensitive."

"Secret?" she guessed.

He shrugged, shutting her out. His glance warned her *no more*.

And he was right. She was being way too interested.

Sucked in was more like it. Turner Kennedy's substantial charm was now layered with something dark and dangerous. Plus there was that chemical-inducing moment of lying beneath him....

Turner shook a cigarette from the pack in his pocket, stuck it in the corner of his mouth and spoke around it. "What are you doing wandering around out here, lingerie-filled suitcase in hand, in the middle of the night, anyway?"

She was tempted to protest that her suitcase was not *filled* with lingerie.

But then she saw it for what it was. Turner was moving the subject, again, away from himself.

She certainly was not going to admit she was escaping him!

"What are *you* doing out here at this time of night?" she asked him.

"I don't sleep well."

It was time for her to go. Really. She had her keys. Her dignity was intact. Why feel sympathetic that he didn't sleep?

But she had something to prove, too. That she could stand out here and talk to him and be completely unaffected by it, even if he had nearly crushed her body under his, even if the dog had stolen his kiss from her lips.

"I don't remember you smoking."

He laughed. "I don't. Not anymore." He took the cigarette, glared at it for a moment, then tossed it over the railing. "But when I can't sleep, I wish I did."

She knew again that there was a dark place in Turner Kennedy that had not been there before.

Casey fought a desire to lighten it somehow—she wasn't sure how. Tell a joke, give a hug, something purely feminine and nurturing. Biology joining with chemistry to make a knockout punch for those who were not careful.

But she was nothing if not careful. Nothing about this encounter was in her script for her completely fulfilling life of solitude and simple pleasures like yoga and calligraphy.

"Smoking is very bad for you," she said primly.

"Thanks, Doc," he said, "I'll take that under consideration."

Something about his voice made her think that whatever he had been doing, smoking paled as a danger.

And something about the way he held himself told her other truths. He felt as alone as she did. And maybe not just at Christmas, either.

"Why are you here for Christmas?" he asked suddenly, abruptly, as if he was irritated that she had decided to come. "You have family."

"There's just my mom. She had, er, other plans."

Something like sympathy crossed the rugged barrier of his closed face, and Casey rushed on. "It's not a big deal. I feel my connection with Emily and Andrea is as strong as a family bond. Besides, don't you think this will be a lovely place to spend Christmas? Almost like a fairy tale."

"Do I look like I believe in fairy tales?" His voice

sounded harsh, not that of a man who had once said, "Just pretend I'm a prince...."

"No, you don't," she said. She would like to add she didn't, either, but she still did, to a certain extent. No prince, but Casey wanted to create fairy-tale Christmases for her child.

Weaknesses she should be happy to unearth!

"How hokey do you think it's going to be?" he asked.

"Terribly."

"Christmas-carols-around-the-fire hokey?"

"Definitely."

"Hell."

"Tut-tut, that's not exactly in the spirit of the season." He smiled reluctantly.

"What were you expecting from a place called the Gingerbread Inn, gladiator games?"

"Touché," he said drily.

"You have a family, too," she remembered. In the days together he had revealed that much of himself. His was as different from hers as night was from day, except that both families had experienced tragedy. Her brother, when she was young; his father in the World Trade Center attacks.

Hadn't that been part of what had drawn her to him, moth to flame? That Turner knew what it was to be part of a normal family? By his descriptions, the Kennedys had been fun-loving, wholesome, all-American.

What kind of weakness was it that she could remember every single word he had said to her?

"I thought your family did hokey," she said thoughtfully. "One year you told me you got a puppy for Christmas, for goodness sake!"

A subtle line of strain appeared around his mouth. "My mom died while I was overseas."

"I'm so sorry. But your brothers? You had two of them,

right? Younger than you?" She smiled. "The backyard skating rink."

Something in his face closed. "Things change."

Her need for self-preservation dissolved, and this time it was Casey who reached out. She placed her fingers on his wrist, then closed them around it. "*That* changes?"

Despite her resolve to place her belief in different things, she felt shocked. A close family, one as close as he had described, could become estranged? By what?

"Everything changes," he said, and his voice was weary and cynical. "That's the only thing you can count on. That everything can change. And it does. You should go inside now."

He slipped his wrist free of her grasp, but she couldn't move. She told herself it was because she was not allowing him to tell her what to do, but she knew that wasn't really it. Not even close.

"You should go inside," he said softly, "before I do something I'd regret even more than lighting that cigarette."

She didn't have to ask him what.

His eyes lingered on her lips and a memory sizzled in the air between them. She felt a disgusting weakness.

A desire to lean toward him and take his lips, and then pull back and say, "Regret, hmm?"

But instead, she pretended she didn't have a clue what he was talking about, pretended she was immune to the pull between them.

She cocked her head. "What would that be?"

CHAPTER FIVE

THE SMILE WAS back. The one that guarded what Turner Kennedy was thinking. He dragged his eyes slowly, and without a bit of apology, away from her lips. "I was going to go shovel off a piece of the lake and go skating."

She saw now that as well as the adoring dog, he had skates at his feet.

"It's three o'clock in the morning!"

"I told you. Can't sleep. That's why I'd regret it if I asked you to come with me. Night can make strange things happen between people. Things that normally wouldn't. Or maybe shouldn't."

He was talking about that night all those years ago when he had impulsively invited her to run away with him. When he had warned her there would be a time limit, and she had allowed herself not to believe it.

"You probably haven't been up at three in the morning since then," he said huskily, and she hated that he could read her mind.

So she said, raising an eyebrow, "Since when?"

Turner just chuckled, not fooled.

She turned and walked away from him, her steps deliberate and unhurried. She picked up her suitcase from where she had dropped it by the door. The screen squealed when she opened it, but it wasn't loud enough to cover the soft sound of his mocking laughter that he'd been right.

That despite the red lace, the only thing wild about her was her hair.

And if the pounding in her heart and the flame in her cheeks were any indication, she was just as susceptible to him.

The next day, she felt so tired. She had fallen asleep, finally, near dawn to the sound of Turner's shovel scraping the ice.

She noticed he looked exhausted, too, as all the friends came together for a simple breakfast of cereal, and to make a plan for the day.

Andrea had made an extensive list of jobs, large and small, that needed to be accomplished, and Casey was relieved that Turner's enthusiasm for the ice had been noted, and he had been put in charge of getting the lake ready for a skating party after the vow renewal ceremony was over on Christmas Eve.

He either took it very seriously or had no desire to be with the rest of them. All day she could hear him shoveling an ever widening space to skate. It seemed as if he would not be satisfied until the whole lake was cleared.

Casey, assigned inside decorating jobs, would go peer out the window and watch him guiltily when it seemed no one would notice,

Watching a strong man tackle all that snow with easy grace and confidence was a shockingly beautiful sight. The lake ice began to emerge from under the blanket of yesterday's snowfall, and it shone, bright as gunmetal.

Sometimes he seemed to grow bored with shoveling. Then he would turn his attention to making a fire pit and building rough benches. He looked as wonderful splitting wood as he did shoveling snow.

He did not come in for lunch or supper. When Emily wanted to go get him, as they all sat around the hearth in the parlor going over the day, eating Carol's amazing apple pie and visiting, Cole just shook his head.

"Leave him be," he said, something troubled in his eyes when he thought of his friend.

Casey went to bed without seeing him, annoyed with herself that she could feel Turner Kennedy's presence at the inn, and a faint agitation that went with it, without even having any face-to-face contact with him.

She woke to pitch blackness, not sure what had woken her, but drawn to the window. Her bedroom was on the back side of the house, facing the lake, and Casey flicked back a heavy curtain that had left the pane frosted, while not keeping out the draft.

Her eyes adjusted to the inky darkness. She was shocked to see Turner was still down at the lake. He sat on one of his benches, but hadn't lit a fire. He had on that ultra-sexy parka with a fur-lined hood. The shovel was propped against the bench and he seemed to be contemplating the rink he'd made.

Then he got up, and she saw he had skates on. He made his way gracefully from the snow-covered bank to the ice.

And he began to skate.

If she had thought watching him pit his power against snow clearing and splitting wood was a wonder, it was nothing compared to this.

Turner was extraordinary on skates. He raced over the ice with effortless grace, his incredible power and energy practically shimmering in the cold air around him.

Harper was skittering along after Turner, joyous at this unusual nocturnal excursion.

Stop watching, Casey told herself. But she couldn't.

All those years ago, with him, she had felt magic. She was not sure she had ever felt it since. He was right; people did not make good decisions in the middle of the night. Because she suddenly wanted to skate.

"I should go skating," she whispered, watching him.

Such an irrational thought shook the scientist in her to her core. It was the middle of the night. She wasn't a great skater. She had not once in her whole life felt compelled to go skating.

She thought of the way Turner's gaze had locked on her lips when he had talked about doing something he would regret. She knew she was playing with fire.

Then, as she watched, Turner stopped for a moment, leaned over and grabbed some snow from the edge of the rink he had cleared. With his bare hands he formed it into a ball, then threw it for the eagerly waiting dog.

Harper scrambled after it, burrowed beneath the snow looking for it, came back to him empty-jawed, with a bewildered shake of her golden head, begging him to throw another, whining that she would do better next time.

He should have laughed. It was funny.

But he didn't. One thing Casey remembered from that night they had spent together was the easiness of his laughter, the goldenness of it, as if it had the power to chase away shadows.

The dog rolled over in front of him, her legs in the air. Still, he did not laugh at her attempt to charm him. He gave her belly a quick pat and went back to work.

Casey knew this was the time to let the curtain fall back into place, and climb back under the cozy, worn feather duvet on her bed.

"After all," she muttered, "he didn't even ask you. In fact, he made a point of *not* asking you."

He was making a point of being by himself.

If ever there was a time in her life to be safe and rational and totally true to her predictable nature, this was it. She finally had a plan for herself. For her future, and her contentment!

She had passed the first test, the first encounter with

Turner. She had passed it despite the fact that she remembered too much, and despite the fact she'd been crushed under his body and, shamefully, had loved it.

She had passed again today, leaving him alone, not seeking him out. Not, she hoped, giving anyone the slightest indication that she had been tense all day at the thought of him joining them, and then oddly disappointed when he hadn't.

So she had passed. She didn't think anyone had guessed that Turner created turmoil in her. That being under the same roof as him felt like a form of torture. Their past history made her feel angry at him. And embarrassed for herself. But that wasn't all she felt. She wished it was. No, she felt confused by him, and by her reactions to him.

So she let the curtain fall, made herself go back to bed, and ordered herself to sleep. But the scientist in her did not like confusion. The scientist demanded a solution.

If she didn't go out there, was she damned to this state of confusion? Had he won in some way? Intimidated her? He was probably even now congratulating himself on how correct his assessment of her had been, despite underwear that screamed the opposite.

That the only thing wild about Casey Caravetta was her hair.

Lying here in bed was the flight option.

It was what he expected of her. And what she expected of herself. And in all honesty, where had that got her, so far? Is this what she wanted to teach her future child? To hide from life and its challenges?

No! She wanted to go into motherhood confident of her ability to be in control of herself at all times, so her children would never know the insecurities of a childhood buffeted by the passions and weaknesses of the adults around them. Casey could not run from challenges. She had to accept them! And conquer them!

Feeling not like someone who had said yes to fun, but like an ancient woman warrior girding herself for battle, she went to her suitcase and found a warm pair of slacks and a wool sweater.

She shoved every single strand of her wildly curling hair under a simple black toque.

Turner had never lost his love of skating. The ice and the work and the solitude he was finding at the inn were a balm to his tumultuous soul.

The lake ice reminded him of his father's backyard rinks—imperfect and lumpy, not like the perfectly made ice in skating rinks at all.

The memory of his father—wanting to honor his father—had driven every major decision of his life since 2001.

So how had it all turned out so differently from what he would have wanted? And certainly differently from what his father would have wanted for him.

Turner remembered only good things from his childhood. Racing his brothers in tight loops around the backyard rink, roughhousing, spending summers haunting the nearby beaches.

He had grown up in one of those wealthy satellite communities, less than a half hour commute to New York City. His family had been fun-loving, traditional and well-to-do. He had never aspired to anything except to follow in his father's footsteps. Turner had had every expectation he would marry, have a wonderful home, re-create for his own children the idyllic childhood he'd had.

He had been in his first year of university when the World Trade Center had been attacked. At 9:59 a.m. on September 11, 2001, the South Tower, where his father worked as a financial manager, collapsed.

The Kennedy family had collapsed at the same time.

Within months, Turner had made a decision to leave university and join the military. He'd felt as if everything his father had stood for was threatened, and he had felt he could not stand by and not try to change a world gone terribly wrong.

In very short order, Turner had been singled out and selected for membership in Tango, an elite and highly classified antiterrorism unit. The cover story was that he handled sensitive "contracts" for the government.

As he had said to Casey, those days with her had been his last in the world he'd known.

He was amazed by how his first discussion with her had been so fraught with the topic of miracles—and that he had started it!

Because he had been in a position many times where he had pleaded for one. And not been on the receiving end. The last time, just a few months ago. It had been an extremely dangerous assignment. The odds had been against them from the start. A far better man than he—Ken Hamilton, a man who had needed to live, for his wife and his family—had died in Turner's arms.

When Turner was young—and hopelessly naive—he had embraced a dangerous way of life, thinking it would give him a sense of meaning, a sense of bringing order to a chaotic world.

Instead, with Ham's death, it had felt as if something broke in him. If he had had even a sliver of faith left, it was gone now. Turner Kennedy was a man who had lost the sense that anything had meaning. Life was random. And unpredictable.

When it was out of your control, you were in trouble. Period.

Now, as he skated, with the dog chasing him joyously, he knew why he had come here. It was different from the reason he had thought.

He had told himself it was to try and get a good night's sleep. It felt like months since he had slept, not been awakened by dreams, soaked in sweat. He always feared he was soaked in the stickiness of blood, until he turned on a light.

He told himself you didn't let down a buddy who asked. And Cole had asked, said he *needed* him to help get this falling-down old inn ready for a special day, the most important day of his life.

"I have an opportunity to make my world right again," Cole had said. "I've been given a second chance. I want the day to be as perfect as it can be for Emily. Will you come be part of it? Will you come help me?"

The possibility that there was such a thing as a second chance had lured Turner here.

He had come to help a friend. That was as engrained in him now as breathing. You helped your buddies when they asked.

But he knew he'd come to help himself, too.

To see if there was any chance at all for normalcy for him. A normal night's sleep. A normal life.

A long time ago he had stood at a crossroad and had taken a turn. The choice had cost him more than he had ever expected to pay.

Could a man backtrack to the same crossroad and choose differently? Could he, who had seen and done so many things that were outside the experience of the average American—certainly outside that of his brothers, who were raising their own families now—could he bring anything back to them except pure poison? A cold, hard heart? A damaged spirit?

What good could that do anyone?

No, maybe his other option was the right one. Sign up again. And again. And again. Until he joined his other brothers, the ones who had shared those experiences. Until all of them lay beneath the ground, where they could be

mourned as heroes, without forcing their families to tolerate them as they were: damaged, cynical, unable to connect with the ordinary things that ordinary people thought
were fun and exciting.

That's why he had come to the Gingerbread Inn. To see
if there really were second chances. And to make a choice.

Out of the corner of his eye, he caught movement.
Through the darkness, in a pink snowsuit that looked almost neon against the white snow, Casey was coming toward the lake.

Now there was a woman who was going to complicate
a simple choice.

There was a woman who could shake his sense of control. And that meant trouble. Period.

And yet all those years ago, when he had spent that
time in New York with her, he had done it with the purest
of motivations. Yes, he'd been intent on making his final
days in the States fun and carefree. Maybe he had known,
at some level, he was leaving a world behind forever.

But it had been more than evident to him that while
he had grown up in a fun and carefree environment—
with backyard skating rinks and puppies delivered by
Santa—that was a side of life she had never, because of
her brother's illness, completely known. Casey had never
been carefree.

He had just wanted to show her something. What life
could be like.

That moment when Casey, drowning in the Waldorf Astoria housecoat, had given in completely, taken his hand
and jumped up and down with him on the king-size bed
in the master bedroom of the suite, laughing out loud, he'd
felt he had succeeded at something.

Setting the rather uptight Miss Caravetta free. In that
moment, the truth he thought he had glimpsed about her
had proved to be wonderfully true.

But it seemed she had gone backward since then. He hadn't been in the inn much, but Casey seemed more up-tight than ever, as if she had rebounded back to where she had been before, and then some.

Because of him? Because he had left her without saying goodbye? Certainly that couldn't be all of it. And just as certainly, it couldn't have helped.

After those three days, he'd had a sense of knowing her, through and through. How sweetly sensitive she was, how deep, how serious. He had known there would be tears if they had a formal farewell.

His fear of tears was not a new one, like his fear of sleeping, and the fear of Christmas that was keeping him out on this lake while everyone else was busy getting ready. By the time he had met Casey that first time, he had had enough tears to last him a lifetime. And so he had just slipped out the door that morning.

So why did he feel faintly but unmistakably happy to see her coming, when it was the last thing he'd expected of her, and when he was a man who did not like to be surprised by life?

Because it meant something of that girl who had jumped on the bed remained.

It meant maybe he had been given a second chance to do the right thing. It meant maybe he could get to see her laugh again.

That part of it had elements of selfishness in it. But a memory of a laugh like hers could hold a man in the light when his life took him to dark places.

This would be the challenge. To bring her back to that place of carefree laughter, without ever letting her see that he could not truly go there with her. Not anymore.

Even back then, maybe he had hoped carefree joy was a baton he was passing to her. The training, though not real, had foreshadowed the real thing. Even before actually going on that first mission, a baptism in blood and fire, Turner had probably known that particular baton—joyous abandon—would not be his to hold again.

She had every inch of her hair tucked up under a toque, and for some reason, her not wanting to give him even a glimpse of those locks that he had confessed to adore made him smile. Getting her to let her hair back down was going to be a challenge.

It felt like the first truly genuine smile he'd had in months.

As she approached the lake, Casey watched Turner skate with a sense of awe. She had not been around people who were athletic, and certainly outdoor sports of any kind were not part of her rather bookish experience.

She paused and looked at him.

He wasn't skating, he was flying. Bent slightly at the waist, legs crossing over each other in the turns, seamlessly moving from skating forward to skating backward.

There was incredible energy in the air around him. This was his confidence and his strength showing in a very outward way.

His proficiency rattled her! She had never even been on skates. She was sure she was about to make a fool of herself, and almost headed back, except that suddenly he threw his weight to one side, and in a spray of scraped ice, came to a halt.

He had seen her. If she retreated now, she had lost more surely than if she had not come down here in the first place.

There was a bench beside the lake and Casey stopped at it to put on the skates she had chosen from the vast array hung on pegs inside the inn's back door, for the use of guests.

While she glared down at the skates, suddenly his dark hair appeared in her peripheral vision.

She braced herself for him to ask why she was here,

what she wanted from him, but he didn't. His dark head bent over her skates. She had to bite her lip to fight the urge to touch it. This was so much like the night he had playfully painted her toenails.

"Red," he'd said, "hidden inside your shoes, like a secret between us."

His hands were on the laces. "Nice and tight," he said. "They're terrible skates. I'll see if the laces are long enough to wrap around your ankles for more support."

She glared at his head. He could at least act surprised that she had come! But then again, she had the feeling he had become a man it would take a great deal to surprise. And a woman wanting to spend time with him would not be one of those things!

"Okay." He gave her skates a little slap. "I think you're ready."

She was not sure what she had pictured, but possibly gliding around him with swanlike elegance had been part of her it.

Too late, Casey realized some skating experience would undoubtedly have helped in creating such a picture.

She waddled from the bench to the ice with about as much grace as a penguin making its annual march.

She was sure once she actually got to the lake, like a penguin making it to water, all that would change, and his next words made her think it would, too.

"Do you believe in miracles, Casey?" he asked softly.

"No," she said, astonished at the quaver in her voice. "Of course not! I'm a scientist."

He regarded her thoughtfully, a faint cynical upturn to his mouth. "I don't believe in them, either," he said softly. "But I wish you did."

"Why?"

He rolled his shoulders. He was obviously exhausted. She was not sure he had slept since he'd arrived here.

"If you give up believing in miracles," he told her quietly, "then you believe only in yourself. And then when you fail there is nothing left to believe in."

She stood there, frozen to the spot, knowing he had just trusted her with something of himself, and the regret he felt was already etched in his face.

He covered it quickly. "So here, Casey, let me give you a miracle."

He held out his hand to her, and tentatively, she took it. And it did feel as if a miracle shivered to life within her.

Everything that had hurt her about love seemed to disintegrate. *Oh, no.* This was the opposite of what she had come here to prove! She should have refused his hand. She should have insisted on doing this herself!

But Turner Kennedy had her now, and he pulled her forward, off the snowy bank and onto the ice.

One foot slid annoyingly away as she tried to anchor the other on the slippery surface. He let go of her hand and she stood there, frozen to the spot.

He was skating backward, as if it was as easy for him as breathing, and watching her. When her leg skittered even farther away, he skated back toward her with a breathtaking burst of speed, leaped forward, took her elbow.

"I'll give you a hand."

It would be churlish to refuse, not to mention there was a very real possibility that without him steadying her she was going to fall flat on her fanny without having skated a single step.

He placed one hand around her shoulder and the other at her waist, and persuaded her to allow her other foot to be guided to the ice.

Even leaning heavily against him, Casey was wobbling. "I feel like an elephant trying to balance on a beach ball," she said.

"What? You don't get the miracle?"

"Miracle?" She was very aware, for the second time since their reunion, that they were touching physically.

And for the second time, she felt as if she could count on him. Lean on him. That he would protect her with his life, if need be.

That was a miracle even if it was quite a lot to read into the fact that he was holding her up so she wouldn't hit the ice with a very painful splat.

"It's a miracle of biblical proportions," he whispered huskily in her ear. "You're walking on water."

Despite herself, she laughed. And then he smiled, and it was a real smile, even lightening the exhaustion around his eyes. He steadied her on her feet. "You've never skated, have you?"

"That's why I'm here," she said mutinously. "I'm all about embracing life's adventures."

He snorted, but gently. "Since when?"

"Hey, I'm the girl who ran away with you once."

"So you are," he said quietly.

"It was the most impulsive thing I had ever done. I lied to my parents about where I was."

"I know."

"I mean, I shouldn't have had to lie to them. I was old enough to do what I wanted."

"Nothing happened that you couldn't tell your parents about."

"That's true. It didn't really work out for me. Embracing adventure. But here I am again. Wouldn't you say that was brave?"

He said nothing.

"Or stupid," she said, as if she had read his thoughts. "You know what the difference is this time?"

He shook his head.

"Me," she said. "I'm different from how I was back then."

He looked relieved and as if he didn't believe her at the very same time.

"I am," she insisted.

"I didn't say anything."

"It was years ago."

"I didn't say anything."

"I'm not needy."

"Okay."

"It just looked like fun. To come out here and skate. No strings attached. Put the past behind us. I don't have a crush on you. That's what I'm saying. That girl is gone."

"Okay," he repeated quietly.

"So, if we've got that straightened away, let's go."

"Let's," he said, and even though he had agreed with every single thing she had said, she was not sure he had believed a word that had come out of her mouth.

And worse…she was not sure that she had, either!

"Someday," she said with grim determination, "I want to teach my children how to skate. That's really why I'm here."

CHAPTER SIX

"I'M GLAD YOU cleared that up," Turner said solemnly, "Now hold on."

He moved the hand around her waist to her wrist. In a blink, he had pulled away, spun around and was facing her.

He took both her hands firmly in his. He had gloves on, she had mittens, but she could still feel a surge of energy pouring between them. He moved effortlessly backward, pulling her toward him.

"Don't look at your feet," he said.

"What am I supposed to look at?"

"Me."

That's what she was afraid of. Because looking into his crystal clear gray eyes made it too easy to forget she was on a mission. That she was here to start laying the groundwork for her child's—or children's—future. She was here to prove something.

To him.

Most especially to herself.

But that mission was feeling like a mirage in a desert. The closer she got to him, the more it seemed to disappear.

"That's it," he said approvingly. "Hey, look, you're skating."

She wasn't really, and she knew it. She was wobbling after him like a baby frantic not to lose sight of its mother.

"Now," he said, "as miraculous as it is to walk on water,

I want you to quit trying to walk. Skating is all about gliding. So push off with your right foot, and let your left one
slide forward. Hey! That was good."

The mission dissolved a little more as she got caught
up in the motion. Push. Glide. Push. Glide. Right foot,
then left one.

"Let go of my hands."

Embarrassingly, he had to pry her hands from his.

"Keep looking at me. Hey! No looking at your feet."

He moved away from her, and she scrambled after him
like a clumsy puppy. He smiled. That smile was a carrot
worth racing toward!

Wait! It wasn't. Her whole future felt as if it could be decided in these moments. She was not leaning! She was not
depending. She was doing it all herself, her way. She was
getting the hang of this thing. She didn't need Turner Kennedy or anyone, and in the interest of making that point,
she turned from him and skated off in another direction.

She made it a few yards before one foot decided to go
one way and one the other, and her arms windmilled in a
crazy attempt to stop herself from falling, but—

Splat.

"Ouch," she said, "That hurt!" Her pride as much as
her derriere!

He skated over and held out his hands. She saw he was
smiling that genuine smile again. Why did she feel it had
become so rare?

She saw no option but to take his hands, and he hauled
her up with easy strength. Strength it would be far too
easy to rely on! Casey swatted his hands away as soon as
she was standing. He raised his palms in mock surrender.

She skated this way and that, experimenting, falling,
getting back up. He gave her instructions, called suggestions, came and grabbed her elbow when she was going

to fall over. Together, they covered every inch of the ice that he had shoveled off.

She realized she may have started out to prove something, but she was having fun! Suddenly, she realized she shouldn't be having fun. She shouldn't be letting her guard down.

In truth, he was setting up the very same dynamic he had that evening of the wedding.

He was the suave and sophisticated slightly older man; she was the gauche girl bowled over by his attention.

He was taking the lead. He was going to decide what happened and when.

Including, like that other time, making a decision never to see her again!

Well, this time it wasn't going to be like that. She was not going to play little sister to his big brother. She had surprised him by showing up on the ice, and she was going to continue to surprise him.

And herself.

She had something to prove! That she could resist his damnable attractions. And at the same time, prove that she was not his little sister, not even close.

Deliberately, she set off across the ice, away from him. She gained confidence. The sensation of flying was quite remarkable. It was fun and exciting to be moving across the frozen surface on her own, but the speed was surprising. Too soon, she reached the end of the shoveled part, and she had not learned anything about stopping yet!

She hit the snowbank at high speed and catapulted into it, facedown, rump in the air. She flipped over and spit snow out of her mouth, looking up at the inky, star-crusted sky.

"Argh." She tried to get up, but the skates made it nearly impossible to get her feet under her. She collapsed back into the snow.

Turner glanced over, then turned and raced toward her. "Are you okay?" He leaned down, held out his hands. She took them and let him yank her to her feet.

He pulled a little too hard and she fell against him, her feet wobbling.

She looked up at him, saw the soft clouds of warm breath leaving his mouth, his eyes lustrous as polished silver in the darkness.

No matter what she had told herself, she knew this was why she was really here. To feel this once again, if only ever so briefly. Uninhibited. Unfettered. Brave, somehow, as if life was an adventure she was willing to embrace.

Without any forethought, she reached up and touched her lips to his. He tasted of ice and magic, of moonlit nights and the sharp cut of skate blades. He tasted of the memory of carefree laughter, and a time when she had let go of all control.

She could feel that control slipping away again, blissfully, completely....

He pulled back from her, but couldn't let her go because she would fall again.

"Casey. What the hell are you doing?"

"Kissing you," she said huskily.

"That wasn't in the lesson plan."

Just as she had figured. He was teacher, she was student. As long as he was in control, everything was great.

"Get this straight," she said firmly, the magic of the kiss dissolving to embarrassment she didn't intend to let him see. "I am not your student. Or your little sister."

He let her go. Her ankles wobbled, but somehow she maintained her balance.

"Okay," he said, his arms folded over his chest, his voice remote. "I think we're clear on that."

And then he skated away from her, went to the edge of the ice, made the transition to the snow easily, and walked to the bench. He took off his skates without glancing at her, slung them over his shoulder, and with the dog's nose an inch from his thigh, headed for the inn.

What had she done? Casey wondered, watching him go. She'd given in to the temptation to be alive fully. But there was no excuse for using her lips to do it!

Besides, she had ended up not at all certain she could resist his appeal if she was put to the test. What had she expected?

That he was going to be helpless in the face of her charm. But why would he be? He hadn't been all those years ago, or he would have stayed, instead of left.

Still, she had a feeling she had just rattled Turner Kennedy, the unflappable, and she couldn't help but feel the smallest satisfaction over that.

Of course, she had rattled herself in the process. Right to the core. She had never felt like that when she'd kissed Sebastian.

Oh, it had been pleasant enough.

When she had confronted Sebastian about his infidelity, he had said woefully that he'd never crossed "the line." He was so sorry. He was just testing the water, looking for something *more.*

When pressed, he hadn't been able to tell her what that "more" was, what it looked like or felt like, even though, presumably, he had been in hot pursuit of it with someone else.

But right now, Casey felt as if she knew exactly what *more* was. It was touching someone else and feeling the sizzle of his energy. It was tasting someone else, and feeling as if you were eating something you could never, ever get enough of. It was a longing, deep and primal, that suddenly felt as if only that one person could satisfy it.

That part Turner never had to know.

He had rejected her, which was sad only because she had planned to reject him first.

"For the sake of future generations," she told herself, as if it was a motto for battle.

She did a few more defiant if graceless spins around the ice, just to show him he could not affect her, that she was still having fun. But there were no witnesses to her lack of grace or her fun-filled effort.

Turner did not glance back.

Not even once.

Casey had kissed him! Hard not to give in to that, Turner thought. Hard not to explore the sweetness of her offered lips until Casey and he were both gasping with need and desire. Thankfully, she had arrived on the ice hard on the heels of his ruthless self-evaluation.

There was no sense him giving her the idea that he was the kind of guy she needed in her life. There was no sense in that at all.

He was not the kind of guy anyone needed in his or her life. That kiss, and the innocence in it, despite the fact she had intended to prove she was now a woman of the world, had led him one step closer to realizing he was too wounded to return to a place like her lips had offered him. Like his boyhood home. Like the homes of his brothers.

Not that anyone was rolling out the red carpet in welcome. His brothers had never felt he was vindicating the murder of their father. They had felt he had abandoned his family when he was most needed, that he had left his mother when she was at her most fragile.

His brothers saw him as going off to save the world when his own family was more in need of saving.

When he had not been able to come back for their mother's funeral, something had broken irrevocably between him and his brothers.

Casey should be careful whose lips she tangled with. With that in mind, Turner headed for the shower, hoping to wash the sweetness of her from his mind. He could not get rid of the dog. She pushed into the bathroom with him, waited in the steamy room until he was done.

An hour later, he hit the stairs at about the same time as another woman.

"Hi," she said, extending her hand. "Not sure why we haven't bumped into each other before. I'm Carol. I run the old place."

"Turner Kennedy."

Her hand was the hand of a woman who worked really, really hard, probably doing all kinds of things women weren't intended to do.

"Nice to meet you. And there's my missing dog! Harper, where have you been?"

"She was with me," Turner said.

"All night? Actually, for two nights?"

"Sorry if you worried. I tried to shake her, but she wasn't having any of it."

"How odd. I mean, she's a goldie, so she likes everyone, but I've never seen her become attached to anyone so completely before. Look, she's not leaving you even now."

Sure enough, after a token tail wag for her owner, the dog sat down beside him, leaning heavily into his leg.

"Poor judge of character," he said, but with a smile.

Carol regarded him with unwanted compassion. "I'd say the exact opposite is true, Mr. Kennedy. The dog knows exactly who you really are, even if you have lost sight of that yourself."

Turner was annoyed that his plan for long, mind-clearing days of hard work and skating had turned into something else—thanks to Casey. It now seemed his tormented soul was so close to the surface anyone who looked could see it.

"Nice meeting you," he said, eager to turn his back on Carol's way too perceptive gaze. He took the stairs two at a time and followed the smell of coffee into the kitchen.

"Hey," Carol said. "Harper, aren't you going to spend some time with me?"

But the dog cast her owner one faintly guilty look before wiggling through the swinging door with Turner just before it closed.

He heard Carol laugh tolerantly. He hoped to sneak into the kitchen and get a cup of coffee, and maybe *try* to sleep for a couple hours before seeing what Cole had planned for them today.

Maybe it hadn't been fair to these people to come here, either.

He'd seen that on Casey's face last night after he'd thought an IED had gone off, and he'd smacked her down to the floor. He might never be able to fit in.

Casey.

He had not succeeded in washing the sweetness of her kiss from his lips. Thinking of her made him ache for the road not taken.

In a way, Casey had been the beginning of his journey away from all he knew, and toward a job that forced him to make choices that hurt people, intentional or not.

Emily was in the kitchen. "Coffee's ready," she sang. "Oh, look, you've got a friend. Good morning, Harper."

The dog wagged her tail, but when Emily slapped her knee to coax her over, Harper sat down stubbornly on Turner's foot.

"I slipped her a doughnut," Turner lied, not wanting anyone making assumptions about the nature of his character just because the dog liked him.

He regarded Emily for a moment, and allowed himself to feel happy for the pure reason that his best friend's wife was happy, that maybe the Watsons were going to make it through the minefields that were relationships and life.

"The coffee smells good." Turner said, shaking the dog off his foot so he could get some.

"You're up early." She looked at him, "I bet you're going skating?"

"I've already been."

"This early?"

"Or late, depending how you look at it."

"Have you been up all night?"

"I have jet lag." It was the convenient lie he told to cover the fact he was having so much trouble sleeping.

"Where are you coming from? Oh, I remember. Cole said something about Turkey."

Turkey was not the exact location, of course. It wasn't even close; just a stop on the way to the end of the world. But he did not correct her.

"I remember you skating," Emily said, "from when Cole and I were dating. You were amazing. Weren't some hockey scouts interested in you?"

A road not taken. A carefree life of playing games. Turner never thought of that, because, inevitably, it would lead him to wonder who he might have been had he chosen a different fork in the road.

"That was a long time ago," he said, a little too harshly.

He rolled his shoulders. All these people, Emily and Cole, Andrea, Casey, despite the problems they might have suffered, still were what he was not.

They were basically good. Wholesome. Uncomplicated. Not one of them had ever had to make a decision about whether another human being got to live or die. Not one of them had ever sat with their best friend's blood soaking into their clothing.

Maybe he should not have come to a place where people were going to begin their sentences with the words *I remember*.

"Good coffee," Turner said, to move the subject away from his recent travels and the past.

"Thanks," Emily said. "It was an early Christmas gift. Melissa's folks sent it from Kona for Andrea and Casey and me. They retired there."

"Have you been to Hawaii?"

She took the bait easily, and Turner was relieved to hear her chatter about the beauty of the islands rather than the places where their histories had touched when she had first met Cole.

Casey came through the swinging kitchen doors, screeched to a halt when she saw him, then flounced by him to the coffeepot. "Good morning, Emily. Good morning, Harper."

No "Good morning, Turner." Well, she was a bright girl, probably the brightest he had ever met, a whole lot brighter than a golden retriever.

"Is this the coffee Melissa's parents sent? It's wonderful. That was so thoughtful of them." Casey took a sip and eyed him over the rim of her mug, while still not acknowledging him. "What can I help with?"

Turner noticed Casey had little smudges under her eyes from being up all night, but other than that she was an unconventional beauty. Her lips looked bruised. How could that be? They had shared about the shortest kiss in history!

She had showered before coming downstairs, and her hair, which looked as if it would take a day to dry completely, was curling as wildly as he ever remembered it. How could a man not dream of burying his hands in those wayward curls?

Had she left it like that because he had said he liked it that way?

She was not wearing a speck of makeup, her olive skin

dewy from the shower, her eyes dark and deep. He looked at the puffy fullness of her lips again and knew it was going to be a long time before he shook off the taste of them, or the longing for it.

She had a beautiful figure, though she had lost some of the endearing chubbiness he remembered of her in her bridesmaid's dress. She still seemed to dress to understate, today in a buttoned-to-the-throat blouse that was too big for her, and a pair of jeans that looked as if she had tried to wrestle her curvy hips into a strait jacket.

"Well, I was thinking omelets," Emily said, a bit doubtfully. "Casey, if you want to start grating some cheese, that would be a big help. Do you remember Turner?"

Casey busied herself slamming through cabinets looking for a cheese grater, and she barely glanced at him.

"We bumped into each other," she said, her voice flat.

Literally, he thought, remembering her soft curves beneath his on the porch the other night, her clinging to him as he'd pulled her from the snow at the edge of the ice.

She managed to convey, without elaborating, that it had not been her favorite experience, which, of course, was repayment for the fact he had rejected her kiss.

For her own damn good.

But she had probably left her hair in that natural glorious state for his benefit, to torment him.

And damn, if it didn't seem to be working!

CHAPTER SEVEN

"I'LL JUST TAKE my coffee and leave you to it," Turner said.

He didn't miss the fact that Casey looked smug that she had managed to make him uncomfortable.

He was pretty sure she knew he was having trouble not watching her as she drew an elastic band from her slacks pocket and began to pull that wild hair back with elaborate care.

He wasn't sure why that was so sexy it was making his mouth go dry. Her hair didn't like being tamed, and little strands were already breaking out of the band, curling wildly.

"No you don't, Turner," Emily said with a laugh. "No chauvinism allowed. The little ladies are not going to fix you breakfast."

Casey snorted with satisfaction.

"I actually wasn't expecting breakfast," he said in his own defense.

"Well, I'm just learning to cook, believe it or not, so I need all the help I can get. I'm regretting telling Carol I'd look after it this morning."

"I hope you're not counting on me," Casey said, slightly panicky. "I'm not a great cook, either."

"What are you good at, Turner?" Emily asked.

Despite the fact he just wanted to escape, he could see they were both in a little over their heads.

Casey looked inordinately pleased that he had been identified as a chauvinist, though her pleasure seemed short-lived when she realized she was going to have to share the kitchen with him.

"I'm pretty good at breaking eggs," he said. Since he had to suck it up, anyway, Turner could show her a thing or two in the kitchen. He set down his coffee, found a carton of eggs in the fridge and a big bowl under one of the counters.

"Harper, would you stop?" he growled, as the dog stuck her nose in every cupboard he opened. He glanced around the kitchen. Where to set up? Casey obviously did not want him anywhere near her.

But she'd started it! That was where the available counter space was, anyway, so he went and set up there, trying to ignore her glare and the shower-fresh scent of her ticking his nose.

"How many eggs do you want?" he called over his shoulder to Emily.

"Let's see, there will be six of us, plus Carol, and I'll invite Martin in, too. Plus Tessa, so we should do three-egg omelets for the guys, two-egg ones for the women, and a one-egg omelet for Tessa."

Harper whined.

"And a little left over for the dog," Emily said with a smile. It looked as if she was going to have to go for a piece of paper and a pen to figure it out, so Casey took pity on her.

"Twenty-two eggs," she said, "which means one for the dog. Not that I think Carol would approve."

"Maybe not of me inviting Martin, either, though he's good for her. She'd resent me saying so, but Carol seems much happier when he's around," Emily noted with satisfaction. "Love is in the air here at the inn."

Casey hunkered down and stared hard at the cheese

grater. Turner tried not to flinch. Had anyone been looking out the window at them skating?

He shot Emily a glance. No, there was no guile in that
girl, and even if there was, he didn't have to worry about
Casey. It was obvious, after he'd rejected her kiss, she had
her defenses up against him. Good!

And it was also obvious she had defenses now. She'd
had none back then on the night of Emily and Cole's wedding, and in the days that had followed. And he was not
going to wonder what had changed her. He wasn't!

No, he was going to do what he did best: do the job
he'd been assigned, quickly and efficiently, and then leave
the kitchen. He wasn't going to think about the fact that
women didn't generally have their defenses up against him.

He glanced at Casey.

And remembered last night when he had said to her,
"Are you happy?"

She hadn't really answered, but she had not been able
to hide the stricken look on her face, either.

For a while, out there skating, she had looked happy.
And before the fiasco of the kiss, he had been deeply grati-
fied by that.

So, what if he made that part of his assignment this
morning? To take the high road? To remember the girl she
had been, a long time ago, a too-big, pure white terry-cloth
robe wrapped around her, jumping on a king-size bed? To
remember the look on her face when he had knelt before
her and painted her toenails candy-apple red?

He was good at missions. Surely he could leave his own
ghosts behind him long enough to show her that even the
most mundane thing could be fun?

His parents had showed him that. The kitchen had been
a playground for them. His dad chasing his mom with a
towel, tossing eggs around like a professional circus juggler, the dog underfoot...

For the first time, Turner was aware of remembering his parents with a sense of the gift they had given him, rather than all he had lost.

He needed to forget the kiss—she obviously now realized that had been a mistake—and coax a little laughter from Casey, to show her there were no hard feelings, and no benefit in taking life too seriously, either.

Maybe he could learn the lesson at the same time, accept his parents gift! Life had been a way too serious matter for him for way too long.

"Casey," he said in an undertone, "you don't need to be mad at me."

Not even a glance.

"Mad at you? Why would I be mad at you?" Her own low response was said way too sweetly.

"Look, we both know why."

She said nothing.

"Because I hurt your feelings."

"Oh, you mean you hurt my feelings because you *rejected* me?"

"I didn't reject you. I acted sensibly," he hissed. "We're only here for a few days. Neither of us needs that kind of complication."

"I don't need you to decide what I need. You *are* a chauvinist."

"Okay, I am. I admit it. Can you lighten up now? Can we leave it behind us?"

"I already have," she said. Obviously a lie, since she continued to ignore him. He picked an egg out of the container, tossed it high up behind his back and caught it effortlessly over his shoulder.

Casey glanced his way, pursed those delectable lips disapprovingly and then squinted hard at the cheese she was grating feverishly.

Still, she could not resist casting him a glance when he

did it again. He smiled when she looked, but her disapproving frown only deepened.

His proficiency with eggs was a morning-after trick that usually impressed, but Casey rolled her eyes as if he was an eight-year-old boy who had presented her with the unwanted gift of a frog. She turned her shoulder slightly, blocking her view of his escapades.

Of course, except for that kiss, it wasn't the morning after.

Turner was stunned by the heat that thought of morning afters created in him: waking up beside her, to that wild tangle of curls cascading across a pillow, her olive skin dark against white sheets, her eyes darker than dark with hunger and wanting....

Stop, he ordered himself. If it was about making her smile, there was no room in there for thoughts of morning afters. Or kisses.

He was a highly disciplined man. He needed to prove that.

"Hey, Casey, catch!"

She turned just in time to catch the egg he tossed at her.

"Nice and light," he said approvingly of her catch. "It's like life. You try to hold it too hard, it breaks and you end up with the very thing you were trying to hold on to running through your fingers."

"Oh," she said, and tossed the egg back to him. "The philosopher king. Who would have known?"

He caught the egg easily, spotted a glimmer of a smile as she turned back to her cheese.

Having seen that faint smile, he felt encouraged to clown around a little, amazed that he still had a part of him that could do so. By coaxing that part of her that he had glimpsed long ago back to the surface, he found a lighter part of himself.

He juggled two eggs, and then three. Casey actually stopped to watch him. So did Emily.

Naturally, being a guy, their attention drove him to new heights, literally. He tossed the eggs higher and higher. And then missed.

One splatted on the floor; he tried to catch the next one and it broke in his hand; the third whizzed by him to explode spectacularly against a cupboard door. He never missed. It had to be these sleepless nights catching up with him.

"We love the juggler best when he fumbles," Emily said.

Turner was not sure he wanted the word *love* bandied about when he was anywhere in the vicinity of Casey, with his judgment badly clouded by sleep deprivation.

"It's like life," Casey said. "You toss it around too lightly and you end up with it running, rather messily, through your fingers."

Harper was thrilled with the fumble, and began to lap eagerly at the mess at Turner's feet.

"She prefers her omelet uncooked," he deadpanned, reaching for a cloth to clean his hands.

And then Casey laughed. It was everything he had hoped for when he had set out to entertain her: the ever-present worry line gone from her forehead, the slight downturn gone from her mouth, the stern disapproval gone from her eyes.

She was lovely, and Turner felt a desire, probably a foolish one, to hear that laugh again. He hoped one more time would be enough.

And another desire, even more foolish, was to finish what they had started this morning, to show her what she had been playing with when she had kissed him that way. It wasn't some dream out of a sweet-sixteen journal.

It was a prelude.

Which was exactly why there would be no kissing,

Turner warned himself. That was well outside the parameters of his mission, which was to get Casey to lighten up.

Since he had managed to break the ice, Turner followed his juggling act, after he cleaned up the mess, by breaking the eggs one-handed, dropping the white and yolk from increasing heights into the bowl.

He shook himself, annoyed with the direction his thoughts had taken. Even though she was not the young, inexperienced girl she had been when he'd first met her, she was still not the kind of woman a guy should have those thoughts about.

Casey was intense, not a girl you could kiss lightly or playfully, unless you wanted to go to hell.

But then again, he reminded himself, he had already been there.

Just to be ornery, because after he'd coaxed that laugh out of her she seemed more eager to resist his charms than ever, he *made* her engage with him, still amazed that there was anything in him that could be this light.

Or maybe it wasn't in him. Maybe it was her. Maybe there was something about Casey that had always inspired what was best about him to rise to the surface.

"I was the boy you didn't like getting as a science project partner, wasn't I?"

"I didn't like getting any boy as my science project partner. I'm sure you would have been as good as any of the other ones. Eager to be my partner because you were guaranteed an A and wouldn't have to do any of the work."

"You were cynical very young," he said sadly.

"And frankly, nothing has happened since to change my mind."

Oh, boy, she was just not going to let him off the hook for what she saw as his defection all those years ago.

All that had happened a long, long time ago. And it hadn't been his fault. He would show her his charming side, and was willing to bet she would forgive him by the time the omelets were up.

"So, Casey," he said casually, getting back to the conversation he'd had with her last night. "What makes you happy? Tell me what you do for fun."

What surprised him was that he really wanted to know.

She glared at him as if he had asked for a peek of her underwear. "I take yoga," she offered reluctantly.

"I've always wanted to try that."

She pursed her lips in disapproval at the lie. "No, you haven't."

He debated telling her about the hazards of frown marks, and decided against it. For now.

"I heard it was great for strength and flexibility." Not to mention the counselor it was mandatory he see right now, because of that gong show on the other side of the world, had told him he should give it a shot. To find *peace*.

Peace was a word that was bandied around a lot. It was supposedly the reason men went to war. Was he the only person who saw how ridiculous that was? Not that it had seemed ridiculous when he was a young man intent on changing the world in honor of his father.

Still, that promise had made him check a yoga class schedule, but he had never quite made it through the doors. The advertisements for the class had showed young women in tights turning their bodies into pretzels.

"Are there any men in your yoga class?" he asked.

"While some of the best yoga masters are men, in my experience," she said primly, "most men aren't good at yoga. They fall asleep during *savasana*. And snore. And they—" She stopped, began to grate cheese with a vengeance.

"They what?"

"You shouldn't eat before doing yoga," she said, not

looking up, "or at least not a ten-ounce steak and a pound of fries. Men never seem to get that."

She shredded cheese; he glanced at her. She was blushing! What would be making her blush about men eating full meals before yoga? Suddenly, he got it, and hooted with laughter.

"Are you telling me you have some flatulent Freddy in your yoga class?"

"It's not funny," she warned him.

"Not even a little bit?"

"Ten-year-old boys find flatulence funny," she said cuttingly, "not full-grown men."

"That shows how many full-grown men you know," he retorted, grinning, hoping to tug a smile out of her.

But she gave him a scathing look, obviously intent on not letting him get her guard down again, and returned to her work.

He should warn her just to give up now. He was on a mission, after all.

"What does *shavasana* mean?"

"Death or corpse pose," she said.

"That's what you do for *fun?*" He was glad he had never made it through the doors of a yoga class. He was searching for peace, yes; death he had seen quite enough of. Especially in Beza-zabur, the worst mission of his career. They had known, going in, the odds were against them. The mission had succeeded, but at an enormous price. He could feel the sadness of loss of good men tugging at him, and tried to shake it off.

"It's a relaxation pose, at the end of class." Casey was watching him closely, as if she knew something had shifted in him.

He pasted on his grin, not liking the sensation of being stripped, as if she could see his soul.

"Well, yoga just doesn't sound fun. Flatulent Freddy

falls asleep during it. I've never known a single person to fall asleep while having fun. I always wondered if downward dog had any potential."

Harper's tail thumped happily at the word *dog*.

"For what?" Casey asked suspiciously.

"Fun. It's got that sound about it." He wiggled his eyebrows at her.

"It's downward-facing dog," she said, but she was still watching him closely, as if she detected he was trying to use humor to slip away from something too intense. "And it's a strength and balance pose."

"Not fun?" he said sadly.

"I think you can eliminate yoga as a source of fun," she said.

"So, what else, then?"

"Pardon?"

She had the snootiest look on her face. Snooty people said "pardon?" instead of "huh?" or "what?"

That expression was endearing for a reason he could not decipher.

"For fun?" he reminded her. "Now that Freddy has destroyed the serenity of yoga class, and you've said yourself it has little potential, what else do you do for fun?"

She was silent.

"Didn't you say you were taking calligraphy?" Emily said helpfully.

"Calligraphy?"

"Not for fun," Casey said defensively. "It helps me relax."

"Look, maybe it's not for me to say—"

"It's not!" she exclaimed, almost panic-stricken at having her ultraboring life exposed.

"But I think you are getting quite enough relaxation in the *shavasana* department."

The cheese grater was put down. She folded her arms

across her chest. "And what would you suggest for fun, Mr. Kennedy? Since you are apparently some kind of expert on the subject."

He ordered his eyes not to veer to her mouth. They did anyway.

She licked her lips uneasily, then, realizing what she had done, pulled her cute little tongue back in her mouth and pressed her lips into a straight line.

She regarded him solemnly, and then said, in a low voice Emily couldn't hear, "Why do I get the impression, for all your talk, it's been a long time since you found life fun, Turner Kennedy?"

"You seemed to enjoy skating with me this morning," he said. "We should try that again. As long as we both understand the limits."

She actually blushed at the reference to her uninvited advance, but looked as haughty as ever at the very same time.

"I understand Andrea has a very ambitious plan for the next few days, so why don't we just leave it for now?"

He stared at her.

Casey Caravetta had just said no to him!

CHAPTER EIGHT

CASEY CARAVETTA HAD said no to him, and Turner told himself just to be grateful. Damned grateful. She'd picked up that particular lesson very quickly.

He'd always known she was about the smartest girl in the world. No doubt she had seen straight through the act—the egg juggling and the one-handed breakage—to the damage beneath.

The damage that would make a man refuse a pretty girl's kiss. For her own damn good.

"Forget I asked," he said gruffly.

And he didn't like the way she was gazing at him, too closely.

"Did I hurt your feelings now?" she asked softly.

Okay, his head was starting to hurt. There were just way too many *feelings* being bandied about.

He shot her a look. "No, you didn't."

She appeared skeptical and sympathetic.

"You can't hurt my feelings."

"Oh, right," she said in a wounded tone. "The girl you can reject has no power over you. How silly of me."

"I thought we left that behind us? You can't hurt my feelings because I don't have any feelings to hurt."

She looked at him, and the sympathy in her eyes deepened. "You can't possibly believe that."

"Believe it? I know it."

She looked sympathetic and then exasperated. But it was like reading an open book. He could tell the moment she realized it wasn't safe to sympathize with him.

"I'm sorry," she said primly, just as if he had said she *had* hurt his feelings. "My not wanting to skate anymore is not about you. It's about me."

He knew a dig when he heard it.

"We don't want things to get complicated, after all," she said sweetly.

"Let's get something straight. Skating and kissing are not the same thing."

"Thanks, Sherlock, now I won't have to look them up in my dictionary."

"I just thought maybe you'd like to have some fun."

"And I need you to do that?"

"Are you always this aggravating?"

For a second, from the spark in her eye, he thought she might just demonstrate true aggravation by throwing the cheese grater at his head. Sadly, she regained control and stepped back from the counter.

"There's enough cheese here for ten omelets, Emily. If you'll excuse me, I have wild adventures awaiting me in the fun department."

"Ha. Rereading *War and Peace?*" Turner muttered.

Casey cast him one more disparaging look. "At least I know how to read."

Emily was watching his reaction as Casey marched by him, nose in the air, and out the swinging kitchen door.

"I don't think she handles being teased very well, Turner."

He turned and gave her his toothiest grin. "I was just trying to be friendly. Who would have thought discussing yoga class could be dangerous?"

"My, my. It's been a long time since anyone said no to you, hasn't it, Turner Kennedy?"

He kept the grin. "The week is young."

"Don't play with her, Turner." Emily bit her lip. "Casey's having a bit of a tough time right now."

He wasn't quite sure why, but he didn't like thinking of Casey having a tough time.

"Why?"

Em hesitated, decided to trust him. "We all lost our friend Melissa this year. Casey also had a breakup. And her dad died."

"Poor kid," he said, surprised by how genuine his sympathy was.

"I don't think she'd appreciate you seeing her as a kid."

"Gotcha."

"Something else is going on. Some reason she doesn't want to spend Christmas with her mom. It seems odd. Her mom's first Christmas alone." Emily shook her head. "It just seems as if it's the wrong time for Casey to be making such a major life decision."

Something prickled along the back of Turner's neck. "What major life decision?" he asked softly.

Emily laughed uneasily. "I shouldn't have said that. I don't think she'd appreciate me mulling over her personal life with a guy she barely knows."

He thought back to the night of Emily and Cole's wedding. Somehow it did feel as if he knew Casey Caravetta, though he knew that assessment was not completely rational.

"So," Emily said, with a soft smile, "don't play with her, but don't give up on her, either."

And as soon as Em said that, he realized he had already decided he wasn't going to.

Give up on Casey. A long time ago he should have sent her a note and hadn't. Was it ever too late to do the right thing?

The play-with-her part was a whole different story.

He took his bowl of eggs, placed them in front of Emily and walked out of the kitchen in search of the uncomplicated companionship of Cole.

Turner's uncomplicated companion, Harper, followed him loyally.

But when Casey didn't appear for breakfast, Turner felt honor bound to track her down.

"Come on, open the door."

"No," she called through the door. "I'm just getting to the really fun part of *War and Peace*."

"There are no fun parts in war. I know from experience." He wished, instantly, that he hadn't said that. "You missed breakfast. I brought you an omelet."

She opened the door and looked at him cautiously. He suspected the door had been opened because he'd let it slip he had firsthand experience with war. He wanted to make her life lighter, not evoke her sympathy.

"I don't want the omelet."

"It's only fair, after all the cheese you grated. Come on. The dog is tormenting me, thinking it's for her."

Harper whined helpfully, as if on cue.

"You've had enough eggs for one day," Turner told her.

Casey folded her arms over her chest, glaring at him. "What part of no don't you get?"

He wafted the steaming omelet under her nose.

"You're not used to women saying no to you, are you?"

"You and Emily are onto me."

"Harper," she said, addressing the dog firmly, "stop fawning over him. You're a disgrace."

"I promise I won't see it as fawning over me if you take the omelet."

"And then you'll go away?"

He nodded insincerely and handed her the plate. She took it, then set it on a dresser beside the door and crossed her arms over her chest again.

He saw it as hopeful that she hadn't slammed the door. "I'm waiting for the going-away part," she said.

She planned to resist his attempts to lighten up a life that seemed to have got bogged down in seriousness. He planned not to let her. For the first time in a long time, he felt almost lighthearted.

He leaned his shoulder against her doorjamb. "I like your hair like that."

"Humph. I just haven't had time to do anything with it yet today."

"Can I touch it?"

"No." She began to ease the door shut. He slid his foot in. She glared.

"You missed all the discussion at breakfast. Andrea is handing out assignments like crazy. The vow renewal is going to be on the steps of the front porch, with the guests seated in a semicircle on chairs below it. She and Carol are making garlands out of real boughs. And wreaths. Cole and Martin are replacing the old Christmas light strings with new ones, LEDs to save the inn money. And you and I—"

"You and I?" she asked, nonplussed.

He nodded.

"How did I end up with you?" she asked suspiciously.

"It was your lucky day?" The truth was most women would have been delighted to have been paired with him. "Look, Casey, we're the only two single people here. I think it's natural we're going to end up together from time to time. Can we declare a truce?"

"What job did we get?"

"Andrea has this idea that it would be fun to have an honor guard of snowmen at the front gate."

"What? A snowman honor guard?"

The wariness faded from her face. She looked, however reluctantly, enchanted by the concept.

"FYI, it doesn't get any hokier," he told her. He had been

tempted to tell Andrea that he wasn't sure about messing
with such tradition as the military arch ceremony, but then
he had reminded himself that if he wanted to help Casey
lighten up, he was going to have to do a little lightening
up himself.

"It's cute!"

"Adorable," he said drily.

"And also very economical. It's very smart of Andrea
to use something free, like snow. Her budget for turning
this place into a winter wonderland is limited."

Somehow he didn't think he would win any points for
saying he thought the budget *should* be limited, for a one-
day event that had no real, pragmatic purpose.

"Can you meet me in the front yard in half an hour?"

"That doesn't give me time to do my hair!"

Good, he thought. Out loud, he said, "There is no sense
doing your hair for snowman duty. It's probably going to
end up wet. Stuff it under a hat."

Obviously, she was torn between outright refusing to
help him, and giving in. And he suspected, when she gave
in, it had nothing to do with his considerable egg-juggling
charm. The snowmen were luring her.

"I'll see you down there, then." And she shut the door
quietly in his face.

Turner stood there for a moment longer. It occurred to
him he had actually been holding his breath, waiting for
her answer.

It occurred to him she had said yes to building snowmen, not to the truce.

CHAPTER NINE

CASEY LEANED AGAINST the door. Hard as it was to admit it, Turner was right. They had to declare a truce. She could not let him get under her skin. If he got under her skin, she could not let him know it!

And, of course, he already had got to her this morning, tossing eggs at her, throwing them around. She had actually laughed when he had broken them, that astonished look on his face saying he couldn't believe he had fumbled.

Sadly, she could not remember the last time she had enjoyed such a good chuckle!

She had come here to find something: a part of herself that could be at peace with her life if she remained single forever.

The truth? Yoga and calligraphy weren't doing it, but she was sure that motherhood would.

Something had drawn her to the inn, as if there was an answer here. In simplicity. In friendships. In the spirit of Christmas itself. These were things she wanted for her child!

And she wasn't going to find that answer locked in her room, hiding from Turner Kennedy and his considerable charms. He was the test, dammit, and she intended to pass it!

She had to give herself over to what the day held, and today that was making snowmen.

And she had to admit, reluctantly, that it did sound fun. It was something she would want to do with her child one day.

And just as reluctantly, she had to admit that somehow Turner had hit the nail right on the head when he had insinuated that fun might be the missing element from her life. What kind of mom would she be if she couldn't just have fun?

Putting her pride aside—she would need her strength, after all—Casey gobbled down the omelet he had brought and then turned her attention to the all-important matter of what to wear for snowman building.

Half an hour later, feeling like a large pink marshmallow in the snowsuit that had seemed so "fun" when she had bought it for this trip, and which now seemed faintly ridiculous, Casey headed out the front door of the inn. She had stuffed every strand of her wildly uncooperative hair under a knit hat that looked like an exaggerated version of what a hippie out of the sixties would have worn.

The sun had come out and made the snow sparkle with a million diamond lights. It was a fairyland of delight.

Turner was already outside, pacing out large steps. He had out a tape measure and ran it from the arbor at the front gate to the stairs. Harper marched up and down beside him, dogging his every step.

"Would you go away?" he said to the dog.

Harper pondered this, decided she had been ordered to sit, and sat down on his foot.

He glared at the dog, but indulgently, and let the tape roll up as Casey came toward him.

"I was thinking eight," he said, "four on each side. But I don't think we have room for them. Not if the chairs start, say, right here."

"Eight snowmen?"

"Too ambitious?"

"Way."

"Well, that's a relief. How about four, two on each side?"

"I hope you know how to build a snowman."

"If I can juggle eggs, I can build a snowman."

"Hmm, I'm not following the relationship between the two, but I'm going to trust you have actually built one before."

"Who hasn't?" he said, frowning down at his tape measure. Her silence made him look up and transfer his frown to her.

"You've never built a snowman?" He seemed astounded by that.

"I grew up in an apartment in New York, so snowmen were not part of my experience."

"You didn't go to the park?"

She shrugged, but could feel him looking at her intently.

"You didn't have a childhood at all, did you?" he said suddenly, his voice husky and deep. "Your brother's illness stole all that from you, didn't it?"

Why did he remember that? Was it just part of his considerable charm? How did she play this game? Give herself over to having fun at the same time as protecting herself from Turner Kennedy?

Casey felt terribly vulnerable all at once, standing there in the pink snowsuit she had never owned as a child. As if she was going to either burst into tears or run.

How could she hope to be a good mother when nothing about her own childhood had given her the kind of experiences she would need?

"I'll show you," he said, way too gently. "I'll show you how to build a snowman, Casey."

She swallowed hard, and said with stiff pride that hid the gratitude blooming in her heart, "I'm sure it's not rocket science."

"Or science of any kind, which puts you at a disadvantage." He smirked, the sympathy gone, or mercifully hidden. "Now watch. Step one." He scooped up a generous mittful of snow. "This stuff is absolutely perfect for it. Not too dry. Not too wet. Slightly sticky, like the rice you make sushi rolls with."

"I suppose you do that, too?" she asked skeptically, watching him form the snow into a smooth, perfect ball.

"What?"

"Make sushi rolls."

"It's easier than you think. And it impresses, er, people."

But she got it. It impressed women people. And no doubt juggling eggs did, also. The touch of aggravation that made her feel—Turner Kennedy, dark, dangerous and suave, the man no woman could resist—was far superior to the way she had felt when he had guessed her brother's death had stolen her childhood.

"You do it, too," he said, holding out his snowball for her inspection.

She scooped up a mitten of snow, clamped her hands around it and watched it squish out either side.

"Make a round ball. Like this." He set his snowball down, scooped up more snow, placed it in her mittens and guided her hands around it. "Pat, don't squeeze."

She wanted to keep her guard up against the man who knew how to make sushi to impress, but it was very hard with his hands wrapped around hers. She kept losing herself in his intensity about the correct procedure for building snowballs.

Was he that serious? Or was he just pretending? It would do very well to remember it was hard to tell when Turner Kennedy was pretending and when he wasn't!

"Hey, Casey, this step is more important than you think. A mistake here could result in a square snowman."

"Maybe we could start a trend," she suggested innocently.

"You can mess with your hair if you have to, but don't mess with snowmen."

She obediently patted the snow together, under his watchful eye. She peeked up at him. He wasn't watching her hands, but her face, a little smile of pleasure on his lips.

She held up the result and he inspected it carefully, standing way too close to her. She found his scent intoxicating, part of the clean crispness of a fresh wintry morning.

"You're a natural," he decided, as he pulled a glove off one hand with his teeth. "Hey, some of your hair is escaping. Wouldn't want that! Like a nun letting some come free of her wimple."

"I told you I was sensitive on the topic of nuns right now," she said, and knew it was a weakness when, despite the mutinous expression on her face, she allowed him to push the little tendrils of hair back under her cap with his ungloved fingers. "What's a wimple?"

"That white thing that surrounds their face. And that is just about the full extent of my knowledge about nuns."

"Thank heaven for small mercies."

"Are you going to tell me why you're sensitive to the subject of nuns right now?"

"No."

"Seriously, I'm intrigued."

"Isn't that just the story of my life," she muttered.

"What?"

"Whenever somebody's intrigued by me, it's always for the wrong reasons."

"Oh. What would you like me to be intrigued about?"

Whether she put bubbles in her bath. What kind of flowers she would prefer sent on her birthday.

"I already know what your underwear looks like, after all. Caught a peek of it when your suitcase fell open."

"Oh, never mind," she said a touch grouchily.

He eyed her. For a man who knew how to make sushi to impress, he seemed a little stupid in the what-to-be-intrigued-about department.

"I'm intrigued about why you aren't married," he said, cocking his head and considering her. "Geez. I hope that's not the connection. You aren't considering becoming a nun, are you?"

"Maybe I am," she said.

"The underwear says no."

"It's old. The new me is more practical." He had sucked her into discussing something very personal with him. She thought he would snort with satisfaction, but he didn't. In fact, he eyed her narrowly.

"Some bastard hurt you."

Her mouth gaped open and then snapped shut.

"When?" he said.

"I haven't even confirmed that!"

"You don't have to. I can tell." He gave himself a little smack on the forehead. "The clues were all there. Yoga and calligraphy. The new revelation about practical undies. Sheesh. You're practically a nun already."

She opened her mouth to protest, to tell him she was going to have a child, not become a nun, but she shut it again, thankful she had regained control, since she did not want that truth about herself open to his dissection.

"When?"

"It's nearly a year ago. I'm so over it."

"Humph," he said, with insulting disbelief.

"I am!" Again there was a temptation to share with him just how she was getting on with her life, but once more she battled it down.

"What did he do?"

"Could we just build the snowman?"

"Okay," he said, tugging his glove back on with his

teeth—was he doing that on purpose making her focus on his all too sexy mouth? "But this is not over."

"What if I say it is?"

He shrugged.

"You're infuriating."

He smiled. "Yes, I am. Okay, set that extraordinary sample of the beginnings of a snowman on the ground and roll it, before you crush it between your fingers pretending it is my head."

She pretended it was his head and set it on the ground, gave it a very vigorous shove.

He sighed. "I'll show you with mine, first."

The dog tried to help him with her nose.

"A little bit this way and then a little bit that way," he instructed. "Harper! So it stays nice and round. Only we'll start on this side of the yard and roll toward the archway so we don't have to move them too far when they're the right size."

Casey watched him for a moment or two. There was something about watching a male apply all that muscle and strength to this task that was at least as lovely as watching him clear snow from the lake and chop wood. Harper's dedication to him was endearing, too. Weren't dogs supposed to be good judges of character?

Then Turner caught her looking, and winked!

Blushing, annoyed with herself, she dropped her own ball of snow and began to push it, first one way, then another. In no time she was totally engrossed in her task, tongue caught between teeth, grunting with exertion, hat askew and hair falling out of it.

The snowball, she saw with pleasure, had picked up every ounce of snow in its wildly weaving path, leaving a trail of naked brown grass in its wake. It was becoming astonishingly large in a very short amount of time. She had to get down on her knees to push it.

"Hey, is that downward-facing dog?" he teased.

"Downward-facing, sweating dog," she said, then gave a mighty push and ended up on her face. He roared with laughter as she sat up, brushing snow off her cheeks and clothes.

"Here, you'll need some 'mus-cull' for this part," he said, making a fist and curling his arm to show her who had the "mus-culls." Even under his jacket, his muscle popped up cooperatively. Casey told herself she was having trouble breathing only because of the heavy exertion of the exercise.

To let him know she was not impressed, and that her heavy breathing had nothing to do with him or his childish display of strength, she rolled her eyes. "A man who quotes Popeye."

"I like a girl who knows her Popeye," he said.

But when he dropped down on his knees beside her, she knew exactly why her heart was beating way too hard. And worse, she surrendered something, as if his closeness was a drug and she was hopelessly addicted.

She surrendered her need to be in control.

She let go of her tight hold on her desire to protect herself.

She did something she had not done in far too long. She gave herself permission to have fun. And she had a feeling it wasn't just for the sake of her future children!

She took the hat off her too-hot head and tossed it aside. Aware of his eyes on her, she shook out the curls.

"Whoa," he muttered, "when you have hair like that you can be practical in every other respect!"

He thought she was sexy. And she had no idea what to do with that!

Thankfully, he tore his eyes away from her freed locks, and put his shoulder to the huge snow boulder. She settled beside him, and together, shoulder to shoulder, with the dog bouncing along, barking and trying to figure out how to insert herself between them, they pushed it into place beside the arch in the fence.

"Okay," he said, "we're on a roll—no pun intended—so now is not the time to rest on our laurels." He deliberately glanced at the "laurels" she was resting on, grinned wolfishly and then raced back and began to maneuver the next ball across the yard. She joined him, huffing, puffing, giggling, slipping.

She noticed with relief that her self-consciousness dissipated as she gave herself over to the pure fun of being on the same team as him.

His shoulder was right against hers. They were pushing together. Their shouts and laughter filled the air.

His feet slipped, the ball trundled away from him and he flipped over on his back, panting. She lay down beside him and for a moment they both watched wispy clouds float through a bright blue winter sky.

Peripherally, she was aware of Carol and Andrea on the porch, making garlands out of a huge heap of evergreen boughs, and fastening them to the railings. Cole and Martin were on the roof, taking down old strings of light.

All that was in the background, but still, she had a sense of being part of something. A little community of people who wanted to make things wonderful for Cole and Emily.

"It feels so good," Turner said quietly. "I feel as if I lived to have a moment like this."

"Me, too," she whispered, and realized they were two people who had come through the battlefields of life to arrive at this moment of utter delight. Of peace. She realized she had laughed out loud.

She had given herself totally to the present moment, something yoga urged her to do, and she had never quite succeeded at until now.

And she knew you had to take those moments when

they were offered. It occurred to her that maybe she and Turner had declared a truce, after all.

Just when she thought the moment could not be any more perfect, he reached over, took her hand and squeezed it firmly, letting her know he felt it, too.

They were on the same wavelength.

Just like they had been all those years ago.

He turned his head to her, gazed at her through the sooty abundance of his lashes. She wondered, her heart beating in her throat, if he was going to kiss her.

He leaned close. Against her better judgment, she did, too. She could feel her eyelids drop. Her mouth puckered.

"So," he said huskily, so close to her his breath stirred her hair, "tell me what he did."

CHAPTER TEN

CASEY REELED BACK from Turner. She set her mouth in a straight line and opened her eyes wide, in a glare. So much for the truce!

Just like all those years ago, he was winning her trust, stealing her secrets from her. To what end?

And that thought spoiled the present moment completely for her. She let go of his hand, found her feet and went back to her next snowball.

"Look," Turner said silkily, "it's probably not even that original. What he did."

"Would you please stop?"

He pursed his lips together grudgingly.

Still, they had to cooperate somewhat, even if it was in silence, to wrestle two large balls to one side of the walkway and two on the other. Since he didn't mention it again, she decided to forgive him in the name of teamwork. Plus, there was something lighter in him. There had been since he had tossed those eggs that morning. It was as if he was making a deliberate effort to push away some shadow.

And she had a feeling the effort was for her. How could you turn down a gift like that, even if Turner was just about the most aggravating man on the planet?

They began to roll the middle balls, slightly smaller, that would form the tummies of their snowmen. They lifted those into place, and she stood panting, regarding their handiwork, as he cemented those second boulders into place by jamming snow where they joined.

"We're good," she decided. She slid him a look. *We.*

"That's right," he said, "a team."

A team. As in her and him. Was it dangerous to be thinking of them as some kind of team? Definitely.

"We're not a team," she said. "We're just two people thrown together in an attempt to make two other people happy."

"There are worse reasons to be thrown together," he said, "Take you and old what's his name—"

He laughed at the grimace she made, then bent, caught up a handful of snow and tossed it in her face. "Lighten up, Doc."

She noticed they were alone in the yard now. Everyone else had gone in. Maybe it was the fact that there was no audience that made her feel so uninhibited.

She spluttered and wiped it away. Glared at his grinning face, Casey bent, scooped up her own handful of snow and stalked toward him with menace.

"Chicken," she called as he made a run for it, then turned and looked at her, ducking this way and that, making it very hard to aim.

"What? You think I'm going to stand there and let you throw snow in my face?"

"You can run, but you cannot hide," she said, and gave chase. She let fly with her snow, shrieked with disappointment when it fell well short of him. He snickered happily. In the time it took her to form a new weapon, he hit her twice with fat wet snowballs.

"This is war!" she declared.

"Bring it," he challenged her, and bring it she did.

Screeching with wild abandon, she chased him around the yard, trying to hit him with snowballs. Only one of hers landed for every six of his.

Finally, panting, she leaned her hands on her knees. She wasn't quite sure how, but somehow while chasing him around the yard, pure frustration had become something else completely.

Joyous. As if she was playing, in a way she never had as a child.

Deliberately, hiding snow behind her back, she fell over and cried out. "Turner!"

"What?" He raced to her side, all playfulness gone.

"I think I twisted my ankle."

"Let me look."

Without hesitation, he sank down in the snow beside her, yanked up the leg of her snow pants. He was scowling with intense concentration, trying to get through the layers of snowsuit and socks and boots to her ankle.

Giggling with evil delight, she yanked her foot away and shoved snow down his back. He shook it out, but when she went to find her feet and scamper away from him, he snagged her ankle and she fell back in the snow.

He flipped her over and straddled her, pinning her arms.

"That was wicked," he said, with a certain amount of approval. "But you know what happens to the girl who cries wolf, don't you?"

Casey squirmed underneath him and then gazed up into his face. He looked, right now, like the boy she had once known, his eyes alight with laughter, and she felt her heart go still.

Suddenly, it didn't seem funny at all as he stared down at her.

"What?" she whispered.

She didn't feel playful. Or peaceful, for that matter.

But she did feel more alive than she had in a long, long time. Could feel the beat of her own heart. Feel air that was scented of him touching her skin, then being drawn inside her, pulled deep within her lungs. Feel the easy strength of his legs, pinning her to the ground.

"I forget," he said, then put his hands on both sides of her face. Her sense of being trapped by him was deliciously complete. And then he dropped his mouth over hers.

Casey met his lips, tasted them and him. What she tasted on his lips was pure, as sparkling as the diamond-crusted snow all around them.

And what she tasted of him was also pure, his essence: strength and playfulness, depth and courage.

He sighed with satisfaction when his gloved hands found her hair, tangled in it, used it to draw himself down even more.

Something unleashed within her as he pulled her in, their snow-damp clothes sticking together. They were generating a world of heat. She wouldn't be surprised to pull away from him and find the snow melted and spring arriving in a ten-foot radius around them!

Then his lips parted hers with tender command, and his tongue explored the soft inner swell there, the hard edge of her upper teeth. And then it darted into the hollow of her mouth.

The potential for meltdown increased. So did the feeling of being intensely alive.

Casey felt as if the blood was turning hot in her veins, and his energy was melding with her own. She could feel herself surrendering despite her every vow not to surrender to this.

It took an iron will to remind herself she had lured him to her because she was losing the snowball fight.

It appeared that if she didn't smarten up now, she was going to lose this other battle, too.

From under the fog of feeling, she allowed a memory of past hurt to surface and strengthen her spine.

She retook control, though she was aware she did it with a sense of loss rather than triumph.

He had loosened his grip on her hands, and she grabbed snow from either side of her and shoved it down his neck.

Turner gave a shout of surprised outrage and leaped off her. He performed a little break dance she might have found hilarious if she wasn't still reeling from the power of what had just transpired between them.

He shook the snow out of his shirt and shot her a dark look that made her shiver.

"You don't play fair," he told her.

"All's fair in love and war," she retorted, and instantly regretted using both words around him.

"Yes, it is," he said with satisfaction.

She frowned at him.

"Because let me tell you something, Casey Caravetta." She waited.

"I found out exactly what I needed to know."

She cocked her head, raised an eyebrow in what she hoped could be interpreted as amusement.

"You," he said softly, "aren't ever going to be a nun."

She dropped any pretense of amusement and glared at him.

"And something else?"

She folded her arms over her chest with what she hoped to pass off as complete indifference.

"It had nothing to do with you. Him cheating on you."

Her mouth fell open. "How could you possibly know that? From a kiss?"

He grinned. "I didn't. The nun part was from the kiss. The other part was just a guess. But I did tell you it probably wasn't even original."

"Consider this truce over!" she said. The source of her intense pain was not even *original?*

"It's not like you did anything to deserve it."

"The truce?"

"The cad."

It was the absolution she had never been willing to give herself, and she felt driven to let Turner know it was her fault. Who had picked him, after all?

"It hurt my pride, okay? I should have been smarter than that! I was engaged to him and never caught on to his deceit. A coworker had a little chat with me."

It was spilling out of her like water against a weakened dam. She realized Turner had sucked her into talking about it.

"Better a bit of hurt pride than a life of misery," he said softly.

"You don't get it! I can't trust myself to make the right choices." She thought of her choice to have a baby on her own. "About men!"

Casey turned and stomped away from him, focused on the snow.

She managed to channel all her angry energy into making snowmen. Without speaking another word to each other they had four snowmen guarding the gate and the walkway by lunchtime.

Turner walked around them, apparently unperturbed by her silent treatment. He was inspecting their morning's handiwork with deep masculine pleasure, picking a leaf or tuft of grass out here and there, smoothing the snow with a gloved hand.

"They look a little naked," she ventured at last, breaking her silence. She reminded herself it was asking for it to use the word *naked* around a guy like him. He'd probably tease her until she blushed.

He didn't rise to the bait. Casey tried to tell herself she was pleased about that, but instead decided he must like the distance between them.

And was sorry he had given in to the temptation to

kiss her, when he had resisted so successfully on the frozen lake.

"Andrea told me she got some top hats from the five and dime, and some cheap vests and neckties," Turner said. "She doesn't want to get them out until the twenty-fourth, though, in case we get more snow."

Casey realized from just a few minutes of standing still that her snowsuit was soaked through and her extremities were freezing. Turner noticed her shivering and shaking her hands to restore feeling.

"Here." He came over to her. "Let me warm them up."

The temptation of having that happen was too much to resist. She gave him her hand, but with a stern warning. "Just don't mistake this for a truce."

"I got it. A truce has to be sealed with a kiss."

He cupped her frozen hand with both his own. How was it they were still so warm?

Then, her hand clasped in his, he lifted it to his lips and blew on her cold, cold fingertips. They burned at first, and then the most luscious warmth crept into them.

Honestly, it was worse than being kissed, and just as intimate. And just as sensual!

She should have pulled away, but really, she was powerless.

"Better?" he asked.

She could only nod.

He released her hand, took the other and did the same thing, his eyes intent on her face.

"Lots of men are trustworthy," he said, finally.

"Are you?" she whispered.

He dropped her hand as if it was hot, but didn't step away from her. It looked as if he was pondering the question, and of course, she already knew the answer, if somebody had to think that hard!

"Hey, you two, everyone else came in for lunch ages ago. It's getting cold."

Carol was standing on a porch that had been transformed into something out of a dream, the railings covered with an abundance of green boughs with beautiful white bows threaded through them. The innkeeper was watching them, a small smile drifting across her lips.

They pulled apart as if a rubber band had held them and suddenly snapped.

Not looking at each other, shaking off snow, they walked up stairs fragrant with evergreen and past Carol, who never quit smiling as she reached out to give her dog a pat as Harper followed Turner into the house.

CHAPTER ELEVEN

"HAM!" THE SOUND of his own voice startled Turner awake. Had he shouted or whispered?

"We making cookies now. Not ham."

Turner opened one eye warily.

He looked into the face of Tessa, Rick's six-year-old daughter. Her eyes were inches from his, huge and solemn.

"I don't make cookies," he said gruffly. He closed his eyes, a hint for her to leave him alone.

It had caught up with him. Poor sleep, lots of physical activity. Casey, her hair straightened to within an inch of its life, was being frostily polite to him, and avoiding him today, one day after they had built the snowmen and he had pried her life's secrets from her.

Maybe not all her life secrets. Nothing she had said to him yesterday seemed even remotely like the major life decision Emily had mentioned.

Though he'd been able to ascertain she wasn't becoming a nun.

And was still hurting enough over some jerk that she wasn't entering into another bad relationship, either.

I don't trust myself. Around men.

And then the all-important could she trust *him?* It was a complicated question, but she had seen his hesitancy as all the answer she needed.

"We got a Christmas tree," Tessa informed him. "It's outside 'cause it's full of snow."

Over breakfast the group had been making plans to go in search of a Christmas tree in the nearby woods.

Casey's eyes had been shining like a kid about to meet Santa for the first time. And then she had shot him a look and bit her lip.

He knew if he said he was going to get the tree with them, she would have found an excuse not to.

For a girl who thought she had been dumb about men, she seemed to be playing it pretty smart with him. After that steaming kiss between them yesterday, she was putting as much space between them as the close confines of the inn would allow.

Turner knew that was good, of course, really good. He just wasn't sure why he felt so grumpy about it. Probably because a kiss had been way outside the parameters of his stated mission.

Not that that explained why he had felt grumpier yet when Casey had announced she wanted to have her turn with the ax!

What was that about? Obviously, Rick, Tessa's dad, and a fireman to boot, would be an expert on safety with an ax. Turner did not have to be there to make sure Casey didn't cut off her foot.

He needed his sleep way more than he needed to be around a woman as complicated and aggravating as Casey Caravetta. He had taken to the couch as soon as the door had shut behind the tree party.

It was better he didn't go. He was still feeling oddly battered and bruised from the snowman building thing. And not physically, either.

It was as if being around her took a run at all his hard-earned cynicism, uncovered longings that he had not been aware he had.

Not to mention threatened his ability to be in control.

He liked being in control, living by his motto, *If It's Out Of Your Control, You're In Trouble*.

And part of remaining in control was not getting sucked in by the fairy-tale vow renewal and Christmas unfolding at the inn. It wasn't reality. It was a manipulation of reality.

To tell the truth, he regretted whatever altruistic motivation had led him to knock on Casey's bedroom door yesterday and coerce her to come out and build snowmen with him.

He probably could have kept it all very big-brotherly and "Let's help poor solemn Casey have fun" if she would have kept her damned hat on and her luscious lips to herself.

"We making cookies *now*," Tessa insisted. "For the wedding."

He opened his eyes and scowled at her. "You're still here?"

The little mite didn't seem the least intimidated by him. She smiled and nodded.

He sighed. "What wedding?"

"Aunt Emily's."

It wasn't a wedding, exactly, but explaining the distinction to a six-year-old was not in his skill set. "What time is it?"

"I don't know how to tell time."

"Didn't your…" He stopped. She didn't have a mom, and because of that he managed to strip a fragment of the unfriendliness out of his voice. "Didn't your dad tell you not to talk to strangers?"

She took his hand and tugged. "You're not a stranger, Uncle Turner!"

He was not her uncle, and he was tempted to tell her so to dampen her enthusiasm, but again he remembered life had been mean enough to her without him chipping in.

The dog, who had also noticed his opening eyes, was

thumping her tail with adoration. Tessa's trust in him, like the dog's, was making Turner feel off-kilter.

He was a warrior, for goodness sake. One look at him and the dogs were supposed to turn and run, tails curled between their legs. People were supposed to hide their children.

"Come make cookies. Please...?"

"Why me?" he said out loud.

"I like you," Tessa declared with utter sincerity.

"Sheesh."

Turner had a niece a little younger than this that he had never met. His brothers had never said he wasn't welcome home for Christmas, but they'd never told him he was, either.

He tried to disengage his hand from Tessa's, but that just made her hang on more mulishly. He closed his eyes again. Was he getting a headache? His mission had originally been to get Casey to lighten up. Why was it shifting? Now he wanted her to face reality?

"Uncle Turner...!"

Oh, definitely a headache.

"I want to make cookies now. Gingerbread, like in the story. That's my favorite story."

The child's voice was becoming more strident. She looked as if she planned to start yelling if she didn't get her own way. Explaining a screaming child to her buff daddy, the fireman, wasn't in his skill set, either.

"I wanted the big one," Tessa said, and the stridency was gone. Her lower lip trembled. "The big gingerbread man in Andrea's store, but he's gone."

She was two seconds away from crying. Turner's aversion to tears was as strong as ever.

So even though it wasn't in his nature, he'd surrender. And while he was in the kitchen, he'd just have a little peek at Casey. If they were making cookies, no doubt she would be in the thick of it.

Maybe he'd say a few words to her, just to find out if she'd discovered cutting down trees was damned hard work, not the stuff of fairy tales at all.

"Okay, okay." Turner sat up, swung his legs off the couch and stood. The dog got on shore with him, and the little monkey was still attached to his hand. Tessa pulled him through the swinging door into the kitchen. Harper sneaked in, too.

Turner stopped and suppressed a groan. "Wrong turn. North Pole."

It did indeed feel like Santa's workshop. A spicy aroma permeated the air. Christmas music was playing and the kitchen was a flurry of colorful activity. Cole, Emma, Rick, Andrea and Casey were all here. Each had on a Christmas apron, and they seemed to be on an assembly line of cookie production.

"I thought you guys would still be busy with the tree."

Cole looked up at him. "That was hours ago, buddy. You've been out like a light."

Turner contemplated that a little uneasily. He had slept, which was good, but so deeply? On a couch in the middle of a house full of people? What had happened to his soldier's gift for sleeping with one eye open?

It occurred to him something was changing. He was being plunged into the things he feared most: sleeping, Christmas, tears. It was like tossing a person who was terrified of water into a lake.

Sink or swim.

And he was swimming. He was not sinking. And it was because of her.

He glanced at Casey. Her cheeks were glowing and pink from being outside; her vigorously straightened hair was clipped back sternly for work in the kitchen. Little curls

were escaping the clip, and she did that thing she did—
blew them out of the way—without having any idea at all
how sexy it was.

So he felt an increasing sense of safety, and about as un-
safe as he had ever felt, at the very same time. His mission
no longer felt clear. Oh, yes, that was definitely a headache
of major proportions developing. He made himself look at
something besides Casey.

Cole, high powered businessman, was working a food
processor, his tongue caught between his teeth in fierce
concentration. Rick, the fireman, was using the considerable strength in his arms to roll out sheets of dark, sugary
looking dough.

The women were using cookie cutters, though really,
it felt as if, despite his efforts to look at everyone else,
Turner could see only Casey, who was moving the freshly
cut cookies onto baking sheets.

Gingerbread men, big surprise.

Her hair being pulled back so severely only served to
show off the amazing height of her cheekbones, the tender curve of her neck.

"So, what woke you up?" Cole said, grinning at him. "I
thought you were going to sleep for a week."

"I had a little nudge from my friend," Turner said, looking down. Tessa was still tugging on his hand, trying to
get him to move along.

"Tess, I told you to leave him alone," Rick said sternly.

"I want him to make cookies with me," Tessa said,
unrepentant. She let go of his hand, finally, and climbed
up on a stool beside Andrea. Grabbing a cutter, the little
girl began to press out cookies randomly from the sheet
of dark dough.

"Are you ever making cookies," Turner said. He noticed
Casey would not look at him, bent over those cookies as
if they were one of her research projects.

So she, too, wanted to take a step back from the intensity of what had leaped up between them yesterday.

The sleep must have made some defenses come down, because when he saw her avoiding looking at him, it was achingly apparent to him he had hurt her all those years ago, so wrapped up in himself that the possibility she might have pined for him had never occurred to him.

He remembered that night so well. Fresh out of training, he'd known he was leaving on his first assignment. It was the first time he had experienced the predeployment intensity, a sense that he was about to embark on a mission that was highly dangerous and probably life threatening. It had given him a heightened awareness of being alive. Each breath had felt exquisite, each encounter lit from within.

And most especially that applied to his encounter with bridesmaid Casey. The few days they had spent together after the wedding had had an almost magical quality. Though they'd stopped well short of physical intimacy, Turner had never felt so alive or so connected to another human being.

Since then, he had experienced that predeployment high on many occasions. True, never quite as sweetly as that first time.

He studied Casey, and knew despite the fact she was a professional, a doctor, a research scientist, at her core was still that sweet, deep-thinking girl who had captivated him that night.

Could he make up for his insensitivity to her? Should he try?

Probably not. Yesterday, playing in the snow with her, should have been a lesson to him. He might not be able to control where the fire went once it started burning.

Besides, it would ask him to be something he was not. His brothers perceived him as colossally insensitive and self-centered, and he had no proof that they were wrong.

Leave that girl alone, he ordered himself.

He had his own wounds to nurse, his own demons to battle, his own hard choices that needed to be made.

But standing here in this kitchen, with good smells all around him, feeling safe, surrounded by people who were cheerful and uncomplicated, he had a sudden memory.

A long time ago, back when the world had worked the way it was supposed to, his dad had shown him over and over what it was to be a good man.

When he was twelve, Turner hadn't made the rep team for hockey that year. He'd been sulking and stewing, breaking things, snapping at his mother and his brothers a whole two weeks after the cut, which was probably a week after he should have been over it.

His dad, without explanation, had ordered him into the car one Saturday morning. Without a word he had driven him to the children's hospital in a neighboring community. Still without a word, his father had gathered packages from the trunk, handing some to Turner to carry.

Once inside it had become clear to Turner, that this was not his dad's first visit. He knew some of the kids by name. He had books and small gifts tucked into his pockets, puzzles and coloring books and NERF toys in the packages.

He'd introduced Turner as a hockey player, and little boys who would never skate plied him with questions loaded with curiosity and envy.

"Do you get it, son?" his dad had asked him as they drove home.

"Yeah, I do." He got it. That he lived a privileged life. That he was fortunate to be able to lace up skates and take to the ice.

His dad hadn't said a word, just reached across and rested his hand on his shoulder, leaving it there for the rest of the trip home.

But Turner realized, since the death of his father, that

his life had not felt quite so privileged. He was not always surrounded by good fortune and luck. He had experienced loss.

What would his father have thought if Turner used that as an excuse not to be a good man? His dad had been a good man. Genuinely, and to the core. He hadn't been good because he needed the approval of others, or to be showy. Being good had come as naturally to him as breathing. Once, Turner had aspired to be just like him. Now?

Was there anything left in him that could be?

Wasn't that what he was here to find out, as he stood at this crossroad, wondering which road to take?

He moseyed up to Casey, saw that she planned to act cool, but then she did a double take.

"What's wrong?" she asked.

"What do you mean, what's wrong?" He didn't like being read. He thought he probably sounded defensive.

"You look like you have a headache."

"I do," he admitted, mulling over how he had been able to keep his vulnerabilities successfully to himself for a long, long time. "Shouldn't have fallen asleep during the day."

"You want something for it?"

Just like he was not used to children and dogs, he was not used to this. Tenderness.

"I'll suck it up." To prove he was strong, not weak.

"Very manly," she said, with a roll of her eyes.

"You know what you look like with your hair like that?" he said, anxious, suddenly, to get her to stop gazing at him with that expression that made him want soft things—a shoulder to put his head on, a soothing hand on his brow.

It worked. She looked wary instead of compassionate. Wariness he could handle.

"Olive Oyl."

"Olive oil?" she said, puzzled.

"Popeye's girlfriend."

"Just because you kissed me yesterday," Casey whispered, casting a glance around her, "don't get any ideas about me being your girlfriend."

Oh, yeah, he had done an imitation of Popeye!

"I kissed you?" he sputtered in an undertone. "You started that! And don't worry. I don't have any ideas about you being my girlfriend."

Even though she'd said it first, now she looked slightly wounded.

Sorry, Dad. Turner's attempt to be a good man had lasted about fifteen seconds. "Not that that's about you," he said hastily, under his breath.

"Thanks, you educated me about the nature of cads and my good fortune around them yesterday," she hissed back.

"Look, it's not about you. I don't do attachment. That's my favor to the world. And you."

She looked perplexed. "What?"

Stop talking, he ordered himself. "I do the kind of work where people come home in bags," he said quietly, for her ears only. "It's not fair to let people love you when you take those kinds of risks."

And he knew. Burned into him, as badly as Ken's blood, were the sobs of the man's wife, the cries of his children.

Turner braced himself. Casey had a perfect opportunity to say she would never love him, anyway. That he had nothing to worry about in that department, at all.

Instead, she did what he least expected.

She reached up and cupped her hand tenderly along his jawline. She looked at him so softly it felt as if his armor was melting.

"Oh, Turner," she said, as if her heart were breaking for him. "Oh, Turner. Now I see what it is about you that children and dogs love."

She glanced at the ever faithful Harper, and kept her

hand on his cheek, oblivious to the other occupants of the room.

"That's ridiculous. I probably smell like a hamburger."

"You don't," she said, and then blushed and took her hand away. He thought she would look around to see if anyone had noticed, but she didn't. She didn't seem at all perturbed that she might have been caught in that easily misinterpreted act of pure tenderness.

Turner felt as if his very survival depended on backtracking, on lightening things up between them. "Hey, I thought that was Harper sniffing my neck while I was sleeping on the couch."

Then Casey blushed *and* smiled. That was a knockout combination.

"Come on," she said. "You showed me how to make snowmen. I'll show you how to make gingerbread men."

He had the perfect excuse to beg off. He had a headache.

Had had a headache. Her touch seemed to have erased it. Was that even possible?

It seemed to Turner that the thing called *love*—the thing he had most tried to avoid, that he had denied needing at every turn—was right here in the kitchen.

With these people that were his friends.

In the uncomplicated affection of a dog. And a child.

In Casey's angel-soft touch against the whisker-roughened surface of his cheek.

It was what he had been running from since the day his father had died. It was what had failed him, and what he had failed, too. He wanted to run from what suddenly seemed to him to be an invitation he did not want to accept.

Turner had complete confidence in himself as a courageous man. He had stood beside buddies in shadowy battles, had stood his ground when others would have run, had said yes a thousand times when other men would have said no.

But now he understood he had only scraped the surface of the meaning of courage.

Suddenly, he couldn't have left the kitchen if he wanted to. He needed to be here. He needed to be here if there was any hope at all for him to ever be the man his father had hoped he would become.

CHAPTER TWELVE

"How was the hunt for the perfect tree? Hokey?"

Casey knew something had just happened. Something unexpected. And important. Turner had told her things about himself that bordered on sacred.

He had set an impossible mission for himself. To protect the whole world from the pain of loving him.

It was heartbreakingly honorable, and if she ever said such a thing to him, she knew he would run for the door.

Even now, his staying here seemed tenuous.

She had to give him room. She had to let him breathe.

And she had to—in the spirit of Christmas, if nothing else—give him a gift. A break from the self-imposed loneliness he wore around himself like an invisible cloak. She had to become the kind of person she wanted the mother of her child to be.

She had known why he hadn't come on the outing for the tree this morning. He hadn't come so that she would go.

Now she felt ashamed that she had been so deeply relieved when he'd bowed out so that she could be more comfortable.

Casey vowed she would not let that happen again.

"It was such good fun," she said with a sigh, regretting that he had not been there. "Did your family do things like that when you were growing up? You and your brothers?"

Somehow, she felt she wanted to reconnect him to what he had lost over the years.

"Sure, we'd go get a tree from the woods. Did they let you touch the ax?"

So, he was as determined not to go there as she was to take him.

"Are you trying to start an argument?"

"What makes you say that?"

"Because you're insinuating I'm incompetent with an ax!"

"They did let you touch it!"

"You're trying to start an argument because you don't want me to delve into the rift between you and your brothers."

He looked at her long and hard. "We have to discuss the terms of that truce."

"We called off the truce."

"Can we just bake cookies then?"

"Ah," she said, knowing it was time to back off. "If I'm not mistaken, you are begging to bake cookies."

"You know something, Casey? You are way too smart for your own good."

"I know," she said, and despite the fact no truce had been agreed on, they settled into the task at hand like two people who had figured out there might be some advantages to being a team.

"Where would you place gingerbread men on the hokey scale?" he asked her.

She glanced up at him. Did his eyes linger on her lips before she looked swiftly away? "Somewhere between snowmen and Christmas trees," she said.

"How come so many cookies?"

"We're going to give them out as guest gifts at the vow renewal. So we're making some gingerbread grooms and some gingerbread brides. And we thought we'd make a

few extras, to donate to the Barrow's Cove Food Bank.
To help fill the Christmas hampers."

"Whose idea was that?" he asked.

Casey shrugged uncomfortably.

"Yours," he said. Casey was a woman his father would
have approved of.

Turner felt the oddest tug of emotion at this humble effort to make the world a better place, one cookie at a time.

It was like her hand on his cheek, and her eyes, soft,
on his face.

Small things.

Almost inconsequential.

It occurred to him such gestures of small kindnesses
were probably far more powerful in bringing about real
change than all the men who marched off to war, set on
making all that was wrong in the world right.

Casey picked that moment to glance up at him.

That night all those years ago, he had thought her dark
eyes saw him in a way no one else ever had.

And despite many predeployment nights since then,
it occurred to him he had never experienced *that* again.

"How many cookies?" he asked.

"We thought half a dozen cookies per hamper, and then
two for each guest, so…" she closed her eyes for a moment
"…about four hundred cookies."

"Wow," Emily said, overhearing, and looking at her
friend with affection and awe. "How do you do that? Math
in your head. And so fast!"

Casey shrugged uncomfortably. "Born geek," she muttered, and shot Turner a look.

But he didn't see a geek. He saw a woman who was brilliant. And beautiful. And trying hard not to be vulnerable.

Could he be a good man, without causing more harm
than good? Did he have a choice? He was here. She was here.

"What do you want me to do?" he asked gruffly.

"Those ones on the counter are ready for decorating. Why don't you and Tessa start icing them?"

"That sounds a little too delicate for me." There were a lot of things in this room that were way too delicate for a man who had killed people for a living. "How about if I start on the dishes?"

But neither of these females was interested in the agenda that would be safest for him.

"No," Tessa said imperiously. "You help me."

"Tessa," Rick said sternly. "Quit being so bossy."

The little girl's face crumpled. Her eyes clenched shut.

"Geez, don't do that!" Turner said. "I'll help you."

The grimace dissolved into a smile.

"Sorry," Rick said. "She has a little issue with being in control."

"It's okay."

"I want you to help, too," Tessa said, tugging on Casey's sleeve.

With the little girl on a stool between them, they took cooled cookies off the pans and laid out row after row of gingerbread men and women.

Andrea popped several full bags of icing in front of them, and one of candy-coated chocolate buttons. "Casey, why don't you and Turner do the faces? Tess can do the buttons."

"No eating the buttons," Turner warned Tessa, and she giggled.

"You're silly," she decided.

"Watch who you're calling silly," he groused, and was rewarded when both she and Casey giggled. "You must call me Master Icer."

He squeezed some icing out of a bag onto the head of a gingerbread man.

"He looks like a monster," Tessa howled, disparaging of Turner's artistic skill.

"Well," he said, "it really doesn't matter. You know why?"

She shook her head.

"Because this is the test cookie. I'm eating it."

He broke the cookie into three pieces, then contemplated them solemnly. "I'm the biggest and the master icer, so I get the biggest piece." He popped the whole chunk into his mouth, then handed Tessa a piece and Casey another.

"You're going to ruin our dinner," Casey protested.

"Oh, boy. Haven't you heard of happy hour? It's time for cookies somewhere, isn't it, princess?"

"Yeah," Tessa said, beaming at him for recognizing her as a princess. "Yum."

"You know what it tastes like?"

"What?"

"Like we should have another one."

Tessa broke into a fit of giggles.

"Master Icer?" Casey said a trace sardonically, "We have four hundred cookies to decorate, so you're going to have to pick up the pace a bit."

He ate faster.

Even Casey laughed, taking in Tessa's delight. "See?" she said. "Kids and dogs."

He realized he felt happy to make her laugh. Happy for this simple moment of changing the world in a simple way, one cookie at a time, one smile at a time, one laugh at a time.

It occurred to him that, for a few minutes, anyway, he had left his baggage behind. And he had fit into this wholesome world just fine.

And liked being here, too.

Turner wondered if that meant he had just moved closer to making the decision he'd come here to ponder.

He and Casey began to put piped, white icing faces on the cookies. Tongue caught between her teeth in concentration, she did the girls, making exaggerated eyelashes and lips for them, while he did the boys. Tessa did buttons.

They all stared at the first completed row of cookies with just a little bit of awe. They looked terrific!

"What would you give this on the hokey scale?" he muttered to Casey.

"Would the hokey scale be out of ten?" she asked.

"Sure."

"How about an eleven?"

"Sixteen."

"One hundred and two," Tessa crowed, determined not to be left out of the conversation.

And then they laughed. It was a small thing, that shared laugh, and yet it felt surprisingly good. Much like Turner had felt yesterday, when they'd built the snowmen. He allowed himself to sink into it.

Sink into the simple pleasure of sharing this warm, fragrant kitchen with friends on a snowy day, trying to make Christmas just a little better for someone else.

He glanced at Casey's shining face.

And was pretty sure he didn't mean the food bank clients, either.

Casey looked at Turner's dark head bent close to Tessa's as he put an icing smile on a gingerbread groom. The little girl waited with the "special" buttons, silver for the vow-renewal cookies.

Despite claiming discomfort, he seemed very at ease with the child. He would be a natural as a daddy, and Casey wondered why he wasn't.

And then told herself, and sternly, too, that was none of her business.

The last two days—building snowmen, everyone pitching in to cook dinners and clean up after, going out in search of a perfect tree—were what she had always hoped for around Christmas as a child. She had dreamed of the kind of days she read about in books and saw in movies, days filled with laughter and fun and a sense of connection with other people.

This was the life she wanted for her own child. It was no surprise to her that she would feel it here. The only times she had ever come close to feeling this way before had always been here, at the Gingerbread Inn.

And in spite of her family, not because of them. The Gingerbread Girls had always given her this gift—creating a sense of the family she wanted and did not have.

She could see Turner had had it, too.

And lost it somehow.

In the very spirit of the Christmas she wanted to believe in for her own child, Casey was determined to help him get it back. Whether he wanted her help or not.

She slid a look at him. He radiated self-certainty and self-reliance. He would not want any help from her.

And that was not going to stop her.

Tonight, she was going to get on her computer and track his brothers down. She looked at his face, open now as he leaned over cookies with Tessa.

Casey had the feeling she might be going where angels feared to tread.

Hours later, she closed her computer and rubbed her eyes. She had found both Turner's brothers on Facebook and sent them a message. I am a friend of Turner's. I need to talk to you. She had hesitated just a second, and then added, URGENT.

She had felt so sure she was doing the right thing, but now, uncertainty hit her. She wasn't even able to repair her own relationship with her mother. What made Casey think she knew what was best for him?

She reminded herself it was only a message. She hadn't actually done anything yet.

She glanced at her bedside clock. Ten at night. She didn't feel tired. She went to her window and looked out, wondering if she might see Turner skating. It was a beautiful night, with a full moon painting the amazing snow-filled world in luminescent shades of silver.

If he was out there, would she join him?

She was aware, as she went to the window, that she was hoping he would be.

What she saw was him heading along the shore of the lake, the dog beside him. Casey hesitated only a moment before grabbing her coat and racing out the door after him.

He sensed her coming and turned, waited for her.

"Where are you going?"

"Just for a walk." After the slightest hesitation, he added, "Do you want to come?"

"Yes."

The silence was companionable, the dog racing ahead and then back. A snowmobile had been by, making a nice, hard-packed trail that was comfortable for two people to walk on side by side.

They passed cabins boarded up for the winter, crossed a little footbridge that spanned a small creek, fast running and deep enough to be not quite frozen despite the frigid nights. They stopped in the middle of the bridge, gazed down at the water, listened to it tinkle over shards of ice.

Casey had never walked at night in the snow. It was a quiet she had never experienced before. When she slipped slightly, Turner took her hand, and even after she had found her footing, he didn't let go.

Harper was sniffing around the foundation of one of the cabins. Suddenly, she broke the silence of the night and began to bark.

"Hey, that's enough," Turner said.

But the dog was now racing back and forth, barking frantically, trying to dig her way under the lattice.

Turner let go of Casey's hand and went to retrieve the dog. But just as he got close, a raccoon shot from under the cabin, the dog hot on its heels.

In seconds they were both on the lake, and then the worst possible thing happened.

The ice, thin there at the mouth of the creek, gave an ominous crack. While the raccoon skittered away, Harper screeched to a halt, stared with doggie consternation at the spiderweb of cracks shooting out around her feet. And then the ice broke and the beautiful dog plunged into the water.

CHAPTER THIRTEEN

CASEY DIDN'T EVEN think. She ran toward the dog, which was paddling frantically in the icy water. Harper was trying to heave herself up onto the ice, but succeeded only in breaking it more. Casey could see the panic on the poor creature's face.

"No! Casey! No!"

She could hear a terrible urgency in Turner's voice, could see him running toward her as if he intended to tackle her. But she felt the same urgency to get to Harper as he felt to get to her. She took advantage of the distance between them and put on a burst of speed.

"Casey, don't!"

She was on the ice now. She could nearly reach Harper. Casey could feel the ice giving, as if it had a faint spring to it like a trampoline. She recognized, suddenly, that she hadn't thought this through. But she was so close!

Some snippet of knowledge about ice penetrated her adrenaline-infused state. She flopped onto her belly, crawled the remaining few feet, dispersing her weight over the fragile surface. The dog, relief in every wrinkle of her loving features, swam to her. Casey reached out for her paws.

Harper flailed and the ice broke.

It was a slow process, like a mirror shattering. First a spiderweb of cracks, then a groan as the ice settled.

Casey tried to wriggle backward but it was too late. Frigid water raced up onto the sinking slab. Then the ice shelf gave way and she plunged into the lake.

The shock of the cold hit her like a sledgehammer as the water closed over her. Somehow, she got her head clear and was able to turn and grab at the ledge of ice. Her breath was coming in great gasping gulps.

Somehow, Turner's voice penetrated her panic.

Don't come, she thought, the silent scream rising above the sheer panic that was enveloping her. It occurred to her he *would* come. That nothing would stop him. And that nobody knew where they were and that they were all going to die out here.

"Listen to me."

His voice was like a life rope, and she turned her full attention toward it. "You have to steady your breath. You are hyperventilating. You are experiencing cold shock. You cannot die from it. Do you hear me?"

Did she nod? She wasn't sure.

"That's better," he said, as she struggled to stop gasping for air, to draw in slower breaths. How could she be so cold and *still* respond to the praise in his voice?

"Casey, you need to get your elbows up on the ice and see if you can pull yourself out of the water, even a bit. Use your legs. Kick as if you are swimming. Casey, do it! I know you can do it."

The firm calm in his voice reached her and she responded to it. Somehow, she found the strength to get one elbow up on the ice. It broke away.

"Kick. Try again."

This time she was able to haul herself up. The ice, miraculously, held.

"Breathe. Listen to me. Breathe in slowly as I count to three. One. Two. Three. Breathe out slowly as I count to three."

The dog had been swimming in frantic circles. Now she came up behind her.

If Harper started to scramble up on her in a panic, it occurred to Casey's shocked mind, they were both going to die.

But Harper put her paws on Casey's shoulders, wriggled up against her and gently clung. They both hung there on a precipice between life and death.

But Casey knew Turner was not going to let them die.

"Keep breathing," he said. His voice was the life rope, calm, assured. "One. Two. Three. Don't try to pull yourself out. Your clothes are going to be too heavy to get yourself out. Keep counting."

And then, to her dismay, instead of coming for her, he turned and ran away from the water's edge.

It seemed like forever before he returned. When he did, he had a ladder. He laid it on the ice, shoved it out to her. She grabbed for it, caught it, held on for dear life. But when she tried to pull herself up on it, she could see he had been right.

Her saturated clothes were way too heavy and the strength had been sapped from her limbs by the excruciating cold.

"I just want you to look at me. Nothing else."

Her eyes locked on his, and though she was so cold, and still partway in the water, it was as if the rescue was complete already.

She knew, with a soul-deep kind of knowing, that in a matter of minutes this would all be over. He was going to save her. He did not have a single doubt, and that confidence ran the length of the ladder to her. It lifted her spirits to a place where she could hang on.

He began to crawl along the ladder toward her. The ice creaked ominously as he crept forward. Once, it cracked loudly and he stopped. But having evaluated that the ladder was distributing his weight across a large surface of the ice, he moved forward again.

Finally, he reached her. He grabbed her wrists and began to scoot backward.

"Just keep watching my face," he said. "Don't look at anything else, don't think about anything else. It's just like skating."

Of course, it was the furthest thing from that magical experience she had had, skating with him, but somehow his invoking that memory was a good thing. He had her. He had her then, and he had her now.

"Kick your legs," he told her. "Kick as hard as you can."

She did exactly as he ordered. She watched his face. She was soothed by the calm in it, by the grim determination.

A man less strong, she knew, would not have been able to do what he was doing. He was literally hauling her out of the water onto the ice. At first it broke away under her weight. She was afraid the ladder would go in, and him with it, but he just waited it out, scooted back, his hands bands of iron around her wrists. When he had her more out of the water than in, he yanked the dog off her shoulders and literally tossed Harper onto more stable ice.

Then he flipped Casey over, sat up, wrapped his legs around her torso and crab-walked backward, dragging her with him.

And somehow she knew this was what he did.

And he did it well. He dealt in life-and-death crises. She suspected he did it all the time. How else could he do it as naturally as breathing?

"Don't even try it," he warned when she attempted, groggily, to get her feet under her. Her mind was not working correctly. Everything was in slow motion.

The dog got on shore, shook herself weakly. Casey took her eyes from his only for a second to watch Harper find solid ground on the embankment and lie down, unmoving.

Turner pulled her backward until they were at the last rung of the ladder. And then he stood up.

The ice groaned.

Panic tried to rear up in her, but he was straddling the ladder, still distributing his weight.

He lifted her, slung her over his shoulder like a sack of potatoes, and ran. The ice snapped and cracked behind them.

And then they, too, were on the shore.

It occurred to her it was not over. She was wet and frozen. How far had they walked? As much as a mile?

"C-could I f-f-freeze to d-death still?" The words took effort, way too much effort.

"Not on my watch," he said, and again his confidence and his competence transferred directly to her. But would that be enough to keep her going until he got them back to the inn?

He was not going back to the inn. He hit the embankment running, not deterred by her extra weight at all. He ran to the cabin, shifted her limp form on his shoulder, and booted the door. With the second kick the wood splintered, and with the third the door crashed open.

She lifted her head. The dog was still lying as if dead, by the shore of the lake.

"H-Harper," she called weakly.

"Forget the damned dog. You nearly died for her."

They were in the cabin's main room. Turner went down on one knee, slid her off his shoulder onto a worn couch. He moved quickly away from her, went through another door, came back with blankets ripped from a bed.

If she had hoped for warmth in the cabin, she was dead wrong. It seemed colder than outside. She had never been so cold. Her body was so numb it was beyond pain.

Wordlessly, working precisely, he began to strip her sopping clothes from her. First her jacket, then her boots.

He grabbed the hem of her sweater, pulled it off her wooden, uncooperative limbs and over her head. It tangled briefly in her hair, and when he tugged it free with urgency, she felt almost thankful to feel the pain of her hair being pulled. To feel anything.

His hands went to her blouse.

"Oh, no," she managed to whisper, mortified. "Don't."

"Get real. Death or modesty. Guess which one is out the window?"

He didn't undo the buttons on her shirt, just yanked, hard, and they all popped free and rattled across the wooden floor.

He tried to peel the sleeves off, but her limbs were not working now, like funny floppy things in no way connected to her. He had to manipulate them, struggling to get the sopping clothes off her pebbled, frozen flesh.

At another time, she might have been more self-conscious, but her brain was feeling sluggish, still moving in slow motion.

This was not the time to be wondering what she had put on for underwear this morning, but wonder she did.

Still, when his hands found the clasp at the back of her bra—and very expertly at that—nothing changed in the professional, cool cast of his face. His expression showed nothing except determination as he pulled apart the clasp and dropped her bra to the floor.

He shoved her down, unsnapped her jeans, peeled them over her hips, down her thighs and off.

He reached for her panties.

"Don't," she rasped. She didn't have the strength to push his hands away.

"Sorry," he said, not very sincerely. The panties were gone.

She barely had time to contemplate her nakedness be-

fore Turner had her wrapped in coarse blankets, tight as
a sausage in a roll.

"P-p-please. The d-d-dog."

He gave her an exasperated look. She began to cry.

Without another word he went out the door and came
back with Harper, dumped her unceremoniously in front
of a cold hearth. Casey noticed the front of Turner's coat
was soaked, too.

"Th-thank you." She meant for getting the dog, but she
was too exhausted to elaborate. It didn't matter. Turner
didn't acknowledge her.

Working quickly, his manner methodical and thorough,
he crumpled paper and reached for kindling, both from
a wood box next to the fireplace. He set them carefully,
played around with the damper and then lit a match, also
taken from the box. He got down on his knees, blowing
gently, reminding her of the time he had blown on her
cold hands.

*Turner. Turner Kennedy. Bringing warmth to a world
gone cold. In so many, many different ways.*

He watched carefully for the first lick of flames, and
only when fire crackled along the kindling did he start
adding wood. And then more.

When that was done, he went and hauled a mattress out
of the bedroom, laid it right in front of the fire. And then
he disappeared and came back with a towel from somewhere. He sat her up in her blanket strait jacket and rubbed
her hair hard with the towel.

"Ouch."

"Hey, suck it up. Compared to what I'd like to do to you,
you're getting off easy." He continued toweling her hair,
squeezing the extra water out of it, toweling some more.

"What?"

"I told you not to go out after the dog," he said sternly.
"What the hell is the matter with you?"

"What would you like to do to me?" she whispered.

"Strangulation comes to mind." But his eyes moved to her lips, and then away. It seemed to her he was extra rough with the towel then.

"Don't be mad." Her chattering teeth made the words sound strangled.

"Yeah, why be mad? You could have got yourself killed over a stupid dog—"

"She's worth it," Casey said stubbornly.

He groaned. "And I've been dying to get my hands in your hair and here we are. Of course, it's not exactly what I expected, but then is anything ever, around you? And it wasn't worth it. No dog is worth a human life."

"I put you in danger, too," she said mournfully. "I'm sorry."

"Not sorry about putting yourself in danger, but sorry about putting me in danger." He snorted with disgust. "You're the one who is going to cure cancer. You're worth ten of me, Casey."

"I am not," she said softly.

"Yeah, well, we'll open the debate later." He tossed down the towel, lifted her easily into his arms, strode across the room with her and set her down on the mattress with a gentleness that belied the sternness in his tone.

"I-I'm not w-w-warming up."

His tone changed completely. "I know, sweetheart. Hang in there."

Sweetheart.

If only all these circumstances were different. To be in a cabin with him, in nothing more than a blanket, and to have him call her sweetheart.

Not like that, though. Not like a person speaking to a child who needed to be comforted.

In the same methodical way that he had rid her of her clothing, Turner began to strip off his own clothes. He tossed off his jacket, wet from the rescue and her hair. His hands flew down the buttons of his shirt, and he yanked it open, revealing the utter perfection of his chest, painted in the golden glow of the strengthening fire.

"Is it normal to feel drunk?" she whispered.

"Yeah, all the girls feel that way when I take off my shirt," he said sardonically.

And he didn't stop at just his shirt, either!

Casey could feel her eyes going round with wonder as his hands went to the snap on his jeans, opened it, and then the zipper. He shrugged out of the pants, stepped from the puddle of denim on the floor.

His fingers found the waistband of his underwear, and through her chattering teeth she gasped.

He hesitated then, for the first time since this whole debacle had started. He stared at her, disconcerted, as if so far he had managed to think of her just as an exercise in survival. After a second, his hands moved away from the band, and the underwear stayed.

Her mind slowed from the cold, Casey couldn't figure out if she was very, very relieved or very, very disappointed.

And then he crouched beside her, tugged up the corner of the blanket and slipped onto the mattress beside her.

"Sorry, babe, it's the best way I know to get some warmth into you. Transfer my body heat. Slow enough not to do harm. Quick enough to prevent hypothermia."

He wrapped his arms around her and pulled her in close.

Her mind processed the information.

Turner Kennedy and I are wrapped in a blanket together. All that is preventing us from total nakedness is the thin fabric of his shorts.

The sad part? The surface of her skin was so cold it was without sensation. He might as well have been a frozen fish.

CHAPTER FOURTEEN

Turner tucked the blankets around them as tightly as he could, and then put his arms around her again, pulling her more closely to him.

The dog whined, and came and lay against his back.

The fire crackled on the other side of him.

"I like your shorts," she decided, and then realized she had said it out loud. "I mean, they're not Jockeys and not boxers. What are they?"

He swore softly and was silent.

"There's got to be a name for that." She giggled. "Not tighty whities, but—"

"Would you stop it?"

"I would, honestly, but I don't think I can. Tighty mighties?"

"Casey, I'm begging you. Stop."

"Just tell me the name."

"If I tell you, you'll never mention it again, ever?"

"I promise."

"Boxer briefs."

"Oh," she said, and then sighed. "I really like them. Were mine okay?"

"Your what?" he asked in a strangled tone.

"My undies. I really wasn't expecting anyone to see them today."

"I didn't really notice."

"Please tell me I was not wearing the full coverage ones that have the days of the week on them."

"You're killing me here."

"Sunday is pink," she prompted.

"Okay. It was not Sunday. Or full coverage."

"So, you did look!"

"Casey, I'm a man. I looked. Not the red lacy ones. White. Bikini."

She felt inordinately pleased that for some reason she had not chosen her practical underwear this morning. Her new leaf was really going all to hell when she thought about it.

But she didn't feel like thinking about it right now!

"You said you didn't notice."

"You caught me then. I was lying. It was one of those self-preserving kinds of lies a man tells when he can't possibly win. Because if I looked—and worse, noticed—I'd be some kind of pervert. And if I didn't notice, then you might think you didn't measure up."

"Did I? Measure up?"

"I'm trying to be professional here."

She pondered that. "Professional what? What kind of government contracts did you say you do?"

"I didn't say."

"Sensitive work," she remembered. "You save people, don't you?"

He snorted. "I'm no hero, Casey. Don't even think it. You have started down the road of disillusionment."

"How can I not think it, when you saved me?" she whispered, suddenly feeling very sober. "Turner, you saved my life. How did you know? How do you know how to do all these things?"

"It's no big deal," he said, and he meant it. "That's what I get paid for. To keep a clear head when all hell is breaking loose."

"You're amazing."

"If I was that amazing, I wouldn't have left home without a cell phone," he said ruefully.

"No," she said. "Turner, you are the most amazing man I've ever met. And that was before I saw you in your boxer shorts. Boxer briefs."

"Yeah, well, survivor's euphoria."

"Is that why I feel like giggling?"

"Unless that's me in my boxer briefs again, yeah, probably."

"Euphoria," she whispered, contemplating it, liking the way the word rolled through her mind like warm mist. And that was exactly what she felt lying there, thawing out, wrapped tightly in a blanket, his naked body sharing his warmth with her. Absolute and utter euphoria, as if she had never had a better moment in her entire life.

"I should be mortified," she said out loud. Were her words slurring slightly, as if she was drunk? "But I'm not. I'm euphoric. And at least I'm not wearing the pink ones that say Sunday on them. Are you euphoric, too, Turner?"

"Oh, sure," he said gruffly, "I'm naked with a beautiful woman under the worst possible circumstances. You have pried personal information from me about my underwear and yours. But as I said before, I have a feeling nothing with you ever goes as expected, does it?"

"Why? Were you expecting this? Were you expecting us to be naked together? Sometime?"

He groaned. "My only defense is a weak one, and I'm falling back on it, even though I've already used it. I'm a man. Men think like that."

"Wow," she said, feeling as if he had announced the discovery of a new planet. "Men think naked thoughts. All the time?"

"Just about," he said.

"With everybody?" She giggled. "Every body—get it?"

"No," he said gruffly, "not with every body."

"So, if you had to get naked with someone to keep them from dying, would you be pretty glad it was me?"

"Casey?"

"Hmm?"

"Quit talking now. I'm begging you."

"If you just answer that one question, I promise I will."

But he didn't answer. He tucked her in even closer, put his chin on top of her head and let her bury her face in his chest.

And it felt like an answer, even if it didn't have words.

The exhaustion had caught up to her. She was sleeping. Cuddled to him as she was, Casey's shivering was beginning to become less violent, her body beginning, just beginning, to feel less like a block of ice. Turner knew that meant they were coming out of the danger zone.

He was keeping his body between her and the fire now. His body heat would warm her up at a good rate; the fire might do it too quickly.

Out of the danger zone? They were lying naked in each other arms, and they had just had a rather intimate discussion about underthings.

So, possibly they were entering a danger zone of a whole other kind, not that he would ever take advantage of what she was feeling.

Gratitude. Relief. Euphoria.

It was probably as close as she had ever come to a near-death experience. He had brushes with them all the time.

But there was a difference here, and he pondered that.

In all those other situations, it had been a mission. Everything rehearsed and controlled, as much as it was humanly possible to do. He knew what he was getting into, what tools and skills he would use, what he could control and what he could not.

He left nothing to that most precarious of things, chance.

Turner believed in himself, and the people he was surrounded with. He believed in carefully calculated odds, even though those odds were not always in his favor.

What he did not believe in was miracles.

And yet, when he looked at what had happened tonight out there on the broken ice, it had the markings of the miraculous. What were the chances that a ladder would be leaning up against the cabin? What were the chances that there would *be* a cabin? Full of every single thing he needed to keep her alive?

What if she'd been out here walking by herself?

A miracle, he thought, and pondered that. Maybe he was experiencing a bit of euphoria, after all.

Turner waited another hour, and then two, feeling warmth sliding back into her body before he finally released her and moved away. The dog protested and Casey mewed in her sleep, but he tucked the blankets tight around her.

Harper, still very wet, was going to try and snuggle into Casey, so he found more towels and dried the dog off.

"Stupid mutt," he said.

Harper kissed him lavishly. Turner went and found an extra blanket, wrapped it around the dog.

Then he got Casey's frozen clothes from the floor by the couch. He took them outside, barely noticing the cold, and wrung them out.

They were not going to be ready for her to put back on in the morning.

Next he rummaged through the cupboards, coming up with broth and crackers. He found a pot. The propane for the stove had been turned off, so he stepped outside, found the tank valve and turned it on.

In moments the soup was bubbling briskly.

He ate some, then against his better judgment got a bowl and spoon-fed some to the dog.

He could go now, and get help.

But just then Casey cried out in her sleep, woke with a start, screaming, and scrabbled out from under the blankets.

He went to her instantly, pulled back the covers, crawled back in beside her, and held her tight. Her tears soaked his chest. He kissed the top of her head, and that seemed to finally settle her down.

"I dreamed I was back in the water," she said.

"It was just a dream. You're safe. Do you want something to eat? I made soup."

"I could have got us all killed," she said. "Instead of a celebration of love, poor Emily and Cole. More tragedy—

"Hey, don't even go there. That's not what happened."

"I could have killed you. One mistake, and you would have been dead. All of us out floating in the water."

"Stop it," he said sternly.

"I-I c-c-can't. So stupid. I'm st-stupid."

"It was an accident. Shit happens. Shhh, you're not stupid. You're about the furthest thing there is from stupid."

"Why couldn't I see? The dog went through the ice! Why did I just charge out there like that? Like an idiot."

"Because, for once," he said softly, "you were thinking with your heart instead of your head."

"That figures," she said. "That just bloody well figures. That's always when I get in trouble."

"Tell me about it," he said. "You tell me all about that, Casey."

Under normal circumstances she would have never told Turner Kennedy about the faulty radar of her heart.

But this wasn't normal.

Nothing about tonight felt normal.

Least of all what she was feeling for Turner. A trust as deep as anything she had ever felt.

"It's a long story if I start at the beginning," she said.

"We've got nothing but time."

"My dad could not be faithful to my mom," she said tentatively, because she knew that really was the beginning. "Some people say it's the nature of Italian men, but I don't think that was it."

She stopped. Heavens, was she really going to get into this? They were naked together, and she was going to discuss her childhood?

No, she was going to discuss the problem of thinking with her heart.

And that was better than the alternative, which she suspected was why he was encouraging her. He wanted her to think about *anything* except that water closing over her head, how close she had come to killing them.

And she wanted to think of anything except how strangely right it felt to be cuddled up in a blanket with a very nearly naked man.

"What do you think it was?" he asked, encouraging her.

"It was my brother getting cancer. I think my dad was unmanned by that. As if he should have been able to save him and protect him, and he couldn't."

"I think every man feels that way," Turner said softly. "As if it is his highest calling to protect what is his."

His voice embraced her, accepted her, encouraged her to go on. But more, she had a feeling Turner Kennedy had just told her who he was.

"Go on," he said, his voice soft in the night, the crackling fire and his nearness lulling her into a place where she wanted to share confidences.

"And then when my brother died, my dad saw that as his greatest failure as a man. He couldn't face it. He kept the pain at bay by having affair after affair after affair. Each one an attempt to get his manhood back. That's my memory of my dad. Even here at the Gingerbread Inn. He was always flirting with my girlfriends' moms."

"You were embarrassed by him," Turner guessed gruffly.

"Oh, yes, but oddly, I was more embarrassed by my mom. She always knew what he was up to. She'd shriek and cry and throw things, but any real action? No. Why did she tolerate that? Why didn't she leave him?"

"It sounds almost as if you've forgiven your dad, but not your mom."

"It's easier to forgive deceased people."

"What's going on with your mom, Casey? How come you aren't spending Christmas with her?"

"How do you know I'm not?"

"Emily told me. She said when she and Cole planned this, they wanted everybody to be able to get home after their ceremony and have Christmas with their families. So, how come you aren't?"

Casey contemplated the fact that Emily had said anything to him about her, but then gave in to the temptation to share it. She said quietly, "Can you keep a secret, Turner?"

"Oh, yeah. That's my life. Keeping secrets."

"When he died, my mom joined a convent. When I asked her to spend Christmas with me, it was no, she was serving Christmas dinner to the poor. But I was welcome to join her. As long as I remember she's Sister Maria Celeste now, and not Mom. She seems much happier being that than she ever was being my mother."

"Oh, boy," he said, his voice a low growl of sympathy. "So there it is, finally. Why you're sensitive to the topic of nuns right now. I'm sorry, Casey."

"I don't want you to feel sorry for me!"

"How can I not? Your life has just been one abandonment after another, hasn't it? Even me, leaving you the way I did."

"Why *did* you leave me like that? Without even a goodbye?"

"Men are jerks. Topped off with the jerk you got engaged to."

"You're not like him, but that's what I mean about following my heart," she said sadly. "How did it lead me right to my father? How could I be so stupid as to pick Sebastian out across a crowded room—or a crowded lab, as it was? How could I be so stupid as to fall in love with a man who was going to be unfaithful? Just like my dad."

"You wanted somebody to love you, Casey. There is nothing wrong with that."

"Yes," she said sadly. "It's that clear to you, isn't it? I was just desperate for someone to love me. Or maybe it's more that I'm desperate for someone to love."

"Don't say that as if it's a bad thing."

"It is a bad thing to want something so desperately it blinds you to reality."

"No, it isn't. Because you were made to love somebody, Casey. Somebody worthy of you. Somebody you can have children with."

"You don't need a man to have children anymore," she said. "I think it's safer to use a sperm donor. It's more scientific, don't you think?"

He swore under his breath.

"What?"

"Remember I told you when I kissed you that I knew you were never going to be a nun?"

"I remember," she said dreamily.

"Well, you aren't going to make babies like that, either."

"I am so," she said stubbornly. "I've already decided. That's going to be my Christmas present to myself. My gift to myself for the rest of my life. A baby. A child. A family. I'm not waiting for some man to come and give me what I want. I am creating my own life!"

"Is this the major decision Emily told me you were making?"

"Emily told you?"

"Don't do it," he implored her softly. "Casey, raising kids is a tough enough job for two people. Wait it out. Wait for the right guy. The life you always dreamed of is waiting for you. I promise."

"You can't know that. You certainly can't promise me that."

"Yes, I can. Some man is going to see you and *know* what you are. He's going to see that you're funny and brilliant and have a heart of pure gold. And he's going to love and cherish you and protect you, and wake up every morning and look into your eyes and see your amazing hair cascading over his pillow, and he's going to thank God for you. He's going to love having wild-haired children with you."

Suddenly, in all this sharing of secrets, Casey needed to tell him the biggest one of all.

Her defenses were so completely gone it felt as if they had been silly in the first place.

"I want it to be you," she whispered. "I've always wanted it to be you. From the night I met you at Emily and Cole's wedding. I want you to be that man."

He touched her hair with infinite sadness, and with no surprise, as if she had never kept her secrets hidden from him at all. "It can't be me, Casey."

"Why?"

"Aside from the fact you're seeing me in a very heroic light right now, I can't give you what you need."

"Why?"

"Casey, I'm so much like your father, you would run."

CHAPTER FIFTEEN

"You are not!" Casey said. Why had she done that? It felt as if she had peeled open her chest and shown him her very heart. But even so, she felt the need to get at his truth. "You are absolutely nothing like my father."

"I don't mean I'm a womanizer," Turner said. "But I have made choices that pulled my family apart as surely as your dad's way of dealing with life did yours."

It penetrated her exhaustion that Turner was doing what he did so well. Trying to distract her. Maybe even to sting her with his rejection, so that she wouldn't focus on him.

"Tell me," she whispered. "Tell me, Turner, about those choices."

"I already did," he said, with a dismissive shrug. "Those days with you in New York were my last days in your world."

"Then tell me about that other world. The one you went to. Tell me where you went and what it did to you."

Suddenly, despite all that had happened to her tonight, Casey did not feel weak, but strong. She felt as if she was seeing Turner as clearly as she had ever seen him, despite his efforts to throw up a smoke screen.

And Casey could see he was struggling, at a deep level, that his very soul was in jeopardy. She knew he was the strong, silent type, and she suspected it was the worst prison of all.

She had just told him her deepest longing. Her deepest secret. That she could love him. Now, she needed to know his. And perhaps, if he told her, some wall would come down from around him, and she could crawl over the rubble, and find him inside....

"Turner, let this cabin be our sanctuary. Let it be the place where we can tell each other anything. Unburden it. And then leave it here."

"Go back to sleep, Casey."

"I'm not going to. Not until you tell me."

"Not even if I beg you?" he said wryly.

"Not even then."

"We could reopen the discussion about underwear."

"You know what? You are trying to use distraction, and it is not going to work. You saved me tonight, Turner. And now it's my turn. To save you. There's something inside you that is eating you alive."

Turner was silent for a long time. And then he sighed, and something in Casey's heart melted, because it was the sigh of a warrior who had found the place, finally, where he could put down his shield.

He was going to trust her, and it felt as if the wall around him had that first all-important crack in it.

"In a way, it's a story like your dad's. Because a tragedy started it. My father died in the 9-11 attacks on the World Trade Center. He was a financial consultant, an ordinary guy, probably a better human being than most, who went to work one morning and got murdered.

"I was in university when it happened. My only goal in life, up until that point, had been to have as much fun as was humanly possible. Someday, though, I assumed I would settle down, have a family and give the same life to my children that he had always given to me.

"But after it happened, I felt like everything he had always stood for was being threatened. I was taken with a rush of patriotic fever, a desire to make a difference, maybe a desire to vindicate my dad.

"Of course, my family did not see it—my becoming part of that rush of young American men who joined the military to make the world right again—as in any way honorable. They saw me leaving when they needed me most, giving my mother one more loss to deal with when she was already at her most fragile. My brothers accused me of leaving because I couldn't stand the pain.

"And it was only a long time later that I could acknowledge how true that was. I couldn't stand it. I couldn't stand all the tears. To this day, I can't stand tears. I couldn't stand wallowing in it. I had to feel like I was doing something about it.

"I pushed to get into an elite antiterrorism unit. I can't talk about what I did, but suffice to say nothing in my rather sheltered and privileged childhood had prepared me for it.

"Even so, I started my career with a great sense of purpose, a sense of taking control in a troubled world. I expected a life of high adventure when I stepped away from everything I knew, and got a life of unfathomable danger and darkness.

"I got a life where mistakes cost lives. Where the people closest to me paid the ultimate price.

"I watched myself change. I became what that kind of work demanded I be. I became a survivor, jaded and cynical. Being emotionally shut down was an asset that was necessary for survival.

"But I'm nothing if not highly adaptable, so I became what I needed to be. And that has meant leaving everything else behind me.

"I was on an extremely delicate, covert assignment when word reached me that my mother had died. It would have jeopardized months of training, and maybe lives, to leave at that moment, so I made a choice.

"My brothers have not forgiven me, and I don't blame them. I'm not the kind of guy who fits into their world anymore. I'm the kind who puts a mission before my own mother. I already told you I'm the kind who ends up in a bag. Better not to let anyone become too attached to me."

"You're protecting them," she whispered. "You think you're protecting them. From you."

He made a harsh sound at the back of his throat. "You can attach an honorable motive to it if you must, but I don't think so."

"How can they not see who you really are?" she asked. "Even Harper can see it."

"That dog nearly killed you. She is missing a few brain cells."

"I can see it," Casey stated, deciding not to hide behind the dog.

"You can, eh?"

"Turner?"

"Hmm?"

"I think I'm falling in love with you." And then she pulled herself in as close to him as she could, and raised her lips to his.

"I just told you all the reasons you can't."

"My heart isn't listening."

He moaned, a low animal sound of pain, deep in his throat. He took her chin in his hand and gazed into her eyes.

And then he brushed her cheek with his lips.

"No," he said firmly. She got the sense it was as much to himself as to her.

He jumped off the mattress so fast he took the blankets with him. And then bent to awkwardly cover her.

"I came here knowing I had to make a decision," he

said. "Do I try to go back to a fork in the road and choose a different path? Could I? Or do I stay on the path that I have chosen already?"

"I don't care which path you take," she said, her voice trembling. "I will support you in either of them."

He snorted. "You don't know the reality of the path I'm on."

"Maybe not," she said firmly, "but I know the reality of you. Turner, couldn't we just give it a chance? Couldn't we just see each other? Couldn't we just see if there's something there? A future for us together?"

It felt as if she had risked everything as she waited for his answer; every ounce of her pride, every bit of who she was was on the line.

For a moment, she saw a struggle behind his eyes, but then it was over.

"Remember when I said you weren't stupid?" he said harshly. "I take it back. You are missing a few brain cells, just like the dog. And I'm not getting any top marks, either. What did I think? That I was at a pajama party, lying here trading secrets? I can tell you are out of danger. I'm going to go."

"Go where?"

"Back to the inn. I'll return with a vehicle and some warm clothes. You should probably go to the hospital."

"I do not need the hospital!"

"Just for observation."

"Please don't do this."

"No," he said, with quiet finality. "Please don't *you* do this. You think you love me because I rescued you. Because you're experiencing that near-miss euphoria.

"I get it all the time. I get it just before I deploy. That heightened sense of awareness. That feeling of being intensely and incredibly alive. The sense that I can see things everyone else has always missed. It's almost like being on drugs.

"You know the first time I felt that way, Casey?"

She shook her head. She had a feeling she really did not want to hear this.

"The first time I ever felt that was with you. Those days in New York. That was the first time I was going to deploy."

She stared at him.

What they had shared that night hadn't been a magical connection between him and her? It had been some kind of intense reaction to heading into danger that had had nothing to do with her?

"You know what else? You know why I rented that presidential suite at the Waldorf? You think it was just to make you feel special? You happened to be in the right place at the right time.

"I'd come into all this money. I had to get rid of it. I had to get rid of that money from my dad's death. Insurance money. Money for the *victims* of 9-11. I hated that money. I hated it as much as I hated the tears. I wasn't going to be anybody's victim."

She felt the shock of it.

And the betrayal.

She could feel her eyes filling with tears.

He looked at her coldly. "Yeah, that's what a woman would get who was stupid enough to fall for a guy like me. A life full of tears. That's why I left without saying goodbye that morning. I knew you'd cry. And I knew it wouldn't change anything.

"You deserve better. You deserve a man who can take your tears and treat them with tenderness.

"You deserve a man who looks at Christmas with something other than dread.

"You deserve a man who can go to sleep with a clean

conscience, who is not afraid of his own dreams. I'm not that man.

"There's soup on the stove. It's still warm. You should probably have some."

And then he turned from her and yanked on his clothes.

"Don't you dare leave me here by myself."

"I'll be back within half an hour."

But somehow, she knew he wouldn't be. Without a backward glance he went out the door and was gone.

The dog dragged herself out of the blanket he had wrapped her in, and went and scratched pathetically at the door.

And then Harper did what Casey wanted to do. She began to howl as if her heart was broken.

Turner didn't come back.

It was Rick and Emily and Andrea who came to find her. It was embarrassing being found naked, rolled up in her blanket like a sausage in a pastry wrapper.

But Rick was a complete professional, and her friends were full of nothing but tender concern.

Casey was too distraught to pretend she didn't care. "Where's Turner?"

"He left. There was some kind of urgent message for him from his brother on his cell phone," Emily said.

"But is he coming back? For the vow renewal?" *For me?*

"Cole said he would never let him down," Emily said.

"But?"

She shrugged and watched Casey uneasily. "But I don't know. There was something about him when he came back…"

"What happened here?" Andrea whispered.

Casey thought about that. The trading of secrets, the deep trust.

But in the end, what had happened was the very same thing as before. She had fallen in love.

And he couldn't wait to get away from it!

"Nothing," she told her worried friends. "I fell through the ice. He saved my life. End of story."

What she didn't let on was that if it was the end of the story, she wasn't sure how she was going to go on, let alone not be a wet blanket for the vow renewal.

The house was a flurry of activity. A dozen times a day, Casey wanted to leave.

But Turner was already going to let down his friends. She couldn't let them down, too! So she stuck with it.

She decorated. And delivered cookies. She scrubbed the inn until it shone. She decorated the tree and hung garlands and did paint touch-ups.

And at night, by herself, not able to sleep, she would go down to the lake and put on that old pair of skates.

She taught herself how to skate. She tried. She fell. She dusted herself off, and she fell again. And got up again.

And somehow, it was the skating that helped her come to terms with it.

Life—and love—were exactly like this. There were moments, if you gave it everything you had, and did not hesitate, when you soared. When you floated joyously through ink-black skies, nearly able to touch the stars.

And then you fell.

But you didn't give up. You brushed yourself off, set your teeth and tried again.

That was what she wanted to teach her child.

A child she suddenly realized she was not ready to have. The greatest gift a mother could give her offspring was to live a whole and healthy existence herself.

When Casey looked at her life, she thought she had played it way too safe. The Gingerbread Girls had been right. She had given her life to a dusty old lab, because there were *rules*. Because it made her life predictable. And to spice it up she had chosen calligraphy? Yoga? Sebastian, for goodness sake?

She needed to skate. And climb mountains. And jump from airplanes.

She needed to love, *fearlessly*.

She had come to the inn searching for something she had searched for her whole life. A Christmas miracle.

Her miracle, it seemed, had come with a crash through the ice, a sudden realization that life could be over in a flash. There was no time to waste on self-pity. Or safety.

Life didn't make any promises. It involved loss and heartbreak.

But, like skating, if you stayed down, if you let the fall cripple you, the joy was gone, too.

She was glad she had laid it all on the line for Turner. She was glad she had risked everything. Because it felt in doing so, she had learned the fall would not kill her.

Not risking at all was what would kill her. In increments, her life getting smaller and smaller as she tried to make it more and more safe and secure.

Casey didn't feel broken by Turner's rejection as she had by Sebastian's. She understood it was about him and not her. She might have risked her heart on Turner, but dammit, she felt as alive as she ever had!

Skating alone, she thought about going through the ice, and the night in the cabin, and she got the gift she had always hoped for.

She knew she was going to be okay. No matter what.

No matter what her mother did. No matter what happened in Emily and Cole's future, or Andrea and Rick's, Casey was going to be okay. No matter what Turner decided to do, she was going to be fine.

Her amazing life had given her the tools she needed to live deeply and fully. To embrace it all, and then to get up and soar on.

And so on Christmas Eve, as Casey put the final touches on the snowmen, she felt loss and joy intermingled, as they often were in the tapestry of life. She adjusted the top hats and ties on the snowmen, and let a few tears fall as she remembered the fun she and Turner had had in the snow.

And then she allowed herself to smile at how adorable the snowmen looked, and to be grateful to have made this contribution to her friend's happiness.

The truth?

Casey had loved her brother. And her father. And her mother. She loved Turner. And even though each of those loves had not been predictable in their paths, each had made her a better person, not a worse one.

Knowing that was her very own Christmas miracle.

And she knew something else. That perhaps she had never loved Sebastian at all. That, in a way even hidden from herself, she had seen him as a means to an end. Perhaps she had seen what she felt for him as safe, because so little of herself had been invested in it.

She had mourned not his loss, but the loss of her own wish for herself: to lead a safe, comfortable, normal life.

And now she saw she had been saved from an unworthy dream. Because love was many things, but "safe" and "comfortable" were not among them.

Real love required people to grow and stretch and become more than they were before, not to stay in a comfortable rut.

"The hairdresser is here," Andrea called, pulling Casey away from her contemplation of the snowmen.

Despite her pleas to straighten her hair, the hairdresser did it in a regal upsweep. When Casey looked at herself in the mirror, it seemed the way her hair was done reflected the great growth she had experienced since her near-death experience on the ice. Her curls had been tamed into the updo, but wayward strands broke free, and the result was breathtaking.

Tears stung her eyes as she looked at herself in the mirror and felt total self-acceptance. Love was breathtaking.

She walked through the inn and on outside. Darkness had fallen and the Gingerbread Inn looked as if it had been restored to all its glory.

It looked like something out of a winter fairy tale. The snowmen were a lighthearted touch at the gate. All the Christmas lights were on. The porch railings were covered in garlands of real fir boughs. A huge wreath hung in the doorway. As darkness fell, Carol and Martin lit the candles in white paper bags all over the yard. They looked like fairy lights and the yard looked like something out of a dream.

Not knowing they were being watched, the two of them paused. Tears stung Casey's eyes for the second time in just a few minutes when Martin swept Carol into his arms and kissed her long and deep.

And then they both turned back and looked at the inn, and whether they were aware of it or not, Casey knew what their future held.

Each other, and the Gingerbread Inn.

The inn had never looked so beautiful as guests began to arrive. Carol and Martin welcomed them and showed them to their seats, arranged in a half moon around the front porch. Carol was glowing with pride and with something else. The joy of a woman who had said yes to love.

Turner wasn't here.

He wasn't coming.

Somehow, Casey had thought she might have one last chance.

CHAPTER SIXTEEN

As SHE AND Andrea stood, gazing at the fairyland of wonder they had created, a cab shot up the driveway and Turner hopped out, suit bag over his shoulder.

"Turner," Andrea said to him, hands on her hips. "Turner Kennedy, you have caused me a great deal of stress."

Casey could feel her heart beating in her throat when she saw him. This was what love felt like, then.

Wanting what was best for him, even if it was not what was best for her. But what if what was best for both of them was the very same thing?

Turner's gaze was like flint. "You don't know the meaning of the word *stress*," he told Andrea.

He glanced at Casey, and the flintiness did not leave his expression.

But she saw the exhaustion around his eyes, the deep weariness.

"You haven't been sleeping again," she noted quietly.

Andrea seemed as if she was going to say something to him, and then stopped, glanced at his face, glanced at Casey beside her, made a sympathetic little clucking noise and flounced into the house, leaving them alone.

Turner brushed by Casey without saying a word. He left her standing on the steps, shaking with so many mixed feelings she felt she might explode. Could love be mixed with so much anger and frustration and confusion?

She went to her room and got ready. The dresses she and Emily and Andrea had chosen were beautiful. Hers and Andreas were navy blue, each with a slightly different cut. With the upswept hairdo and the elegant dress, Casey was not sure she had looked so beautiful at Emily's first wedding. After a final twirl before the mirror, she went downstairs.

She reminded herself, firmly, that this night was about Emily and Cole. Her personal agendas had to be set aside.

A few minutes later, Turner was also back downstairs, looking unfairly amazing in a beautifully cut suit that showed off the tremendous masculine power of his physique.

He looked at her, his gaze taking in everything. She shivered from the hunger she thought she saw there. But, no, now it was gone, if it had ever been there at all. His face was carefully schooled in a calm mask.

"We need to talk," she said to him in an undertone.

The grim line deepened around his mouth. "Yeah, we do. About you interfering in my life. You sent a message to my brothers?"

"You won't have to worry about that happening again."

"You can't unring a bell." But for all the harshness in his tone, for a moment she saw something baffling in his eyes. A woman determined to be dumb might mistake it for regret.

But the flurry of last-minute instructions from Andrea, and their respective duties, drew them apart.

The yard was completely dark now, except for the golden light on the porch, the Christmas lights on the house and the flickering candles, luminescent in the white bags. People were seated in a semicircle around the porch. The wedding party stood inside the door.

Andrea pressed Play on the CD player, and a song by a children's choir came on. Their voices were soaring and joyful, and filled the night. The song was about love being a light to follow through the darkness.

When it was over, Andrea signaled to Casey and Turner. They went out the door together, then parted, moving to either side of the porch. Andrea, and Cole's other best friend, Joe, did the same.

And then Cole stepped out, and waited for Emily.

Emily had decided on a simple ivory frock and a matching cashmere sweater. She was carrying a single bloodred rose as she stepped toward her husband.

A collective sigh went up from all assembled.

There was no mistaking the look of exquisite tenderness Cole gave Emily. There was no mistaking her absolute love for him, as she rose on her tiptoes and brushed her lips against his cheek.

They were both shining from within.

In a simple ceremony that took only ten minutes, Cole and Emily took those sacred and ancient vows. Cole did not have to repeat them after the minister, but said them as though they were written on his heart.

"I, Cole," he said in a voice strong and true, sure and steady, "renew my vow to you, Emily, to love you as my wife, to have and to hold, for better or for worse, for richer or for poorer, in sickness and in health, to love and to cherish, until death do us part."

Then Emily, quiet, strong, said those vows also.

It was as if every bit of hard work they had all done to the inn disappeared, and every single person. It was as if Emily and Cole stood alone, wrapped in their love for each other.

When their lips met, for a moment there was only silence.

And then a cheer went up, as those invited realized they had been part of a miracle, the affirmation of love in a world where it could be so hard to find it, so hard to sustain it, so hard to keep its light from going out.

Wasn't that really what Christmas celebrated, after all? The very thing these two people were reaffirming on this beautiful Christmas Eve?

The way Cole and Emily continued to look at each other—as if each was brand-new to the other—made Casey's throat close.

Turner put his hand on Cole's shoulder. It was a gesture of solidarity, and it made Casey glance at him.

And what she saw made her heart stand still.

For one unguarded moment, as he looked at his friend, the remoteness left his face. And in its place was the deepest yearning that Casey had ever seen.

Turner wanted what his friend had just said such a resounding yes to.

But then he glanced at her, and the look was gone. He took his hand from Cole's shoulder and shoved it deep in his pocket. Turner narrowed his eyes and held hers coolly, daring her to believe what she had just witnessed.

But she did believe it.

It was as if the Christmas miracle she had waited for her entire life had been delivered in that one unguarded second when she'd seen the yearning in a strong man's face.

But the moment was swept away as people left their chairs and surged around Cole and Emily, hugging, crying, congratulating, laughing.

Everyone was invited in. The house was as it was meant to be, at last. Filled to the rafters with people laughing, and loving each other.

"I can't thank you all enough," Emily said, after a while, silencing the mingling crowd with a lift of her hand. "My two best friends, Casey and Andrea, have made this day perfect for me and my other best friend, Cole. And I am humbled that so many of you were willing to spend your Christmas Eve with us.

"There's skating outside, and hot chocolate by the barrel, so I'll see you out there for our first dance in about ten minutes."

Casey joined the crowd who watched from the bank. Emily and Cole had elected not to change their clothes. They looked like pairs skaters waiting to take their turn in a fancy competition.

What followed was poetry. A dark night, white snow, Emily and Cole skating hand in hand. And then he pulled her to him, and she twirled into his arms, and they skated seamlessly, a gold medal performance because of the genuine love that shimmered around them.

It was one more beautiful moment in an evening that had strung together beautiful moments like pearls on a thread.

Casey couldn't help but fantasize that it was she and Turner out there skating, but then jerked herself to reality. He had disappeared as soon as the ceremony was over. But he had arrived by cab, and one hadn't returned to pick him up.

Was he still here?

She pulled herself away from the crowd and went to change out of the beautiful dress and remove the pins from her hair.

She couldn't go out there to the rink, and visit and drink hot chocolate and show off her new skating skills, and pretend everything was all right. She couldn't. She had to find Turner and talk to him now. She wondered if maybe he had slipped away already.

She knocked on the door of his room. At first she was relieved that she could hear him in there, and but then there was sudden silence.

No answer.

She tried the door, and it opened. She took a deep breath and stepped in.

Turner had not changed from his suit, though he had stripped off the jacket, loosened his tie at his throat. He was sitting on the edge of the bed with his head cradled in his hands. When she entered, he shot up off the mattress, his position defensive.

She knew she had caught him at a vulnerable moment. "We need to talk."

He shrugged, all his defenses in place now.

"Being found in that cabin, naked except for a blanket, was one of the most embarrassing moments of my life," Casey said, hoping she had stripped every bit of the hurt and despair of the last few days out of her tone.

"Then you've led way too sheltered a life. I am so angry about you sending a message to my brothers. That situation was none of your business. What on earth made you think you should contact them?"

"I could see you were dying of loneliness."

He drew in his breath sharply. For a moment, he couldn't speak. When he did, much of the anger was gone from his voice.

"You scared the hell out of them. An urgent message from someone they had never heard of? They thought something had happened to me."

"And they contacted you to make sure you were all right?"

"The message was waiting for me when I got back from the cabin."

"It seems to me that would be an indication your relationship with them is not as damaged as you thought. They care about you. It was as good an excuse as any to hightail it out of here, though."

He was squinting at her dangerously. She was sure it was a look he could have used to intimidate the enemy.

But she could not let it work on her. It felt as if her life—and his—depended on that.

"I figured it out," she said softly. "It's not about them. And it's not about me. It's about you. The big, tough soldier. Terrified."

He looked at her warily.

"For a smart woman, I can be kind of dumb sometimes."

"You're preaching to the choir. I saw you nearly die trying to save a dog."

"Hmm," she said. "Dumb about matters of the heart."

His look of wariness increased.

"I meant it when I said I was falling in love with you." How had this happened? She was saying the exact opposite of what she had planned to say if she ever saw him again!

But what could possibly be gained by lies?

She suddenly understood the absolute necessity of standing in her truth, of being who she really was, of not hiding.

"Well, there's the dumb part," he said.

But she looked right past the harshness of the words.

"Remember when you told me you were like my dad? And I said you weren't? You are in this one way.

"I figured out you think you have to protect everyone and everything. You feel it's your highest calling to protect what is yours, don't you? You even said that."

He didn't answer.

"You said, 'I think every man feels that way. As if it is his highest calling to protect what is his.'"

Turner was silent, and so she went on.

"You told me you had come to rely only on yourself. And when that failed you believed in nothing anymore. What happened?"

His lips pressed together in a hard line.

"What happened?" she said again, dangerously.

"The last mission went bad." He choked this out.

"And was it your fault?"

"No. But a good man died. The best. And it was a reminder."

"Of what?"

Turner glanced at the door. He looked as if he was going to put his hands on her shoulders and push by her without answering.

But she leaned on the door, blocking it with her body.

"It was a reminder that when it matters most, a man is powerless. I couldn't save my dad, and I spent all those years trying to change that. Only to arrive in the same place. I couldn't save anything.

"Don't you see what a man who has lost all faith would bring to you?" He asked this desperately.

And she knew, then, that she had won.

That he was breaking wide-open in front of her.

She crossed the distance between them and looked up into his face.

"Poison," he told her, desperately. "I would bring all the ugliness I have seen and been to you. And to my brothers. I'm going back after the holidays. I am going back to what I do."

"What was his name?" she asked softly.

There was a long silence, and when his voice came, it was a whisper.

"Ken. Ken Hamilton. We called him Ham because he was such a practical joker. He had a wife, Casey, he had kids."

"I'm so sorry."

"I didn't protect him."

She let that fall into silence. For a long time, she said nothing. A huge shudder shook him.

"Who protects *you?*" she asked.

"What?"

"You are trying so hard to protect everyone, to save the world. Who protects you? Who saves you?"

He stared at her silently, as if he did not comprehend the question, or was afraid of the answer.

"I do," she said. She held out her hand.

He stared at it for a long time. She did not take his hand, or move hers. She waited. This step had to be his. And then, hesitantly, he put his hand in hers. And she drew him to her, and guided his head to her breast, and felt him give a great sigh against her.

"I do," she said again. "I do."

In the distance, she became aware of people calling out farewells to one another, the air full of Merry Christmases.

Car doors began to slam, engines to start.

For a while there were the sounds of things being put away downstairs. And then that, too, was gone.

Casey held Turner Kennedy, and was aware she would hold him for as long as it took. She guided him to the bed and he lay down, and then she lay down beside him and stroked his face.

"Not just for tonight," she whispered. "I'm going to wake up beside you tomorrow, and every Christmas after that for as long as we both shall live."

"You need to know who I really am before you say that."

"You think I don't know that?" she said, gently scoffing.

"I come with a lot of baggage," he warned her. "Unusual fears. I'm terrified of tears."

"You're a man that dogs love," she told him tenderly.

"And I have problems sleeping." But for a man who had problems sleeping his voice was growing husky, and he yawned deeply.

"Children love you, too," she said with deep satisfaction.

"I have a job that is hard on the people who love me."

"I'm sure your brothers and I will bond over that. But yes, if you want, we'll take it slowly."

"I think we should go serve dinner with your mother tomorrow night," he said.

"We could put that off for a bit."

"No, we couldn't."

She could feel all the tension draining from him.

"I think I owe you a few days at the Waldorf." His eyes were closed. The steady in-and-out of each breath was coming further apart. "Do you want to run away with me?"

"Yes," she said. "Yes, I do."

"Not for three days. Not this time, Casey. Do you want to run away with me forever?"

"Yes," she said, without a moment's hesitation. "Just be warned. The next time you get down on your knees in front of me?"

"Yeah?"

"It won't be to paint my toes or tighten my skates."

"All right," he said, his voice husky. "I consider myself warned."

And then he slept, and she slept, too. His sleep was dreamless, but a different dream began that night.

It was a dream realized, a dream of being safe. And loved. It was a dream of belonging. And it was a dream of coming home.

It was a dream all the more cherished for the fact that it had once been given up on, seen as unobtainable and dismissed as impossible.

That was what love did—made the cynic a believer, made the fearful brave. Made a man who had lost faith in everything embrace the possibility of miracles.

EPILOGUE

"UNCLE TURNER, THE fireworks are starting in two minutes. Come outside."

"Just a sec."

"No. *Now.*"

Turner dragged his eyes away from the book he was studying, and looked at Tessa. She was eight, as bossy as ever, and the unchallenged queen of a new set of Gingerbread Girls that included his own seven-year-old niece, Hailey.

"Hasn't your dad told you not to go into people's cabins without knocking?"

"The door was open," Tessa said. "And I'm not really *in.*" She waggled a foot at him to demonstrate it was outside the door. Hailey giggled approvingly.

It was the Fourth of July, and the Gingerbread Inn was full. He and Casey had rented one of the new cabins that Martin and Carol had added last year. They were quaint little log buildings facing Barrow's Lake, set back from the main inn. Turner had hoped for a bit of privacy so that he could study for a particularly tough exam.

He had left all the doors and windows open, not just for a pine-scented flow of air on the hot summer evening, but because he liked the background noises. The quiet lap of the lake water against the shore. The evening cries of birds. The snap and pop of a bonfire at the water's edge.

But the sounds were mostly the cries of lots of children. Carol had inherited a passel of grandchildren when she had married Martin. Emily and Cole's daughter was two. Turner's brothers and their wives, and his three nieces and nephews were here.

Next year, at this time, there would be a new baby. He and Casey had chosen not to find out if it was a girl or a boy, but to let life surprise them.

So far, life had surprised them a lot, and maybe especially him.

With its capacity to delight. With its opportunities for love.

That first Christmas he had spent with Casey had been a baptism by fire into the opportunities for love. They had joined his brother David at his brother Mitchell's place to watch the kids open gifts. And then they had gone to help Casey's mother serve dinner to the homeless.

After that was over, Turner had needed a rest. He'd booked a whole week in the presidential suite at the Waldorf.

And they'd done it all again.

Jumped on beds, and worn the white housecoats, and walked to museums and theaters, and eaten wonderful food.

Only this time there was no predeployment intensity in the air. And he'd still felt it: as if every single moment was infused with light.

He'd known the truth then.

Excitement was one kind of high.

And love was another. Quieter. Deeper. More lasting. All those years ago, he'd experienced the dropout punch of them both combined.

Of course, in time, as he wooed Casey in earnest, they had reached that place where he'd had to deploy.

And instead of feeling any of that intensity he usually

experienced, he had felt only the sadness of leaving her to deal with a great unknown all on her own. But Casey was the strongest woman he had ever met. And at least he had been working on becoming the man he had always wanted to be.

Because when she cried, he held her and dried her tears tenderly. He saw what an honor it was that a man like him, who had almost turned his back on this most precious of things—love—would be so trusted, so cared about.

It had been easy to make the decision that he had wrestled with for so long. It had been easy to say goodbye to one life, and open the door for a new one.

The easiest thing he had ever done was get down on one knee and ask Casey to walk with him down the winding road that was life.

Were there wounds that he would never quite recover from, no matter what was said about time?

Yes.

But Turner had come to know he had no corner on tragedy. Each of these people who came here, his friends who were closer than friends, his family of choice, had known tragedy. Or defeat of some kind.

Each of them: Cole, Emily, Andrea, Rick, Casey, his brothers, had been tested by life and had known some devastating loss. That was probably the thread that had drawn them together that Christmas when Emily and Cole had renewed their vows.

And yet, woven into the fabric of that loss, were threads of light. Those threads were courage. Compassion. Patience. Forgiveness. Against the fabric of darkness, those threads of light shone as if they were the only important things.

Turner had come to this inn, like those wise men who had followed a star to a stable. He had not been sure what he would find, and he had not even been sure what he was looking for.

What he had found was the miracle he had stopped believing in.

It wasn't a water-into-wine kind of miracle.

It was a quieter kind.

It was the ability to see that the human animal had an amazing resiliency of spirit. People could slog through loss and disillusionment and discouragement to come to this place.

A simple place, where they could pause and stand in the light.

They could come to these moments of pure and joyous life.

The Gingerbread Inn had been restored to being that place where everyone wanted to be with their families.

A place of simplicity in a complex world.

A place of serenity in lives that were full.

A place of utter safety in a world that could be dangerous and unpredictable.

In a few weeks, Turner would be finished with an accelerated program to get his master's degree in business.

He had taken a detour from the life he wanted, but he was not sure that, given the choice, he would change a thing.

Out of all the people here, he suspected he had a deeper sense of how precious all this was.

Of the miracle of peace.

Children's laughter floated in the warm night air. Above it all, he suddenly heard Casey's, which rang out like a kind of truth.

"Are you coming?" Tessa demanded.

He put away the books and stood up and stretched. At the door, Tessa took one hand and Hailey took the other, and they pulled him eagerly to where a fire burned brightly on the shore of the lake.

In the distance, he could see Martin preparing the fireworks that he would shoot off over the black, still waters.

Turner moved toward the sound of Casey's laughter, with the eagerness of a warrior who had been allowed to lay down his sword, who needed to fight no more.

He headed toward the sound with the heart of a man who had lost his way, and then found it.

As if she knew he was coming, Casey turned and searched the darkness until she saw him.

He headed toward the welcoming light in her eyes with the firm and utterly fearless step of a man who knew his way home.

* * * * *

SWEET SILVER BELLS

ROCHELLE ALERS

Honour the Lord with your wealth, with the first
fruits of all your crops.

—Proverbs 3:9

Prologue

Reunion

"Attention, passengers," the pilot's voice echoed throughout the jet cabin, "this flight to Miami will terminate at Palm Beach International due to a security breach at our scheduled airport. All passengers will be rescheduled to other flights once flights are allowed to land and depart from Miami."

The jet landed smoothly and Crystal Eaton and her baby daughter, Merry, made it into the terminal to find people standing around staring at the electronic boards. All flights to Miami were delayed indefinitely.

"Oh no," she whispered under her breath. That meant she didn't know when she would get home. Sitting and balancing Merry on her lap, she retrieved her cell phone. "Mother, I'm at the Palm Beach Airport. All flights going into Miami are delayed."

"I know, darling. I just heard the news report."

"I'm going to rent a car and drive down. I'll call you again when I get into the city."

"How's Merry?"

Crystal smiled for the first time in hours. "She's a real trouper. She hasn't cried or fussed the whole time."

"Drive carefully, Crystal. Please don't make me worry about you and my grandbaby, too."

"I will." It wasn't until she walked in the direction for car rentals that her mother's plea resonated with her. She professed to worry about her daughter and granddaughter but also about her ex-husband, who'd been admitted to the hospital with chest pains. Several arteries had been found clogged, necessitating immediate heart surgery.

There were long lines at the rental car counters and Crystal set the car seat on the floor. She wanted to put Merry down but decided against it. Her daughter had just taken her first steps several days ago and she didn't trust her not to fall and hurt herself on the marble floor.

The line moved slowly and Crystal wondered if taking a taxi would be a better choice.

She'd just moved out of the line when she went completely still. Walking into the terminal was the man she'd never expected to see again. She turned around, but it was too late.

He'd recognized her.

Closing her eyes, she whispered a silent prayer that he wouldn't make a scene. A shiver snaked its way up her back as his moist breath swept over the nape of her neck.

"You're a liar!" His accusation lashed at her like the stinging bite of a whip.

Crystal turned slowly to face the man who still had the power to make her heart beat a little too fast for her to breathe normally.

She watched Joseph as he stared at her little girl. Even if Crysal hadn't changed, he had. His face was leaner, his cropped hair grayer, and she detected new tiny lines around his large, deep-set, intense eyes. It was as if there was no more boyishness left in Joseph Cole-Wilson.

"I didn't lie to you," she countered.

Grasping her upper arm, Joseph steered her away from the crowd to a spot where they couldn't be overheard. "I asked you to let me know if you were pregnant, and you said you weren't."

When she tried extricating her arm, he tightened his grip. "I'm not going to stand here and debate with you. I have to get to Miami. My father had a heart attack and—"

"I'll take you to Miami," he volunteered, cutting her off.

Crystal shook her head. "That won't be necessary. I'm taking a taxi."

Joseph pushed his face within inches of hers. "Please don't

fight with me, Crystal. As soon as I call someone I'll take you." Reaching for his cell phone, he punched in a number. "Diego, I need Henri to come to the airport to pick up Zach. His flight is due in at any moment. I'm going to call and tell him. Thanks." He tapped another number. "Hey, bro. I'm not going to be able to pick you up, but I have someone coming from ColeDiz who'll meet you. I have a family emergency, but I'll be in touch."

Even though Crystal only heard one side of Joseph's conversation, she knew it was futile to argue with him. He'd said that he had a family emergency. Well, he was wrong. Raleigh was her and Merry's family, not his. He might have fathered her daughter, but legally he had no claim to her.

Joseph extended his arms. "I'll carry her." Crystal reluctantly let him take Merry.

The little girl reached out and patted Joseph's clean-shaven jaw. "Dada," she crooned, laughing and exhibiting a mouth filled with tiny white teeth as Joseph buried his face in her black curly hair.

"Yes, princess. I am Daddy."

Crystal closed her eyes. Merry had a vocabulary of about twenty words, and Dada had been the first one; Crystal hadn't exposed her daughter to many men, yet Merry hadn't called any of them Dada.

Crystal followed Joseph out of the terminal to the parking lot, strangely relieved that she didn't have to go through the ordeal alone.

Joseph set the car seat on the second row of seats in the Range Rover, then placed Merry in it and secured the harness while Crystal got in beside her. She was exhausted. Not physically but emotionally. She stared at the back of Joseph's head when he got in behind the wheel and maneuvered out of the parking lot.

Joseph slipped on a pair of sunglasses as he followed the signs for the airport exit. Glancing in the rearview mirror, he noticed Crystal had closed her eyes. "What's her name?"

"Meredith, but I call her Merry."

"How old is she?"

"She turned one October tenth."

He smiled. "An October baby like her mother."

Although he wanted and needed answers, Joseph decided to wait. Crystal's father's health crisis was a lot more pressing than uncovering why she had decided to conceal the fact that he'd fathered a child. Fate had intervened, bringing them together, and he had no intention of letting Crystal walk out of his life again.

Chapter 1

Destiny

Crystal Eaton took a quick glance at the navigation screen on the Ford Escape. She was thirty-three miles from Charleston, South Carolina, less than half an hour from her destination, and if she hadn't had to drive down to Miami earlier that morning, she would've arrived much sooner. As she unclenched her teeth, the lines of tension bracketing her mouth vanished.

Her mother had called crying hysterically as soon as Crystal had maneuvered out of the parking garage at her Fort Lauderdale condo. She hadn't been able to understand a word her mother was saying, and in a panic she'd driven south instead of north.

It wasn't the first time in her life Crystal wished she hadn't been an only child. If Jasmine Eaton hadn't been able to reach her, then she would have been forced to contact her son and/or other daughter whenever she had an emotional meltdown.

If it had been a medical emergency, Crystal would have postponed her plan to meet with the owner of several luxury hotels, but she then discovered the cause of her mother's latest hissy fit. Jasmine's current boyfriend had refused to take her with him on a business trip to Las Vegas, leading Jasmine to accuse him of cheating on her.

Biting her tongue and instead of telling Jasmine she was too old for adolescent histrionics, Crystal smiled, issuing her usual mantra, "Mother, this, too, shall pass."

This was followed by another crying jag until Crystal reminded her mother that her eyes were swollen and her cheeks blotchy.

It was as if someone had flipped a switch when Jasmine raced to her bathroom to examine her face, declaring no man was worth sacrificing her beauty.

Crystal knew her own reluctance to marry was because of her parents' inability to form lasting relationships. Her fifty-four-year-old father had been married four times and her mother, only a year younger than her ex-husband, had had so many dates with a steady parade of men coming and going that Crystal stopped counting.

However, Jasmine was quick to inform anyone who labeled her a serial dater that she was very discriminating when it came to sleeping with a man. Jasmine's gratification came from being seen on the arm of a handsome gentleman, not sleeping with him.

Crystal's cell rang and she glanced at the number on the dashboard. Activating the Bluetooth feature, she said, "Hey, Xavier."

"Where are you, Criss?"

"I'm about forty minutes outside the city."

"Selena and I expected you hours ago."

She'd promised her cousin she would stop and spend some time with him, his wife and their toddler daughter. "I would've been here sooner if I didn't have to drive to Miami and check on my mother. She just broke up with her latest male *friend,* and that always sends her into drama mode. I believe she liked this one more than she's willing to admit."

"Isn't she a bit too old to have tantrums?" Xavier asked, chuckling softly.

Crystal rolled her eyes, although her cousin couldn't see her. "Please, Xavier, don't get me started. My mother should've become an actress instead of an art dealer."

Xavier laughed again. "Your mother is drama personified."

Crystal frowned. "I don't know why I mentioned her, because talking about my mother's antics always gives me a headache. It's too late to stop by tonight," she said, deftly changing the topic of conversation, "so I'm going directly to the hotel. I have meetings tomorrow and Friday, but I'm free this weekend."

"Why don't you come spend at least Saturday or Sunday with us?"

"That sounds wonderful. I'll call to let you know when I'll be there. See you soon."

"We'll be here," Xavier said.

Tapping a button on the steering wheel, Crystal ended the call. Crystal smiled for the first time in hours. She was about to embark on a project she'd dreamt about since decorating her first dollhouse. But this project wasn't about dollhouses but two historic landmark buildings the owner planned to turn into an inn and a bed-and-breakfast.

The original owners of the three-story, early-nineteenth-century structures had used them as their secondary residences whenever they relocated their families from the cotton, rice and indigo plantations built along the creeks and marshes in order to escape the swamp fevers so prevalent at the time during the intense summer heat.

She knew she'd taken a big step when she left her position with a prestigious Fort Lauderdale architectural and design firm to set up her own company—Eaton Interior and Design. She'd come to the realization she'd been overworked, overlooked for promotions, underpaid for her expertise, all the while being subtly sexually harassed by one of the partners. Rather than initiate a lawsuit against him and the firm, she'd decided it was time to leave.

Despite Jasmine's occasional histrionics, Crystal had to thank her mother for giving her the encouragement she needed to strike out on her own. Jasmine might have been impetuous when it came to her relationships, but she was the complete opposite when buying and selling art. Jasmine revealed that she, too, was thirty when she'd sold her first painting, so it would stand to reason that her daughter would start up her own company at thirty.

Two years later Jasmine opened a thriving and exclusive art gallery in an upscale Miami neighborhood with a growing clientele that included celebrities who wanted to decorate the walls of their sprawling mansions with works of art.

Crystal didn't have a shop—not yet—but she did have recommendations from several of her father's clients and one from her mother. Not once had she harbored any guilt about using her parents' name to further her career. It was the least they could do for emotionally abandoning her as a child. She'd found herself competing with her father's wives for his attention, while her mother had never recovered from losing her husband, the man she considered the love of her life.

Crystal spent more time at her cousins' house than she did her own. Levi, Jesse and Carson Eaton were more than cousins. They had become her surrogate brothers.

The lights of downtown Charleston came into view as she listened to the automated voice issuing directions, driving through cobblestone streets lined on both sides with elegant homes still festooned in Christmas lights and decorations. It was the second week in January and it was as if the residents were reluctant to let go of the holiday.

Maneuvering up to the hotel's entrance, she slowed, coming to a complete stop in front of a valet wearing a white shirt, red bow tie, black vest and slacks.

"How long are you staying, ma'am?"

"I'll be here for a couple of months."

"Are you Ms. Eaton?" the young man asked.

She nodded. "Yes, I am."

The valet opened the driver's-side door. "I'll park your truck and have someone bring in your luggage." Reaching into the back pocket of his slacks, he removed a walkie-talkie. "I need a bellhop out front."

Crystal reached for her handbag and the tote with her laptop and then slipped from behind the wheel. She managed to smother a moan. Her legs were stiff and her shoulders ached. She'd driven nearly six hundred miles, stopping in St. Augustine to refuel and order a fruit salad. The entire drive had taken her nearly twelve hours.

What she wanted now was a leisurely bath before climbing into bed to sleep undisturbed throughout the night.

She made her way into the lobby and over to the desk to

check in, admiring its sophisticated opulence. Marble flooring, several glittering chandeliers and a massive glass-topped table in the center of the lobby cradled an enormous hand-painted ceramic vase filled with fresh flowers. Queen Anne chairs were positioned at round pedestal tables for guests to sit and relax.

A woman with flawless brown skin, neatly braided hair and an infectious smile greeted Crystal as she approached the front desk. "Welcome to the Beaumont House. How may I help you?"

"I'm Crystal Eaton," she said, "and—"

"Oh, Ms. Eaton, we've been expecting you," the woman said. "Your accommodations will be handled by concierge." She picked up the telephone, speaking quietly into the mouthpiece.

In less than a minute, a tall man in a black tailored suit approached the desk. There was something about his bearing that reminded Crystal of her father. Raleigh Eaton's good looks, refinement, charm, and legal and financial acumen had made him a very wealthy man *and* a magnet for women regardless of their age.

Two years ago he'd divorced his fourth wife, and his current fiancée was thirty-five, only five years older than Crystal. Wherein Raleigh might have been unable to maintain a successful marriage of any duration, he wasn't so reckless as not to have had his prospective wives sign a prenuptial agreement. The exception had been his first wife. The alimony payments deposited directly into Jasmine's bank account like clockwork afforded the mother of his only child, coupled with her successful art business, a very comfortable lifestyle.

The concierge extended his hand, while offering Crystal a friendly smile. He lowered his gaze rather than let her see the admiration in his gaze. Crystal Eaton was stunning. Her pixie-cut hairstyle, unblemished face, the color of polished mahogany, radiated good health, and her dark brown wide-set slanting eyes, pert nose and full, sensual mouth were enthralling.

The perfection of her body matched her face: tall, slender and curvy in a pair of fitted black jeans, matching pullover sweater and leather flats.

"Welcome, Ms. Eaton. I'm John Porter, your personal concierge. Mr. Beaumont has asked me to take care of all of your needs during your stay."

Crystal took his hand, finding it as soft as her own.

"Thank you so much, Mr. Porter."

John reluctantly withdrew his hand. "Mr. Beaumont has arranged for you to stay in the penthouse. You will have the privilege of twenty-four-hour room service that includes laundry, dry-cleaning, housekeeping and meals." He angled his head, smiling. "All of which are gratis. The penthouse staff is aware they're not to accept tips from *you*. Don't look so alarmed, Ms. Eaton," he said when Crystal's gave him a stunned look, her delicate jaw dropping. "They are compensated far beyond what the other employees earn," he added when her mouth closed.

She forced a smile she didn't feel at that moment. "That's good, because I wouldn't want to take advantage of their services."

John cupped her elbow, directing her to the bank of elevators, and stopped in front of one with a sign indicating floors 8-PH. "Mr. Beaumont treats all of his employees quite well. I'm going to give you two room card keys. The red one will permit you elevator access to your floor and the green to your apartment."

He handed her an envelope with her name, punched the button and waited for the doors to open. Crystal walked into the car. He entered behind her and, reaching into the pocket of his suit jacket, removed a master key and inserted it into the PH slot. The doors closed, and the car rose silently.

When she agreed to the terms in the contract between Beaumont Hotels and Eaton Interior and Design in which the owner of the hotel chain would provide lodging for the duration of the project, Crystal had expected to occupy a suite, not a penthouse apartment. She knew Algernon Beaumont was anxious for her to decorate the two boutique hotels before spring and the influx of tourists to the Lowcountry, and because she wasn't married, didn't have a fiancé, boyfriend or children, Crystal was able to accept the commission that would take her away from home for weeks at a time.

The elevator doors opened and she stepped out into a carpeted hallway.

John remained in the elevator. "You're in penthouse two, which is on the left," he informed Crystal. "The bellhop will bring up your luggage. If you need anything, please dial fifteen and either I or someone from my staff will procure it for you."

Crystal smiled at the very formal man. "Thank you. I doubt if I'll need anything tonight." All she wanted was a bath and a bed. Anything she did need would wait until the next day.

John nodded. "Good night, Ms. Eaton."

"Good night, Mr. Porter."

She walked the short distance to the door labeled PH 2, opening the envelope and taking out one of the card keys.

Crystal's hand halted as she caught movement out the corner of her eye. She stole a glance at a tall, slender man dressed in a pair of cutoffs, a T-shirt and flip-flops closing the door to the other apartment as he walked toward the elevator. The contrast of the white shirt against his olive complexion was attention-grabbing. He was like a bronze statue come to life.

After several seconds Crystal realized she was staring when their eyes met and held. Even from the distance she noticed the perfection of his features.

"Good evening, neighbor," he said.

She went completely still as a shiver of awareness swept over her body. The man's voice was deep and as utterly sensual as he appeared to be. "Good evening," Crystal replied, smiling.

"Are you checking in?" She nodded. Closing the distance between them, he extended his hand. "Joseph Cole-Wilson."

Shifting the card key to her left hand, she took the large, groomed hand with long, slender fingers. "I'm Crystal."

"It's nice meeting you, Crystal."

Nodding, she withdrew her hand from his loose grip. "Are you Joseph or Joe?"

He smiled, drawing Crystal's gaze to his sensual mouth and the slight cleft in his strong chin. "I've always been Joseph. I'm not going to hold you up settling in, but I just want you to know I'll be next door if you need anything."

Crystal wanted to tell Joseph that if she *did* need anything, all she had to do was pick up the telephone and dial two digits. She didn't know if Mr. Drop-Dead Sexy was attempting to come on to her, but at present his mojo definitely wasn't working. She was much too tired to carry on an exchange of witty repartee with him, and the reason she was in Charleston took precedence over any- and everything in her life.

"Thanks, Joseph. I'm sorry, but I have to get some sleep or I'm going to fall on my face."

Joseph's eyebrows lifted a fraction. Light from a wall sconce illuminated the face of the tall, slender woman with the killer body. Only those in his family knew his legal name: José Ibrahim Cole-Wilson. His mother had always called him Joseph, so the name stuck.

Crystal put up her hand to smother a yawn, and it was then he noticed her exhaustion.

"I'm sorry to hold you up. Have a good evening." That said, he turned and walked to the elevator.

Crystal stared at him until he disappeared into the car. Then she inserted the card key into the slot, waited for the green light and pushed open the door.

If the furnishings in the lobby reflected a bygone era, it was the same in the penthouse. The chairs, tables, lamps, wall mirrors in the living and dining rooms were uniquely art deco, one of her favorite decorating styles.

Dropping her handbag and tote on an oversize ottoman, she walked into a modern, state-of-the-art kitchen with double stainless steel sinks, cooktop stove, double oven, eye-level microwave, dishwasher, French-door refrigerator/freezer, trash compactor and cooking island. There was also a fully stocked wine cellar with three dozen bottles.

Crystal opened the refrigerator stocked with dairy products, the vegetable drawers with fresh fruit and salad fixings. The freezer was also filled with packaged and labeled meat. The shelves in the pantry were stocked with everything she would need for breakfast, lunch and dinner. A door off the kitchen revealed a half bath.

She continued her tour, mounting a flight of stairs, discovering two bedroom suites with adjoining baths. Each bedroom was constructed with sitting and dressing areas. Wall-to-wall silk drapes were open to offer an unobstructed view of night-time Charleston and a lit rooftop deck.

She returned to the first floor at the same time the bell chimed throughout the apartment. She opened the door and the bellhop carried her bags up the staircase, leaving them in the hallway outside the bedrooms. He returned, gave her a slight bow and then left, closing the door behind him.

Crystal turned off all the lights on the first floor with the exception of the table lamp in the entryway. Her footsteps were slow as she climbed the staircase for the second time, wondering if she would remain awake long enough to take a shower.

After a hot shower, she crawled into bed, pulling the sheet and comforter up to her neck.

She hadn't drawn the drapes. Daylight coming in through the windows would become her alarm clock. Eight hours of sleep would give her everything she needed to face the day and the most comprehensive commission of Eaton Interior and Design thus far.

Chapter 2

Joseph lost count of the number of times he swam the length of the Olympic-size swimming pool on the lower level of the Beaumont House. He'd also stopped cursing his cousin for banishing him to South Carolina to start up ColeDiz Tea Company, ColeDiz International Ltd.'s first U.S. mainland venture since their great-grandfather established the company ninety years ago. He was solely responsible for the oversight of the ongoing operation of the tea garden, as well.

This wasn't his first trip to the Lowcountry. Two years ago, Joseph had met with Harry Ellis to survey one hundred acres of land between Kiawah and Edisto Islands the real estate agent had purchased on behalf of the Cole-family-owned conglomerate. Not only had Harry bought the land, but five years earlier he'd also brokered a deal with a Ugandan cotton grower for Diego, making ColeDiz the biggest family-owned agribusiness in the United States.

Subsequently an engineering company had drained the swampy area to prepare it for growing and processing tea leaves, all the while Joseph insisting they not upset the ecological balance of region's indigenous wildlife.

He'd argued with his cousin that he was a lawyer, not a farmer, but Diego was quick to remind him that he also wasn't a farmer, yet had familiarized himself with the entire process of growing and harvesting coffee, bananas and cotton. Joseph had been under the impression that tea wasn't grown in the States, but Diego told him about the tea garden on Wadmalaw Island, South Carolina. Once ColeDiz Tea Company harvested their first yield, there would be not one, but two tea gardens in the United States.

It'd taken him a while, but he had adjusted to spending the last two years of his life in Belize, Mexico, Jamaica, Puerto Rico and Brazil, educating himself with the cycle of planting, cultivation, harvesting and processing coffee and bananas in order to learn everything he could about the different varieties.

It hadn't been only about planting trees, but also soil quality, insect control and irrigation. He had logged thousands of hours in the air, crossed various time zones and grown accustomed to sleeping in strange beds and ordering room service. Several of his college buddies and fraternity brothers claimed they envied his jet-setting lifestyle, but Joseph had been quick to remind them it was work and not fun.

However, he did take time off to have some fun when he stayed with his landscape-architect cousin Regina Spencer in Bahia, Brazil. Regina and her pediatrician husband hadn't been to Carnival in years, yet had offered to accompany him. Joseph witnessed firsthand the once-in-a-lifetime frivolity. Partying nonstop for three days offset the months, weeks, days and hours he spent learning to become a farmer.

Now he was back in Charleston to oversee the first planting of ColeDiz Tea Company's tea garden. He'd grown fond of the incredibly beautiful historic port city and its friendly populace. He returned not as an attorney but as a farmer and an astute businessman. Although assigned to the legal department, he'd been groomed to eventually take over as CEO when Diego retired. His cousin failed to realize that Joseph preferred the legal component to running a company. Whether it was negotiating contracts or spending hours researching and interpreting international tariffs, law had become his jealous mistress.

He didn't want to think about jealous mistresses or past relationships. His four-year liaison with Kiara Solis had run its course the third day into a two-week Hawaiian vacation when he'd tried to make the best of what had become a highly volatile situation.

Kiara had been under the impression they were going on a romantic holiday where he would propose, although he'd told her repeatedly he hadn't been ready for marriage. At twenty-eight his life wasn't stable. He'd just resigned his position clerking for a Florida appellate judge to join ColeDiz. He had also purchased land in Palm Beach with plans to build a home, but even that had been placed on hold until after he curtailed traveling.

Joseph's father had lectured him about dating a woman for more than two years without committing to a future together. His father failed to understand that although he loved Kiara he hadn't been in love with her. If he had, there was no doubt he would've married her.

Joseph swam the length of the pool, then pulled himself up at the shallow end. He was breathing heavily, his chest rising and falling from the exertion. Picking up a towel from the stack on a wooden bench, he dried off before pulling on his shorts and T-shirt. Swimming was the perfect alternative to sitting up watching late-night infomercials.

Joseph walked to the bank of elevators. Living in the penthouse wasn't a perk but a requisite befitting his lifestyle. He'd grown up privileged, and having the best life had to offer was something for which he never apologized. As a Cole and a member of the purportedly wealthiest African-American family in the country, he accepted everything that went along with the distinction.

Kiara had called him a "spoiled rich boy" and a few other epithets that he would never repeat to anyone, and it was her vicious and spiteful outburst that reminded him why he'd been reluctant to ask her to marry him. It hadn't been the first time Kiara had gone off on him when she couldn't get her way, but it was the last time Joseph decided to turn the other cheek. Although laid-back and easygoing, he wasn't a masochist.

He was certain his parents had had their disagreements, yet he couldn't remember a time he was privy to them. Joseph shook his head as he stepped out of the elevator car, and walked to his apartment, unlocking the door. He vowed to remain single until he met the woman with whom he felt he wanted to spend his life. After all, he was only thirty and in no immediate hurry to settle down and start a family.

Climbing the staircase to the second level, he stripped off

his clothes, leaving them in a hamper, and then stepped into the shower. By the time Joseph got into bed, he had mentally prepared himself to oversee the project he'd been entrusted with. Despite his initial objection to setting up a tea garden, he knew failure was not an option.

Crystal woke rested and clearheaded. Her appointment with Algernon was scheduled for nine in the hotel restaurant; he'd informed her they would meet with the contractor in downtown Charleston to inspect the interiors of the recently restored properties.

When she first came to see the abandoned buildings, she'd found herself hard-pressed to contain her excitement. Despite the faded, peeling wallpaper, warped floors, weakened window sashes and the pervasive odor of mold, she was able to imagine the beauty and elegance of the renovated spaces. Algernon, or Al, as he insisted she call him, wanted the interior to replicate the furnishings of 1800s Lowcountry city residences.

After brewing a cup of coffee, she unpacked, putting everything away, then stepped into the Jacuzzi for a leisurely soak. The hands on the clock on the bathroom's vanity had inched closer to eight-fifteen when she stepped out of the tub. At eight forty-five she entered the restaurant off the hotel lobby, the hostess greeting her with a friendly smile.

"Good morning, ma'am. Are you a guest?"

Crystal nodded. "Yes, I am."

"What is your room number?"

"I'm in penthouse two."

The hostess punched several keys on a computer. "Ms. Eaton?"

"Yes," she confirmed. "I have an appointment to meet Mr. Beaumont here at nine."

"Ms. Eaton, I don't know if anyone told you, but as an elite guest you'll take your meals in the private dining room. Mr. Beaumont will meet you there." The young woman motioned to a passing waiter. "Patrick, please escort Ms. Eaton to Mr. Beaumont's table."

Crystal followed the waiter to the rear of the restaurant and to a door with a plaque reading Elite Hotel Guests Only. The space was half the size of the restaurant for other hotel guests and the general public, and furnished in the manner of a formal dining room with cloth-covered tables and place settings of china, silver and crystal. Classical music flowed from hidden speakers as waitstaff moved silently, efficiently picking up and setting down dishes.

She thanked the waiter when he pulled out a chair at a table in an alcove, seating her at the same time her cell phone chimed softly. Reaching into her handbag, Crystal retrieved the phone and glanced at the display. It was Algernon. Tapping in her pass code, she answered the call.

"Good morning, Al."

"Crystal. I'm glad I reached you. I rang your room, but it went directly to voice mail. I'm on my way to the airport to catch a flight to Vancouver. My daughter was injured on a movie set, and even though I'm told it isn't serious, I need to see her. I'm not certain when I'll be back, but I'll keep you updated. I'm sorry you had to come and—"

"Please don't apologize," Crystal said, interrupting him. "Take care of your daughter and don't worry about me. I'll be here when you get back. The last time I was in Charleston I didn't get to do much sightseeing, so I intend to tour the city until you return."

"Thanks, Crystal, for being so understanding."

"Have a safe flight and I'll see you when you get back."

She ended the call, exhaling an audible sigh. Although anxious to see the restored buildings, Crystal also understood an unexpected personal predicament. And taking care of your family always took precedence over everything. There were Eatons living in different parts of the country, but whenever there was a significant occasion, they all came together as one whether it in sickness, tragedy, marriage or a new birth.

She'd attended so many weddings over the years Crystal needed a scorecard to document which first cousin had married whom. It began with Belinda marrying her brother-in-law sports attorney/agent, Griffin Rice. Belinda and Griffin had become guardians of their twin nieces after the death of their parents, who were Belinda's sister and Griffin's brother. Belinda made Griffin a biological father for the first time after giving birth to a baby boy.

The marriage bug then bit Belinda's brother, Myles, when he married his ex-fiancée after a ten-year separation. Myles hadn't known Zabrina was pregnant with his son, because she'd been blackmailed into marrying another man. They added to another generation of Eatons with a daughter.

Myles and Belinda's sister Chandra married celebrated playwright Preston Tucker, and they were now the parents of a daughter, and Xavier and his wife, Selena, also had a daughter. All the Eatons were wagering whether Denise and Mia and their husbands would have boys once they decided to increase their family, because it looked as if girls were outnumbering boys in the latest generation of Eatons.

Crystal still did not picture herself a wife or a mother. The closest she'd come to a committed relationship was when she lived with a man after enrolling in graduate school. Her parents disapproved of her living or *shacking up* with a man, because they claimed they'd raised her better than that.

Jasmine lamented, why would the man want to buy the cow when he could get the milk free? Her comeback was that she didn't want to be bought, because her goals did not include becoming a wife.

Her relationship with Brian worked well; he also didn't want to marry or father children. As a child he'd been physically abused by his parents, spent years in foster care and feared he would turn out like them. He and Crystal had lived together for three years before Brian was offered a teaching position at a Los Angeles college. Crystal encouraged him to accept the position, and after graduating she gave up their miniscule New York City Greenwich Village studio apartment and moved back to Florida.

She lived with her mother until she secured employment with a Miami-based design firm. Once she transferred to their

Fort Lauderdale office, she purchased a two-bedroom condo in a gated community.

Living alone was a wake-up call that she was in complete control of her life and future.

She beckoned a waiter as he finished filling a water goblet at a nearby table. "Is it possible for me to change tables? Mr. Beaumont won't be joining me." Crystal didn't want to sit in the grotto-inspired alcove alone.

The waiter glanced around the room. "There's an empty table near the window."

Crystal nodded. "I'll take it."

It wasn't until she was seated near a wall of glass that she saw her penthouse neighbor. Joseph sat at a table several feet away. Their eyes met and she returned his open, friendly smile with one of her own.

"Good morning, neighbor," Joseph said in greeting.

Her smile grew wider. "Same to you, neighbor."

"Did you sleep well?" he asked.

"Yes, I did. Thank you for asking."

Joseph stared boldly at the woman, who'd exchanged her jeans and sweater for a navy blue pantsuit and white silk blouse. A light covering of makeup enhanced her best features: eyes and mouth. His gaze lingered on Crystal's flawless dark complexion. He took a quick glance at her hands. She wasn't wearing a ring, but that still didn't mean she wasn't married or involved with someone.

His interest in the woman occupying the neighboring penthouse was a reminder of how, for the past two years, his life had not been his own to control. He hadn't found time to embark on another relationship since his breakup with Kiara, but now that he was stateside his days and nights were more predictable.

"Are you expecting someone?" he asked Crystal.

"No, I'm not. Why?"

"I see several people waiting for tables, and if we sit together, it would free up one for them."

Crystal's gaze shifted from Joseph's deeply tanned face to the couples standing at the entrance. She was seated at a table for two while he sat at a table seating four. "You may sit with me."

As he moved over to sit opposite her, Crystal inhaled the subtle scent of his masculine cologne. It was if she were seeing Joseph for the first time. Last night she hadn't realized he was so tall. She was five-nine in her bare feet, and estimated he had to be at least three or even four inches above the six-foot mark. He was casually dressed in relaxed jeans, black Timberland boots and a white button-down shirt, opened at the collar under a navy blue blazer.

The hint of a smile softened her mouth. "I see you're Greek."

Attractive lines fanned out around his large dark eyes when he smiled. "Alpha Phi Alpha," he said proudly, glancing at his belt buckle with the Greek alphabet. "Are you also Greek?"

Crystal nodded slowly. "Alpha Kappa Alpha."

Joseph smile grew wider. "Well, Miss AKA, where did you go to school?"

"Howard. And you?"

"Cornell."

Her eyebrows lifted. "So you're an Ivy Leaguer. I'm impressed." It wasn't often she met many African-American men who'd attended Ivy League colleges. Most she knew had enrolled in historically black colleges. "Are you active?" she asked Joseph.

He flashed a set of straight white teeth. "Active *and* financial." Since his return to the States, Joseph had rejoined his local chapter. He planned to drive to West Palm Beach one weekend each month to attend chapter meetings.

Crystal glanced at a spot over Joseph's broad shoulder. She didn't want him to think her rude for staring. Despite the stubble on his lean jaw, there was something about his features that made Joseph almost too pretty to be a man. "I'm financial but inactive. Unfortunately," she admitted, "I don't have the time to attend my chapter meetings."

"Where is your chapter?"

"Miami."

Leaning back in his chair, he crossed his arms over his chest. "So you're a Gator."

Crystal wasn't able to discern from Joseph's expression whether he was being derisive or complimentary. "Is there something wrong with being a Gator?" she asked defensively.

"Hell no, because you're looking at a fellow Gator. Palm Beach," he said before she could ask.

She laughed softly. "It looks as if we're truly neighbors in every sense of the word." Crystal paused, and then asked, "What are you doing in Charleston?"

Joseph picked up the menu, studying the selections rather than looking at Crystal. He'd never been one to engage in what he deemed inane repartee in order to glean information from a woman, yet that was exactly what he was doing with Crystal.

"I'm here on business."

"So am I," Crystal concurred.

He glanced up, meeting her direct stare. "It appears we have a lot in common. We're both Greek, Floridians and we're in Charleston on business."

"That's three for three."

Joseph angled his head. "What about your marital status?"

"What about it?" she asked, answering his question with one of her own.

"Are you single?"

"I'm single *and* unencumbered."

A beat passed. "Is that the same as not having any children?" Joseph asked

"It is."

He went completely still. "That's four for four."

"What else do you want to know about me, Joseph?"

There was another pause before he asked, "How long do you plan to be here on business?"

"I estimate a couple of months."

The slow smile that spread over his features did not reach his eyes. Joseph thought about the odds of meeting a woman, an incredibly beautiful woman who was staying in the same hotel as his, on the same floor and with whom he shared much in common. If he'd signed up with an online dating service, Crystal would've been the perfect candidate. He wasn't looking for a relationship, but friendship––something he hadn't had in a while.

And for him it had never been about how many women he could sleep with, because there had been more than he could count or remember who were more than willing to become his dessert after he'd taken them to dinner. He didn't know why, but Joseph always thought about his sister and the lengths he would go to if some man sought to take advantage of her. His mantra of protect a woman as if she were your sister was never that far from his mind, and he knew that was why he'd continued to stay in his past relationship longer than necessary.

"Five for five," Joseph drawled. He'd planned to live at the hotel for the next four months; the tea garden's manager who was overseeing wanted to return to Nebraska with his wife, where she would give birth to their first child.

Crystal smiled as she glanced at the menu. It appeared as if she had more in common with Joseph than she'd had with Brian. The man with whom she'd lived eschewed fraternities and sororities, claiming they were socialized cults. The subject always started an argument where they wouldn't speak for days. It wasn't their only disagreement, but it was one subject she refused to allow him to vilify. Her mother had been an AKA and her mother before her.

Her stomach rumbled loudly and she hoped Joseph hadn't heard it. She motioned to a waitress standing several feet away. "I'm ready to order now. I'll have grits with soft scrambled eggs and one slice of buttered wheat toast."

The waitress scribbled on her pad. "Would you like coffee, tea or juice, ma'am?"

Crystal closed the binder. "I'd like green tea and grapefruit juice." Joseph had just given the woman his order when an ear-shattering piercing sound reverberated throughout the room.

The waitress slipped her pad into the pocket of her apron. "I'm sorry, but you're going to have to leave the hotel. That's the fire alarm."

As if on cue, everyone began filing out, Joseph reaching for

Crystal's free hand as she gripped her handbag with the other. Hotel personnel were escorting guests down the staircases, because the elevators were shut down, through the lobby and out to the parking lot. The wail of sirens in the distance came closer and closer. Members of the police and fire departments were now on the scene, urging everyone to leave the parking lot and move across the street.

Joseph tucked Crystal's hand into the bend of his elbow as they followed the crowd away from the building. An elderly woman complained loudly that someone on her floor had been smoking in their room and she thought it shameful they'd ignore the hotel's smoke-free policy.

"It looks as if we're going to have to forgo breakfast," Joseph said softly, leaning closer to Crystal.

Her stomach rumbled again at the mention of breakfast. "Maybe you can, but I have to get something to eat. The last time I had solid food was more than eighteen hours ago."

He went completely still, his eyes meeting hers. "Do you have an eating disorder?"

Chapter 3

It took several seconds for Crystal to process what Joseph had just asked her. She wasn't underweight and she definitely didn't look emaciated, either. "No!" she said. "I didn't get a chance to eat yesterday. I drove up from Miami and I wanted to get here before nightfall," she explained when he continued to stare at her. "And there's nothing anorexic-looking about me."

Joseph blinked slowly before a slow smile spread over his features. His gaze moved over her body. "No, there isn't." He sobered quickly. "I know of a small restaurant not far from here."

Crystal wasn't immune to the hungry look in his eyes, and wondered if Joseph knew how much his eyes mirrored what he was feeling. It was apparent he hadn't learned to hide his emotions behind a facade of indifference. "How far is not far?" she asked.

"It's about ten blocks. If we start out now, maybe we can get there before it gets too crowded."

Crystal eased her hand from his loose grip, reaching into her handbag for her phone. She had no intention of walking ten blocks in four-inch heels. "I have a cousin who lives downtown and I'm going to call him and let him know to expect us."

Joseph narrowed his eyes. "Are you certain he's not going to be put out with bringing a stranger into his home?"

"He's not going to be put out. We *Eatons* have an opendoor policy when it comes to family." She'd proudly stressed her family's name.

His smooth brow furrowed when she mentioned the name Eaton. "Are you related to Judge Solomon Eaton?"

"You've heard of him?" Crystal asked.

"Are you kidding?" Joseph couldn't keep the excitement out

of his voice. "I clerked for him for a year before joining my family's business."

Crystal couldn't stop her hand from shaking as a shiver of unease eddied up her back, making her more than apprehensive. She did not want to believe she was indirectly connected to a man she'd met less than twenty-four hours ago. "You're a lawyer." The query was a statement of fact.

He nodded. "Yes."

"And you're certain it was my uncle you clerked for?"

"Yes," Joseph said emphatically. "We happen to be fraternity brothers."

She ran a hand over her short hair. Her uncle had pledged Alpha Phi as a Howard University undergraduate. "This is much too weird. If I didn't know better, I'd say you were stalking me."

Crossing his arms over his chest, Joseph gave her a direct stare. "I can assure you that I'm not stalking you. In fact, I didn't know you existed before last night. And the name Eaton isn't that common. And with you being from Florida, I just assumed you were related."

His former boss had distinguished himself as a federal prosecutor before he was appointed to the bench, and still held the distinction of presiding over more drug cases than any other U.S. attorney in south Florida's history. He indicted a drug kingpin, several traffickers responsible for high-end deals and midlevel dealers caught with large amounts of cocaine and marijuana.

"Solomon Eaton is my uncle," she confirmed. And he was also Levi, Jesse and Carson's father.

Reaching into the breast pocket of his blazer, Joseph retrieved his cell phone. "I'll call a car service while you call your cousin."

Walking away to put some distance between them, Crystal turned her back, tapping the screen for Xavier's number. "Good morning, Crystal," Selena answered in greeting.

"Good morning to you, too," she replied. "Selena, I'm afraid I'm going to have to take you up on your offer to hang out with you guys earlier than I'd anticipated." She told her cousin's wife about her aborted meeting with the hotel owner and having to evacuate the hotel because of a fire situation. "I hope you don't mind if I stop by for breakfast."

"Crystal, please. You know you don't have to ask."

"I'm asking because I'm bringing someone with me."

"That's not a problem. I was just preparing brunch for Xavier. He doesn't have classes until this afternoon. I'll hold off cooking until you guys get here."

"Thanks, Selena."

Crystal ended her call at the same time Joseph ended his. "My cousin says you're welcome to come with me."

He smiled. "Thank you. The car should be here in about fifteen minutes."

Staring at him in the bright sunlight, she noticed flecks of gray in his coarse, cropped black hair. Crystal doubted whether he was that much older than she, which meant he was graying prematurely. She also wondered how many times Joseph came to Charleston on business for him to have had a local car service programmed into his phone.

There was so much more she wanted to know about him, yet was reluctant to ask. She just wasn't prepared to accept any more revelations. And because he knew her uncle, there was also the possibility he had been familiar with her aunt and cousins.

She wrapped her arms around her body as much to ward off the morning chill as to protect herself from someone she wasn't prepared to possibly become involved.

What-ifs nagged at her like exposed, inflamed nerves. If her mother hadn't had a meltdown delaying her arrival, she would've spent the night with her cousins instead of the Beaumont House. If Algernon hadn't had a family emergency, she would have shared a table with him instead of Joseph. Now she was exacerbating the situation by inviting him to meet her cousins.

Crystal didn't get the overt vibe that Joseph was coming onto her, but even if he was, she knew his efforts would be fruitless, and not because she had qualms about establishing a friendship with a man.

Her sole focus was the exclusive commission to decorate the

historical structures with exquisite antiques and reproductions. She'd spent months in furniture warehouses and at estate sales looking for pieces with which to decorate a nineteenth-century Lowcountry residence. It wasn't just furniture she'd sought but also accessories, including candlesticks, vases, rugs, apothecary jars, clocks, linens, teapots and other collectibles.

She'd recommended Algernon rent a storage unit. Several pieces she had purchased at an estate sale were carefully wrapped, crated and shipped to him at the Beaumont House, where he arranged for them to be stored in the unit that was quickly filling up with sets of china and silver. Once she inspected the restored buildings, Crystal would be faced with what to put into each room. And in keeping with the time period, she'd planned for the walls to be covered with wallpaper, tapestries or even fabric.

She was anxious to begin her first significant commission.

"A dollar for your thoughts."

Joseph's soft, drawling voice shattered her reverie. Smiling, she turned to face him. "I thought it was a penny."

"That was before inflation," he countered. Slipping out of his jacket, he placed it over Crystal's shoulders. "You look cold."

Tugging on the lapels, she inhaled the cologne clinging to the cashmere fibers. "Thank you, but aren't you going to be cold?" She had on a suit, while he was in his shirtsleeves.

"No. After spending so many winters in upstate New York with lake-effect snow, I rarely feel cold."

"When I was here last January it was much warmer than it is now."

"Last year was unusually warm." Joseph stared at Crystal's distinctive delicate profile. "Did you bring winter clothes with you?"

Crystal nodded. "Yes. However, I didn't expect to stand outside when I got dressed this morning." Her wool gabardine pantsuit wasn't adequate for the low-forties temperature. As someone who lived in Florida year-round, anything below fifty degrees was cool to her.

A Lincoln Town Car maneuvered up to the curb, and Joseph, resting his hand at Crystal's waist, led her to the rear of the limo as the driver alighted. "I'll get the door, Mr. Wilson," the chauffeur called out.

Joseph stepped back, permitting the driver to open the rear door. Crystal got in first, and he followed, sitting beside her on the leather seat. Waiting until the man was seated behind the wheel once again, she gave him the address to her cousin's house.

Sitting close to Crystal, feeling her feminine heat and inhaling the hypnotic scent of her perfume was a bonus Joseph hadn't anticipated when he suggested they share a table.

The ride was much too short when the driver stopped in front of a classic example of a Charleston single house. The wrought-iron and stone pinecones atop ornate brick gates guarded the three-story structure with tall, narrow black-shuttered windows and first- and second-story white porches. The street address and 1800, the year the house was erected, were engraved into a brass plate affixed to one of the brick gate columns.

"Nice," Joseph crooned sotto voce. The house was surrounded by palmetto trees and several ancient oaks draped in Spanish moss.

Crystal smiled. His reaction was similar to her own when she first saw Xavier's house. "Wait until you see inside." Selena had decorated the interiors in an iconic Lowcountry style.

The driver came around to open the door and Joseph stepped out, extended his hand and assisted Crystal until she stood beside him. Reaching into the pocket of his jeans, he removed a money clip, peeling off a bill and handing it to the man. "I'll need you to take us back to the Beaumont House later this afternoon."

The chauffeur pocketed the money, smiling, then handed Joseph a business card. "Thank you. Call me when you're ready to go back."

Joseph put the card and money clip in his pocket. He rested a hand at the small of Crystal's back as they walked together to the front door. He stood off to the side. She'd just raised her hand to ring the doorbell when the door opened.

Ex-marine Major Xavier Eaton smiled at Crystal. He shifted the little girl he cradled on one hip. Extending his free arm, he pulled Crystal close and kissed her forehead. "Welcome back to Charleston."

Crystal pulled back, staring at Xavier's deeply tanned face. He wore a white tee, jeans and running shoes, and his ramrod-straight posture signified he'd had military training. "Thank you. You wear your vacation well."

Xavier, Selena and their daughter, Lily, opted out of spending Christmas with the extended family when they'd flown down to Puerto Rico to stay with one of Xavier's Marine Corps buddies who'd retired there once he was medically discharged. Xavier was also forced to resign his commission after a bullet had shattered his leg when he was deployed in Afghanistan. He'd been the quintessential bachelor whose dimples winked whenever he smiled until he stared through the plate glass of Sweet Persuasions to catch a glimpse of Selena Yates, the owner of the patisserie on King Street.

He laughed softly. "I'm still in vacation mode."

Crystal rubbed noses with Lily Eaton, eliciting high-pitched giggles from the toddler. "Hi, sweet Lily." Shifting slightly, she smiled at Joseph. "Xavier, I want you to meet a…a friend." She didn't know why she was stammering, but for an instant she didn't know how to introduce him. "This is Joseph Wilson." Reaching for Joseph's hand, she eased him closer. "Joseph, this is my cousin Xavier Eaton. And the beautiful little girl is his daughter, Lily."

The two men shook hands. "Nice meeting you, Xavier."

"Same here, Joseph. Welcome and please come in."

Xavier noticed Crystal was wearing Joseph's jacket over her suit, wondering if the man was the reason his cousin had changed her mind, deciding instead to spend several nights at the hotel. He successfully hid a smile. It'd been a while since Crystal appeared remotely interested in a man, and if she'd decided to bring Joseph to meet her relatives, he suspected he was more than a *friend*.

He was deployed when his sister told him Crystal had relocated to New York to pursue her graduate studies, and Xavier found it hard to accept that she was living with a man, because it had been drilled into the heads of every Eaton, every generation whether male or female, if a man or woman was good enough to live with, then he or she was good enough to marry.

Crystal slipped out of Joseph's jacket, handing it to him as they followed Xavier along the length of the porch and through another door leading into an entryway with a solid oak table cradling a collection of woven sweetgrass baskets. Selena's decorating trademarks were everywhere in the carefully chosen furnishings in the expansive living and formal dining rooms. She'd teased her cousin's wife that if Selena retired as a patissier, she would hire her as an assistant.

"Did Selena tell you we had to leave the hotel?"

Xavier glanced over his shoulder as he led them down a narrow hallway to the kitchen. "She mentioned something about a fire but didn't go into detail. What happened?"

"Joseph and I overheard one of the guests complaining about someone smoking in their room."

"If you guys can't get back into your room, then you're more than welcome to stay here."

Crystal exchanged a glance with Joseph. She noticed Xavier said *room* instead of *rooms*. He assumed she and Joseph were sharing a hotel room. "I don't think that's going to be necessary—"

"What's not necessary?" asked a familiar feminine voice. Selena stood at the cooking island in a bibbed apron, her hair concealed under a blue-and-white-checkered scarf as she sprinkled flour on a ball of dough. Her lips parted in a wide grin. "Wow!" she drawled. "Look at you. You cut your hair."

Crystal smoothed down the short strands on the nape of her neck. "I decided I needed a new look." She'd affected a hairstyle that was virtually maintenance free. She didn't have to use a blow-dryer, curling iron or flatiron. It was what she thought of as wash and go. A trim every six weeks kept the style fresh.

Wiping her hands on a towel, Selena approached Crystal, arms outstretched. "Good seeing you again. He's gorgeous," she whispered under her breath, hugging her husband's cousin tightly.

Crystal knew Selena was referring to Joseph, and she had to agree with her. He *was* gorgeous. "Selena, I would like you to meet Joseph Wilson. Joseph, this is Selena, who just happens to be the best pastry chef in the entire city."

Smiling, he took Selena's hand. "My pleasure. Your home is beautiful."

Selena's dark, almond-shaped eyes in a face the color of toasted hazelnuts crinkled attractively when she smiled. "Thank you. It's going to be at least fifteen minutes before everything is ready, so if you'd like, Xavier can give you a tour of the house." She cut her eyes at her husband. "Honey, please put that child down. Once you leave she's going to wild out because I refuse to carry her around."

Xavier tightened his hold on Lily as he gestured for Joseph to follow him, deliberately ignoring Selena. "If you don't have any plans for Super Bowl Sunday and if you're going to be in Charleston, then I'd like you to come over for a little get-together."

Crystal waited until she was certain the men were out of earshot before turning to look at Selena, who'd opened the refrigerator/freezer, taken out a small dish filled with freshly cut fruit, set it and a fork in front of her and then gone back to rolling out dough for biscuits.

Sitting on a stool at the island in the ultramodern chef's kitchen, she said, "It's not what you're thinking."

Selena met her eyes. "What exactly is it I'm thinking, Crystal?"

Between bites of cantaloupe and honeydew, she carefully formed her thoughts. "There's nothing going on between me and Joseph." She told Selena how they met and what they'd discovered about each other while sitting in the hotel's restaurant. "Belonging to a sorority or fraternity isn't extraordinary, but knowing he'd clerked for my uncle is eerie."

"It's not as eerie as it is serendipitous. It's as if you were destined to meet," Selena drawled, trying not to laugh.

Slipping out of her suit jacket, Crystal draped it over the back of the stool. "I don't believe in serendipity."

"What do you believe in?"

It was a full minute before she said, "I believe everyone is born with certain gifts and it's up to us or for others to recognize those gifts in order to make the world a better place."

Selena picked up a pastry brush, dipping it into a bowl of melted butter, and then brushed the tops of the biscuits in a baking pan. "What about love, Criss?"

"What about it?"

"Don't you believe in love?"

Crystal smiled. "Of course I believe in love. Look at you and Xavier. You guys are living proof of the adage 'love at first sight.'"

Selena placed the baking sheet on the shelf of a heated eye-level oven. She wiped her hands on the towel tucked under the ties of the bibbed apron. Resting a hip against the countertop, she angled her head. "You're talking about me and Xavier, but what about you, Criss? I heard about the man you lived with when you went to school in New York. Were you in love with him?"

"I don't think so. My relationship with Brian was more of convenience and companionship."

"For whom?"

Crystal stared at the granite countertop. "Brian and I were like a two-headed coin. We were interchangeable." A wry smile flitted over her lips. "He wasn't looking for a serious relationship, and it was the same with me. I didn't want to get married and neither did he. He also didn't want children, because he'd grown up in an abusive home and he feared he would also abuse a child, while I definitely wasn't and still am not looking to become a mother."

"You don't want to get married or have children?" Selena asked.

She wasn't marriage-phobic, but she didn't see it in her immediate future. "Right now I'm concentrating on growing my business. We didn't have to go looking for a date, and whenever men tried coming onto me, I told them the truth. I was living with a man," Crystal continued as if Selena hadn't broached the subject of marriage and children. "We were museum junkies. When Brian wasn't teaching and when I didn't have classes, we spent all of our free time seeing how many museums we could visit. One summer we drove to Vermont and hit every museum as far south as D.C."

Selena's eyes grew wider. "It sounds as if you had the perfect relationship. Didn't you ever argue?"

"Oh, we had our disagreements but nothing that monumental. He didn't believe in sororities or fraternities and he invariably left the toilet seat up and dirty dishes in the sink."

Scrunching up her nose, Selena drawled, "Thankfully Xavier is a neat freak. Now back to Joseph. It looks as if you two have a lot in common, so if he does ask you out, would you accept?"

"I think my busybody cousin already took care of that. Unless Joseph gives him the four-one-one about us, Xavier assumes we're sharing a hotel suite. And I'm certain you heard *your husband* invite him here for the Super Bowl party."

Selena sucked her teeth. "You didn't see it the last time you were here, but we turned the top floor into a theater and media room. I told Xavier if any of his friends have too much to drink and can't make it downstairs, then they're going to stay up there until they're mummified."

Crystal laughed until her sides hurt and tears ran down her face. She and Selena were still laughing when Joseph and Xavier entered the kitchen, both holding Lily's hands as she urged them to swing her higher.

She stared at him, marveling that he appeared so comfortable with her family. When Xavier released his daughter's hand, Joseph swung Lily up as she emitted a high-pitch squeal of delight. Black curls had escaped the two elastic bands holding her hair in place, and in that instant Crystal wondered if Joseph would be a stern or indulgent father. Judging from his interaction with the toddler, she knew it would probably be the latter.

Lily, breathing heavily, her face flushed, screamed, "I have to do potty!" Joseph set her on her feet and she raced to the half bath off the kitchen.

"She goes by herself now?" Crystal asked. Selena had begun toilet training her daughter at fourteen months, but Lily refused to sit on her potty unless her mother sat in the bathroom alongside her, reading fairy tales and nursery rhymes.

Selena chuckled softly. "Miss Grown wants to do everything by herself now that she's two. Every morning we bump heads because she wants to pick out her own clothes."

"What's wrong with that?"

"She forgets we're in Charleston and not Puerto Rico. She wants to wear sandals, shorts and bathing suits. I try to tell her we're not in the Caribbean, but she doesn't seem to understand." Lily emerged from the bathroom, her hands dripping water, and Xavier handed her a paper towel. The toddler dried her hands and then ran over to Crystal, raising her arms for her to pick her up.

Selena shook her head in exasperation. "When it gets to the point where I'm not going to be able to do anything with her, I'm going to send her to Florida to spend time with you."

Cradling the little girl to her chest, she dropped a kiss on her hair. "You know I'd take her in a heartbeat. Titi Criss will make certain she'll have the most tricked-out dollhouse imaginable."

Lily clapped her chubby hands. "I want a dollhouse."

Joseph sat on the stool next Crystal. "You build dollhouses?"

Xavier cracked eggs into a mixing bowl, then whisked them until they were light and fluffy before turning them onto a heated stove-top griddle. "You didn't know your girlfriend is an interior decorator?"

"I'm not his girlfriend," Crystal countered quickly.

"My bad," Xavier said with a sheepish grin.

Joseph stared at Crystal's profile. He didn't know why, but he wanted her to be his girlfriend only because he felt they were destined to connect. "I never would've thought you were a decorator."

She shifted slightly to look at him. "Why not?"

He lifted a shoulder. "Somehow I got the impression you were in Charleston to audit some company's books." There was something about her demeanor that called to mind the no-nonsense accountants at ColeDiz.

"You're not even close. I'm here to decorate the interior of an inn and B and B for the owner of Beaumont House," Crystal said.

Now he knew why she was living in the penthouse. He stayed at the Beaumont House because it was rated as one of the best hotels in Charleston. And if the owner of the hotel had elected to have Crystal decorate his other establishments, then there was no doubt she was at the top in her field.

"Congratulations."

She flashed a wide grin. "Thank you."

Thoroughly exhausted, Lily pushed two fingers in her mouth and closed her eyes. Within seconds she was asleep as Crystal savored the warmth of the small body molded to her chest. She closed her eyes for several seconds and when she opened them she was shocked by the tender expression on Joseph's face as he watched her rock the child. Seconds ticked as they continued to stare at each other.

Xavier shattered the spell as he gently extricated his sleeping daughter from Crystal's arms. "Let me take her."

"Does she usually take a nap this early?" Crystal asked him.

"Her sleep patterns have been haywire since we came back from vacation."

Xavier placed Lily in a playpen in the corner of the kitchen while Selena removed the pan of golden-brown biscuits from the oven, setting them on a warm plate. Temporarily fortified by the dish of fruit, Crystal stood up, washed her hands and assisted Selena in setting a bowl of grits and a platter with crisp bacon, julienned ham and country links on the table in the breakfast nook in the large eat-in kitchen, while Xavier ladled fluffy scrambled eggs into a serving bowl. Crystal had to do something so as not to sit and stare at Joseph.

* * *

Joseph, seated next to Crystal, took surreptitious glances at her. Each time she asked him to pass her a dish, their shoulders brushed, making him more than aware of her feminine scent.

He was surprised at how comfortable he felt interacting with her and her cousins.

It had to be an Eaton thing because he had experienced the same thing when meeting Solomon for the first time. He'd been referred to the judge by one of his law professors who'd attended law school with Solomon.

Although passing the bar on his first attempt, Joseph found himself mildly intimidated working for the former celebrated U.S. prosecutor, who struck fear in defendants and the opposing counsel whenever he entered the courtroom. Solomon never went to trial unless he was certain of a victory. Joseph's mentor jurist treated him as an equal, and he learned more about the law working with Solomon than he had in three years of law school.

Joseph swallowed a forkful of grits and eggs, savoring the piquant flavors. "Do you guys eat like this every morning?" he asked.

"I wish," Xavier intoned. "Most mornings I have breakfast at school. It's not as appetizing as it is health-conscious."

Selena smiled at Joseph. "I save the grits, eggs and pork for the weekend or whenever we have houseguests. If I ate like this every morning, I'd end up going back to bed instead of working."

Joseph slathered apple butter jam on a fluffy biscuit. "Xavier told me you have a home-based mail-order business."

She nodded. "Yes, I do. I closed my shop on King Street and went completely mail order after Lily was born. We expanded the house and installed a commercial kitchen. Working from home allows me to spend time with Lily and to do what I love."

He picked up the small jar of jam, staring at the label printed with the Sweet Persuasions website. "Do you sell these, too?"

Selena nodded again. "Those I give away as complimentary gifts for first-time customers. Most times they order the larger size whenever they place subsequent offers."

"Do you also make them?"

"No," Selena said, smiling. "I can't take credit for the jams, jellies and preserves. My grandmother makes them for me and I sell them in two-, four- and six-ounce sizes."

"How large an order can you accommodate?"

"How large are you talking about?" Selena asked.

"I'd like to begin with an assortment of at least five hundred jars. My family own and operate a number of vacation resorts throughout the Caribbean, and a variety of gourmet jellies and preserves would be perfect for breakfast breads and high tea. The larger sizes could be sold in the gift shops."

"Which resorts?" Crystal had asked the question before a seemingly stunned Selena could respond to Joseph's offer.

"ColeDiz International Limited." Joseph's expression was deadpan.

A soft gasp escaped Crystal's parted lips. "You're one of *those* Coles?" Even though it'd never been substantiated, the Coles were purported to be the wealthiest African-American family in the United States. It was then she remembered he'd introduced himself as Joseph Cole-Wilson.

The hint of a smile flitted over his mouth. "And you're one of *those* Eatons."

Xavier's gaze shifted from his cousin to Joseph. "Am I missing something here?"

Joseph told Xavier he'd been a law clerk for Solomon Eaton and that they also belonged to the same fraternity. "Now I'm a true believer that it's a small world, but I never would've expected to meet the judge's niece when I checked into the Beaumont House."

Xavier nodded. "Fate is a fickle woman. You never know what to expect from her."

"Why does it have to be a woman?" Crystal and Selena chorused in unison. Sharing a wide grin, they exchanged a fist bump.

"I think we'd better quit while we're ahead, brother," Joseph suggested, as he and Xavier executed their own handshake. He redirected his attention to Selena. "Do you think you'd be able to meet my request?"

She closed her eyes for several seconds. "I…I don't know. I have to think about it."

He nodded. "Take all the time you need. However, I'd also like to invest in your company. Just name your price. While you're thinking about it, can I place an order and have you overnight it to Diego Cole-Thomas. He's the CEO at ColeDiz."

A heavy silence descended on those sitting in the kitchen as Crystal stared at the contents of her plate instead of the man sitting next to her. He definitely was one of *those* Coles, she mused.

She didn't know if Selena was willing to give up a portion of a business she'd worked to grow over the past three years, and if she did agree to Joseph's offer, then the Eatons and Coles would be linked even further.

Crystal knew Joseph's family guarded their net worth like a top-secret government document, and had elected to remain a private company instead of going public like many billion-dollar conglomerates. People such as Joseph sealed deals with a single phone call or with a stroke of a pen.

And he had it all: looks, brains, wealth and power. Something told Crystal to run in the opposite direction, that when they returned to the Beaumont House she should end her association with him. But realistically she knew that wasn't possible. Xavier had invited him to their Super Bowl party.

Although Crystal did not want to become involved with Joseph, fate, destiny, providence or external circumstances had intervened. He would become a part of her existence while in Charleston and possibly beyond because of her uncle.

Chapter 4

It was after one when Joseph and Crystal returned to the Beaumont House.

When he called the front desk and was told the smoky condition had been extinguished, Joseph made arrangements for the driver to take them back. They hadn't exchanged a word during the return ride.

He reached for Crystal's hand, guiding her through the throng of guests to the elevators. Aside from reconnecting with his parents and siblings, he couldn't remember when he'd spent a more enjoyable morning since returning to the States.

The cooking skills of the owner of Sweet Persuasions were superior and the interchange between Crystal and her cousins light, lively and easygoing. He listened closely when Xavier talked of his intent to become a career officer, but after being seriously wounded he'd smoothly transitioned to civilian life and moved to Charleston to teach military history at a prestigious military prep school.

His interest in history was evidenced by the memorabilia in Xavier's home/office that included military maps, books on military history and black-and-white photographs of players from the Negro Leagues, and different countries and cities he'd taken while on leave.

Selena recounted her career from actress to pastry chef, and now mother of a precocious two-year-old. She admitted to being a frustrated interior decorator, teasing Crystal that whenever she decided to give up her mail-order enterprise she wanted to assist her at Eaton Interior and Design.

Joseph had waited patiently for Crystal to open up about her life and career, but she appeared more interested in her cousins talking about themselves. He still didn't know her age, if she'd been married or why she'd decided to become an interior decorator. He was also puzzled about her reaction when he'd revealed he was a Cole. He felt her withdraw when it was quite the opposite for him once she revealed she was an Eaton.

Both of them belonged to prominent black Florida families but hadn't crossed paths. He'd come to Charleston to oversee a business venture and had unknowingly come face-to-face with his mentor's niece. Joseph wasn't certain what she'd heard or read about the Coles that made her refer to his name with so much aversion.

It was another five minutes before they were able to squeeze into one of the three elevators. His arm went around her waist, easing her back against her body as a large man settled his bulk against Crystal's slender frame. His sigh echoed hers when they finally exited the car at their floor.

When he'd gotten up earlier, Joseph had planned to eat breakfast and then drive over to the tea garden to meet with the manager of the tea garden, not spend the morning and early afternoon with a woman who was as intriguing as she was stunningly beautiful.

Reaching into her handbag, Crystal removed her card key, while the hint of a smile played at the corners of her mouth. "Let's hope the rest of the day goes a lot more smoothly than this morning."

Joseph wanted to tell her there was nothing remotely wrong with his morning. Circumstances beyond his control had connected him with his penthouse neighbor and a plan he never would've been able to devise even if he'd mulled it over for days.

"It wasn't a total loss. At least not for me," he added, smiling. "And thank you for allowing me to tag along with you for brunch. I'd like to return the favor and prepare dinner for you tomorrow night." He'd heard Crystal tell Selena she would see her Saturday afternoon.

Crystal's fingers tightened on the card key. "You can cook?"

His expression changed, vertical lines appearing between his eyes. "Why would you ask me that?"

Cocking her head to the side, she drawled, "Your being a Cole, I thought you would've grown up with live-in cooks and housekeepers."

Joseph's frown vanished quickly. "So you think because I'm a Cole I'm completely helpless and that I need someone to cook and pick up after me?"

"I don't know what to think," Crystal countered. "What I do know is that you've overdosed on entitlement pie. You hadn't known my cousin an hour before you expected her to accept your offer to invest in her company."

Joseph stared at the carpeted floor for several seconds; then his gaze came up and his eyes met Crystal's. "I asked her because I'm a businessman."

"I thought you were a lawyer."

"I am a lawyer, a farmer and also a businessman looking for new opportunities in which to expand my family's company." He realized that two years ago he never would've admitted to being a businessman or a farmer. Joseph had challenged the CEO of ColeDiz when Diego gave him the responsibility of adding the tea company to the list of other ventures under the corporate umbrella with the argument that he wasn't a farmer.

The disclosure that he was a farmer shocked Crystal. "What are you growing?"

Joseph's expression closed. "We can discuss that when you have dinner with me. Tomorrow night, seven o'clock, my place, casual attire."

Much to her chagrin, Crystal laughed. She'd just accused Joseph of having OD'd on entitlement and he'd just assumed she would share dinner with him because he wanted it. "What you need to consider is eating a slice of humble pie," she said laughingly.

Splaying the fingers of his right hand over his heart, he managed to look contrite. "I'm so very sorry, Miss Eaton, but will you do me the honor of sharing dinner with me?" He lowered his hand. "Is that humble enough?"

"It'll do—for now," she said, biting back more laughter. Even though she thought Joseph slightly arrogant, she had to add charming to his other obvious assets.

"Do you like Italian food?"

"I love it."

"Then Italian it is," he said with a wide grin.

"Do you want me to bring anything?" she asked.

"No. I have everything I need."

"Tomorrow night at seven," she repeated.

Turning, she walked the length of the hallway to her apartment. Crystal felt the heat from Joseph's gaze on her back, and seconds before she slipped the card key into the slot, she turned to find him watching her. He hadn't moved. Their eyes met, gazes fusing for a nanosecond; she glanced away, opened the door and then closed it behind her.

Kicking off her shoes, she placed the card key on the table in the entryway and set her handbag on the leather-covered bench seat next to the table.

Walking on bare feet, she made her way into the living room. Flopping down on an inviting club chair, she rested her feet on the matching ottoman and closed her eyes at the same time her cell phone chimed. Pushing off the chair, Crystal went to retrieve the phone from her handbag.

Swallowing back a groan, she tapped the screen. "Hello, Mother."

"Why did I have to wait almost twenty-four hours just to hear your voice?"

Walking back to the chair, Crystal sat down again. She'd promised her mother she would call her once she arrived in Charleston, but she didn't because she didn't want to hear Jasmine go on about her latest breakup. "Mama, please don't start."

"Please, Crystal. You know better than to call me by that tacky title."

She rolled her eyes upward even though Jasmine couldn't see her. "How are you today?"

"Wonderful. I'm leaving for the airport to fly out to Vegas

to meet Philip. He called early this morning to say he wants me to join him."

Crystal clenched her teeth to keep from spewing curses. She didn't want to believe she'd driven down to Miami to console her mother just to have her reconcile with her latest beau the very next day. "What happened to you breaking up with him, Mother?"

"I changed my mind. Of all of the men I've dated, Philip is someone I'd actually consider marrying."

"He must really be exceptional if you're willing to give up your alimony payments."

"I did say *consider.*"

Crystal stared at the chipped polish on the big toe of her right foot as her mother talked incessantly about the plans Philip had made for them. "I told him I wanted to take a flight over the Hoover Dam and Grand Canyon," Jasmine continued without pausing to take a breath, "but he said he's not certain whether we'll have enough time."

"When are you coming back?"

"Wednesday night. Enough talk about me. Have you seen Xavier and his adorable baby daughter?"

Smiling for the first time since answering the phone, Crystal said, "Yes. But Lily's not a baby anymore. She's a toddler who's walking, talking *and* potty-trained."

"I really miss seeing Raleigh's family."

She registered the longing in Jasmine's voice. "Remember, Mother, you divorced Daddy, not the Eatons. Whenever they invite you to family reunions, you always decline. And I've lost count of those who've asked about you year after year."

"I don't come because I can't abide those tramps hanging on to Raleigh as if they can't breathe without him. He needs to be told to stay away from strip joints when looking for a new wife."

"You're preaching to the choir, Mother." Crystal didn't understand how her father could take up with women who were the complete opposite of his first wife. Jasmine had more class in her little finger than all of her ex-husband's ex-wives collectively.

"I know you don't like talking about it, but why don't you ask Xavier to introduce you to some of his single guy friends? If you're going to spend a couple of months working in Charleston, you should have some fun, too."

Crystal rolled her eyes upward again. "I came here to work, not look for a boyfriend."

"There's nothing wrong with a little casual dating."

"I'll think about it, Mother," Crystal lied smoothly.

Two months was hardly enough time for her to meet and become romantically involved with someone, and what Jasmine termed as casual dating usually meant seeing someone for a month. It would take her more than a month to truly feel comfortable enough to take their casual dating to the next level.

"Hold on, darling. The gatehouse is ringing me." Seconds later, Jasmine said, "I have to go. My driver is here."

"Have fun, Mother."

"I will. Love you, darling."

"I love you, too." She ended the call, staring at the live fern in a painted glazed pot on a corner table. The words her mother found so difficult to say when Crystal was a young girl now came so easily from Jasmine. She'd wanted Jasmine to be like the mothers of her friends and cousins who got up and prepared breakfast before seeing their children off to school. Or when she came home after classes, she wanted to find freshly baked cookies waiting for her as she sat down to do her homework.

What she did remember was Jasmine sleeping late, chain-smoking and visiting her therapist, while handing over the responsibility of taking care of her daughter to a series of nannies. Once Crystal turned eight, there was no longer a need for a nanny or babysitter; she had unofficially moved in with her uncle Solomon and Aunt Holly.

Shaking her head to banish painful childhood memories, Crystal pushed off the chair and climbed the staircase to the upper level. Restlessness assailed her, akin to an itch she couldn't scratch. She needed a full-body massage. She didn't know why, but she always experienced unease whenever Jasmine called her because she never knew what to expect. Why, she mused, couldn't they just have a normal mother–daughter discussion without Jasmine bringing up the topic of dating?

What the older woman did not know was that she did date, although it had been a while. Over the years she'd dated a few handsome and not-so-handsome men, those who were well-to-do and others whom she suspected lived from paycheck to paycheck. Their looks and the size of their bank accounts were never prerequisites for Crystal to agree to go out with them. It was always their confidence and manners—the latter taking precedence over the former. Even before she was old enough to date, her mother had lectured her constantly about home training.

Even behind closed lids Crystal could still see the image of Joseph's deeply tanned face, his dark eyes and tall, toned slim body. He was the epitome of tall, dark and handsome. And the fact that he was wealthy didn't begin to play into the equation.

She didn't want to think about Jasmine or Joseph. Rolling her head, she attempted to ease the tight muscles in her shoulders and upper back. It was time for a massage. Having access to an on-site health club was one of the reasons, along with the unisex salon, spa and boutique, was why she'd decided to buy property in the Fort Lauderdale gated community.

Picking up the phone, she dialed the number to the hotel's Serenity Silk Day Spa. Her call was answered after the second ring. "Good afternoon, Ms. Eaton. How may I help you?"

"I'd like an appointment for a facial and a mood-makeover massage. Is it possible for me to combine the massage with hot stones?"

"Of course, Ms. Eaton. What time would you like to come in?"

Crystal glanced at her watch. "I can be down in less than half an hour."

"We'll be waiting for you."

Ending the call, she went upstairs to her bedroom to change out of her suit and into a pair of sweatpants, a shirt and a pair of flip-flops. The sound of something hitting the windows caught her attention. It was raining. Even if she'd wanted to do some sightseeing, Crystal realized she would've had to change her plans.

She slipped the two card keys, a credit card and cash onto a wristlet before leaving.

Crystal walked across the marble floor of the lobby to the spa discreetly located at the end of a narrow hallway. She felt the calming atmosphere the instant she opened the door to the candlelit space, finding herself enveloped in the sounds of a waterfall, soothing New Age music flowing from hidden speakers and the tantalizing scent of essential oils.

The white-coated receptionist escorted her to a dressing room, where she stripped down to her panties and put on a thick terry cloth bathrobe. She was given a cup of herbal tea and a questionnaire asking about her health status, including whether she was pregnant and/or had any implanted devices.

Twenty minutes later Crystal knew she'd made the right decision visit the spa. Her face anchored in the cushioned doughnut on the massage table, she closed her eyes and moaned softly when hot stones lined the length of her spine. She had her mother to thank for her turning her onto the practice of using heated stones dating back five thousand years to the Ayurveda, an ancient Indian healing tradition.

She found herself succumbing to the strong fingers of the masseuse easing the tightness in her shoulders and upper back, falling asleep and waking only when told to turn over.

The hot stone massage was followed by the application of oils made up of lavender and patchouli, and then a shower and a facial that left her moisturized face glowing. She lingered long enough for a mani/pedi.

After paying for the services, Crystal gave the masseuse and esthetician generous tips, feeling better than she had in weeks.

As she left the spa and walked through the lobby, Crystal had to decide whether she wanted to cook dinner for herself, order room service or eat in the hotel's restaurant. Her step faltered as she headed in the direction of the elevators to find Joseph in a passionate embrace with a petite woman with a café-au-lait complexion and hair the color of ripened wheat.

Joseph lifted the woman off her feet at the same time his eyes met Crystal's. She saw an expression of surprise freeze his features as he stared at her. She didn't know why, but she felt like a voyeur even after she'd pulled her gaze away from the couple. Joseph had promised to cook for her the following day, and she wondered if the attractive blonde would join them.

Entering the elevator, she inserted the card key into the PH slot. *Two's company and three is a crowd.* The familiar adage came to mind as the car rose quickly to the top floor.

Perhaps, she mused, Joseph should've waited to invite her to dinner before checking whether his girlfriend would show up. It was obvious her neighbor was faced with a dilemma, and because Crystal detested confrontation she was more than willing to accept his suggestion to cancel dinner. The ball, as the saying goes, was definitely in his court.

Joseph went completely still as he held his sister. When Bianca called from the concierge's desk asking him to come down, he'd been surprised to hear from her. Then he saw Crystal stroll across the hotel lobby in sweats and flip-flops.

Once he and Crystal returned to the hotel, he hadn't been able to stop thinking about her, or comparing her to Kiara. He found himself transfixed by her soft drawling voice, her low, sensual laughter, the genuine affection she appeared to have for Xavier and Selena and the sparkle in her eyes whenever she interacted with Lily. He was completely mesmerized by the confidence and poise that seemed to come so naturally to her. And after comparing her to Kiara, he realized he'd wasted four years of his life with a woman with whom he had so little in common.

As a Cole, he would always put family first, but not with Kiara. Once she left Baltimore she refused to return or interact with her parents or anyone in her extended family. And whenever he mentioned meeting her family, she would fly into a rage, then not speak to him for days.

"Joseph, please put me down." Bianca's command broke into his musings.

"Sorry about that." He gave her a long, penetrating stare. "How did you find me?" he asked.

A slight frown appeared between Bianca Cole-Wilson's brilliant gold-green catlike eyes. "Diego told me you were going to be here for a few months. I need to talk to you."

Joseph hadn't seen his sister since Thanksgiving. Bianca, a premed senior at Duke University, hadn't celebrated Christmas and New Year's with the family because she'd spent the holiday in California with her sorority sisters with whom she shared off-campus housing.

Holding on to her hand, he steered to the bank of elevators. "We'll talk upstairs."

Bianca pulled back. "Can't we talk down here?"

He gave her a questioning look. "What's the matter?"

"Henri is waiting in the parking lot to drive me back to college."

"Why are you going back so early? Don't you have another week before classes begin again?"

"Yes, but I need to clean up my bedroom. I left clothes everywhere. It's also my week to clean the kitchen and bathroom."

"Why aren't you flying up?"

"The jet is being serviced."

Joseph nodded. Henri had been hired as Diego's driver and bodyguard. The mandate that anyone with Cole blood was prohibited from flying on a commercial carrier was still in effect more than forty years after Regina Cole's kidnapping. Instead of arriving at the airport hours before departure time, or going through long lines at the security gate, Bianca and her sorority sisters were seated in the Gulfstream G650 business jet within minutes of arriving at the Raleigh-Durham International Airport for their nonstop flight to LAX.

"Okay," he said conceding. "We'll talk in the lounge area. Would you like me to order something for you to eat or drink?" he asked when they were seated next to each other on a tan leather love seat.

"No, thank you. We stopped to eat in Savannah, so I'm good."

Joseph wanted to tell his sister that aside from her deep suntan, she didn't look that good. Standing five-four and usually tipping the scales at one ten, she appeared much too thin. The natural blond hair she inherited from her Puerto Rican maternal grandmother made her a standout among the many dark-haired, dark-eyed Coles.

"Talk to me, Bianca."

Lacing and unlacing her fingers together on her lap, Bianca revealed she had second thoughts about going to medical school. "It's not that I don't want to become a doctor, but I'm thinking of taking a year off after I graduate in May."

Joseph's expression did not reveal his shock at this disclosure. For as long as he could remember, Bianca had always talked about going into medicine. "Are you pregnant?" he asked. It was the first thing that popped into his head.

She gave him an incredulous look. "No!"

He angled his head. "Then why the change of mind?"

Bianca closed her eyes. "I think I'm burning out." She'd accelerated in high school taking advance placement classes, graduating at fifteen, and would be a month shy of her twentieth birthday when enrolling in medical school. "My brain is fried, Joey," she whispered under her breath. Bianca was the only one in the family who shortened his name.

Draping an arm around her shoulders, Joseph eased her closer to him and pressed a kiss on her hair. "Should I assume you haven't mentioned this to Mom and Dad?" She nodded. "Have you decided what you want to do while you're taking the year off?"

Bianca's cheeks puffed up as she emitted an audible sigh. "I want to spend six months in Brazil with Regina and Aaron, and the next six in New Mexico with Emily and Chris."

"Why are you telling me this instead going directly to Dad?" Joseph asked. "After all, he's still legally and financially responsible for you."

Bianca raised her chin, staring directly into the eyes of her favorite brother. It wasn't that she didn't love her other three brothers, but it was Joseph with whom she felt closest. Nathan, Harper and Anthony, who were twenty-six, thirty-two and thirty-five respectively, never seemed to find the time to play or listen to her.

"I have saved some money, and I would've had more if I hadn't gone to L.A., but what I need is your reassurance that you'll loan me enough to hold me over for the next year because Daddy's going to cut me off once I drop out of school."

Orthopedic surgeon José Cole-Wilson Sr. laid the ground rules for his children with regard to their education. He would underwrite the cost of their college, law or medical school tuition, provide them with a car and gas cards and deposit enough money into a checking account to take care of personal incidentals. And if she did take a year off, then she would be forced to move back home and rely on her parents for her day-to-day support.

"You're not dropping out, Bianca," Joseph argued softly. "You'll graduate in May."

"But I don't plan to go to medical school for a year, and for Daddy that's the same as dropping out."

"I think you're being a little overdramatic, Bibi."

She closed her eyes. "You know I'm not."

"If you decide to take a year off, I doubt Dad will cut you off financially. But if that's what you believe, then I want you to open a separate account when you get back to Durham. Call me with the account number and I'll arrange to transfer money from my account into yours. How much do you think you'll need?"

She opened her eyes, smiling. "I'm not certain, because I'll be staying with Regina and Emily."

"Have you told them of your plans?"

Bianca nodded. "They're both in agreement. What I have to do is tell Dad."

"When are you going to do that?"

"I'm going home for spring break. I'll tell him then."

"Do you want me to be there when you tell him?"

Bianca kissed his stubble. "No. I don't think I'm going to need backup, but thanks for offering."

Joseph rested his chin on her head. "Regardless of what happens I want you to remember that I'll always be here for you."

She smiled, willing the tears pricking the backs of her eyelids not to fall. She came to Joseph rather than her other brothers because she knew he would not only hear her out but also take her side. Nathan, Anthony and Harper were too involved in their careers and whatever woman they were dating at the time.

"I know that." Bianca glanced at her watch. "I think I've kept Henri waiting long enough."

"I'll walk you to the car."

Joseph put his arm around Bianca's shoulders. He'd always felt very protective of his sister from the moment his parents brought her home from the hospital.

They reached the parking lot and as if on cue Henri exited the limousine, opening a large black umbrella. A rare smile parted his lips with his approach as he extended his free hand. "Good afternoon, Mr. Wilson," he greeted in slightly accented French.

Joseph grasped the proffered hand in a firm handshake. "Good afternoon, Henri. How have you been?"

He hadn't seen the driver/bodyguard since before the Christmas holiday. The man with the shaven dark brown pate and strong features reminiscent of carved African masks appeared as taciturn as his boss. He and Diego were well suited for each other; both were men of few words—Henri even less than Diego. Only Diego knew his last name, and whenever he picked up the phone to call Henri he made himself available twenty-four/seven.

"Bien, señor."

Joseph smiled as Henri lapsed fluidly into Spanish. There were occasions when he overheard the man speaking fluent French, Creole or Spanish. He shifted his attention to Bianca. "Call or text me when you arrive. And don't forget about the account number."

Going on tiptoe, she kissed his chin. "I will."

Taking a step back, Joseph watched Henri hold the umbrella over Bianca's head as they walked to the black Mercedes. He stood in the same spot watching the red taillights disappear before going back into the hotel. He had to come up with a menu for a dinner he would prepare for the most beguiling woman he'd ever met. The South Carolina Eatons had offered him their Southern hospitality, and in a little more than twenty-four hours a Palm Beach Cole would return the favor when he prepared dinner for Crystal.

Chapter 5

Crystal massaged scented cream cologne over her body, followed with dots of a matching perfume at all of her pulse points. She'd taken a bubble bath, luxuriating in the Jacuzzi until the candles lining the bathtub's ledge flickered wildly, then sputtered out.

The clock on the table in a corner of the expansive bathroom chimed the half hour. It was six-thirty—thirty minutes before she was scheduled to meet Joseph for dinner.

He planned for a casual encounter, and after going through her closet she selected a pair of black stretch cropped slacks, matching long-sleeved cashmere sweater and black leather ballet flats.

As promised, Algernon had called, giving her an update. He planned to return to Charleston late Monday evening; the contractor overseeing the renovations to the adjoining historic buildings would meet with her and the owner Tuesday at noon.

Anxious to begin decorating the rooms for the inn and B and B, Crystal estimated completing the project hopefully within eight weeks.

Her next commission would take her to New York City, where the owner of a one-hundred-fifty-seven-year-old Tribeca residence planned to turn the town house's basement into a late-night jazz club; she looked forward to returning to the city she'd called home while attending Parsons New School for Design, where she'd earned an MFA in interior design.

Pushing her arms into the sleeves of a thick terry cloth robe, Crystal belted it and sat at the vanity; picking up a sable brush, she opened a makeup palette with foundation, concealer and bronzer in shades matching her skin tone and another with eye shadows in muted shades ranging from sienna to smoky grays and black.

Adjusting the lighting around the perimeter of the mirror, she lightly swept the tip of the brush over the foundation, gently blew off the excess and then dusted the velvety bristles over her forehead, cheeks and chin.

Peering closely at her reflection, she surveyed her final handiwork, pleased with the results. The smoky gray shadow on her lids and the soft black mascara on her lashes made her eyes appear larger, dramatic. The coat of raspberry lip gloss matched the barely perceptible matching blush on her high cheekbones.

Staring at her reflection, she recalled Joseph hugging the blonde. She'd expected him to contact her to cancel their date, but as the time drew closer she went through with the motions of readying herself as originally planned.

Crystal experienced a range of emotions whenever she thought about Joseph. Despite his being born into wealth and privilege, there was nothing ostentatious about him, and if he did give off vibes of entitlement she credited it to his being a Cole. And she was also curious to find out more about his family. Even with their supposedly great wealth, they'd managed to remain discreet, inconspicuous, unlike some privileged scions stalked by the paparazzi.

What truly puzzled her was his disclosure of being farmer. Why, she mused, would he give up practicing law to farm? And what was he growing? Crystal hoped she would have the answers she sought before the night ended.

The chiming of the doorbell echoed throughout Joseph's apartment. Taking long strides, he crossed the living room to the entryway and opened the door, certain Crystal could hear his audible intake of breath when he stared at her upturned face. Her dramatic yet subtle makeup, her black attire, the modified spiky hair style and the scent of her perfume silently screamed *sensuality*. It took herculean strength for him to pull his gaze away from her mouth.

"Am I too early?" she asked.

Crystal forced herself not to gawk at Joseph. The absence of stubble made him appear boyish. He'd exchanged his jeans and boots for a pair of dark blue tailored slacks and black leather slip-ons. His light blue shirt with white contrasting cuffs and collar was open at the throat.

Joseph blinked as if coming out of a trance. "No...not at all." Stepping aside, he opened the door wider. "Please come in."

Crystal handed him the decorative bag with several bottles of wine. Not wearing heels made her aware of the differences in their heights. The top of her head came to his chin. "I didn't know if you were serving meat, chicken or fish, so I brought zinfandel, pinot noir and a sauvignon blanc."

He peered into the bag. "Thank you, but I have wine."

"Please keep it," she said when he attempted to give her back the bag. "I have more than I'd ever attempt to drink in a year."

Placing the bag on a side table, Joseph escorted Crystal into the living room, seating her on the love seat facing an unlit fireplace. The layout and furnishings in his apartment were identical to hers. He hadn't drawn the wall-to-wall drapes, and lights from office buildings and streetlights shimmered eerily through the nighttime mist. A steady downpour had left the city with more than two inches over a twenty-four-hour period.

Her gaze shifted to the table in the dining room set for formal dining with china, silver and crystal. It was apparent dinner was going to be anything but casual.

She turned to face Joseph staring at her, wondering what was going on behind his dark eyes. Crystal asked herself why she'd accepted his invitation when it would have been so easy to decline. As soon as the thought entered her head she knew the answer. Not only was she curious about Joseph, but she also had to acknowledge the physical attraction. Everything about him: face, body, the hypnotic scent of his cologne and the sensual timbre of his voice radiated blatant sensuality.

"Did you ever work in a restaurant?" she asked him.

Folding his hands together behind his back, Joseph angled his head. "Yes. Why?"

"Just asking."

A smile tilted the corners of his mouth. "Why are you 'just asking'?"

Pushing to her feet, Crystal walked into the dining room. "Only someone with restaurant or catering experience would know how to arrange silver and glassware for a formal dinner." The place settings included salad, dessert and fish forks and dinner and butter knives, water goblets and red wineglasses.

Joseph followed Crystal, resting his hands on her shoulders. "My mother owns a restaurant. The year I turned fifteen I worked there as a dishwasher. At sixteen it was busing tables, and at seventeen I'd graduated to waiting tables."

She froze for several seconds before relaxing under the light, impersonal touch. Crystal peered at him over her shoulder, smiling. She'd misjudged him. He wasn't a rich kid whose parents had indulged his every whim. Washing dishes and busing tables were the least glamorous jobs in the restaurant business.

"Where's her restaurant?"

"Palm Beach. It's called Marimba in honor of my grandfather who was a percussionist with a Latin band back in the day."

"You're Cuban?"

Tightening his hold on her shoulders, Joseph turned her around to face him. "I'm African-American, Cuban and Puerto Rican." Reaching for her hand, he laced their fingers together. "Come with me into the kitchen and I'll give you a brief overview of the Cole-Wilsons."

The sight that greeted her in the gourmet kitchen rendered her temporarily mute. He'd prepared an antipasto with prosciutto, Genoa salami, roasted peppers, mixed olives, fresh mozzarella, sliced tomatoes and a Caesar salad topped with parmesan shavings. There were also small cubes of marinated beef kabobs on a plate next to the stove-top grill.

Moving closer to the cooking island, she stared at a baking sheet with risen dough sprinkled with garlic, rosemary, olive oil and coarse salt. Joseph had poked shallow indentations and sprinkled grated Parmesan over the top of the focaccia bread.

"There's a lot of food here," she remarked.

He pulled out a high stool at the island, seating her. "It looks like a lot because I enjoy different courses. I grew up eating soup, salad, bread, rice, beans, meat, chicken or fish for dinner, plus dessert. There's enough here for two servings from each course."

Joseph continued to surprise Crystal. His culinary prowess was definitely impressive. "You must have spent all day putting this together."

"I got up early to put up the dough, but it took me less than half an hour to make the antipasto and salad. I cooked the main dish of baked rigatoni with a tomato-basil sauce and meatballs last night, so it just has to be reheated."

Resting her elbows on the granite countertop, Crystal watched Joseph unbutton and roll back the cuffs on his shirt. Her gaze lingered on his hands. They were as exquisite as his face. "Who taught you to cook?"

"*Mi madre y abuela.* My mother and grandmother," he translated quickly. "I hope you brought your appetite."

"I did," Crystal answered truthfully. Her caloric intake for the day included yogurt topped with granola, an apple and bottled water.

Joseph opened the refrigerator and removed a pitcher of clear liquid filled with sliced white peaches and green grapes. "We'll start with peach sangria and the beef kabobs."

She stood up. "Do you need help with anything?"

Leaning closer, he ran his forefinger down the length of her nose. "Yes. I want you to help me eat this food."

Crystal rolled her eyes at him. "That's not what I meant and you know it."

"Do you know that you're real cute when you pout?" he whispered, filling two glasses with sangria and handing her one. He touched his glass to hers and took a swallow.

For several seconds she had no comeback. "I never pout."

"Yeah, you do," Joseph insisted. "You push out your lips and roll your eyes upward."

"Pouting is sucking teeth, closing your eyes, while rolling your head on your neck. Like this," Crystal added, demonstrating the motions.

Throwing back his head, Joseph laughed loudly. "You remind of Wanda. The Jamie Foxx character from *In Living Color*."

Crystal's laughter joined his. "I love watching reruns from *In Living Color* and *Martin*. And to see those actors transform themselves into characters that became icons is genius."

"Now, that takes real talent," Joseph agreed. Turning on the stove-top grill, he sprayed the surface with cooking oil. "How do you like your meat cooked?"

"Well. How do you like yours?" she asked.

He placed the skewers on the heated surface. "Why? Do you plan to cook for me?" he teased with a wide grin.

Crystal flashed a sexy moue. "Could be yes, could be no."

"Which one is it, Crystal?"

The uneasiness she'd felt when first walking into Joseph's apartment disappeared, replaced by an easygoing emotion that made her feel as if she'd met him weeks ago instead of two days. "I'll cook for you if you want."

His wide grin showed straight white teeth. "I want."

"Are you certain your girlfriend won't mind?"

The teasing glint in Joseph's eyes vanished. "Why would you mention a girlfriend?"

Crystal also sobered. "You said you're single, but you could still have a girlfriend."

He lifted a skewer, testing the meat for doneness before turning it over. "I don't have a girlfriend."

"Do you like women?"

Joseph's expression was a mask of stone as he glared at Crystal, unable to believe she would ask him something so ridiculous when he was practically salivating over her. It had taken every ounce of his self-control not to kiss her and satisfy the yearning to see if her mouth tasted as sweet as it looked.

"Yes, I like women. In fact, I like them a lot. It's just that I'm not seeing anyone right now."

"And why not?" she asked, pressing the issue.

Joseph turned four of the eight skewered cubes of beef over. He preferred his meat medium-well. "I was in a relationship for four years."

"What happened?"

"She wanted marriage and I wasn't ready for it at that time." Leaving his position at the courthouse to work for ColeDiz entailed longer work hours and a great deal more responsibility.

Crystal recoiled as if she'd been struck across the face. "You date a woman for four years and then decide she's not worth marrying?"

A frown furrowed Joseph's forehead. "Don't put words in my mouth, Crystal. I never said she wasn't worth marrying."

"What exactly are you saying, Joseph?"

"Kiara and I met in law school. We saw each other off and on, then hardly at all after graduation because I was studying for the bar. We reconnected when she relocated from Baltimore to Orlando. She was offered a position with the public defender's office at the same time I began clerking for your uncle."

"Had you moved to Miami?"

He shook his head. "No. I kept my West Palm Beach condo."

"You commuted the seventy miles between West Palm and Miami?"

He nodded. "Driving a minimum of three hours roundtrip every day isn't what I'd call a walk in the park, but I did it because I loved what I was doing." Joseph exhaled an audible breath. "I regretted having to resign clerking for Judge Eaton because criminal law had taken over my life. I ate, breathed and slept it."

Crystal took a sip of sangria, waiting for Joseph to continue. She wondered what would make a woman date a man for four years hoping, wishing and praying he would marry her. "Why did you resign?"

"Unfortunately, ColeDiz's general counsel was murdered when he walked in on a home invasion, and my cousin Diego needed someone in the legal department he could trust because he'd restructured to take the company global. I was able to set up an African international division, which allowed Diego to pay cash on delivery to a Ugandan cotton grower with an extra-long staple crop. It resulted in ColeDiz becoming the biggest family-owned agribusiness in the States. I traded commuting for jetting around the world.

"One month I'd be in Mexico or Belize. Then a couple of months later it was Jamaica, Brazil, Puerto Rico or Africa. Kiara complained we didn't see enough of each other, but there was nothing I could do about it because of my commitment to ColeDiz. I took her to Hawaii for a vacation to try and make up for the time when we couldn't be together, but she misconstrued my intent, believing I was going to propose marriage. When I didn't, all hell broke loose. The only thing to do was cut the trip short and return to the mainland."

"You never reconciled?"

"No." The single word was adamant. Joseph would never reconcile with Kiara because she had cursed not only him but also his entire family.

A beat passed before Crystal spoke again. "What else are you involved in besides cotton?"

"We have banana plantations in Belize and coffee in Mexico, Jamaica, Puerto Rico and Brazil. Two years ago we established Cole Tea Company, our first North American–based enterprise. It's only the second tea garden in the United States."

Crystal stared, surprised. "You're growing tea here in South Carolina?"

An expression of triumph brightened Joseph's eyes. "Yes."

"That means you're going to compete with the Charleston Tea Plantation."

Joseph sobered. "I don't know about competition, but ColeDiz has done very well with coffee, so tea was the next logical choice. Our tea garden covers one hundred acres between Kiawah and Edisto islands, and we plan to harvest our first crop in a couple of months."

Crystal sparingly sipped the sangria. "Is that what you meant when you said you were a farmer?"

"I now think of myself as a farmer because before the tea garden I knew absolutely nothing about bananas, coffee or tea except to eat or drink them. I spent a couple of years studying everything I could find about irrigation, soil composition, disease control and various methods of planting and harvesting these crops."

"Why did you decide on South Carolina? Why not Georgia or Florida?" she asked.

"The Lowcountry has the perfect environment for tea because of its sandy soil, subtropical climate and an average rainfall of over fifty inches a year. And there's a common myth that different types of teas are produced from different tea plants."

"Aren't they?" she asked.

"No. All types of tea are produced from the same plant, although there are two different varieties. The differences between them are the result of the different processing procedures. Sinensis sinensis thrives in the cool, high mountains of central China and Japan and sinensis assamica in moist, tropical regions of northeast India, the Yunnan provinces of China and here in the Lowcountry."

Crystal's eyebrows rose in amazement. "Are you saying green, black and oolong tea all come from the same plant even though they don't taste the same?"

"Yes. If you have some free time I'd like to take you to see our tea garden."

Although Crystal wanted to see the tea garden, she knew it couldn't be this weekend because she'd promised to spend that time with Xavier and Selena, and she was also scheduled to meet Al and the contractor Tuesday afternoon. "Monday is the only day I'm free this coming week."

"It's all right. We can put it off until a later date. By the way, do you have boots?"

Crystal nodded. "I have a pair of rain boots."

"They'll do because most times the island is a little muddy."

"What about your resorts?"

"What about them?" Joseph countered.

"How many do you have?"

"Eight. That's why I offered to invest in Selena's company. Her gourmet jams and jellies when marketed as duty-free souvenirs will make her a very wealthy woman. ColeDiz of course will be responsible for exportation, tariffs and other fees."

Crystal closed her eyes for several seconds. Now she understood how the Coles had amassed their wealth, and she wondered how many people outside their family were privy to this information. When she opened her eyes Joseph had placed four kabobs on a plate with a tiny cup of dipping sauce for her along with a knife and fork.

Setting down the glass of wine, she picked up the knife, cutting a slice of the grilled meat and popping it into her mouth.

"Oh my word!" she gasped. "This is so good."

Joseph dipped his cube into the leftover marinade, slowly chewing the tender buttery sirloin. It was only the second time he'd attempted the recipe, and he had to admit to himself it was delicious. "Not bad."

"Don't be so modest, Joseph," Crystal chided. "You're an incredible chef."

"Cook," he corrected. "My mother is the professional chef. Enough about me," he said, deftly steering the topic away from him. "Is there someone special in your past?"

Crystal stared at the precisely cut raven-black hair lying close to Joseph's scalp, wondering, if he let it grow, if it would curl or stand up like brush bristles. The seconds ticked while she composed her thoughts.

"I lived with a man for three years when I was in graduate school." The disclosure seemed to shock Joseph. "Brian taught art at New York University. We met at a sports bar in the Village where students and faculty from NYU and Parsons hung out on weekends."

"If you lived together for three years, why didn't you get married?"

The censure in Joseph's voice sounded so much like Raleigh Eaton she thought she'd conjured him up. "There were a number of factors. I was twenty-three and felt I was too young to settle down. Brian was thirty-nine and he didn't want children."

"Damn, the dude was too old for you."

"He wasn't *that* old." Crystal knew she sounded defensive, but it wasn't what it seemed. Brian might have been sixteen years her senior, but he looked years younger.

"I still say he was too old for you," Joseph whispered under his breath. "Should I assume you wanted children?"

"Not then. However, I'd like to have one or two sometime in the future."

"Why did you break up?"

Crystal caressed the granite surface under her fingertips. "We really didn't break up. He was offered a teaching position in California and I encouraged him to take it. After I graduated I gave up our Greenwich Village apartment and moved back to Florida."

Joseph placed his hand over Crystal's. "How did your family react to you shacking up with a man?"

She rolled her eyes at him again. "You could've said cohabitating instead of shacking."

"It is what it is, Crystal."

"To answer your question—my parents didn't like it for a number of reasons. First, they felt I was too young to *shack up* with a man and second, Brian was too old for me. It was sort of a test for me because I grew up as an only child and if it hadn't been for my aunt, uncle and cousins I probably would've had abandonment issues. My parents divorced not only each other but also me. They were so caught up in their own lives at that time they'd forgotten they had a child."

He tightened his grip when she attempted to extricate her fingers. "How old were you when they divorced?"

"Eight."

Joseph stared at his hand covering her much smaller one. "That's very young."

Crystal smiled wryly. "I managed to survive without having to spend thousands of hours on a therapist's couch. Now that I'm an adult, I'm cool with my parents. It's better they're not married because they get along better as friends than husband and wife."

"Did you ever think you lived with a man who was that much older than you because you were looking for him to replace Daddy?"

Crystal clenched her teeth as she gave Joseph a long, withering stare. "I definitely wasn't looking for another father. Brian and I were together because we offered each other what we needed at that time in our lives.

Joseph released her hand. "Sex?"

In spite of herself, Crystal burst out laughing. "Is that all you men think about?"

His gaze traveled over her face, then moved slowly to her chest before reversing direction. "It's not all *I* think about, but it is necessary if you want a satisfying physical relationship."

Resting an elbow on the countertop, she cradled her chin on the heel of her hand. "I prefer a *healthy* physical relationship to a satisfying one. Don't forget there are methods men and women can use to bring themselves to climax or ejaculate."

Choking sounds came from Joseph as he reached for his glass of sangria and took a deep swallow.

"Did I embarrass you?" Crystal laughed. "Come, now, Joseph. We're both adults, so the subject of masturbation shouldn't be off the table." Growing up around three male cousins and overhearing them talk about sex helped her to have a healthy attitude about what went on between men and woman in the bedroom.

Joseph narrowed his eyes. "I'm not embarrassed," he said defensively. "I just didn't expect us to talk about masturbation."

"You were the one who mentioned sex."

"You're…" His words trailed off when the phone rang. "Excuse me, Crystal, but I have to answer that." It wasn't often someone called him on the hotel's line. Striding across the kitchen, he picked up the receiver to the wall phone. "Hello."

"Hi, Joey. I tried calling your cell, but it went to voice mail."

Joseph was too annoyed with his sister to tell her he left his cell phone in the bedroom. She had promised him she would call when she got to Durham. "Don't tell me you're just getting in, because I left you a voice mail this morning."

"I got in last night but couldn't call you because one of my sorority sisters found out that her boyfriend got another girl pregnant and we were up all night talking her off the ledge. She's threatening to buy a gun to shoot him and the girl."

"Tell her to save her money and the bullets because neither of them is worth her spending the rest of her life in prison."

"That's what we've been saying. Hopefully it will sink in. By the way, you don't have to send me any money. I spoke to Daddy a few minutes ago and told him everything."

He smiled. Apparently Bianca had decided to take a stand with their father. "How did it go?"

"He wasn't too happy, but said he understood where I was coming from. He must be mellowing out in his old age."

"Dad's only sixty-two, so he's not that old." Joseph half listened to his sister talk nonstop about the plans she'd made when she took the year off as he stared at Crystal, watching him. There was no doubt he'd misjudged her. Under her reserved exterior was a woman who wasn't afraid to speak her mind. And she was right when she accused him of bringing up the topic of sex.

"Joey, are you still there?"

"Yeah, Bibi. I'm here."

"You sound distracted. Do you have company?"

"Yes."

"Why didn't you say something?" Bianca admonished. "I'll text you with an update on the drama that's going on here."

"Tell your soror that I'm not licensed to practice law in North Carolina, so she shouldn't do anything crazy. Remind her if she's charged with murder one, that carries a life sentence or the death penalty."

"I'll let her know. Bye, Joey. I love you."

"Love you, too, Bibi."

Joseph ended the call, returning to the cooking island. "That was my sister. I told her when she came to see me yesterday to call when she got back to school, but she had other pressing issues than phoning her brother."

Grimacing, Crystal bit down on her lower lip until she felt a pulse. "That was your sister I saw you with in the lobby yesterday?"

"Yes. When I introduce Bianca as my sister, folks always ask if she's adopted. My brothers and I tease her saying we found her on the back porch and decided to take her in."

"I guess you and your brothers look alike."

"We look like most Cole dudes, while Bianca resembles the Reyes side of the family. At almost twenty, she's the mirror image of our Puerto Rican grandmother at the same age." Joseph noted the time on the microwave. It was almost eight o'clock. He and Crystal had spent the past hour talking. Rounding the island, he eased her off the stool. "It's time I feed you or you'll think I'm a terrible host."

Chapter 6

Dinner concluded, Crystal sat across the table from Joseph wondering if she'd been involved with him at twenty-three how different her life would be now. She knew he never would've agreed to live together without marriage. And if they'd married they would have at least one child.

Unlike his ex, she wouldn't complain about not seeing her husband enough. Growing up an only child, she learned early on to entertain herself. Whenever she wasn't with her cousins, she escaped between the pages of a book. In middle school she began making up stories, filling volumes of cloth-covered journals.

Once she entered adolescence, subscribing to magazines had become her drug of choice. She filled out countless order cards and when the first issue arrived along with the bill, Crystal gave it to her father, who promptly wrote a check.

Stacks of magazines devoted to fashion, travel, cooking and design and architecture eventually took over all the available closet space in her bedroom. Then her mother issued an ultimatum: get rid of all but her favorites. She bundled all except the issues devoted to décor and design. Thus began her love affair with interior decorating.

"What made you decide to go into interior decorating?"

Joseph's voice broke into her musings. It was as if he'd read her mind. "I love beautiful things," she said, smiling. "I suppose it comes naturally because my mother is an art dealer."

Leaning back in his chair, Joseph angled his head. "A lot of people like beautiful things, yet they don't become decorators."

"For me it is taking an empty space and filling it up with

pieces that not only complement one another but also reflect the owner's personality."

"I'm planning to build a house."

Crystal sat up straight. She didn't have to be clairvoyant to know Joseph was going to ask her about decorating ideas. "What do you want to know?"

"Will you consider decorating it once it's completed?"

She schooled her expression so as not to reveal her excitement. Joseph asking her to decorate his home, if she accepted the commission, would be her first nonreferral. "If you hadn't met me, who would you have chosen?"

"My aunt, who just happens to be a retired decorator, gave me a list of recommendations. She stopped working for the family a couple of years ago because she's spending more time with her great-grandchildren."

"Who did she recommend?" A cold shiver snaked its way up Crystal's spine when Joseph mentioned the architectural and design firm in Fort Lauderdale where she'd been sexually harassed.

Joseph's expression mirrored confusion. "What's the matter, Crystal?"

"What are you talking about?"

"You look as if you just saw a ghost when I mentioned Bramwell and Duncan Architectural and Design."

She lowered her eyes, staring at the tablecloth. "I used to work for them before I went into business for myself."

Joseph leaned over the table. "Why did you leave?"

"I was passed over for promotion one too many times."

"What else, Crystal?"

She looked up at him, meeting his eyes. "What makes you think there's something else?"

"I may be a few things, but a fool is not one of them. I saw something in your eyes that says there's bad blood between you and your old employer."

Crystal had underestimated Joseph. It was apparent he was quite perceptive. "One of the partners sexually harassed me, and rather than sue, I resigned."

"You never told anyone?"

She shook her head. "No."

"You leave so he can sexually harass another woman?"

Joseph's accusatory tone grated on her nerves. "You have no right to be judgmental when you don't know all of the facts. I wasn't the first woman to be targeted, and there's no doubt I won't be the last. An assistant architect told me in confidence that another woman had threatened to sue, but she was paid well for her silence. Bramwell and Duncan have deep pockets and enough clout to keep any case tied up in the court for years. And because I wasn't willing to take a bribe, I left. Think about it, Joseph. How many companies would hire someone with a history of suing her employer?"

Joseph ran a hand over his face. "I suppose you did the right thing when you resigned."

"Even if I didn't do the right thing, I know I made the right decision to go into business for myself."

"Lucky me," he drawled. If Crystal was good enough to decorate hotels for the preeminent Charleston hotelier, then she had to be very good at what she did. "Now, Miss Businesswoman, will you accept the commission to decorate my house once it's completed?"

"What's the projection date for completion?"

"It probably won't be until sometime next year."

Crystal traced the design on the handle of the dinner fork with her forefinger. She did not want to commit to decorating a home that was still in the planning stages. "We'll talk once you get closer to completion. No more, please," she said, placing her hand over her wineglass when Joseph attempted to refill it. Smiling, she said teasingly, "If I drink any more I'll have a problem making it down the hall."

Light from the overhead chandelier bathed Joseph in gold as he ran a forefinger around the rim of his wineglass. "You don't have to go home. I do have an extra bedroom."

Her gaze grazed his mouth. "I was only teasing about not making it back to my apartment. What I'm not is much of a drinker."

His eyes opened wider. "And I'm serious about you staying over. If or when you can't make it back to your place, I'll either carry you or put you up here."

A shiver of awareness snaked its way up Crystal's back when she realized she was about to embark on something for which she wasn't quite ready. Joseph embodied the essence of the perfect bachelor—if there was such a thing. He was tall, dark, handsome, intelligent, elegant and wealthy. "Is that something you do with women who've had too much to drink? Put them up at your place?"

Joseph dabbed the corners of his mouth with the linen napkin. "No. I can't afford to have an intoxicated woman in my home and later on have her accuse me of taking advantage of her. When I suspect she's had too much to drink I usually call a car service to take her home. The driver knows not to leave them until they're safely behind a closed and locked door."

She gave him a bright smile. "I don't think you'll ever have to deal with that problem with me, because two drinks is usually my limit."

He gestured to her glass. "You only drank half your wine."

Crystal touched her napkin to her lips. "That's because I had the sangria."

His expression didn't change. "Are you ready for dessert?"

She looked at Joseph as if he'd suddenly taken leave of his senses. "I'm so full I'm going to have to pass on the dessert."

Rising, Joseph came around the table and pulled back Crystal's chair. He hovered over her head longer than necessary, her warmth and scent wafting to his nostrils. "I'll wrap it up so you can take it with you."

Crystal stood, resting her hand on his shoulder. "I'm not leaving yet. I'm going to stay and help you clean up."

He shook his head. "No, you're not. Someone from housekeeping will take care of everything." A knowing smile played at the corners of Crystal's mouth, bringing his gaze to focus there. "What's so funny?"

She averted her head to conceal her smirk. Joseph had denied having someone pick up after him. "Nothing. No!" she screamed. He'd picked her up, holding her above his head as if she weighed no more than a child. "Put me down, Joseph!"

"Apologize."

Crystal closed her eyes, praying he wouldn't drop her. "For what?"

"For what you were thinking."

"What was I thinking!"

"You know right well what you were thinking."

"Okay. I'm sorry." She shook uncontrollably when he finally lowered her until her feet touched the floor.

Joseph felt her trembling. Pulling her against his chest, he pressed his mouth to her forehead. "It's okay, sweetheart. I wouldn't have dropped you."

Crystal curved her arms under his shoulders, holding tightly as if he were her lifeline. Temporarily traumatized, she couldn't react to the softly whispered endearment. "I'm afraid of heights," she admitted tearfully.

Cradling the back of her head, Joseph closed his eyes. "I'm sorry. I didn't know." Lowering his head, he pressed a kiss to her ear, and then trailed kisses along the column of her neck. "Will you forgive me?"

Crystal sniffled. "I'll think about it."

Joseph cradled her face in his hands. His heart turned over when he saw the unshed tears in her eyes. He touched his mouth to hers, making certain not to increase the pressure to where she'd pull away. "I'm very, very sorry," he whispered over and over, placing light kisses on her parted lips.

The soft caress of his mouth reminded Crystal of the gossamer wings of a butterfly brushing her face when she'd lain on the grass long ago, staring up at the clouds in the sky. At first it'd startled her, but it flew back and landed on her forehead; she lay completely still so it wouldn't fly away again. Those were the happiest days in her young life—before her parents' divorce.

It had been a long time, much too long since a man had held and kissed her. Before she'd slept with Brian, there had been one man—a student at Howard University—and no one after Brian. She dated a few men but refused to sleep with them because she'd convinced herself she didn't have time for romance in her life when she had to concentrate on her career.

Spending the past few hours with Joseph had proven her wrong. She wanted romance, passion and to experience again why she'd been born female. Lowering her arms, she pushed against his chest. "I think I'd better go now."

Reluctantly, Joseph released her. "Don't you want to wait for your dessert?"

A rush of heat suffused her face as she grew conscious of his scrutiny. "Will it keep?"

"Yes."

Crystal forced a smile. "Bring it to my place Monday. If you don't have anything planned for Monday evening, then I'd like to have you over for happy hour."

His eyes caressed her face. "What time does happy hour begin?"

"Five."

"I'll be there."

Rising on tiptoe, she kissed his cheek. "Thank you for a wonderful evening and an incredible dinner."

Joseph stared at her, committing everything about her face to memory. Resting a hand at the small of her back, he led her out of the dining room. "I'll walk you back to your place."

"Don't be silly. I'm less than two hundred feet from you."

He took her hand. "Didn't I tell you I always make certain my date gets back home safely? And because I don't have to call a driver, I'm going to see you to your door."

Crystal realized it was futile to argue with Joseph. "I didn't know I was your date."

"You don't get out much, do you?"

She gave him a sidelong glance. "Why would you say that?"

"When a man invites you to share dinner with him, it's a date."

"What if I invite you to dinner? Is it still a date?"

"Yes, ma'am."

Crystal stared at the toes of her shoes for several seconds. "I'm glad we cleared that up."

Joseph left his door unlocked as he walked with Crystal to her apartment. He waited while she took the card key from the pocket of her slacks and slipped it into the slot. The light glowed green. Reaching over her head, he held the door open for her. "I'll wait until you close and lock the door."

Crystal didn't understand Joseph's rationale for escorting her to her apartment. The penthouse floor was the most secure one in the hotel; they were the only guests occupying the apartments, and only employees assigned to the floor were allowed access. "I think you're being ridiculous."

"Please indulge me."

"Good night. And thank you again for a wonderful night."

Joseph winked at her. "You're welcome, beautiful."

She closed and locked the door; pressing her back against the solid surface, she slid down to the floor, her heart hammering against her ribs. *I like him. I really like him!* She'd come to Charleston to decorate hotels, not become involved with a man who'd claimed confidence as his birthright.

"If you're going to spend two months working in Charleston, you should have some fun, too." Her mother's words came rushing back in vivid clarity. "Well, Mother," she whispered, "I'm about to have some fun."

Joseph picked up the iPhone, answering before it rang a third time. He knew it was Diego. *"Hola, primo. Cómo estás?"*

"That's what I should be asking you, *primo.* I left a couple of voice mails for you to call me back."

Joseph had been watching a comedy on television

"I was indisposed, Diego." It was a half-truth.

Diego's resonant chuckle came through the earpiece. "I hope she was good."

A shadow of annoyance crossed his face. "It's not what you think." He and Crystal had shared dinner, not a bed, and if she'd been any woman other than the niece of Judge Solomon Eaton, Joseph definitely would've made it known to Crystal he was romantically interested in her.

While in college he'd had one-night stands, but they usually left him unfulfilled. Waking up next to a woman he'd just met hours before, unable to remember much about her, sometime not even her name, was relegated to his undergraduate party days.

"Lo siento, José. Quise decir sin faltarle el respeto," Diego replied in Spanish.

"No disrespect taken," Joseph countered.

"Who is she, Joseph?"

"What makes you think it was a she?"

There came another chuckle. "If it wasn't a she, then you would've said you were tied up with something."

Joseph smiled. "You think you know me that well?"

"Well enough since you decided to leave the dark side and work for ColeDiz."

"I didn't have much of a choice when it came to leaving the dark side as you call the justice system. If you hadn't lost Barry I still would be helping to lock away the dregs of society for lengthy sentences."

There came a pause, and then Diego said, "I really like your suggestion about selling the gourmet jams, jellies and preserves in our resort gift shops."

It was apparent Diego had received the order he'd placed with Sweet Persuasions. "Have you sampled them?"

"Hell yeah. That's why I'm in agreement. Do you have a firm offer from the manufacturer?"

"Not yet," Joseph said confidently. He knew he had to create a business plan, outlining their partnership before meeting with Selena.

"You're a brilliant lawyer, but you've also become a helluva businessman."

There was another pause, this time from Joseph. "Are you all right, Diego?"

"Of course. Why?"

"You usually don't give out compliments." Diego had a reputation as a hard-nosed, take-no-prisoners businessman. He wouldn't let anything or anyone stand in his way if he wanted something. A few of the employees referred to him as the SOB instead of the CEO, but never to his face. Diego expected those who were fortunate enough to work for ColeDiz to give the company 110 percent effort. However, their hard work was always rewarded with generous year-end bonuses.

"I shouldn't have to blow up your ego because we're *sangre*."

Joseph nodded, although Diego couldn't see him. They were blood, and for a Cole that meant everything. Anyone with even a drop of Cole blood was *familia*. "Word."

"I had a long talk with Vivienne a few days ago and I want you to be the first know that I'm thinking about going into semi-retirement at fifty and retire permanently at sixty. That means you should prepare to become CEO-in-training."

Joseph held his breath, not exhaling until his lungs were close to exploding. Diego held the distinction of being the fifth CEO of ColeDiz since Samuel Claridge Cole had established the company in the mid 1920s.

"Are you sure there's nothing wrong with you? Vivienne? The kids?"

"Slow down, Joseph. There's nothing wrong with either of us. I suppose you can say I had an epiphany."

"What about?" he asked, listening intently as his cousin talked about making changes in his life.

"I'd like to spend more time with my family before my kids grow up and have lives of their own. In ten years they'll be teenagers and will probably want nothing to do with their old man except use me as their personal ATM. I don't want to miss their soccer and Little League games or dance and music recitals because Daddy always has to work."

Joseph tightened his grip on the phone. He wasn't ready to assume control of a billion-dollar international conglomerate. He didn't need that responsibility, even if shared. When would he find the time to complete the construction on his home? And when finished, would he have time to enjoy it?

"What if we compromise, Diego?"

"How?"

"I limit my traveling to South Carolina, Puerto Rico and Jamaica. No more crossing time zones and datelines. Even though I'm not married or have children, I'd like to think about having them by the time I'm thirty-five. And that's not going to happen if I continue to jet around the world at a moment's notice."

"Have you met someone special, Joseph?"

Joseph's jaw clenched. *If* he had met someone special he doubted whether their relationship would be deemed even close to normal. What woman would be willing to put up with him not celebrating her birthday with her because he was thousands of miles away? And if married, miss the birth or birthdays of their children?

"No," he said emphatically.

"Are you looking?" Diego asked.

"Not consciously, but I don't want my life so bogged down with work that I won't be able to give her the emotional support she's entitled to as my wife. I bought that parcel of land almost a year ago with the intent of building a house, yet it hasn't happened. I've put off meeting with the architect so many times he probably thinks I'm crazy. I'm scheduled to meet with him once again, but it'll have to be after the tea harvest."

"I didn't realize you were ready to settle down."

"It's not so much about settling down as it is experiencing a semblance of normalcy. Hanging out here in Charleston for the next three months is the first time since I joined ColeDiz that I can actually plan what I want to do two or three days in advance. I may not have a family, but I do have a life. When you asked me to come and work with you I didn't hesitate because you're *familia.* And now you want me to take on more responsibility."

"It won't be that much more."

"That's bull, Diego, and you know it. I'm not agreeing to anything unless you're willing to compromise."

"Let me think about it."

"You do that," Joseph countered. Diego wasn't the only Cole with a stubborn streak a mile wide. "I'm going to draft a proposal for Selena Eaton, so hopefully we'll be able to invest in her company. I'll send you a copy before I present it to her."

"Eaton? Is she by chance related to your Judge Eaton?"

Joseph's annoyance with his cousin eased with the mention of his former mentor. Diego knew how he had felt when he had to resign his position at the courthouse. But instead of pouting and sulking he sucked it up and did what so many in his family did when summoned to come work for the family-owned business. They did it without question.

"Yes. She's married to his nephew."

"Damn, *primo*. It looks as if you can't get away from the Eatons."

A wide grin spread across Joseph's face. He doubted if he would ever have met Selena if it hadn't been for Crystal. "You're right about that. I guess you can say it's a small world."

"When it comes to you and the Eatons, it's a small, small world," Diego countered. "And there's no need to send me a draft of the proposal, because you'll just have to explain the legalese, which by the way bores the hell out of me. And, Joseph?"

"What, Diego?"

"I'm going to check with H.R. to see who in legal would like to do a *little* traveling every now and then."

"Gracias, primo. Adios."

Ending the call, Joseph wanted to remind Diego that it wasn't just a little traveling, and whoever he selected would probably have to renew their passport every two to three years instead of the requisite ten. He also realized he'd turned a page on a chapter in his life when he'd challenged Diego. It was something he wouldn't have thought of doing two years ago. However, Diego wasn't the only one who'd had an epiphany. It was time he took control of his life *and* his future.

Palming the phone, he made his way to the area where a home/office had been set up. Instead of using the hotel desktop, he opened his laptop and entered his password.

Hours later Joseph printed out the draft agreement. He would wait a day or two and then review it for additions and/or deletions.

Chapter 7

Crystal dropped her overnight bag on the floor in the entryway, her gaze lingering on the exquisite bouquet of flowers on the table.

"Gorgeous flowers," she remarked as she followed Selena through the living room.

"They're a gift from Joseph," Selena said. "He sent the flowers along with a dozen honeybell oranges as thank-you gifts for brunch. It's nice to find a man our age with some home training. Most times they want to take from a woman instead of giving or sharing. In my opinion he's a keeper."

Crystal placed a hand over her mouth to conceal a yawn. She'd spent a restless night, tossing and turning, then finally getting out of bed after recurring dreams about Joseph. In one of them they were in bed together, limbs entwined, while his mouth explored every inch of her body. In another she saw herself walking away from him while he yelled at her to come back. The visions were both erotic and frightening, foreshadowing a short-term relationship.

"I can't keep what I don't have."

Reaching for her hand, Selena led her into the kitchen. "But you could have him. I saw the way he was looking at you."

"Which way was that?"

"Like he couldn't believe what he was looking at. Would you go out with him if he asked you?"

Crystal didn't tell Selena that although she would go out with Joseph she definitely wasn't looking for something long-term. "Why not? After all, it's not as if I have a trail of men knocking on my door. And as you said, he does have home training."

"You should have a trail of men knocking down your door,"

Selena said, giving her a sidelong glance. "Everyone says you and Mia are the family's high-fashion models."

"Yeah, right," Crystal drawled. "It's because we're so tall." The former Mia Eaton had relocated from Dallas to Jonesburg as a medical resident. She fell in love and married Selena's cousin Kenyon Chandler, sheriff of the historic Mingo County, West Virginia, mining town.

"Tall and beautiful," Selena continued as if Crystal hadn't spoken. "In fact, you and Mia look enough alike to be sisters now that you've cut your hair. I know you said you had breakfast, but will you join me for a cup of latte?"

Settling herself on the chair at the table in the eat-in kitchen, Crystal nodded. "Of course." She looked around, not seeing any of the toys usually scattered about the floor. "Where's Lily?"

"Out with Xavier. He took her to Murrells Inlet."

Crystal stared at her cousin's wife in a pair of gray sweatpants and an oversize white tee. She'd pulled her hair back into a ponytail. "What's there?"

"Brookgreen Gardens. It has nature trails, sculpture gardens and the Lowcountry Zoo. Lily's a little young for the trails and gardens, but I'm certain she'll enjoy the zoo."

Crystal smiled. "So the outing is more for Xavier than Lily?"

Selena turned on the espresso machine. "You really know your cousin. Every Saturday he takes Lily out to give me a break. Even though he selects places that are child-friendly, they still appeal to him if they're connected to history. And that means you and I have the rest of the day to ourselves."

"Don't you have orders to fill?"

Selena opened an overhead cabinet, taking down two mugs. "I stayed up late last night making six dozen chocolate amaretto and coffee-flavored truffles for a customer who'll pick them up in an hour for her twin daughters' twenty-first birthday."

"Have you given any thought to Joseph's offer to invest in Sweet Persuasions?"

Selena nodded. "Xavier and I talked about it, and he's warming to the idea. I called Myles and spoke to him about it. He said not to commit or sign anything until he looks the agreement. It pays to have a lawyer in the family."

Crystal agreed with Selena. There were a number of Eatons who were doctors, several lawyers and teachers and her CPA/financial analyst father. "If Myles gives you the go-ahead, will you be able to meet the demand?"

Resting a hip against the countertop, Selena gave Crystal a direct stare. Her expression changed, her gaze softening. "That depends. I'd have to hire someone, even if it's part-time, and buy several automatic jam and jelly makers. The machine can produce about four half pints of each at a time. The problem is I don't want to give up being an at-home patissier, because it would mean putting Lily in day care."

"What would you do?"

"I may have to expand the commercial kitchen."

"How long does it take for a batch of jam to cook?"

"About thirty minutes. One machine can produce one hundred twenty-eight ounces an hour. Multiply that by four hours and you have five hundred twelve ounces. Packaging them in two-ounce jars will yield more than two hundred fifty of them. I have Grandma's recipe, so there's not a problem of duplicating the final product. I thought about copackaging it, but the recipe is a closely held secret, and it would take years to get a patent, so I have to keep it in the family."

Crystal smiled. "Good for you." Her smile faded. "What about your employee? Will he or she be privy to the ingredients in the recipe?"

"No. They'll know everything but the ingredients for the pectin. That's Grandma's secret." Selena waved her hand. "Enough about me. What do you want to do today?"

"Shopping."

"I was hoping you'd say that," Selena said, smiling. "There's a new boutique that opened a month ago off Calhoun Street that I'd like to check out."

Crystal's smile grew wider as she cupped a hand to her ear. "I can hear it calling my name."

* * *

Joseph eased off the accelerator, slowing the Range Rover as he maneuvered along the narrow, rutted, unpaved road leading to the tea plantation.

Each time he came to the sparsely populated island during the summer months, Joseph felt as if he had stepped back not only in time but also into another world. It was primordial with ancient live oaks draped in Spanish moss, towering cypress trees, swamps and marshes teeming with poisonous snakes, alligators, snowy-white egrets and eagles. Eagle Island—one of more than a thousand in the Lowcountry running from Charleston, South Carolina, to Savannah, Georgia—was environmentally sensitive, and the engineers ColeDiz hired for the tea garden were instructed to clear land only necessary for planting.

The summer air—heavy and dense—always seemed to smother him like a leaded blanket, making it difficult to draw a normal breath. But in autumn it changed, becoming clearer, softer and lighter, although the mornings were heavy with dew. The winter months were Joseph's least favorite time of the year. What had been lush and alive now appeared gray, bleak.

He drove past a small house erected on stilts, returning the wave of the elderly man sitting on the porch. Several hundred feet away stood another house, this one larger with a screened-in wraparound porch. There were more houses, all built off the ground in typical Lowcountry architecture. Most front doors were painted light blue, which at first he found odd until the proprietor of the island's only store explained it was a Gullah custom. The color blue kept away the bad spirits.

If Joseph thought many of the Gullah customs and traditions peculiar, it was their language he found intriguing. The term Gullah, believed to be derived from Angola, was an English dialect interspersed with several African languages. Books devoted to the Gullah culture and language now lined the shelves of the bookcase in his ColeDiz office, along with those devoted to every country and culture he'd visited. Joseph knew success only came from immersing himself in the culture of the country or region in which he conducted business.

A road sign pointing the way to the Cole Tea Company came into view. Reflective letters warned it was private property and trespassers were subject to arrest. Unseen to the naked eye were close-circuit cameras protecting the property and monitored by a local resident who also worked for the tea company.

Executing a smooth left turn, he maneuvered over a wide, paved roadway and then came to a complete stop. A carpet of green stretched across the landscape for as far as he could see.

Seeing acre upon acre of tiny shoots pushing up through the damp earth made two years of sacrifice all the more profound. Joseph had given up the career he coveted since he was a child to take his place in the family-owned company. He'd sacrificed years of not having a normal relationship with a woman because of his commitment to a project initially he wasn't certain would come to fruition. Twenty-six months, to be exact.

Staring at the tea plants filled him with an indescribable feeling of pride. A law degree notwithstanding, Joseph had become the latest farmer in a family spanning five generations.

Pulling into the driveway alongside a modern two-story Lowcountry house, he turned off the engine. The sound of a door opening and heavy footfalls caught his attention as he stepped out of the Range Rover. Joseph's smile matched the wide grin belonging to the man who'd taught him everything he needed to know about growing tea.

Standing six foot six and tipping the scales at two sixty, raven-haired former NFL defensive tackle Shane Knox was an imposing figure.

Extending his hand, Joseph mounted the porch steps. "Happy New Year."

Ignoring the proffered hand, Shane pulled him close in a rib-crushing bear hug. "Back at you, Wilson. How the hell have you been?"

Joseph pounded his back. "Yo, man, ease up before you break my ribs."

A rush of color suffused Shane's face. "Sorry about that."

"How's Marci?" The move to the Lowcountry hadn't been easy for Shane's wife. She missed her family, and the isolation was exacerbated by a pregnancy plagued with nausea and vomiting.

Shane ran a hand over his face. "She's resting. Her sleep patterns are off because the baby sleeps during the day and does gymnastics at night. Do you want me to let her know you're here?"

Joseph shook his head. "No. Let her rest." Reaching into the breast pocket of his jacket, he handed Shane an envelope. "These are your arrangements. Someone from the car service will call you tonight to confirm the time you and Marci will be picked up Sunday morning. The jet will be at the airport when you arrive. The only thing you'll need to board is your ID. I've also arranged for a doctor and nurse to be onboard if Marci needs medical assistance."

Shane tapped the envelope against his palm. "I hate to leave now with harvest only months away. What if I send Marci now, and fly out closer to her due—"

"Come on, man, let's not go through this again," Joseph said, cutting him off. "Your wife has been begging *you* to take her to see her parents—her mother in particular—because Marci needs to see and talk to someone other than you. This tea garden will not wither and die because you're not here. Mervin, Willie and I will make certain of that."

"But—"

"No buts, Shane" he interrupted. "If your ass isn't on that plane tomorrow morning, then you're fired!"

When Shane asked him if he could take Marci home to Nebraska to await the birth of their son, Joseph quickly approved the request.

The blood drained from the former athlete's face, leaving it an ashen shade. "You're kidding," he whispered.

A scowl distorted Joseph's features. "Do you see me laughing?"

A beat passed. "No, I don't," Shane countered.

"So we're in agreement?"

Shane offered his hand. "Yes."

Smiling, Joseph took his hand, then landed a soft punch on Shane's hard-rock shoulder. "Thank you." His smile vanished, replaced with a hardened expression belying his youth. "My grandfather told me a long time ago that nothing, and that includes personal desires, is more important than family. Marci and that baby she's carrying are your family. *They* are your priority, not this tea garden. Take care of them."

That said, Joseph turned and walked back to his truck. Pressing a button on the remote device, he started the engine. He'd questioned his cousin's management style over and over, and within the span of thirty seconds he'd threatened a prospective father with dismissal because Shane challenged his mandate.

He hadn't wanted to step into the role as a badass, but if the tea garden failed he would be culpable, not Shane. Diego had entrusted him with the venture, and no one wanted the tea garden to succeed more than Joseph, but not at the expense of a man neglecting his family.

Crystal took a step back, surveying her handiwork. The smile parting her lips reached her eyes. She hadn't lost her touch. All of the dishes on the buffet server had met, and several exceeded, her expectations.

Rather than offer Joseph the usual happy hour fare, she decided on a cheese platter with red and white seedless grapes, sliced strawberries and stone-ground crackers. There were hot and cold hors d'oeuvres with a Mediterranean medley of grape leaves, red sweet peppers, pepperoncini and mixed pitted olives. Cocktail meatballs, sesame shrimp toast, pork dim sum and barbecue spare ribs cut into bite-size pieces were kept warm atop an electric buffet server.

Housekeeping had come earlier that morning to dust, vacuum and clean the apartment while Crystal made a supermarket run to purchase the items she didn't have on hand. Her decision to cook for Joseph was twofold: she wanted to return the favor of his preparing a scrumptious dinner for her, and she wanted to see if she hadn't lost her touch hosting a dinner party.

The doorbell chimed and she walked out of the dining room to answer the door. She opened the door to find Joseph leaning against the door frame, grinning from ear to ear.

"Welcome to Club Chez Crystal." She'd affected a French accent.

He inclined his head. *"Merci, Mademoiselle Eaton,"* he replied, extending his right hand with the bag with the wine she'd given him. "I thought you could use a little more libation." He tightened his grip on the handles of the smaller bag in his left. "This one has a cannoli, your dessert from the other night, and a few samples of gelato from your favorite shop."

Crystal's jaw dropped slightly as she stepped aside to open the door wider. "Paolo's?" Joseph nodded. "Who told you it was my favorite?"

Joseph smiled, glancing around the candlelit living room. She hadn't drawn the drapes, and the light coming in through the wall-to-wall windows lent itself to an evening for romance.

His gaze shifted to linger on her, moving slowly from her face to her shapely bare legs in a pair of black pumps that put her height close to the six-foot mark. He smiled again. It was obvious she was very secure about her height. "Xavier."

Crystal took the bag with the dessert from his outstretched hand. "You and Xavier were talking about me?"

"Not really. I asked him if I wanted to take you out what restaurant was your favorite. And he said you really liked 39 Rue de Jean on John Street, and you never ate dessert there because you preferred ordering gelato from Paolo's."

Her eyes narrowed in suspicion. "Is that all you talked about?"

Taking several steps brought Joseph mere inches from her. His hands went to her bare shoulders. The ubiquitous little black dress hugged every inch of her tight body, making him more than aware of her feminine curves. "That's all," he said softly. "I like surprises."

Crystal froze. There was something so potently masculine about Joseph she found it difficult to draw a normal breath whenever he touched her. She'd lived with a man many years older than her, yet she never felt this uncomfortable around Brian.

She closed her eyes for several seconds. "You think of me as a surprise?"

He dipped his head and pressed a kiss alongside her neck. "Everything about you is surprising," he whispered against her silken skin. "When you opened the door I didn't know what to expect, but it certainly wasn't to be wined and dined at Chez Crystal by the owner herself."

Crystal let out an inaudible sigh, grateful he'd said wined and dined and not seduced. Seducing Joseph wasn't something she consciously thought about, because that had never been her style. She liked dating and courtship.

"I had to do something to try and match your incredible cooking prowess." Her smile and the timbre of her voice belied her quaking innards. Everything about Joseph seeped into her: the warmth of his body, the feathery touch of his mouth against her neck and the scent of his sensual cologne.

Joseph's hands moved up, cradling her face. "There shouldn't be a competition between us, Crystal."

Her gaze searched his face, lingering on the cleft in his strong chin. "What do we have?"

A sweep of long black lashes concealed his innermost feelings for a woman whom he felt he'd known forever instead of less than a week. "Something very special," Joseph said after a pregnant silence.

Another beat of silence ensued. "And what's that?" Crystal asked.

"A family connection."

She didn't know what she'd expected him to say, but he was right. Neither knew of the other days ago, yet circumstances beyond their comprehension deemed one day their paths would cross. "How true. You're going to have to let me go so I can put the gelato in the freezer before it's a soupy mess."

It was with reluctance Joseph lowered his hands. If possible, he would hold her indefinitely. "Do you want me to help you with anything?"

"Yes. I want you to help me eat this food," she said, repeating what he'd told her Friday night.

Joseph had no comeback as he watched the sexy sway of Crystal's hips and her long legs that seemed to go on forever. He watched her walk, and suddenly it hit him. He wanted to make love to Crystal. The image of her lying naked in bed, arms outstretched to welcome him into her embrace, flooded his mind like fast-moving frames of film.

Making love with Crystal was something he didn't want to think about only because it would ruin their easygoing friendship. Besides, she was the first woman he'd known since becoming sexually active with whom he could be himself. He'd long tired of women who either were vapid or came on too strong, and Crystal was neither. Shaking his head as if to banish the erotic musings, he followed her into the kitchen.

However, he felt like a voyeur, staring at the outline of her firm backside in the fitted dress as she leaned over to place the gelato in the freezer drawer. Turning around, he walked out of the kitchen and into the dining room, not trusting himself to occupy the same space with Crystal. He had to leave or she would've seen his growing erection. Buttoning the suit jacket, he stood at the window staring at the many steeples of the churches in the Holy City.

"Would you like something to drink?"

Not willing to risk turning around to face Crystal, Joseph smiled at her over his shoulder. "I'll have what you're having."

She moved closer, standing next to him. "I'm going to make a virgin planter's punch because I have to work tomorrow and I need to be clearheaded."

It seemed like an interminable length of time before he was able to look directly at her. "I'll have the same."

Looping her arm over the sleeve of his jacket, Crystal steered Joseph over to the bar. "Whenever I want to drink something nonalcoholic I usually ask for a virgin planter's punch or piña colada."

Joseph watched, awed as she measured orange juice, lemonade and grenadine syrup into a shaker filled with ice. Once the shaker was frosty she added ginger ale, then poured the concoction into two ice-filled Collins glasses, finishing them off with a pineapple spear, a maraschino cherry and an orange slice.

"Where did you learn to tend bar?"

Crystal handed him a glass. "I used to fill in at my mother's gallery whenever her regular bartender couldn't make it to the openings."

He shook his head in amazement. "What did I say about surprises? It probably would take me years to figure you out."

"I'm not that complicated, Joseph. What you see is what you get." She touched her glass to his. "To happy hour."

Joseph smiled. "Here's to more surprises."

Crystal took a sip of her drink. It was perfect. "I don't know about you, but I'm ready to eat."

Moving over to the buffet server, he picked up a napkin and a plate. "What can I serve you?" he asked her.

"I'll have one of everything, thank you."

Joseph and Crystal cuddled spoonlike on the sofa, his chest rising and falling against her back. She'd kicked off her shoes and lay on the sofa after what had become a leisurely eating affair, and he knew he'd surprised her when he joined her on the sofa, molding her body to his like a trusting child.

Many of the candles lining every flat surface in the living and dining rooms were sputtering and going out, leaving the space in near darkness. Twin lamps on either end of the table in the entryway provided the only illumination on the first floor. Joseph was loath to move because he didn't want his time with Crystal to end. Lowering his head, he pressed a kiss to her soft, fragrant hair.

"Are you going to sleep?" he whispered.

Crystal opened her eyes, smiling. She felt the strong beating of Joseph's heart against her back. Happy hour had stretched into more than two, and unlike Joseph, who'd prepared enough of each course for two servings, she had plenty of leftovers.

"No, but I don't know how long I'll be able to stay awake, because I'm as full as a tick."

Throwing back his head, he laughed loudly. "It's been years since I've heard that expression."

She giggled like a little girl. "Well, I am. You know I'm going to have to stop hanging out with you, because every time we get together we eat."

"What's wrong with that?"

"What's wrong is I won't be able to fit into my clothes, and I don't have the money to replace some of the garments in my closet with a bigger size."

"Not to worry, sweetheart. If I'm responsible for you gaining weight, then I'll buy you a new wardrobe."

Crystal pulled her lower lip between her teeth. This was the second time Joseph had called her sweetheart. She wondered if it was just a slip, or if he called all of his female friends sweetheart, or did he actually think of her as his sweetheart? She didn't know if she wanted to be his sweetheart, because it'd been too long since she'd been physically close to a man to whom she found herself attracted.

And she didn't want or need Joseph to pay for her clothes or anything else. All of her life men had indirectly taken care of her. Although her parents were divorced, her father had made certain to provide for her financial support. Then it was Levi and his brothers who put the word out that no one better mess with Crystal or they would have to answer to them. It continued with Brian, offering her his protection months after she'd moved to New York City.

However, the one time she needed a man to take care of her, he wasn't there. She knew that if she had made it known that she was being sexually harassed, things would've turned out differently for her. The partners would not have retaliated by firing her, but no doubt would've made certain she would never advance at the firm.

"I'm not a pauper, and the clothes I have I like very much."

Joseph kissed the nape of her neck. "And you look incredible in your clothes."

A wave of heat swept up her chest to her hairline. "Thank you. Maybe that's because they fit."

"But you have to admit we make a pretty good pair when it comes to throwing down in the kitchen. I'd prepare the entrées and you the hors d'oeuvres and cocktails."

Shifting, Crystal turned to face Joseph. "Yeah, we could hire ourselves out as caterers for small, intimate dinner parties," she said, laughing.

He traced the curve of her eyebrow with his forefinger. "That sounds like a plan."

"That sounds crazy. I like cooking, but not enough to give up decorating interiors."

Joseph stared at Crystal's upturned face in the diffused light, committing it to memory. He wanted to remember everything about her: face, voice, body and mannerisms. Once she completed her commission he didn't know when or whether their paths would ever cross again. Although he'd talked about her decorating his home, he knew that was just conjecture. The architect still had to draw up plans for the proposed property. And once it was completed, there was no guarantee she would accept his offer or be available for the project.

"It could be your Plan B once you decide to give up decorating."

A shimmer of amusement filled her eyes. "I'm still working on Plan A while you're talking about a Plan B. The difference between you and me is that you're involved in a successful family business at the same time I'm growing mine."

"If you're looking for clients I'm certain I can send a few your way."

Crystal wanted to tell Joseph that if she needed referrals, all she had to do was call her parents. She forced a smile she didn't feel. "Please don't think I'm ungrateful, but I'd rather build a reputation based on referrals from prior clients. Eventually I want Eaton Interior and Design to be a brand."

Joseph stared at her, complete surprise freezing his features. "Are you in business to make money or become a brand?"

"Both," she confirmed.

"If that's what you want, then why wouldn't you accept help from someone who could help you—"

"Stop it! Please stop," she pleaded in a softer tone. "I have to do this my way." Pushing against his shoulder, Crystal slipped off the sofa, coming to her feet. "Excuse me, but I'm going to clean up the kitchen."

He also stood. "I'll help you."

"No, you won't. I know you don't like washing dishes."

Taking a step, Joseph curved his arms around Crystal's waist. "Are you that perceptive, or am I that transparent?"

Resting her hands on his chest, she rose on tiptoe and brushed a light kiss to his cheek. "You are very, very transparent, Joseph Cole-Wilson."

Transparent enough to see that I want to make love to you, he thought. He found himself so physically attracted to Crystal it was palpable. "You're right," he confirmed. "I don't like washing dishes."

"And you don't have to, because I don't mind doing them." She paused, suddenly at a loss for words. Crystal knew when Joseph walked out the door it would be a while before they would get together again. It probably wouldn't be until Super Bowl Sunday. Decorating the historic residences meant conferring with workmen and visiting antique shops and furniture warehouses as far as away as North Carolina. "Would you like me to pack up some of the leftovers?" she asked after an uncomfortable silence.

Joseph moved even closer, their chests a hairbreadth apart. "No, thank you." Placing his hands over hers resting on his chest, he gave her fingers a gentle squeeze. "Thank you for an incredible happy hour. And if you can find time in your very busy schedule, would you be opposed to taking in a concert or going to the movies with me?"

She flashed a sexy moue. "I'd love to go out on a date with you."

Slipping into his suit jacket, Joseph reached into the breast pocket and handed Crystal his cell phone. "I'm going to need your cell number so I won't have to go through the hotel operator."

Crystal took the iPhone, programming her number. She

offered him a tentative smile, handing him back the phone. "Thank you for being a wonderful dinner guest."

Raising her hands, Joseph kissed each of her fingers. "Good night, Crystal."

Her smile widened. "Good night, Joseph."

Crystal felt his loss within seconds of his releasing her hands. Proper etiquette stipulated she walk him to the door, yet her legs refused to follow the dictates of her brain. She didn't know how long she stood there, waiting for the sound of the door opening and closing. When it didn't she followed him. He stood at the door, his hand resting on the doorknob.

"Joseph?" His name came out in a shivery whisper.

Without warning he turned and approached her, but Crystal didn't have time to catch her breath when she found herself in his arms, his mouth on hers in an explosive kiss that stole the very breath from her lungs. Her arms came up in slow motion, circling around his neck, holding him fast.

Being in Joseph's embrace, his mouth on hers, inhaling the sensually haunting scent of his body felt so good and so right. Her lips parted under his searching tongue, and she inhaled his warm, moist breath. She heard a moan and realized it had come from her. Crystal moaned again, this time in frustration. She wanted more, and the more was to sleep with him.

The kiss ended as abruptly as it had begun. Joseph released her, her arms falling away from his neck, and he retraced his steps. This time he opened and closed the door behind him without a backward glance.

It happened so quickly Crystal thought she'd imagined it, but the lingering taste of Joseph's tongue on hers, the heaviness in her breasts and the throbbing and moistness between her legs said otherwise. She knew if he hadn't ended the kiss she would've begged him to make love to her.

Walking on wobbly legs, she managed to find her way to the sofa without bumping into the coffee table, collapsing on the butter-soft leather cushion. Fists clenched, eyes closed and heart pounding a runaway rhythm, Crystal replayed the pleasure of Joseph's slow, drugging, possessive kiss in her mind over and over.

Opening her eyes, she came back to reality. The hotel owner's return to Charleston could not have come at a better time. Work was the perfect alternative to fantasizing about sleeping with a man she'd met only five days ago.

Chapter 8

Crystal found herself totally engrossed in decorating the twelve suites in the Beaumont Inn and the eight bedrooms with en suite baths in the Beaumont Bed-and-Breakfast. A hallway on the first floor permitted access between the adjacent buildings. The Charleston earthquake of 1886 that left a hundred dead and destroyed a number of buildings in the city caused little or no structural damage to the proposed inn and B and B.

She and the contractor, Roger Kincaid, were like kindred spirits because he knew exactly what she wanted whenever she explained the pieces that would go into each of the rooms. Roger and his crew had restored the interiors to their former beauty with hardwood floors, wainscoting and crown molding.

All of the fireplaces were converted from wood-burning to electric to eliminate the risk of potential fires. The upgrading of the electric and plumbing had passed inspection and all that remained was painting, hanging wallpaper, installing light fixtures and filling the rooms with furniture and accessories.

She and Roger sat at a makeshift worktable, going over paint swatches. "Miss Eaton, you'll have to let us know what colors you want in each of the rooms."

Crystal gave the contractor—a diminutive man with a ruddy complexion, shock of white unruly hair and a voice that was perfect for radio—a sidelong glance. The timbre of his voice reminded her of Joseph's—deep, velvety and beautifully modulated. Spending hours on the phone with vendors and endless trips to local antique shops had kept her so occupied she hardly gave him a passing thought until she returned to the hotel.

Once there, Crystal looked for him in the parking lot, in the lounge area off the lobby, in the elevator or on the penthouse floor whenever she left or returned. The one time she spotted him, he'd been in the lounge with several couples, and he'd acknowledged her with a nod and wave before turning his attention back to those at the table.

"That's going to be easy. I want to mix paint with wallpaper," she said, tapping a key on her laptop. A color design was displayed on the monitor. "I'm using a signature fabric with a color palette that will become the thread throughout the entire inn or B and B."

She tapped another key with splotches of paint samples with hues ranging from oyster white, French gray, pale powder blue and blue-gray cashmere. All of the rooms were numbered with a corresponding numbered color palette. Crystal suggested the owner identify each room or suite by name instead of a number. The rooms in the B and B would be named for Revolutionary War patriots and the inn for U.S. presidents. It was easier for guests to know they were staying in the Paul Revere or Thomas Paine room or George Washington or Thomas Jefferson suite than room 145 or 216.

Roger scratched his stubbly chin. "Where do you want the wallpaper other than in the bathrooms?"

"Only the inn's living room suites will be papered. Based on the architect's measurements, I've ordered enough wallpaper with some to spare. I'll stop by the shop after I leave here and let them know to deliver the rolls tomorrow at a time that's convenient for you."

The daily room rate at the inn, twice the daily rate of the B and B, included amenities of a buffet breakfast, a sit-down dinner and late-night cordials in the proposed drawing room.

Reaching into a leather portfolio, Crystal handed the contractor a loose-leaf binder with printouts of what she'd saved on her computer.

"I'm usually here at seven, so anytime after that is okay. Roger flipped through the pages, his snow-white eyebrows lifting. "You're very thorough."

She nodded, smiling. Everything she'd put in the binder was

detailed and self-explanatory. She'd labeled every wallpaper pattern, indicating in which rooms they would be hung.

"It saves a lot of time and my client's money. When do you think your crew will be able to finish painting and hanging the paper?"

Roger angled his head. "If I hire one or two more painters, I believe we can get everything done in a week. The guys who hang the paper are fast, so I know they'll finish quickly."

Tapping another key and opening the page for the calendar, Crystal typed in the date for painting and paper under the column labeled Projected Completion. Meeting the projected construction completion date meant the inn and B and B could open for business as scheduled, and more important, offset cost overruns.

"If you can achieve that, then I hope to complete decorating everything sooner than planned," she said.

"Do you have another project after this one?" Roger asked.

She nodded, smiling. "Yes, I do."

"If it is here in Charleston, then you're going to make quite a name for yourself once these hotels are up and running. Mr. Beaumont showed me the pictures of the proposed rooms, and they look like they did two hundred years ago."

"I'm just giving him what he wants," she confirmed. "The buildings are historic landmarks, which mean the interiors should embody and complement the exteriors."

Roger scratched his cheek, the raspy sound reminding Crystal of fingernails on a chalkboard. "They're going to become quite the showpiece once you decorate them."

That's what I'm hoping, Crystal mused. Decorating the inn and B and B would be her first commercial commission, and she looked forward to turning the New York City Greenwich Village town house basement into a jazz club with an excitement she found difficult to contain. It'd been four years since she was in the city that pulsed with a flutter of restless activity night or day, summer or winter.

She powered down the laptop. "Call if you need me for anything," she told Roger.

Roger stood, pulling back her chair as she rose to her feet. "No problem."

Crystal had just gotten behind the wheel of her vehicle when her cell phone rang. Reaching into her tote, she stared at the display. Tapping the talk feature, she said, "Happy New Year, Emerson." She and the highly skilled architect at Bramwell and Duncan spoke several times a year, and always exchanged birthday and Christmas cards.

"Same to you, my friend."

"Are you calling to tell me you've finally decided to strike out on your own?" Emerson Russo confided to her on more than one occasion he was seriously thinking of resigning to set up his own firm but wanted to wait until he found a competent partner.

"I wish it was about that," he said cryptically.

There was something in Emerson's voice that sent a shiver up her spine. "What's the matter?" Crystal listened, stunned, her heart pumping painfully in her chest when he revealed another woman at the firm hadn't just been harassed but sexually assaulted by the same partner who'd attempted to come on to her. "Did she report it to the police?"

"No."

"Why not?"

"Because Gillian doesn't have proof."

Unconsciously her brow furrowed. Gillian Stuart had joined the firm as an intern a month before Crystal resigned. And Emerson was talking in riddles. "You're telling me she was assaulted, yet she can't prove it? Why?"

There came a beat. "What I should've said is that she can't remember the assault because she believes she was drugged."

"Please tell me that she went to the hospital for them to test for DNA and have blood drawn and tested."

"No and no."

Crystal's heart rate kicked into a higher gear as something she didn't want to believe stabbed her brain while Emerson offered other details of the assault. "She's pregnant." The question was a statement.

"How did you know?" Emerson asked.

"Other than vaginal bruising or trauma, it's the only logical conclusion. She plans to have the baby?"

"That's what she told me. She doesn't believe in abortion. I've worked at B&D long enough to hear all types of stories about Hugh going after women, but this is a new low."

"What's Gillian going to do?"

"She plans to charge him for rape *and* sue him for paternity. I know your uncle is a judge, so hopefully because of this you'd know a lawyer who Hugh Duncan doesn't have in his pocket."

Crystal knew Emerson was right. Hugh Duncan came from an extremely wealthy and prominent political family. His father and grandfather were both U.S. representatives, and their sphere of influence was legendary throughout the state of Florida. He'd also retain a battery of attorneys to protect him personally *and* professionally.

However the Duncans weren't the only Florida family with wealth and prominence. To her knowledge the Coles might not have been as politically connected, but their name carried enough clout to make people stand up and take notice.

"Let me talk to someone, and I'll try and get back to you in a few days."

"Thanks, Crystal."

"I can't promise anything, but I'll try."

"That's all I can ask. Every time I hear about Hugh going after a woman, I relive the horror of my sister being stalked and raped."

Crystal understood Emerson's driving need to have his boss charged with rape because his younger sister took her own life the day after a jury acquitted her ex-boyfriend of unlawful kidnapping and rape because he claimed they'd had consensual sex. "Hugh has hidden behind the facade of being a family man and a pillar of the community for far too long. If Gillian can get someone to take on her case, then tell her she can count on me as a material witness."

Crystal ended the call and then sat staring through the windshield. Joseph had chided her for leaving Bramwell and Duncan rather than sue the pervert, which left him to harass other women. It was as if his words had come to fruition, because not only had he drugged a woman but he had also gotten her pregnant.

Crystal called Joseph's cell. Despite the gravity of the call, she smiled when hearing his mellifluent voice. "How are you?" she asked.

"That's what I should be asking you, neighbor. It's been a while."

"That is has. I've been busy."

"Good for you. What's up?"

Crystal sobered quickly. "Can you come to my place? I need some legal advice."

"I'll see you in about… Let's say twenty minutes."

"Thanks, Joseph." She hung up, hoping and praying he would be able to help her stop a sexual predator.

Joseph stepped into the shower stall and turned on the faucet to the programmed temperature setting. He'd spent the past hour in the hotel pool, swimming laps. Hearing Crystal's voice reminded him of how much he'd missed their easygoing camaraderie. He thought he would see her during his comings and goings, yet she'd proven elusive except for the one time he spied her walking across the lobby.

He had also been busy making frequent trips to the tea garden while also conferring with the assistant manager. An above average rainfall for the month caused drainage problems wherein an unseeded section of land flooded, but the problem was remedied by redirecting the flow of water when the man flipped a switch in the factory's engineering room.

After showering, he dressed quickly in a pair of jeans, a navy blue long-sleeved tee and running shoes, wondering why Crystal would need his legal advice when she could've called her uncle or her cousin Myles. Slipping his card key and cell phone into the back pocket of his jeans, he left the apartment.

Crystal had left her door ajar, and Joseph walked in, closing it behind him. He went completely still, staring at her descending the staircase in body-hugging black jeans and an emerald-green mock turtleneck. A smile tilted the corners of his mouth as she smiled at him.

Extending his arms, Joseph wasn't disappointed as she came into his embrace. Lowering his head, he pressed his mouth to her damp hair. She smelled delicious. Holding her reminded him of the last time he kissed her. He knew he shocked her with the impulsive action, yet he couldn't resist tasting her incredibly sexy mouth one more time. The crush of her breasts against his chest stirred the flesh between his thighs and he eased his hold on her body before she detected the growing bulge in his groin. He wondered how Crystal would react if she knew how easily she turned him on with a glance or a touch.

Reaching for her hand, he led her to the sofa, sitting and pulling her down to sit beside him. "What's the matter, sweetheart?"

Leaning against his shoulder, Crystal told Joseph what her ex-coworker had revealed to her earlier that afternoon.

Anger and rage merged, twisting his features when he clenched his teeth. "Had anyone told her about him before she agreed to let him into her home?"

Crystal shook her head. "Apparently not."

"Is she certain he drugged her?"

"She had to be, Joseph. She said Hugh called her early Black Friday to ask if she'd finished a project he needed for a Monday morning meeting. When she said no, he offered to come over and help her. Gillian told Emerson that Hugh didn't do or say anything that would make her feel uncomfortable, so she was completely relaxed when he called his favorite restaurant for dinner to be delivered to her house. Halfway through dinner she began to feel sick, believing it was something she'd eaten or drunk. Hugh told her to lie down on the sofa. Once there she must have passed out, not waking up until Saturday morning."

Back in control and shifting slightly, Joseph repositioned Crystal until she lay between his outstretched legs, his chest molded to her back. "Was there any physical evidence he'd had sex with her?"

Crystal shook her head. "No."

"What about DNA? He had to have left it on something."

"She woke up on a leather sofa, so he must have raped her there rather than in her bed, where he could've possibly left DNA. She knew he'd given her a bath because she found wet towels in the hamper. So the cretin cleaned her up and put back on the same panties in an attempt to make her believe he hadn't touched her."

"Without DNA she has no case," Joseph stated.

"Yes, she does," Crystal countered. She paused. "She's six weeks pregnant. And before you ask, no, she wasn't sleeping with another man. She broke up with her boyfriend just after Labor Day."

Joseph came out of his relaxed position as if pulled up by a taut wire. "Is she certain it isn't her boyfriend's baby?"

"Quite certain, because he always used a condom."

He quickly did the math in his head. Given eleven or twelve weeks, Gillian would've known whether she was pregnant or not. "Did she tell the bastard that she's carrying his baby?"

"Yes, and he terminated her with the excuse she was delusional, paranoid and completely burned out. However, he did give her a generous severance package, aka hush money."

"She intends to have the baby?"

Crystal nodded. "She doesn't believe in abortion," she said, repeating what Emerson told her.

Wrapping an arm around her waist, he again settled Crystal against his chest. "She's got him, sweetheart. But only after she delivers the baby can she sue for paternity. Either he'll give up his DNA if he's innocent, or he'll refuse because he knows he's the father of her child."

"If he was devious enough to drug a woman and clean up after himself, why didn't he use a condom? Didn't he think about contracting a STD?"

Joseph exhaled an audible breath. "I don't know much about sexual predators except they have little or no impulse control. Duncan probably didn't think about using protection before or during the act, but once it was over he was clearheaded enough to methodically cover up his crime. And maybe he didn't get the other women pregnant, or if he did they accepted his hush money, opting for an abortion instead of having the baby."

There came a swollen silence.

"You were right, Joseph."

"What about?"

"If I'd sued Hugh instead of resigning, Gillian wouldn't be carrying a baby as a result of rape."

Joseph kissed her hair. "It's too late to second-guess yourself. Duncan is a serial sexual predator who should spend the rest of his life in prison."

Crystal closed her eyes, wishing she had confronted Hugh rather than resign, although he would've come up with the excuse that she was either delusional or burned out like with Gillian.

For Crystal, it hadn't been what he said or did but what she perceived. On several occasions he stood too close for propriety, would deliberately cover her hand with his whenever they met to review a project and compliment her on what she was wearing. Invariably his forearm brushed her breasts when he leaned over her shoulder to place a report on her desk. It was then she noticed his erection.

Perhaps he hadn't reached the stage where he'd invite himself to her home or out to dinner, drug and rape her because she was Judge Solomon Eaton's niece. Rather than allow his continual subtle violation, she resigned.

She opened her eyes. "Who's going to put him there? No lawyer in Florida would risk going up against the Duncan family political machine."

There came another prolonged silence, and then Joseph said, "I think I know someone who would be willing to take her case." Crystal turned over, resting her chin on his breastbone. He saw a shimmer of excitement in her eyes. "I'm familiar with a lawyer specializing in sex crimes. In his former life he was a forensic psychologist, so it's the perfect marriage when it comes to defending sex crime victims."

The light in Crystal's eyes faded. "Do you think he can get her a fair trial?"

"What he'll attempt to do is *not* go to trial because Duncan's defense team will try and dissect her sex life from her first encounter to the last. And if the baby is proven to be his, they'll turn it around and say it was consensual sex, or she deliberately seduced him and got pregnant so she could sue him for paternity."

A flicker of apprehension coursed through Crystal. "Please don't tell me you're talking about a plea deal. He'll pay restitution, and then get off with a slap on the wrist so he's free to rape another woman." There was a hint of panic in her voice.

Joseph placed a hand alongside her delicate jaw. "Seth will not let him get off that easily. In order to spare Duncan's family the embarrassment of a trial, he'll suggest he plead guilty to misdemeanor rape and register as a sex offender. His offender status will depend on how many women are willing to come forward and testify to being victimized by him, and if they agree to a class-action lawsuit and win, hopefully Hugh Duncan will have a lot fewer zeroes when it comes to his net worth."

Her jaw hardened under his light touch. "This may sound vindictive, but I want him to pay for everything he's done."

Joseph's mouth replaced his hand. "He will."

"How can you be that certain?" Crystal whispered.

"I know people who can get someone to snitch on their mothers or firstborn just to save their behinds."

She froze. "What are you going to—"

"No more questions," he warned, stopping her words with a light kiss. "You asked me to help you, so please leave it at that. What I'm going to need is the phone number of your friend Emerson so I can pass it along to Seth."

Crystal nuzzled his throat, breathing a kiss there. "Thank you."

"Thank me once your predator gets what he deserves. However, I will accept a little kiss right now."

Crystal melted against his body, losing herself in the pleasurable sensations of his mouth on hers. Joseph deepened the kiss and within seconds she forgot why she'd called him. And in a moment of madness, nothing mattered except the man holding her to his heart.

She wanted him with the hunger and thirst of someone deprived of food and water. Joseph was a constant and nagging reminder of what she'd missed and had been missing for far too long. She'd been so intent on growing her interior decorating business she denied the strong passions within her.

However, if she were to become involved with Joseph, both knew it would be brief. Anything short-lived and personal fit nicely into Crystal's current lifestyle; her upcoming commission would take her away from home for prolonged periods of time and thankfully she didn't have to answer to anyone as to her whereabouts.

She'd known a few women who'd sacrificed advancing their careers because their boyfriends or husbands weren't willing to accept their need to travel for their jobs. Spending four years in a city as racially and culturally diverse as New York City and living with a man sixteen years her senior had forced Crystal to mature at a faster rate than her same-age female counterparts. There were times when she felt this gave her an advantage and other times when she found herself quite cynical about the opposite sex. And like many thirtysomething women, she looked forward to marriage and motherhood, but didn't feel an all-encompassing need to find Mr. Right before her biological clock started ticking.

A slight gasp escaped her parted lips when she felt Joseph's fingers feather under her sweater, his hands coming to rest over her breasts rising and falling heavily under the lacy fabric of her bra. "You smell and taste wonderful," he whispered, swallowing her breath as she exhaled.

Laughing softly, she began her own exploration, her hands searching under the front of his tee, encountering hard-rock muscle. "So do you," she countered in a husky whisper. Crystal bit down on her lip to keep from laughing aloud when he jerked as if burned as her thumbs grazed his nipples, the tiny buds hardening like pebbles. Within seconds, her mouth replaced her hands. She gasped again, this time when Joseph hardened quickly, the solid bulge in his groin pressing against her middle. "Jo-se-ph," she whispered, his name coming out in three syllables.

Reaching for her shoulders, Joseph managed to extricate her mouth with a minimum of effort. Lowering his head, he fastened his mouth to the side of her neck. "You see what you're doing to me, Crystal?"

She buried her face between his neck and shoulder. "What am I doing?"

"I just have to look at you or touch you and I get a hard-on."

"This isn't as one-sided as you think."

"Are you telling me you're ready to take what we have to the next level?"

Crystal gave him a long stare. "I need to know what you mean by the next level." She hadn't lied to Joseph. Her body said yes while her head still said no when it came to sharing a bed.

A smile played at the corners of his firm mouth. "I'm surprised you're asking me that. I want to make love to you, but it has to be on your terms."

Her eyes opened and Crystal couldn't stop the smile parting her lips. "Are you certain you want to hear my terms?"

Joseph eased back, his eyes searching her expression for a hint of guile, and finding none, he nodded. It was the same thing he'd said to Kiara, but with unexpected dire consequences. He knew it would be different with Crystal. She was older, more mature and secure enough to speak her mind.

"I'm very sure," he answered after a comfortable silence.

Crystal stared at the cleft in Joseph's chin, pausing as she chose her words carefully. "If we do happen to sleep together, then it would be like the Las Vegas commercial. What happens here stays here." Joseph smiled, attractive lines fanning out around his large eyes. She sobered quickly. "You wouldn't have to concern yourself about me asking you for a commitment or a declaration of marriage because I don't want or need either at this time in my life, and I'd like you to promise the same."

He knew she was referring to his disclosure to why he'd ended his relationship with Kiara. Although his life was more predictable than it had been two years ago, he still wasn't ready to marry or start a family.

"I promise."

"I'm not on birth control, so you're going to have to assume responsibility for protecting me from an unplanned pregnancy. That is, if we *do* decide to make love," she added softly.

Joseph wanted to tell Crystal the only thing better than going to bed with her would be waking up with her beside him. And it had nothing to do with sex—that was something he could get from any willing woman. Whenever they were together he experienced a level of comfortableness he hadn't thought possible.

"So I can look forward to the time when we can become friends with benefits?"

Crystal's arms went around his neck. "Yes."

"Don't worry about contraception. I'll take care of it."

Exhaling an audible breath, Crystal met his eyes. "I said all that because I need you to understand where I'm coming from."

Reaching up, he gently removed her arms. Joseph had asked Crystal what she wanted, and it was something he could very easily live with.

Joseph knew instinctively that if he'd met Crystal years ago, fallen in love with her, he would have seriously considered proposing marriage. That is, if she thought him worthy of becoming her husband.

"I understand and accept your terms. Let's go out."

Crystal sat up. "Where?"

"The Watering Hole is a local sports bar that's within walking distance from here. I want to warn you that it's a little noisy."

Rising on tiptoe, she kissed his cheek. "I don't mind noisy. I'll be right back. I have to change my shoes and get a jacket."

Cradling the back of her head, Joseph brushed a light kiss on her mouth. "I'm going to my place to get a jacket. I'll meet you at the elevator."

Chapter 9

Crystal sat next to Joseph in the booth instead of opposite him in order to hear what he was saying. When he said the Watering Hole was a little noisy she didn't know it would be from decibel-shattering music.

A dozen wall-mounted, muted televisions were tuned to various sporting events, a few displaying closed captions. Shouts of triumph and/or collective groans followed a hockey goal or basketball sailing through the net. Motown hits and '60s and '70s R&B blared from speakers as several couples seated at the bar got up to dance to Smokey Robinson and the Miracles' "Ooo Baby Baby."

Thursday night at the pub was advertised as wing night, and the rustic establishment offered more than ten different varieties of Buffalo wings, attracting hoards of college students paying a twenty-dollar flat fee each for all-you-can-eat wings with unlimited pitchers of domestic tap beer.

She and Joseph ordered fresh guacamole with grilled corn, salsa, crisp tortilla chips and virgin margaritas. They were watching the Miami Heat in a back-and-forth scoring battle with the New York Knicks.

"Yes!" Crystal said between clenched teeth while pumping her fist. The Heat's point guard had just scored his fourth three-point basket within the span of five minutes, ending and winning the game.

Joseph found it hard to conceal his own excitement. Both he and Crystal were into the basketball game, and it was the first time he saw her that relaxed. So, he thought, the prim and proper decorator did know how to let down her hair.

"That was swee-eet," Crystal crooned.

Joseph smiled. "You really like basketball."

Crystal gave him a sidelong glance. "I do. I played basketball in high school."

"Come dance with me," Joseph said close to Crystal's ear when the classic love song segued into the Temptations singing "Just My Imagination."

She didn't have time to accept or decline as Joseph grasped her hand, pulling her off the well-worn vinyl booth and leading her to the area dance floor. She had to quicken her step to keep up with him. He eased her to his chest at the same time her arms circled his slim waist inside his jacket.

Crystal rested her head on his shoulder, inhaling the lingering fragrance of his cologne that mingled with his body's natural scent. Crystal felt as if she were being pulled into a sensual vortex from which she did not want to escape.

Lowering his head, Joseph pressed his mouth to her ear. "Do you have anything planned for Friday night or Saturday?"

"What do you have in mind?" Crystal asked.

"The Heat are playing the Bobcats in Charlotte Friday night. I figure we'd drive up, stay overnight and then come back here Saturday, when we'll have dinner at the Ordinary. If you like seafood, then you'll love this place. When I make the hotel reservation I'll ask for a suite with adjoining rooms."

Crystal nuzzled his warm throat. Joseph had just gone up several approval points when he mentioned adjoining bedrooms. He hadn't assumed because they were going away together she would automatically fall into bed with him. Crystal was forced to admit to herself the more she saw Joseph the more she wanted to sleep with him. In him she found everything lacking in the men with whom she'd become involved.

Involved! She shook her head as if to banish the word. What she didn't want was to become emotionally involved with Joseph. If and when the time came that they did sleep together, she wanted it to be no more than a slackening of the sexual tension wound so tight it kept her from a restful night's sleep.

"Your offer sounds very, very tempting," she murmured.

He spun her around and around. "Tempting enough to take me up on it?"

"I think I'm going to need a little convincing."

Cradling her face in his hands, Joseph met her eyes in the semidark space. "How much convincing do you need, sweetheart?"

Crystal felt as if she and Joseph were the only two people in the crowded restaurant. Everything else ceased to exist: the music, the images flickering across the many television screens, pub regulars, college students and waitstaff. Within seconds of the question flowing from her lips, she realized it sounded like a subtle challenge for seduction. And as much as her body craved intimacy, she was ambivalent about sleeping with Joseph, wishing she was more like some women who were able to sleep with a man without becoming emotionally involved. If she and Joseph were to make love, then she had to make certain not to confuse love with lust.

"Tell me, how are you going to get tickets?"

Joseph chuckled. "I have season tickets. They were my brother's, but he gave them to me just before he left the country. Is that convincing enough?"

Pressing her forehead to his shoulder, Crystal nodded. The noise escalated when another crowd of students pushed their way into the pub, and yelling to be heard was getting annoying. "Can we please get out of here?"

Tightening his hold on her waist, Joseph led her off the dance floor and back to their booth. Signaling for the waitress, he pressed a bill into her hand.

Crystal sucked in air when they walked out of the Watering Hole. Afternoon temperatures peaking in the high '70s had dropped to mid-'60s with nightfall and the streets were filled with pedestrians taking advantage of the warm night.

Tucking her hand into the bend of his elbow, Joseph steered her out of the path of a group of rowdy teenage boys playing a game of chicken by pushing one another off the sidewalk and into the flow of traffic.

She gave him a quick glance. "How well do you know this city?"

Slowing his stride, he stared straight ahead. "Well enough to get around without getting lost." Joseph told Crystal about coming to the Holy City for the first time when he negotiated purchasing land to set up the tea garden, then again while conferring with the engineers hired to drain the swamp and surrounding land for cultivation. "Instead of commuting between here and Palm Beach, I decided to live at the Beaumont House, and whenever I have some downtime I become a tourist."

Crystal huddled closer to Joseph's side. "Would you ever consider living here permanently?"

He patted her hand. "Not really. It's not that it isn't beautiful, but I like living in Florida. How about you? Would you ever consider leaving the Sunshine State again?"

"Yes," she said truthfully, "only because I'm unencumbered."

"Unencumbered," he repeated under his breath. "I like your way of saying you're single with no children."

"It's because I have options some women my age don't have. Either they're in relationships, are married, going through a breakup or divorce or have children. All of which would make it more difficult to pick up and relocate. If I were to get my big break, the only thing I'd have to do is put my condo on the market."

They left the avenue, turning down a cobblestoned side street lined on both sides with houses with decorative wrought-iron gates and white porches. The flickering glow from streetlights reminded Crystal of Victorian-era gas lamps. "If it were raining and this street were lined with town houses, it would be the perfect setting for a Jack the Ripper–type movie," she murmured, her tone pensive.

Something within Joseph quieted; he suddenly saw what hadn't been as apparent to him as it was to Crystal. He knew that, as a decorator, she looked at everything with an artist's eye. "You're right. I think Charleston's charm is its architecture. Whenever I come here I always feel as if I've stepped back in time. It's the same when I go to Eagle Island."

"Is that where you've set up the tea garden?" Crystal asked.

"Yes. An elderly man who claims he's a direct descendant of one of the oldest black families living on the island told me about stories passed down by the griots, who talked about hundreds of large birds with wings that were wider than a man was tall that had built their nests high up in the pine and cypress trees, hence the name Eagle Island. But when the European landowners decided to build homes, they cut down many of the trees, disturbing their habitat. Later it was the pesticides that greatly reduced the numbers.

"Are there any eagles left on the island?" Crystal asked.

"I've seen a few."

"Didn't putting in the tea garden disturb their habitat?"

Joseph patted the hand tucked into the bend of his elbow. "No. That is one thing I insisted upon when the engineers dredged the land. They were not to upset the balance of nature. Although I negotiated for the sale of one hundred acres, we cleared only the land needed for planting. The rest of the garden is surrounded by water and swamp that's home to gators, water snakes, egrets and of course fish. Watching the sun rise over the swamp is an amazing experience."

"It sounds primordial," Crystal remarked reverently.

"It is," Joseph said, agreeing with her. "I did promise to take you on a tour, so anytime you're ready just let me know."

"I'm off until Tuesday, so I'm available to take the tour whenever you want to take me."

"If that's the case, then we can go either Sunday or Monday." Joseph was anxious to show Crystal the undertaking that had taken over every phase of his life for the past two years. And once the tea was harvested and processed, his focus would turn to the construction of his new home.

"How do you get to the island?" she asked.

"The way is the ferry. Unlike with Wadmalaw, there's no road connecting it to the mainland. I have to warn you that it's very rural."

"If I can play competitively on a girls' basketball team, then I'm certain I'll be able to adjust to a rustic countryside."

"Do you have another commission after this one?" he asked after a comfortable silence.

A shiver of excitement swept over Crystal. "Yes. I'm going back to New York City to decorate a jazz club. The owner inherited the town house from his grandparents, who ran a speakeasy during Prohibition in an adjoining property."

"They were never busted by the police?"

She laughed softly. "You don't get busted when you have high-ranking police officers on the take. After the repeal of Prohibition they turned it into a rooming house. Unfortunately someone smoking in bed started a fire that nearly destroyed the three-story building. Renovating it was too costly for the owners, so they boarded it up and many years later a high-profile actor bought and renovated it because he wanted homes on both coasts. By the 1980s the Lower Manhattan neighborhood was transformed into an upscale, trendy residential area.

"Last year my client decided to convert the basement into the Speak Low late-night jazz club. It's probably the only concert venue in New York City with a doorbell. Just like with a speakeasy, you'll have make reservations and be buzzed in through the front door. Then you head downstairs through a narrow, chandelier-marked hallway and into the club."

Joseph found himself intrigued with the idea of running a modern-day speakeasy.

"Have you seen it?" he asked Crystal.

She shook her head. "Not yet. However, I did see a video of the entire house and it's magnificent. It was built in 1860, a year before the start of the Civil War, but wasn't completed until 1866, because some of the men working on the house had enlisted in the Union army. I'll show it to you when we get back to the hotel. Tell me about your brother," Crystal said, deftly changing the topic of conversation. "Where is he living now?"

"Harper and two of his friends bought an uninhabited island in the Caribbean they plan to turn into a vacation retreat."

"That sounds exciting. What did he do before becoming part owner in a private island?"

Joseph waited for the light to change before he and Crystal

crossed the street leading down the block to the hotel. "He was a sports agent."

She smothered a laugh under her breath. "It looks as if your family is really into vacation resorts."

"It works for those who run them."

Crystal thought she detected a hint of wistfulness in Joseph's voice. "What about you, Joseph? What would you have done if you hadn't gone into law? Would you be managing one of the resorts?"

"No. I always knew I wanted to practice law."

"You didn't have a Plan B?" she drawled teasingly.

Dropping her hand, Joseph put his arm around Crystal's waist, pulling her closer to his side as they made their way up the path to the Beaumont House. "Not at that time. Little did I know I'd become a farmer. Now I'm going to ask you the same question. What would you have been if you hadn't become a decorator?"

"A dancer."

Joseph stopped in midstride, causing Crystal to stumble. He caught her before she lost her balance, and then stared at her as if she'd taken leave of her senses. "You're kidding."

She recovered quickly, her smile spreading to her eyes. "No! My mother decided dance lessons would make me graceful, so she signed me up for ballet and modern dance. What she didn't know was that I wanted to be an Ikette or a fly girl, and when I told her I wanted to take hip-hop classes she stopped paying for the classes. I could've gone to my father for the money, but I didn't want them arguing with each other again, so when I went to Italy and France in my junior year as an art student, I spent more time in the clubs than I did at the museums or on field trips."

"Did your parents know you were out clubbing when you should've been studying?"

"Of course not, or I would've had to beg, borrow or steal to pay for my senior year's tuition. Daddy is pretty laid-back but not so laid-back that he would approve of me clubbing when I should've been studying."

Joseph laughed loudly. "Did you pass, Miss Dancing Queen?"

"It wasn't a pass/fail course, but that's not to say I didn't keep up with my coursework."

"It's still not too late to become a rump-shaking, twerking diva," he teased.

"It is too late, Joseph. Number one, I'm too old and it's been a while since I've gone out clubbing, and I really don't need any of my clients seeing me shaking my butt like a backup dancer in a hip-hop video."

"They don't have to see you if we don't go out. Instead of hanging out at Chez Crystal, we'll go to Club José," Joseph said, grinning from ear to ear. "I'll arrange for dinner to be served in my apartment. That way we don't have to cook or clean up afterward, and then we'll dance."

Crystal's heart made a crazy flip-flop motion as she anticipated dancing again. It wasn't that she hadn't danced recently, but it was always alone.

Stopping, she turned slightly and grasped the front of Joseph's jacket. Going on tiptoe, she fastened her mouth to his, deepening the kiss before ending it. "Thank you."

Joseph's arms went around her shoulders. "You're very welcome."

He liked Crystal's spontaneity, yet what he was beginning to feel for her went beyond a mere liking. He'd asked her to establish the requisites for their relationship and she had determined the parameters as to where it would lead and end. However, the more time he spent with Crystal, the more he wanted to spend with her because it was no longer about wanting to make love to her. He wanted to do and share all of the things couples experienced when dating: weekend trips, going to the movies, dinner, dancing and eventually extended vacations.

Joseph realized his time with Crystal was limited, but he intended to take pleasure in the shared encounters she parceled out like sips of water to a man dying of thirst, while attempting to make the best of it, knowing he would be left with the memories of their time together.

"Good evening, Mr. Wilson, Miss Eaton. Beautiful night

for a walk," drawled the liveried doorman standing at the entrance to the Beaumont House. His warm greeting matched his inviting smile.

"Yes, it is," Crystal and Joseph said in unison as the man opened the door for them.

The hint of a smile tweaked a corner of her mouth. She enjoyed what little time she and Joseph were spending together. He treated her like an equal, unlike other men her age who were hell-bent on power-tripping.

Despite being born into wealth, Joseph did not flaunt it, Crystal discovered. His clothes, sans designer labels, did not come off a department rack, and other than a watch, he wore no other jewelry. There were no visible tattoos or piercings, which led her to believe he was a very conservative thirtysomething.

As they strolled hand in hand across the lobby, she experienced a measure of safeness and protection she hadn't had in a long while, and she had to admit, once again, Joseph was right when he mentioned her living with a much older man had been the result of her not growing up with her father. Crystal had thought of herself as a young sophisticate. After all, she'd grown up in Miami, spent six months in major European cities and lived in Washington, D.C., as an undergraduate student, so the decision to go to graduate school in New York City had been an easy one for her.

When she met Brian in a local coffee shop, they began an easygoing friendship that eventually led to their sleeping together—Crystal's life changed the moment he suggested she share his studio apartment. The arrangement was advantageous for both. Brian didn't have to troll clubs looking for someone with whom to sleep, and she had a live-in lover and protector. And because she wasn't his student, Brian didn't have to concern himself with reprisals from college administrators if their liaison ended badly.

Despite the differences in their ages, Crystal had a normal relationship with him. He didn't relate to her as her father and herself as his daughter. And since meeting Joseph she wondered, if they'd met years ago, how changed would she have been from the connection? At that time and even now she still felt she wasn't ready for marriage, and she didn't have to go to a psychic to know her reluctance was the result of her parents' unstable relationship with others.

She'd grown up listening to Raleigh accusing Jasmine of deliberately getting pregnant so he would marry her. What Crystal didn't understand was that if her father was so opposed to marriage, then why had he married so many times? She knew the volatile and spiteful allegations had shaped her views toward marriage, and secretly vowed she would never coerce a man into marriage because she was carrying his child.

The elevator arrived and they entered the car along with several other hotel guests. It rose quickly to the top floor. Joseph held the door as they exited. They walked abreast along the carpeted hallway. Crystal slipped the card key into the slot, waiting for the green light, and then opened the door. Kicking off her running shoes, she left them on the thick floor mat, and then hung her jacket on the coat tree by the door.

Slipping out of his jacket and dropping it on one of the chairs in the entryway, Joseph followed Crystal through the living room and into the space set up as an in-home office. He smiled when he saw her workstation. Unlike his—strewn with paper, books, newspapers and magazines—Crystal's was free of clutter.

Selena had returned the proposal he'd sent her with a number of legal queries and a cover letter from Myles Eaton. Earlier that morning he'd begun drafting a response. Crystal's neat desk, her leaving her shoes on the mat at the door and not waiting for housekeeping to come and clean up the kitchen, spoke volumes about the woman who now occupied his waking thoughts. She was a neat-freak.

Crystal pulled over another chair over to the workstation. "Come and sit down."

He stared at her enchanting profile, wondering if Crystal knew how innocently sexy she was. Joseph hadn't missed the admiring glances from men when they entered the Watering Hole. Although slender, she had curves in all the right places.

His cell phone chimed a programmed ring tone as he was sitting down. The call was from one of his frat brothers. "Excuse me, but I have to take this," he mumbled, rising slightly to take his phone out of the pocket of his jeans. "Hey, Drew. What's up?" He placed his free hand over Crystal's much smaller one while giving it a gentle squeeze.

"Frank's leaving for Denver on Tuesday, and the rest of us decided to give him a surprise send-off this weekend. We contacted his fiancée about the get-together and she's flying in Friday night. Frank still doesn't know she's coming."

Geothermal engineer Francis Lynch had accepted a position with a Denver-based energy company after his cardiologist fiancée moved from Miami to Denver. "I already have plans for this weekend." Crystal tapped Joseph's arm, garnering his attention. "Hold a minute, Drew." He placed his thumb over the mouthpiece. "What is it, baby?"

"We can take in a game some other time."

He shook his head. "No."

"Yes, we can. If you have season tickets, then we can always go to other games together," she said sotto voce.

Joseph paused, mentally weighing his options. He looked forward to spending three consecutive days with Crystal and he also wanted to see his frat brother and former college roommate once more before Frank moved across the country. Winking at her, he mouthed a thank-you. If she was talking about other games, then perhaps they would continue to see each other once they'd returned to Florida.

He removed his thumb. "I'm back, Drew. I thought Frank wasn't supposed to leave until April."

"He got the call earlier this morning that they want to bring him on board early," Drew explained.

"What are you guys planning to do?" Joseph asked, his gaze meeting and fusing with Crystal's. Light from the desk lamp cast a flattering glow over her flawless dark skin, causing him to hold his breath for several seconds. She was breathtakingly beautiful with or without makeup.

"We need you to run interference."

A slight frown appeared between Joseph's eyes as he pulled his attention back to the voice on the other end of the connection. "What do you want me to do?"

"We're going to tell Frank that everyone's coming up to Charleston Saturday night to celebrate your birthday with you."

"My birthday isn't until next weekend," Joseph reminded him.

"Next weekend is the Super Bowl and some of the brothers are flying out to the West Coast for the game. That's why we decided your birthday is the perfect excuse to hang together."

The seconds ticked off as Joseph mulled over the plan. "Okay. Count me in."

"Thank, bro. Now, I need you to give me the names of a few restaurants where we can party."

"Forget about a restaurant. If it's my birthday, we'll party here at the Beaumont House."

"Are you sure you'll have enough room? The brothers are bringing their wives and girlfriends."

Joseph smiled. "There's plenty of room. I'll arrange for the hotel to cater the party."

"Thanks, brother. We'll reimburse you later."

"Forget about it. What time should I expect you?"

"We're renting a party bus so we don't have to come in separate vehicles and—"

"And you don't have to worry about designated drivers," Joseph quipped, perceptively finishing Drew's sentence.

"Bet to that," Drew countered, laughing. "Look for us to arrive around seven."

Ending the call, Joseph placed the phone on the desk. "I'm sorry about—"

"Please stop apologizing," Crystal admonished, interrupting him. "Think about the fun you'll have with your friends when they celebrate your birthday prematurely."

He draped an arm over her shoulders. "It will only be fun if you're with me."

Easing back, Crystal stared at Joseph, committing everything about his face to memory. And she knew she would only have memories once they parted. "No, Joseph. They're your friends and they'll just view me as an interloper."

Picking up his chair, Joseph moved it closer to Crystal and cradled her face between his hands. "When you asked a stranger to come with you to your cousin's house for brunch, did you think of me as an interloper?"

"No."

He smiled. "I rest my case."

Crystal affected a sexy moue, bringing his gaze to linger on her mouth. "You like saying that, don't you?"

"Only when I have to," Joseph drawled, pressing a kiss on the bridge of her nose.

"One of these days I'm going to overrule you, counselor."

Joseph's smile grew wider. "Should I be afraid?"

Crystal rubbed noses with him. "You should be very, very afraid, because you're not going to win every difference of opinion."

Curbing the urge to kiss her mouth, Joseph lowered his hands because he didn't trust himself not to take Crystal into his arms, carry her up the staircase to her bedroom, strip her naked and bury his flesh so deep inside her they'd become one in every sense of the word.

Aside from her beauty, Joseph wasn't certain what it was about Crystal that drew him to her like a moth to a flame. Perhaps it had something to do with her outspokenness. Under the veneer of poise and sophistication was a woman in complete control of her life—something he'd just come into. Joseph left the court to take on a role at ColeDiz because of family loyalty. It hadn't been easy working with Diego, whom he initially regarded as a despot. Whenever he challenged his cousin, Diego's stance softened and their working relationship had become one of mutual respect. When the CEO accused him of not being a risk taker like so many other Coles working for the family-owned company, Joseph reminded Diego his mind-set was law, not business.

He'd become a businessman who'd found himself enthralled with a businesswoman, although they were like ships passing in the night, acknowledging each other for a while before sailing on to other ports of call.

"I'm ready to see what you plan to do with the former speakeasy."

Crystal inserted the thumb drive in one of the ports on her laptop, clicking on the file for Speak Low. Joseph stared, awed by the before photos and after renderings of the basement in the Tribeca residence that had been transformed from a dark, brick-lined empty space to one with strategically placed lights between the coffered ceiling and brick walls, creating a soft, inviting atmosphere.

He shook his head in amazement. "It's stunning."

Crystal highlighted the wall with framed photographs, enlarging it. "Do you recognize these jazz greats?"

Joseph peered closer. "I know Scott Joplin, Duke Ellington, Miles Davis, John Coltrane and Charlie Parker." He paused, shaking his head. "I can't recall the others."

She pointed to the three remaining photographs. "Sidney Bechet, Fats Waller and Artie Shaw."

"How do you know so much about jazz musicians?"

"My father is a jazz enthusiast. He has a priceless collection of rare recordings of jazz greats dating back to the 1920s."

To say Joseph was in awe of Crystal's talent was putting it mildly. She was more than good at her craft. She was brilliant. "You must decorate my home once it's built, and I'm not going to take no for an answer."

Crystal closed the file, her jaw hardening as she clenched her teeth. Joseph was back to flaunting his belief in entitlement, that she couldn't or shouldn't deny him whatever he wanted. "You have no idea how long it's going to take to build your house, and I don't know where or what I'll be doing then. You have my number, so whenever you're ready, give me a call and I'll let you know if I can or can't accommodate you."

Joseph went completely still as if he'd been struck across the face. Crystal's retort was cold, waspish. "I'm sorry if you believe I'm pressuring you," he said.

A beat passed as Crystal looked at Joseph in what had become a stare-down. Twin emotions assailed her. She didn't know why he excited and exasperated her all within the same breath. "It isn't what I believe, Joseph. You were emphatic when you said you weren't going to take no for an answer."

"I shouldn't have put it that way."

Crystal tried to soften her response. "I'll let you off this time, but please don't let it happen again."

A frown marred Joseph's even features. "Damn, girl. Can't you cut me some slack? I said I was sorry."

She had no intention of relenting, not until Joseph learned that being a Cole wasn't the answer to getting everything he wanted in life. "I'll have to think about it."

It was Joseph's turn to engage in a stare-down, his large, dark eyes boring into Crystal. "Why is it I find myself completely enthralled with a woman whose beauty is comparable to the most exquisite, delicate rose? Yet when I try to touch her she's quick to remind me she has sharp thorns that draw blood. What do I have to do for you to let me in?"

"You don't have to do anything. You're already in," Crystal said in a hushed whisper. She wanted to tell Joseph that she'd allowed him to scale the wall she'd erected to keep men at a distance.

Joseph moved closer, his breath warm and moist against her cheek. "Am I really in?" he questioned. Crystal blinked, and then nodded. "Please spend the night with me." She blinked again, staring at him as if he'd spoken a language she didn't understand. "Nothing's going to happen that you don't want to happen," he continued.

Please spend the night with me. The passionately spoken query caused Crystal's breath to solidify in her throat, choking her with a raw emotion that wouldn't permit her to speak. He hadn't asked to make love to her, but just to be with him. His arrogance and entitlement aside, she knew Joseph was different, unique from the other men with whom she'd become involved. He made her more than aware of the strong passions within her, and that she'd denied her own physical needs for far too long.

He'd asked her to establish the terms of their short-lived relationship and she knew if they were going to make love, then she would have to make the first overture.

Exhaling an inaudible breath, Crystal knew she couldn't continue to ignore the truth. She wanted the man. A secret smile stole its way over her parted lips. She and Joseph had reached a point in their friendship where it had to be resolved.

"Please wait for me to pack an overnight bag."

Joseph sat stunned, unable to move, when Crystal stood and walked out of the room. She'd become an enigma, keeping him emotionally off balance. It wasn't vanity that communicated she enjoyed his company as much as he enjoyed hers; however, the hours, minutes and seconds they'd spent together hadn't totaled a full day.

He wanted more time, time in which to discover if what he felt for her was real or imaginary, only because José Ibrahim Cole-Wilson believed he was falling in love for the first time in his life.

Chapter 10

Crystal knew the moment she walked through the door to Joseph's penthouse to spend the night that she and her life would change forever. She shifted her bag from one hand to the other in an attempt to stem a sudden flash of nerves, unable to believe she was reacting like a frightened virgin about to embark on her first sexual encounter. *Pull it together, girl,* she told herself. After all, she was a thirty-year-old, sexually experienced woman who in her early twenties had lived with a man almost twice her age. Even though there hadn't been anyone since Brian, she still shouldn't be shaking like a fragile leaf in a storm.

Reaching for her bag, Joseph placed it on the floor. His eyes never left hers as he cradled her face in his hands, and she was certain he could hear and feel the runaway pumping of her heart. "If you don't want to do this, then I'll take you back to your place."

Crystal lifted her chin in a gesture he probably had no problem interpreting as defiance. "If I wasn't certain, I never would've agreed to spend the night with you."

Lowering his head and hands, taking her into an embrace, Joseph breathed a kiss under her ear. "You're certain, yet you're afraid."

"I'm not afraid," she countered.

"If you're not afraid, then why are you trembling?"

"Perhaps it comes from the anticipation of sharing your bed," she half lied.

Crystal knew Joseph had offered her the option of their sharing a bed without making love.

It was just that while her head said no, her body was screaming for a release of sexual tension and frustration building up for longer than she could remember. And she had to remind herself that both were responsible, consenting adults who were aware of where a sexual encounter would lead. There would be no declarations of love or promises of a future together. In other words, they would be friends with benefits.

"Would you feel less apprehensive if we don't make love tonight?"

Crystal tried making out his features in the muted light in the entryway. "Why are you giving me mixed messages? Didn't you say nothing's going to happen that I don't want to happen?" He nodded. "Then I say we should start with sharing the same bed." Smiling, Crystal rested a hand on his chest. "Please show me where I can shower and change."

And it wasn't for the first time Joseph felt he was falling in love with an enigma. The trembling woman in his arms was nothing like the one who'd stunned him when she broached the subject of men and women masturbating. He pressed a kiss to the soft, fragrant strands covering her head. "Come upstairs with me."

Like a trusting child, Crystal held Joseph's hand as he led her up the staircase to the second floor and into his spare bedroom. He set her bag on the padded bench at the foot of the bed, turned and walked out, closing the door behind him.

Puffing up her cheeks, she blew out a breath. She stood without moving, staring at the bag on the bench seat. Joseph had referred to her as a delicate rose with thorns, but the thorns were a necessity to keep him at a distance. And what Crystal knew as surely as she knew her own name was that she had feelings for Joseph. She could imagine herself falling in love with him. But, unlike his ex, she wouldn't try and pressure him into marrying her. However, she did think him selfish for continuing to date a woman for that long when he wasn't ready to put a ring on her finger.

Shaking her head as if coming out of a trance, Crystal opened the bag and took out her grooming supplies. Minutes later she stepped into the shower stall.

* * *

Joseph stared at his reflection in the bathroom mirror as he drew the electric shaver over his jaw and chin, knowing he'd turned the corner in his relationship with Crystal when he'd practically begged her to spend the night with him. It wasn't sex he needed from her as much as it was companionship.

He'd chided Diego time and again about being married to ColeDiz, but he'd become his cousin's clone when over the past two years he'd thought of nothing else but the overall success of the tea garden.

This time when he'd returned to Charleston, Joseph could never have predicted he would meet someone like Crystal. If he were looking for the ideal woman, then she would be it. She embodied beauty, grace, intelligence and passion. However, she'd accused him of being somewhat arrogant with an inflated sense of entitlement when in reality he wasn't either. What she thought of as arrogance was confidence to Joseph—something that had been instilled in him from childhood. His father constantly reminded him that as a Cole he was a descendent of survivors who'd endured unspeakable cruelty so that he would exist today, and at no cost should he dishonor their sacrifice.

As for entitlement, it was synonymous with his family's legacy. His great-grandfather Samuel Claridge Cole, the grandson of slaves, had established a foundation wherein his children, their children and their children's children would never have to look outside the family for financial stability.

He ran his hand over his face and throat, finding it free of stubble. Reaching for a bottle on the vanity, he uncapped it and poured a small amount into his cupped hands, then patted his cheeks, wincing against the stinging sensation. Not wanting to linger any longer, Joseph stepped into the shower stall, switched on the radio hanging from the showerhead and sang along with the latest Bruno Mars hit.

Knocking lightly on Joseph's bedroom door, Crystal entered at the same time he walked out of the bathroom in a pair of black cotton pajama pants. Her eyes widened as she stared at his smooth, broad chest. His upper body was magnificent: broad shoulders, long, ropy arms, muscled pectorals and defined abs and biceps. The drawstring waistband to his pants rode low on a pair of slim hips. She smiled. Joseph wasn't that conservative; the scales of justice were tattooed over his left breast.

"I was hoping you were decent," she said, smiling.

Joseph glanced down at his bare toes peeking out from under the hem of the pajama pants. "I usually sleep nude, but because I have company I decided it best I cover up."

She nodded. "Thank you." If she walked into the room and found him nude, Crystal wasn't certain how she would react. Seeing him in a state of half dress was enough to make her heart beat a little too quickly. When going through her lingerie drawer, she had to decide whether to wear a nightgown or pajamas, deciding on the latter at the last possible moment because she didn't want to show too much flesh. The pink-and-white cotton pants and a matching sleeveless top were definitely not risqué.

Joseph pulled back the quilt, blanket and sheet on the far side of the bed. "I like to sleep near the door. If that's okay with you," he added quickly.

"It's okay."

Crystal wasn't about to debate with Joseph which side of the bed she preferred, because even if she slept on the right side, by morning she'd find herself on the left. She strolled fluidly across the bedroom, placed her slippers next to the bedside table and got into bed. Reaching up, she turned off the lamp on her side, then settled down against the mound of pillows cradling her shoulders.

Joseph hadn't closed the wall-to-wall drapes and millions of stars winked in the clear nighttime winter sky. She went completely still when he got into bed next to her, dimming rather than turning off his bedside lamp. The warmth of his body elicited sparks of awareness that eddied throughout her.

Resting his head on a folded arm, Joseph turned on his side to face Crystal. "What's on your calendar for tomorrow?"

Shifting slightly, she stared directly at him. Light from the lamp illuminated his smooth clean-shaven jaw, while drawing her gaze to linger on his mouth. Crystal stared at Joseph through the eyes of an artist. He would've made the perfect model for drawing classes, because with his balanced features and beautifully proportioned body he was certain to have become a favorite for those drawing the male nude figure.

"I have a one o'clock appointment at a textile factory over in Goose Creek." She had to order sheets, tablecloths and towels for the inn and B and B. "What about you?"

"I'm free all day," he answered, his minty toothpaste breath sweeping over her face.

"How often do you go to the tea garden?"

"Four or five times a week, now that the project manager is in Nebraska awaiting the birth of his first child."

Her eyebrows shot up as she focused on the tattoo on his chest. "Don't you have someone else to step in for him if you're not there?"

Smiling, Joseph flashed his straight white teeth. Crystal was thinking in business mode. "There's an assistant manager who is an environmental engineer, but he's not full-time because he teaches environmental studies at the College of Charleston. I have someone who's retired and living on the island who acts as a backup and security. We've installed closed-circuit monitors in his house, and at any time of the day he's always aware of any activity at the garden."

"When do you expect to harvest your first crop?"

"Mid to late April."

Her eyes came up, meeting his. "So, you're going to hang out here until that time?"

Joseph nodded, his fingers playing in the curls touching the top of her ear. "That's the plan. I can't go back to Florida now even if I wanted to, with Shane gone. Marci's due to have her baby in another two weeks, so by the time she and baby are medically cleared to travel, they'll be back for harvesting."

Crystal couldn't believe she could feel so comfortable sharing the bed with a man of whom she'd had erotic dreams. He smelled of soap and an aftershave that matched his cologne, and she wanted to press her body to his in a silent plea for him to make love to her.

"How old will you be next weekend?" she asked after a pregnant silence.

"Thirty-one."

She smiled. "You're eight months older than me."

"When's your birthday?"

"October thirty-first."

"Damn, baby. You came out with the witches and ghouls."

"Tell me about it," she snorted delicately. "I usually celebrate it November first."

Joseph stared at her fresh-scrubbed face, wondering if Crystal knew she didn't need makeup because her complexion was flawless. "All Saints' Day was a school holiday for me growing up."

Crystal assumed Joseph would be Catholic because of his Latin ancestry. "You have Latin roots, yet your name doesn't reflect it."

"My legal name is José Ibrahim Cole-Wilson, but the only person who calls me José is my grandmother. My uncles refer to me as Joe Jr. and my sister calls me Joey."

Easing away from him and sitting up, Crystal gave him a long, penetrating stare. "I like José better than Joseph or Joe. It's softer sounding."

Pushing into a sitting position, Joseph pressed his shoulder to Crystal's. "*Abuela* would love you for saying that because she wanted all of her grandchildren to have Spanish names. My parents decided before they had their first baby that my father would name their boys and my mother their girls. My oldest brother is Anthony instead of Antonio. Then there's Harper, and the youngest is Nathan. When my mother had two boys back to back, she overruled my father because she thought they would never have a girl. So she got to name me and my sister, Bianca."

"It must have been fun growing up in a big family." There was a hint of wistfulness in Crystal's voice.

"It was chaos personified, especially when we pretended we were professional wrestlers and jumped off sofas and tables. If we didn't break lamps or some little figurine that was my mother's favorite, then it was an arm, wrist, leg or occasionally we'd dislocate a shoulder. Dad, who's an orthopedic surgeon, would put us back together and then ground us for as long it took for whatever was broken or dislocated to heal. Unfortunately for me I broke one leg and then the other in two consecutive summers, so I spent two school vacations in a cast and indoors. All of the roughhousing stopped when Marimba opened for business and Mom put us to work. I'd complain that she was breaking the law because we were too young to work, so she had us sign up for working papers and put us on the payroll."

"I suppose she rested her case," Crystal teased. Joseph cut his eyes at her, but she pretended she didn't see the threatening look. "Speaking of food, what do you plan to serve Saturday?"

His expression changed, softening. "We're going to entertain between sixteen and twenty, so it should be buffet-style." Turning over, Joseph picked up a pad and pen with the hotel's logo off his bedside table. "I like what you made when I came to your place for happy hour. Maybe we can add a few more dishes."

Crystal noted it was the second time he'd said *we.* "You can order a cheese and fruit platter. A raw bar with clams, oysters, lobster and sushi is always a big hit. I'm partial to prosciutto-wrapped asparagus and melon, prawn with various sweet and spicy dipping sauces, spinach and bacon-stuffed mushrooms and sliced tomatoes and mozzarella. That's just for the ladies."

Scribbling quickly, Joseph listed the various dishes. "What's for the guys?"

"Chicken wings, ribs and pigs in a blanket."

"What you trying to say, baby? That we're carnivores?"

Crystal folded her hands at her waist. "Who're you trying to fool? If I gave you a choice between a walnut salad in endive and a rib eye steak, you'd go for the steak."

"Man cannot live by salad alone," he quipped.

"Speaking of salads, what do you think of a Cobb salad?"

Joseph added it to the list. "Anything else you can think of?"

"Deviled eggs topped with caviar."

"Beluga, sevruga or osetra? What's the matter?" he asked when she gave him a look of astonishment.

"Beluga. I didn't think you were that familiar with different types of caviar." It was only on very special occasions and depending upon the artist that Jasmine served caviar during a showing.

"I remember my mother nearly having a meltdown when she catered a private party at the restaurant and the woman who wanted to surprise her husband insisted she wanted to serve sevruga caviar to her fancy guests. Beluga or osetra wouldn't do, because she'd heard somewhere that the golden osetra was the rarest and most mature of the osetra sturgeon. My mother contacted a gourmet shop that sold sixteen-ounce tins for twenty-five hundred dollars a pop."

Crystal did a quick calculation in her head. "That would only serve eight to sixteen, depending on the portions."

"Mom had to order enough for at least eighty. The bill alone for caviar was more than twelve thousand dollars."

Crystal shook her head in amazement. She didn't understand how some people threw away money in order to impress others. "How much was the entire bill?"

"Over a hundred grand. Mom closed the restaurant to the public, so she had to adjust the final cost. Champagne flowed like water, along with vintage wine and top-shelf liquor. There was a live band, a D.J. and rolling bars. Several couples left with someone they hadn't come to the party with, and I witnessed firsthand how drinking too much destroyed a few marriages when men and women who were married to others were seen coming out of the private party rooms adjusting their clothes."

"Damn!" she drawled, scrunching up her nose. "That is so low. The only thing worse is having sex in an airplane bathroom."

"That depends on the plane," Joseph replied, deadpan.

Crystal's jaw dropped. "You've have sex on a plane?"

Joseph did all he could not to laugh at her shocked expression. The bathroom on the Gulfstream G650 had a shower *and* enough room for a couple to make love without having to be

contortionists. "No. One of these days I wouldn't mind joining the mile-high club, but only on a plane with a bathroom
large enough where I don't have to straddle a toilet to get my
freak on."

She scrunched up her nose again, unaware of how much
Joseph had come to watch for the charming expression. It reminded him a little child smelling something malodorous.

"That's one club I don't need to join, thank you." Crystal
gestured toward the phone. "I think you'd better call concierge
to place your food order," she suggested.

"You're right," he agreed. Reaching for the phone, Joseph
punched in the number for the concierge. He knew he wasn't
giving the hotel chef a lot of time in which to prepare what he'd
need for Saturday night; however, it was the Beaumont House's
pledge to their penthouse guests to fulfill their requests.

"Concierge. John Porter speaking. How may I help you, Mr.
Wilson?"

It took fifteen minutes for Joseph to give him the proposed
menu. "I'm going to need at least two servers and one bartender.
I'd really appreciate it if they can set up twenty minutes before
my guests are scheduled to arrive. They're coming in together
around seven, and I'd also like someone from the hotel staff to
allow them access to this floor."

"That shouldn't be a problem. Is there anything else you'll
need, Mr. Wilson?"

"That's all for now. Thank you so much, Mr. Porter," Joseph
said, ending the call.

Turning off the lamp, he lay beside Crystal, pulling her
hips against his groin, while hoping he would be able to sleep
through the night without making love with her. In that in-
stance he felt like Job, being put to the test and praying he
would succeed.

He pressed a kiss to the nape of her neck. "Good night,
sweetheart."

Crystal smiled in the darkened space. "Good night, darling."

It was Joseph's turn to smile. "Am I really your darling,
sweetheart?"

"Tonight you are."

"What about tomorrow morning?" he asked.

"Let's take this one day at a time."

He sobered quickly. Joseph wondered if that was how their relationship would play out—one day at a time. He'd asked her to let him in and she countered saying he was in, but somehow he felt it wasn't enough. With Crystal it had to be all or nothing for him, and he wasn't prepared to accept nothing. Exhaling an inaudible sigh, Joseph closed his eyes, waiting for sleep to overtake him.

His last thought before slipping into the comforting arms of Morpheus was of his growing old with Crystal.

Ribbons of sunlight crept over the bed, caressing Crystal's cheek with warmth. She came awake with the realization she was alone. The pillow beside hers bore the imprint of Joseph's head but none of his body's heat. Moaning softly, she turned over to peer at the clock on a side table. It was minutes before eight.

Pushing into a sitting position and raising her arms above her head, she stretched like a languorous feline emerging from a long nap. Sharing a bed with Joseph certainly had its advantages. She'd slept through the night and Crystal felt more rested than she had in a while.

Her arms were still above her head when he walked into the bedroom carrying a bed tray with covered dishes from which wafted mouthwatering aromas. He'd pulled on a white tee over the pajama pants. Seeing him like that was a sight she could easily get used to.

Lowering her arms, she ran her fingers through the short strands pressed against her scalp. "Good morning."

Joseph placed the tray on the table on his side of the bed. Leaning down, he brushed a light kiss over her parted lips. "Good morning. I thought it would be fun if we'd have breakfast in bed."

Easing back, Crystal swung her legs over the side of the

mattress. "I'd like that. But I have to wash my face and brush my teeth first."

"I put your things in my bathroom," he said as she headed for the door.

Crystal stopped midstride and turned around slowly to face him. A beat passed. "Thank you."

She didn't want to read more into the action than necessary, as she turned toward the bathroom, wanting to anticipate when they would possibly share the intimacy of a bath or shower. She was realistic enough to know when they did make love it would change her. An even more terrifying realization would be falling in love with him. Shaking her head as if to banish the thought, Crystal entered the bathroom.

Crystal completed a modified ablution in record time and returned to the bedroom.

Joseph had set another tray on her side of the bed. "Come and eat before everything gets cold." Quickening her step, she practically jumped into bed, smiling as he adjusted the pillows behind her back and shoulders before settling the bamboo bed tray over her lap.

She uncovered a dish and gasped. He'd prepared a mushroom-and-spinach omelet topped with fragrant grated truffle. A smaller dish held country links and strips of crispy bacon, and another grapefruit sections.

Crystal picked up a knife and fork resting on a snowy white damask napkin, cutting into the omelet. An explosion of flavors lingered on her tongue and palate even after she'd chewed and swallowed the eggs.

"I truly can get used to eating breakfast in bed if this is what I have to look forward to," she remarked lightly.

Attractive lines appeared around Joseph's eyes when he smiled. "That can easily be arranged, sweetheart." The endearment rolled off his tongue as easily as involuntary breathing.

"Every morning I could prepare something different. It could be chicken and waffles, eggs Benedict, shrimp and grits, scones, frittatas, croissants—"

"Stop it, Joseph," she interrupted, in an attempt not to burst out laughing.

"You interrupted me before I could finish. There are also pancakes, crepes, steak and ham and eggs."

Crystal gave him a sidelong glance. "Yeah, right, and I'd end up so full that I'd never get out of bed."

"Lingering in bed can be quite pleasurable when sharing it with someone you love."

Crystal froze. The four-letter word had the same impact as a large hand going around her throat and not permitting her to swallow, breathe or even utter a sound. However, she was able to shake her head before finding her voice. "No, Joseph," she whispered. "You're not abiding by the terms."

Joseph chewed and swallowed several grapefruit sections. "What are you talking about?"

"We promised there would be no mention of love."

It was his turn to go completely still. Nothing moved. Not even his eyes. "You're wrong, because the word *love* never came up in that conversation. And what is so wrong with me saying I love being with you—in and out of bed?"

Crystal felt properly chastised. Being presumptuous, she'd misconstrued his meaning. She flashed a bright smile. "And I enjoy being with you."

Joseph touched his napkin to the corners of his mouth. "What's the matter? Does saying the word *love* bother you?"

"No. It's just that I believe it's bantered about much too freely."

"What if I tell you that I love you?"

"But you don't," she countered, and then continued eating.

A pregnant silence followed her retort until the space vibrated with tension as Joseph struggled to control his rising temper. Crystal was the most incredible *and* exasperating woman he'd ever met. "Are you a psychic, Crystal?"

She blinked. "Say what?"

"Did I stutter?"

A shiver of annoyance shimmied up her back. "No, you

didn't stutter, *Joseph.*" Crystal stressed his name. "Why would you ask me that?"

"I asked because if you're able to read minds, then I applaud you. But if you can't, then don't tell me what I feel. Or is it you don't feel you're worthy to be loved?"

She snorted delicately. "Now who's being presumptuous?"

Picking up a pot of coffee, Joseph filled Crystal's cup with the steaming brew. "Will you please answer my question? Do you feel worthy of a man loving you?"

"Of course I do," she said much too quickly.

Joseph decided to press the issue. He'd found the woman in bed with him so easy to love, yet she continued to put up barriers to keep him from getting too close. "If you believe that, then why would you live with a man who didn't love you enough to marry you? And please don't tell me again that he didn't want children. I know a few married couples who've decided not to have children, but that doesn't mean they're not a family."

Biting down on her lower lip, Crystal mentally beat herself up for telling Joseph about living with Brian. Her past was her past and he had no right to pass judgment about her former lover. "Brian and I had a very satisfying relationship."

"Open your eyes, sweetheart. The man used you. Imagine his ego when as a middle-aged man he got to flaunt a beautiful young woman nearly half his age every time you were in public together. He didn't have to pay for sex because he had you." Joseph leaned closer. "I never would've treated you that shabbily."

Crystal pretended interest in adding cream to her coffee. Joseph's assessment of her relationship with Brian was similar to her parents'. "How would you have treated me?"

"If I wanted you to live with me, then I would marry you."

"Even if you weren't ready for marriage?" It was her turn to remind Joseph of why he'd ended his relationship with his longtime girlfriend.

"Maybe it wasn't so much that I wasn't ready but perhaps I'd chosen the wrong woman with which to engage in a long-term relationship."

They fell silent, concentrating on finishing breakfast. Joseph knew he'd waded out into dangerous waters bringing up the topic of marriage with Crystal. He knew her stance on the issue, but since meeting her, his had changed drastically. He wasn't the same man who'd checked into the Beaumont House in late November, and he had to thank Crystal for that.

Before meeting her, his focus had been on himself and his accomplishments. Walking into the federal courthouse alongside her uncle amid cameras and reporters on the first day of a drug kingpin's trial gave him a rush of unquestionable power. The high continued throughout the trial, ending when the jury rendered a guilty verdict.

It was ironic that his association with Solomon Eaton never crossed the line from professional to personal. It wasn't until Joseph handed in his resignation that Solomon revealed he'd received several death threats, threats targeting friends and family members. He also hadn't told Joseph that members of the U.S. Marshal Service had provided around-the-clock protection for him during the trials in which Solomon had served as a lead prosecutor for the government against high-level drug traffickers.

When he walked out of the federal courthouse and into a private office at ColeDiz International Ltd., Joseph's life took another turn he hadn't anticipated when instead of becoming immersed in corporate law he'd become a businessman and farmer.

Now his life was about to change again, and he thought of Crystal as his good-luck charm.

Everything he wanted seemed to go in his favor. Diego had found someone at ColeDiz willing to travel, leaving Joseph to concentrate on eventually taking over as CEO.

He'd revised the proposal for the jams and jellies, either deleting or updating the points set down by Myles Eaton and emailing it to him for his review. Within hours he'd received a reply. Myles had approved the proposal and final contract between ColeDiz International Resorts and Sweet Persuasions.

He hadn't lied when he told Crystal she was special, and for him she was special enough to make her a part of his life and his future.

Chapter 11

Pressing her palms together, Crystal stood next to Joseph, watching the bartender set up his bar. His arm went around her waist and she pulled her gaze away to meet his eyes. "Do you think I lit too many candles?"

"No, baby. Everything looks perfect. You're perfect." She'd placed white candles in various sizes in the fireplace and along the mantel. Watching her instruct the waitstaff where she wanted them to set up the buffet indicated this wasn't the first time she'd hosted a dinner party.

If he was pleasantly surprised as to her hosting ability, it was her appearance that rendered him mute. She'd selected a silk-lined midnight-blue cocktail dress with a slightly flaring skirt ending at her knees. Four inches of matching strappy pumps put her at the six-foot mark.

"Be careful, sweetie," she whispered, "or you're going to give me a big head."

"We'll be all right as long as I don't end up with a big head before our guests get here," he whispered in her ear.

It took a few seconds before Crystal realized what Joseph was referring to. "I don't like quickies," she whispered back.

Joseph chuckled deep in his throat. "That's something else we have in common."

Crystal nuzzled Joseph's ear with her nose. "I think your friend is going to be very surprised."

Earlier that afternoon two men from maintenance had come to set up tables near the wall-to-wall windows spanning the width of the living and dining room, leaving enough space for people to walk around.

The dining table provided seating for eight; the sofa added

three and a love seat another two, and an additional dozen padded chairs were set up around the living room to accommodate those wishing to sit.

Joseph had turned a satellite radio to a station featuring slow jams from the '80s and '90s, and the melodious sounds flowed from hidden speakers installed in rooms throughout the first floor.

The apartment phone rang, preempting Joseph's reply. He picked up the receiver on the table in the entryway. "Our guests are here," he announced softly.

Crystal stood beside Joseph, smiling, shaking hands and exchanging air kisses with his frat brothers when he introduced her as his girlfriend. Like their host, all of the thirtysomething men wore suits or blazers, tailored slacks, shirts or sweaters, sans ties. They exchanged rough hugs with Joseph while pounding his back.

Their female companions, less effusive and very chic in tailored suits, dresses and designer shoes and matching handbags, were dignified and gracious. All of them had left their purses and totes on the table in the entryway.

When Joseph introduced her to Frank Lynch, his former college roommate, Crystal wondered if the tall, handsome, red-haired, green-eyed engineer was aware the gathering was for him and not Joseph.

Frank held her hand, dropping a kiss on her knuckles. "If I wasn't engaged, I would seriously consider stealing you away from Wilson."

Joseph forcibly removed Crystal's hand from his friend's, tucking it into the fold of his elbow. "I know you're not trying to hit on my woman," he teased with a wide grin.

Frank's fiancée, a very pretty petite woman with a light brown complexion and a profusion of reddish brown, shoulder-length twists, glared at him. "Francis Patrick Lynch, I hope you're not disrespecting me and Joseph by flirting with his girlfriend!" A chorus of guffaws followed her reprimand.

"Easy there, Brother Lynch. When your woman calls you

by your government name, then you better watch out for what comes next," mumbled Andrew "Drew" Andrews. He grew up being teased because he had the same first and last name.

"Word," drawled another of Joseph's frat brothers. "You're a better man than me, Lynch. There's no way I would upset a woman who knows how to use a scalpel, then lie down next to her and close my eyes." Francis turned a beet-red while his future wife glared at Drew.

"If you're ever in Denver and need medical assistance, don't come to my hospital, Mr. Andrews," she threatened, flashing a grin at the stocky man sporting a dark brown shaven pate and a neatly barbered goatee.

Joseph knew it was time to end the lighthearted teasing before it escalated. "Ladies and gentlemen, the bar is open. Once everyone is served we'll have a toast."

"Damn, Wilson," Drew drawled, following Joseph to where the bartender waited to take their beverage requests. "This place is outrageous. Brother, you're really living the high life."

"It'll do," Joseph said, winking at him over his shoulder.

Crystal beckoned the women closer. "Ladies, please follow me. For those who need to use the restroom, there's one just before you come to the kitchen, and there's another to the left of the staircase."

"I'm so glad Joseph came to his senses and stopped seeing that cow that used to work my last nerve," whispered Lucretia Moore, an incredibly beautiful full-figured woman with close-cropped hair bleached a becoming platinum.

Dr. Anaïs Woods nodded in agreement. "I second that, Lucie." She gave Crystal a direct stare, smiling. "You're such a welcome change from Kiara Solis, who believed her you-know-what didn't stink. We only tolerated her because she was seeing Joseph."

"How did you meet him?" asked Maria Acosta in slightly accented English.

"He used to work with my uncle." She wasn't ready to divulge that she and Joseph occupied neighboring penthouse apartments. Her answer seemed to satisfy them as they made their way toward the bar.

* * *

Glasses in hand, everyone stood in the middle of the room waiting for Joseph to make a toast. Crystal stared at the man who, despite her efforts to put up barriers to keep him at a distance, had managed to scale the hurdles to soften her heart. He'd called her a thorny rose and she had been. Now the thorns were gone and she was ready to acknowledge that she was falling inexorably in love with him.

Smiling, Joseph raised his glass of amber liquid. "First of all, I'd like to thank everyone for coming to my temporary humble abode for an evening of friendship and goodwill." This was followed by a roar of laughter. "All of you know why you're here," he continued once the laughter faded. "Except for one person. It is not to celebrate my birthday prematurely, but rather to honor a friend and brother who in another week will wake to look at the face of his beautiful future wife and the majestic Rocky Mountains." He extended his glass. "Brother Lynch, we'll miss you, man."

The shocked expression on Frank's face was priceless when his jaw dropped. "Why, you sneaky—"

"Don't blame me," Joseph said quickly, interrupting him while taking a backward step.

Drew held up a hand. "Blame me, Frank. We know how you hate goodbyes, so the brothers decided a little get-together would be the best way to show you how much we're going to miss your corny-ass jokes."

"My jokes aren't corny," Frank retorted. All of the frat brothers knew he was a frustrated standup.

"Just don't quit your day job!" someone yelled out.

Joseph laughed with the others. "Speaking of day jobs. Frank, we wish you and Anaïs all the best life has to offer."

"Frank and Anaïs!" chorused the assembly.

Frank kissed his fiancée, eliciting a round of applause. He signaled for silence. "Even though I'm here under false pretenses I still would like to thank everyone for giving me a send-off I know I'll never forget." Shifting slightly, he stared directly at Joseph. "He's probably going to try and kick my ass, but I'm going to tell it anyway." He paused. "I wouldn't be standing here if it hadn't been for Brother Wilson." Frank ignored Joseph when he shook his head.

"When I moved into my dorm room and saw Joseph Cole-Wilson standing there, my first impression was I'm going to have to compete with this pretty SOB for women because he had no idea I liked my honeys with a little color." Everyone laughed, including Joseph. "Once he found this out, he encouraged me to pledge a Black Greek Letter Organization, and that way I would become his brother in every sense of the word. We were halfway into our junior year at Cornell when I got a letter from the bursar's office saying I wouldn't be able to attend classes because my tuition payment was overdue. When I asked my father if he'd sent the check, he broke down and told me he'd lost his savings in a Ponzi scheme and that I would have to drop out. I started packing and that's when Brother Wilson told me he could get the money. I thought he was crazy, but three days later I was reinstated. At first I thought my roommate was into some funny stuff, but he finally had to admit that he asked his father to give him the money for the rest of my junior year. What I didn't know at the time was that he'd also paid for my senior year." Frank paused again as he stared down at the floor. "I owe everything I am today to Brother Wilson. Because of him I was able to graduate. Because of him I became an Alpha, which led me to meet the woman whom I love more than I ever thought possible." He extended his glass to Joseph, and then to the others in the room as tears filled his eyes. "Frat, sorors. I love you all."

There came a moment of silence. "You should be glad you're leaving, because from the look on Brother Wilson's face I know he's thinking about kicking your ass," Drew called out.

Lucretia waved her free hand. "Brother Wilson, I have a nephew who wants those new Jordans. Is it possible for you to spot him some chedda so he can style like the other kids in his class?" Her plaintive entreaty elicited another round of laughter.

Maria sucked her teeth loudly. "I'd have to be crazy to spend four hundred dollars on a pair of sneakers for my son when he'll need another pair less than six months later because he's grown out of them."

Most of the women were grumbling loudly about the cost of so-called designer sneakers, while Crystal's gaze met and fused with Joseph's as he stared at her over the rim of his glass. She'd thought him arrogant, entitled, yet in an act bordering on courage and selflessness, he'd gone to his father on behalf of his friend and roommate to ask for money.

She'd tried much too hard to tell herself that she was totally immune to him, but that was a lie. And Crystal knew she had to stop lying to herself and face reality. She wanted Joseph, all of him, for the short time they would have together.

She hadn't moved, so he wended his way through those lining up alongside the table with the food. A secret smile curved her mouth with his approach. "I like your friends," she said softly.

Lowering his head, Joseph pressed a kiss along the column of her neck. "I like them, too, but I like you a lot better. I should warn you that most of the women are also Greek, and you'll find a few AKAs among them."

Looping her arm over the sleeve of his jacket, Crystal took a sip of her wine. "Greek love," she said softly.

Joseph nodded. "Phi-Skee."

"Skee-Phi," she replied, acknowledging the bond between the Alphas and the AKAs of being the first Black Greek fraternity and sorority respectively.

It was two in the morning when she and Joseph said their goodbyes; the bartenders and waiters were clearing away all food and drink, and the maintenance staff had come to stack chairs on trolleys and reposition furniture.

Resting his hands at Crystal's waist, Joseph turned her in the direction of the staircase. "Go to bed, baby. I'll wait down here until everyone's finished."

Crystal flashed a lopsided smile. "Thank you," she slurred, leaning in and patting Joseph's chest. She knew she'd drunk too much wine when she was forced to hold on to the railing as she attempted to climb the staircase in her bare feet.

Frank's farewell celebration was nothing short of perfection. Copious amounts of food were consumed, and the bartender was kept busy filling drink requests.

Joseph changed the radio station to one featuring rap and hip-hop, Frank and Drew rolled back the rug and the living room had become a dance floor with couples dancing. As soon as the dancing began, Crystal shed her shoes and so had most of the women wearing stilettos.

Stepping off the top stair, she walked slowly along the hallway and into the master bedroom.

Folding his body down to the chair in the entryway, Joseph stretched out his legs, crossing his feet at the ankles. Given the short notice, Frank's impromptu going-away celebration was a rousing success. However, Joseph would've preferred Frank not disclose his involvement in securing the money needed for the engineering student to complete his undergraduate education at Cornell.

His thoughts shifted from Frank to Crystal when he spied the stilettos she'd taken off once the dancing had begun. He smiled. Club José had become Joe's Joint when the guys shed their jackets and the women their shoes. Joseph noticed Crystal bonding with the wives and girlfriends of his frat brothers—something Kiara had never been able to do.

He'd felt a measure of smugness when his frat brothers spoke of her beauty and graciousness. A few were bold enough to remark that Crystal was a refreshing change from his ex. Hearing their comments made him question himself as to why he'd continued to date Kiara when he knew marriage wasn't in their future. And in the end he had to admit to himself he'd been wrong to string her along, hoping he would never have to experience what he'd put Kiara through.

"Mr. Wilson, we're finished here."

Coming to his feet, Joseph nodded to the maintenance workers. They'd loaded tables and chairs on two trolleys. The bartender with his cart and the waiters were right behind them.

"Thank you, guys."

The bartender flashed a wide grin. "Awesome party." The waiters nodded in agreement.

"I agree," Joseph said without a modicum of modesty. It was one of the better get-togethers his friends had had in a while. Only the destination weddings were better. He closed the door, locking it, picked up Crystal's sexy heel, and went in and out of rooms extinguishing lights, leaving on the lamp on a side table near the staircase.

Joseph climbed the staircase, following the lingering scent of Crystal's perfume to his bedroom. Placing her shoes on the floor beside the door, he kicked off his own. She'd dimmed the lamps to the lowest setting, and there was enough light for him to see her neatly folded dress and underwear on the bench at the foot of the bed.

Undressing, he made it a concerted effort not to leave his shirt, slacks and socks scattered about the room.

Wearing only a pair of boxer briefs, he made his way to the bathroom. Crystal reclined in the Jacuzzi amid a profusion of bubbles up to her neck. She gave him a sexy, inviting smile.

"Hey, you," she said softly.

Leaning against the door frame, Joseph returned her smile. "Hey, yourself, beautiful. Would you like company?"

"I don't mind if you don't mind smelling like a girl."

Pushing away from the door, Joseph approached the tub, his thumbs anchored in the waistband of his briefs. "It will take more than smelling like a girl to make me feel less than a man," he drawled confidently.

Moisture had curled Crystal's short hair and spiked her lashes. "Bragging?" Bending slightly, he shed his underwear and stepped into the warm water. Her breathing stopped, her gaze lingering on the heavy semierect sex hanging between Joseph's muscled thighs. His genitals were an overt testimony to his masculinity.

Her gaze came up, resting on his face as he sat down opposite her in slow motion. The heat from the water spread up her chest to her face. The wine hadn't dulled her senses so much she didn't know he was giving her an up-close and personal view of his magnificent naked body. Crystal wished she could read minds, because Joseph's impassive expression gave nothing away.

"It was very noble of you to pay your roommate's tuition." She'd said the first thing that came to mind.

"That's something I really don't like to talk about."

"Why?"

Joseph closed his eyes. "I didn't do it to be noble. And I'm certain if the roles were reversed, Frank would've done the same thing for me."

"Are you certain he would've been able to come up with that much money?" she asked.

He opened his eyes. "It wasn't my money, but my father's."

"You asked your father?"

A cynical grin twisted Joseph's firm mouth. "I begged him. However, he agreed on one condition. That when I gained control of my trust I would have to pay him back plus fifty percent interest. Of course his demand was excessive, but he hadn't given me much of a choice. Two days after my twenty-fifth birthday I wrote him a check. Dad shocked me when he tore it up, saying he was proud I hadn't welched on my debt, and if he needed one friend, he'd want me to be that friend. Now, can we please drop the subject?"

Crystal now knew why Joseph was uncomfortable talking about it. He hadn't been comfortable with his father's compliment. "Yes."

She shifted slightly, the motion allowing Joseph a glimpse of a firm, rounded, water-slicked breast through fading bubbles. He hardened quickly, grateful for the remaining bubbles concealing his erection.

Crystal picked up a bath sponge and handed it to him. "Do you mind washing my back?"

Staring at her under half-lowered lids, he beckoned her. "Come down here and turn around." Joseph realized he should've refused her request when she scooted down to the opposite end, presenting him with her back. His erection brushed the small of her back, the sensation making him even harder.

He tried concentrating on drawing the sponge over her flaw-less dark brown skin, but his body refused to follow the dic-tates of his brain.

Around and around, up and down, he counted each time he touched her and after a while he lost count as the sponge moved lower down the curve of her spine to the roundness of Crys-tal's buttocks. Then he heard it. Her breathing had quickened. He dropped the sponge, cupping her hips, and his fingers mas-saged the firm flesh.

Crystal managed to escape the hold Joseph had on her bot-tom. Turning around, she went to her knees. Days, nights, months and years of denial surfaced, allowing her a newfound boldness when it was her turn to explore Joseph's body.

Resting her hands on either side of his face, she brushed her mouth over his in a whisper of a kiss. She tasted one corner of his mouth, then the other, knowing she was frustrating him when he brushed her hands aside and held her head captive. His explosive kiss sucked the air from her lungs, leaving her light-headed and struggling to breathe.

Looping her arms under his shoulders, Crystal pressed her breasts to his chest in an attempt to get even closer. She was on fire, the area between her legs throbbing uncontrollably. Her hips moved sensually over his groin, silently communicating how much she needed him to assuage a rising passion threat-ening to incinerate her.

"Joseph." His name was a whisper.

"I feel you, baby."

Joseph released her head, pulling her to straddle his thighs before grasping his erection and slowly, methodically easing himself inside Crystal. He was met with a slight resistance, so reversing their positions and pushing his knee between her thighs, he drew back and with a strong, sure thrust of his hips buried his hardness in the hot, moist, tight flesh pulsing around his own.

The world outside ceased to exist as he lost himself in the sensual pleasure taking him to a place where he'd never been. Even when he'd fantasized about making love to Crystal, that hadn't come close to the ecstasy he now found in her arms. Fastening his mouth to the base of her throat, he pulled the tender flesh between his teeth. Then without warning he felt it. The tightening in his scrotum indicating he was going to come when he'd wanted it to last much, much longer.

"Joseph!" Crystal called his name. "Please stop!" Panic rushed through her like molten lava. She'd been so caught up in passion she'd forgotten he'd penetrated her without using protection.

Something in her voice shattered the sensual fog holding Joseph captive. He'd promised to protect her. He pulled out, every muscle in his body screaming in frustration. He held his engorged flesh tightly, struggling to stop the flow of semen straining for release. Unable to believe he'd been so irresponsible, he pressed Crystal's head to his shoulder.

"I'm sorry, baby," he apologized over and over. "Will you forgive me?"

Crystal nodded, grateful he'd stopped in time. She placed her fingers over his mouth. "Yes, I forgive you." She pressed a kiss under his ear. "Remind me not to accept an invitation to take a bath with you again."

He caught her hand and kissed each finger. "I promise it won't happen again."

"We have to be careful not to get caught up in the moment."

Joseph smiled, the gesture not meeting his eyes. Crystal didn't know his level of frustration had gone into overdrive, and he knew if they didn't get out of the Jacuzzi he would break his promise and take her again without protection.

Punching the button to turn off the Jacuzzi, he stood, bringing Crystal up with him. Stepping out of the tub, he picked her up and walked out of the bathroom. He placed her damp body on the bed, his following hers. His rapacious mouth charted a course from her mouth to the soles of her feet, seemingly wanting to taste every inch of her silky skin. And as much as he wanted to be inside her, Joseph wanted to bring her to completion.

Crystal pulled her lip between her teeth to keep from screaming. The pleasure of Joseph's tongue and teeth made her feel as if she was coming out of her skin. Closing her eyes, she arched when the heat from his mouth seared her closely trimmed mound. A scream, torn from the back of her throat, filled the bedroom as the tip of his tongue made tiny circles around her swollen clitoris.

"Please," she pleaded shamelessly, over and over, the plea becoming a litany of neediness only Joseph could assuage.

Stopping his temporary sensual assault on her body, Joseph opened the drawer to the bedside table, took out a condom and slipped it on. Spreading her legs wider with his knee, he reached for Crystal's hand and placed it on his erection; together they eased it into her vagina, both groaning in unison.

Crystal gloried in the feel of her lover's skin against hers, his touch sending tingles up and down her body, and the hardness sliding in and out of her body setting her afire. He quickened his thrusting; she followed his pace. Heat shot through her like an electric current; throwing back her head, she screamed his name, followed by long, surrendering moans of ecstasy. A peace she'd never experienced swept over her as Joseph collapsed on her body. The raspy sound of his heavy breathing reverberated in the room. After what seemed like an eternity when it was only seconds, he rolled off her and lay on his back, a muscular arm covering his face.

A secret smile curved her mouth. Her period of enforced celibacy had been more than worth it. Making love with Joseph had awakened the dormant sexuality of her body, and she looked forward to when they would make love again and again until they parted. Her smile grew wider when he reached for her hand and laced their fingers together.

"Did I hurt you?" he asked.

"No," she answered truthfully.

"You're very small."

"I'm probably tight because it's been a while since I've had sex."

Joseph didn't want to engage in a debate about how small or tight she was, but made a mental note to wait a few days before making love to her again. And he didn't want to correct her about having sex. What they'd shared went beyond sex. Letting go of her hand, he sat up and swung his legs over the side of the bed. "Don't run away," he teased softly.

"Where am I going?" she asked.

"I don't know. Maybe you're a vampire and you have to get home before the sun comes up."

Rolling over, she placed her hand over his latex-covered penis. "As long as I don't bite this, you'll be okay."

Joseph forcibly removed her hand. "We will not pretend we're vampires."

"You're the one that brought it up."

"My bad," he drawled, rising to stand.

Crystal stared at his gloriously naked body as he headed for the bathroom. She'd wanted to tell him she wasn't as small as he was large. A moan slipped past her lips when she shifted her legs. The muscles in her groin were on fire. She needed to soak in the Jacuzzi again—this time without company.

Turning over on her side and pulling the sheet up to her neck, she closed her eyes. She was drifting off to sleep when Joseph returned, molding his chest to her back. They lay together like spoons, their breathing coming in unison until they fell into a dreamless sleep.

Crystal woke at dawn to find Joseph on his back, snoring softly. She managed to slip out of bed without waking him, completing her morning ablutions in the other bathroom.

Dressed in a pair of sweats and thick cotton socks and carrying the bag containing her clothes, she went downstairs to the kitchen. She'd drunk two glasses of water while waiting for the coffeemaker to finish the brewing cycle.

"Good morning, baby."

Spinning around on the stool at the cooking island, she smiled at Joseph standing a short distance away in his bare feet and pair of jeans and long-sleeved tee. She hadn't heard him enter the kitchen. "Good morning."

He kissed her forehead. "What are you doing up so early?"

Crystal nuzzled his ear. "I had to get something to drink. My mouth is as dry as the Sahara Desert. I OD'd on cheese, caviar and sushi, which led me to drink more wine than usual."

Wrapping his arms around her waist, Joseph rested his chin on the top of her head. "How many glasses did you have?"

"I stopped counting after the second one. I suppose that's why I was slow reacting when we got caught up in the moment."

Joseph sobered suddenly. He recalled their impromptu coupling in the Jacuzzi. "I hope I pulled out in time."

Crystal said a silent prayer he had, because they'd picked the wrong time of the month to have unprotected sex. "I think I'm all right," she said with more confidence than she actually felt.

She didn't want history to repeat itself, like her parents, if she found herself carrying Joseph's baby. Jasmine had vehemently denied she'd deliberately gotten pregnant to trap Raleigh into marrying her; instead she'd accused him of getting her pregnant because he'd believed she was breaking up with him.

Despite the accusations, they married and then spent the next six or seven years blaming each other until they finally divorced. All Crystal remembered from her early childhood was the "he said, she said" rants, and it was something she vowed never to repeat with any man.

"Will you tell me if you're not all right?" Joseph asked.

"Why?"

"Because *if* you are pregnant, then we would have to get married."

Pushing against his chest, she extricated herself from his arms. "That's where you're wrong, Joseph. I doubt if I'm pregnant, or if I were to get pregnant by you, then we don't *have to do* anything except become parents to a baby girl or boy. I will not repeat with you what my parents went through. One blaming the other because my mother was pregnant with me."

Joseph froze as if he were a statue. "We are not your parents, Crystal."

Her eyes flashed fire. "I know we're not, because I'd never marry you or any other man because of a child."

Joseph refused to back down. "Don't you believe a child needs both parents?"

Crystal also refused to concede. "Not when they're at each other's throats. Every time my parents disagreed about something, they'd pull out the pregnancy card." She shook her head. "That's not going to be me. I won't be the first single mother and I definitely won't be the last one, either. And I don't know why we're arguing about marriage and babies when it isn't something we're both not ready for."

"We're not arguing," Joseph insisted. "We're having a discussion."

She rolled her eyes upward. Okay, she mused, they weren't yelling at each other, but they were having a disagreement. Unwilling to prolong the conversation, Crystal picked up the cup, filling it from the carafe with steaming black coffee. She set it down on the saucer in front of Joseph before reaching into an overhead cabinet and taking down another cup for herself.

Joseph watched Crystal intently as she spooned a teaspoon of sugar into her cup and then added a generous amount of cream. "Will you let me know? One way or the other?" he asked.

Her eyes came up, meeting his. "Yes," she answered. "I'll let you know one way or the other."

She didn't drop her gaze as she took a sip of coffee, savoring the taste and warm brew, wondering why Joseph wouldn't let it go. And for someone claiming not to be ready to embrace marriage, he'd become like a dog with a bone, insisting on it if she were actually carrying his baby.

"Thank you," he drawled.

Crystal cut her eyes at him, clenched her teeth to keep from spewing curses, all the while counting slowly to ten. She had to leave before she said something she would no doubt later regret. "As soon as I finish my coffee I'm going back to my apartment. I have quite a few things I have to take care of."

"Don't you want breakfast?"

She shook her head. "No, thank you. I'm still full from last night." Taking a sip from the cup, she met his eyes over the rim.

"I probably won't see you until tomorrow, so if you're going to the tea garden I'd like to go along with you."

"There's a prediction of rain for tonight, and if it does, then we'll have to put it off until Tuesday."

"It can't be Tuesday because I'm going up to North Carolina." She'd planned to visit many of the furniture manufacturer stores and outlets in High Point, Hickory and Jamestown for furnishings with which to decorate the inn and B and B. "I have to shop for furniture, and I probably won't be back until next weekend." Setting the cup on the countertop, Crystal rested both hands on his chest, registering the strong, steady beating of his heart under her palms. "I'll make certain to return in time for your birthday and the Super Bowl party"

Joseph covered her hands with his larger one. "I'm going to miss you."

She affected a sexy moue. "I'm going for less than a week."

His fingers tightened slightly on hers, holding her captive. "I'm still going to miss you."

Crystal knew her feelings toward Joseph were intensifying and she was becoming more confused every minute they were together. That meant their eventual separation would be even more difficult—at least for her. "And I you," she whispered.

"I'll walk you back to your place." Dipping his head, Joseph fastened his mouth to the side of her neck.

Crystal smothered a moan as she closed her eyes. What had happened to the levelheaded woman who'd come to Charleston to decorate two renovated residences for the owner of one of the city's most luxurious hotels? What she couldn't understand was why she'd permitted herself to fall under the spell of a man whose caresses, kisses and lovemaking upset her balance and rekindled a passion she'd believed impossible.

"Please, Joseph. I have to go now." He complied, picking up her bag. They walked the carpeted hallway in silence. Joseph waited until she unlocked the door, handing her the bag, then turned and retraced his steps.

Chapter 12

Crystal stared at her reflection staring back at her in the hotel's bathroom mirror. Her fervent prayer had been answered. She wasn't pregnant! Her eyes filled with tears of relief as she compressed her lips to suppress a sob.

Since coming to North Carolina, she hadn't had a restful night's sleep in four days. As long as she was busy, placing orders for only the merchandise the manufacturers had in stock, she didn't have to dwell on whether she was carrying a baby.

At night it was different when she lay in bed, trying to imagine what was going on in her womb. What she feared most was repeating her mother's life. However, the difference was that when Jasmine discovered she was carrying Raleigh Eaton's baby, they'd been seeing each other off and on for years, while with her and Joseph, it wasn't quite a month. And for her that amounted to little more than a one-night stand.

Crystal had planned to spend one more day in North Carolina before returning to Charleston. She'd ordered beds, side tables, tables and chairs, desks, chests and armoires for the inn at a company specializing in reproductions, and the furnishings for the B and B at three other furniture companies selling exclusively to wholesalers, both who had promised a two-to-three-week turnaround for delivery.

She had an appointment with several dealers selling rugs and framed prints and with another specializing in curtains and shades. Crystal had ordered floor and table lamps from local Charleston dealers, and once the items in the storage units were delivered, she would then arrange each space according to her meticulously thought out floor plans.

Her step was light, close to skipping, when she picked up her cell phone and punched in Joseph's number. She'd promised him she would let him know one way or the other as to her physical state. His phone rang four times before going to voice mail.

Crystal paused. "Joseph, this is Crystal. I'm calling to let you know I'm not..." She paused again, clearing her thoughts and mulling over how to phrase the news he would not become a father from an unplanned pregnancy. "I'm not pregnant," she finally blurted out. "I'll see you when I get back."

Joseph rolled over, loathing getting out of bed. He hadn't gotten back to the hotel until three in the morning after spending hours at the Watering Hole. He managed to get a seat at the bar and had sat there watching basketball played on the West Coast while the three glasses of beer he'd ordered sat untouched and eventually went flat. He hadn't come to drink, but for the feverish commotion that helped him forget about Crystal.

Even after some of the college students stumbled out, he continued to sit at the bar staring at the wall-mounted screen. First it was the basketball game, then an encore of a hockey game followed by continuous commentary from sports analysts and former players.

Instead of walking back to the Beaumont House, he'd hailed a taxi for the short trip. Not bothering to shower, he tossed his clothes on the floor in a heap and fell across the bed.

Reaching for his cell phone, he peered at the display. He had two missed calls. Punching in his pass code, he listened to the voice mail. Crystal's voice was flat, a monotone when she announced, "I'm not pregnant." One part of Joseph wanted her to be, because it meant they would have a lifelong connection, but Crystal was adamant about not marrying a man because she was carrying his child. And for Joseph, there was never a question of him taking care of his responsibility. He wouldn't be the first Cole male to get a woman pregnant before exchanging vows, but what he didn't want to be was a baby daddy. Even if he and Crystal didn't marry while she was pregnant, he would be more than willing to give her time to change her mind after she delivered their son or daughter. Knowing he wasn't going to be a father permitted Joseph a second chance—a chance to prove to Crystal he wanted her for herself, to show her—if she gave him a chance—how much he'd come to love her.

He listened to the second voice mail, smiling. Seth Allen had agreed to represent Gillian Stuart. He stated he was currently interviewing other women who'd worked at Bramwell and Duncan Architectural and Design who were also sexually harassed by Hugh Duncan.

Unfortunately for the perverted architect, he didn't know he was about to confront an attorney with the doggedness of a pack of wolves stalking prey.

After he tapped in Seth's number, Joseph's smile grew wider when he heard his friend's unorthodox greeting. "Talk to me."

"I got your voice mail. Thanks for taking on the case."

"What's your stake in this, Wilson?"

Joseph told him about Crystal's experience, without mentioning her name, when she worked at the architectural and design company.

"So this is personal."

"Very personal."

"What is she to you?" Seth questioned.

A beat passed. "The only thing I'm going to say is that she's very special."

Seth's whistle reverberated through the earpiece. "It sounds like you're ready to hand in your playa's card since you broke up with your ex."

Joseph wanted to tell his friend he was wrong. He'd never been a playa—hadn't even come close to ever being one. Not when he'd dated one woman exclusively for four years. "The only thing I'm going to say is I'm seriously thinking about settling down and starting a family in the very near future."

"Good for you, friend. Send me an invitation if you decide not to go the Vegas route."

"She's not the Vegas type, and I'm certain she'll want all of her family in attendance."

Joseph chatted with his friend for a few more minutes, then rang off.

It was after ten and time he got out of bed to start his day. It was Friday and Crystal had promised to return to Charleston before Sunday. Whipping back the sheet and quilt, he swung his legs over the side of the bed and made his way to the bathroom, whistling a nameless tune.

Crystal stopped at the concierge to pick up her mail before going up to the apartment. The young woman handed her a shopping bag with her name attached. Peering into the bag, she saw several magazines and the package containing the gift for Joseph's birthday.

She'd planned to leave High Point Saturday afternoon to return to Charleston, but the vendor with whom she was scheduled to meet the day before had put her in his calendar for Saturday instead of Friday.

Her decision to check out early and be on the road by sunrise on Sunday morning proved beneficial because she was able to avoid the subsequent backup on Route 17 when several vehicles collided, blocking traffic.

Pulling her wheeled suitcase, she walked into the elevator and inserted the key into the slot for the top floor. A feeling of accomplishment swept over her as the car rose quickly and silently. Crystal had managed to purchase everything she needed to complete decorating the interiors. All that remained was the delivery of the furniture and arranging them according to the approved specifications. The commission she'd estimated would take three months would be accomplished in two. Al was excited because he would be able to advertise his grand opening well in advance of the beginning of the tourist season.

The elevator doors opened at the penthouse floor, and when she exited the car Crystal took a quick glance to the right as if she expected to see Joseph. She'd sent him a text Saturday night informing him that she'd been delayed and wouldn't return until late morning.

Although Selena had insisted she not bring anything for the Super Bowl party, Crystal had decided to use some of the ingredients in the refrigerator before she had to discard them.

She planned to make an assortment of wonton dumplings filled with gingered ground pork, chicken and beef and a chili-soy dipping sauce.

Leaving her bags in the entryway, Crystal picked up the receiver to the house phone and dialed Joseph's room. He answered on the first ring, her stomach muscles tightening slightly when she heard his voice. "Honey, I'm home," she said into the mouthpiece.

"Bienvenido a casa, mi amor!"

Crystal understood *bienvenido* because of the signs in the Florida airport welcoming passengers to the various cities. And she needed no translation for *home* and *my love.* "Thank you."

"What are you up to?" he asked her.

"I have to shower before I make some appetizers for the party."

"What are you making?"

"Wonton crescents with gingered meats and a chili-soy dipping sauce."

"That sounds a lot more exciting than what I plan to make."

"What are you making?" she asked.

"Guacamole and salsa."

"I'm completely clueless when it comes to making salsa. Mine always comes out much too watery."

"Do you want me to show you how to make it?" Joseph asked.

"Yes. Why don't you come over and we'll cook together?"

He chuckled. "That sounds like a plan."

"Give me half an hour, and then come on over. I'll leave the door unlocked."

Crystal's head popped up when Joseph walked into the kitchen. He placed a wicker basket on the countertop. Seeing him again made her aware of how much she had missed him. Time away from Joseph had also forced her to acknowledge that she was falling in love with him.

If he'd thought her perfect, then she thought him spectacular—in and out of bed. She'd watched his interaction with his friends and they appeared as fond of him as he was of them. He was three *G*'s: gorgeous, generous and gracious.

Wiping her hands on a terry cloth towel, she picked up the gaily wrapped box from the shelf under the cooking island. Rounding the granite-topped island and going on tiptoe, she pressed her mouth to his ear. "Happy birthday to you," she sang softly.

Smiling, Joseph set the basket on the countertop. "You didn't have to get me anything."

"I know, but I wanted to get you a little something." Crystal held her breath as she watched Joseph unwrap the box. The expression on his face was something she should've captured with her camera phone when he gently removed the engraved monogramed Waterford crystal basketball paperweight from its packaging.

Joseph felt the solid weight of the multifaceted glass on his palm while staring at the block-lettered monogram. His gaze shifted from the paperweight to Crystal's charming expression. "You think you know me that well?" he teased.

Picking up a knife, she chopped scallions, adding them to the crushed garlic, grated ginger, soy sauce and sesame oil in a food processor. "Don't play yourself, Joseph. You know you're a basketball fanatic. I'm willing to bet that the plans for your new house will include a basketball court."

A sheepish expression crossed Joseph's features. "I'm sure it will."

"I could walk around butt-naked while a Heat game is on and you wouldn't even bat an eye."

He returned paperweight to its box, then held out his arms. "Come here, baby."

Crystal walked into his embrace, burying her face against his warm throat. She anchored her arms under his shoulders and closed her eyes. Everything about the man with whom she'd found herself captivated seeped into her. He was so indelibly imprinted on her heart and mind that she would be able to pick him out in a darkened room with hundreds of other men.

Resting his chin on her head, Joseph dropped a kiss on the

short, damp strands clinging to her scalp. His right hand moved up and down her sweatshirt-covered back as if he were comforting her. "Nothing in this world could make me ignore you with or without your clothes." He kissed her hair again. "Thank you so much for the gift. I'll treasure it forever."

Crystal wanted to tell him it wasn't easy buying a gift for a man who had everything and could buy whatever he wanted given his net worth. The wives and girlfriends of his frat brothers were forthcoming when they talked among themselves about Joseph's ex-girlfriend bragging about dating a very wealthy man. Lucretia, the most vocal in the group, admitted she had accused Kiara of being a wannabe gold digger who'd probably end up marrying a freeloader.

"You're very welcome." Crystal delighted in his strong embrace, his familiar scent, the way the contours of his body complemented her curves. She didn't want to think of the time when they would exchange goodbyes.

Pulling back slightly, Joseph angled his head, his nose nuzzling her ear, trailing kisses along her neck. She gasped softly when his teeth closed on the tender flesh as he suckled her. "Did I tell you how much I missed and love you?" he asked between clenched teeth.

Crystal closed her eyes, willing the tears pricking the backs of her lids not to fall. He loved her, while she couldn't tell him how much she'd come to love him. "You don't have to say anything. I don't know how, but there are times when I know what you're thinking."

A chuckle rumbled in Joseph's chest. "What am I thinking now?"

"Something X-rated."

He laughed again. "Wrong, sweetie. It's triple-X-rated."

"Should I be scared?"

"Not today."

Crystal opened her eyes, meeting his. "When?"

"That's up to you. You have to let me know when we can make love again."

She glanced up, mentally counting when she would be finished with her menses. "Wednesday."

Joseph counted on his fingers. "Sunday, Monday, Tuesday. I hope I can hold off—"

"Don't you dare say it," she interrupted, placing her fingers over his mouth. "If you need some release, I believe I can help you out."

"No, no and no!" he protested through her fingertips.

She dropped her arms and pushed out her lips. "Well, I did offer."

"There's no need to pout."

"I'm not pouting!"

"Yes, you are, baby."

Leaning into Joseph, Crystal ran the tip of her tongue over his lower lip, then suckled it. "To be continued."

Joseph released her. "To be continued," he repeated, as he emptied the basket with avocados, tomatoes, red and yellow onions, limes, garlic, jalapeño and cilantro.

They spent the next ninety minutes listening to the radio while preparing a concoction of spicy guacamole and salsa. Joseph assisted Crystal filling, folding and crimping wonton wrappers with pork, beef and chicken. She would wait until they got to her cousins' house to fry them in a wok.

Crystal experienced a comfortable peace while cooking alongside Joseph. Was this, she mused, how it would be if they married? That he would serve her breakfast in bed, then linger long enough to make love before they left for their respective offices?

And would they eventually have a child or maybe children raised by two loving parents? She was certain they would be gracious hosts when opening their home to friends and family.

Crystal beckoned to the man who had stolen her heart. "May I have this dance?"

Joseph took her in his arms, twirling her around and around. "So you like old-school music?"

Tilting her chin, she stared into a pair of eyes the color of rich, dark coffee. "Not really, but I like this song."

He smiled. It was Bobby Caldwell's classic blockbuster hit, "What You Won't Do for Love." Pulling her closer, Joseph pressed a kiss to her forehead.

The song ended but they continued to hold on to each other. "What do you use on your hair that makes it smell so good?" Joseph asked after a comfortable silence.

Crystal smiled against his shoulder. "Argan oil."

"I love the smell and I love you." It was the second time he'd uttered the simple declaration.

And for the second time that morning Crystal felt like crying. Falling in love should've filled her with joy, not regret, and she knew the closer the time came when she would have to leave Charleston, the more difficult it would be to keep her fragile emotions in check.

Joseph maneuvered into the driveway and around the rear to Xavier and Selena's home, parking between a minivan and a late-model SUV. Unbuckling his seat belt, he got and came around to assist Crystal. "Go on in, baby. I'll bring the food."

She grasped the handles of the tote with the ingredients she needed to cook the dumplings. "Are you sure?"

Cradling her face between his hands, he kissed her forehead. "Very sure."

Crystal climbed three steps and opened the door leading into the kitchen. Mouthwatering aromas filled the space as Xavier stood at the stove top grilling baby lamp chops.

"Hey, cuz," she called out.

"Hey, yourself. Where's your boyfriend?"

Her cousin referring to Joseph as her boyfriend didn't bother her as it did the first time they'd come to his home. "He's coming." She glanced around the gourmet kitchen. "Are we late?"

"No. Everyone got here about ten minutes ago."

"Where's Selena?"

"She's upstairs putting Lily to bed. It's a little early, but baby girl didn't take a nap this afternoon because the doorbell was constantly ringing. This year we decided to cater most of the meat dishes."

"What did you…" Her words trailed off when Joseph entered the kitchen carrying two oversize shopping bags. Moving quickly, she approached him, taking the bag with the pan of wontons. She took them out of the bag, setting them on the countertop.

Xavier lowered the flame on the grill. "Let me take that," he said to Joseph. Reaching into the bag, he removed two large glass bowls filled with guacamole and salsa. Lifting the top on the bowl with the salsa, he blew out an audible breath. "Damn! This stuff is guaranteed to singe a few eyebrows."

Joseph laughed. "Nothing a few ice-cold beers can't cure."

"No lie," Xavier drawled, grinning.

"He shouldn't have brought anything." Everyone turned to find Selena standing at the entrance to the kitchen, hands folded at her waist. She walked in and hugged and kissed Crystal. "I specifically told you not to bring anything," she said. She turned and hugged Joseph. "Thank you for coming, partner."

Joseph gave her a warm smile. "Back at you, partner."

Waving her hand at Xavier in a gesture of dismissal, Selena picked up a pair of tongs, testing the lamp chops for doneness. "Darling, I'll take over here. Why don't you and Joseph take the salsa and guacamole upstairs? Criss and I will finish up, and then we'll join you."

"Are you certain you don't need us?" Xavier asked.

Selena nodded. "*We're* very certain." Waiting until the two men were out of earshot, she turned to Crystal. "You're sleeping with him, aren't you?"

Crystal recoiled as if she'd taken a punch in the nose. However, she recovered quickly. "Why would you ask me that?"

Pulling out the collar on the man-tailored shirt, Selena traced the slight bruise on the area above Crystal's collarbone. "You have a love bite right here."

Crystal's blood warmed, her cheeks burning as she recalled Joseph biting her neck. However, she hadn't noticed the mark when getting dressed. Her hands were shaking noticeably when she fastened a button. "I guess he got a little carried away," she mumbled. Walking out of the kitchen, she washed her hands in the sink in the half bath.

"Please don't tell me you're embarrassed," Selena said when she returned.

"I'm not embarrassed that we slept together. What I don't want to do is to advertise it. Why are you looking at me like that?" she asked when the other woman shot her an incredulous look.

"What's the big secret? It's only a matter of time before your families find out you're involved with each other."

Crystal shook her head. "That's not going to happen. Whatever we have now will end once I leave Charleston." She told Selena about returning to Florida for a brief stay before traveling on to New York City and another commission. "Joseph will be here at least until late April or early May."

Selena removed the meat from the grill, placing it in a warming drawer. "So, you won't see him for a while. What's wrong with that?"

"I'm just beginning to grow my business and I can't commit to an ongoing relationship at this time."

"Is Joseph asking for a commitment?"'

"No." Crystal told Selena about the terms she and Joseph agreed to with regard to their temporary liaison. "Joseph isn't ready for marriage and neither am I. We enjoy each other's company, so what happens in Charleston stays in Charleston."

"So." Selena snapped her fingers. "You're going to walk away from someone who appears so suited to you."

Opening a drawer under the countertop, Crystal took out an apron, slipping it on over her blouse and jeans. "I'm not walking away, Selena. I just can't afford to get sidetracked when it comes to my career."

"Look at me, Criss. I'm married and a mother, yet I still have a successful career."

Reaching up, Crystal took down a wok and its cover from an overhead rack. "How much do you know about my parents?"

Selena lowered her eyes. "I know your father has been married four times."

"And he's about to embark on a fifth."

"No!"

Crystal couldn't help laughing at Selena's shocked expression. "My mother and father met in college. They dated, broke up and reconciled so many times they had to have lost count. During their last separation, Daddy heard she was seeing someone in New York and he managed to woo her back. She'd stopped taking the pill, so she relied on him to protect her from an unplanned pregnancy. Within a month of earning her MFA she was scheduled to move to New York to work as an appraiser with a Manhattan auction house, but she had to decline the position once she discovered she was pregnant. She blamed Daddy for deliberately getting her pregnant to keep her from moving to New York to advance her career, while Daddy blamed her for tricking him into marriage, because he'd always said he didn't want to father a child out of wedlock."

Selena watched as Crystal poured a small amount of sunflower oil into the wok, waiting for it to heat before she placed the crescents in the hot oil. "If your father was so against marriage, then why has he married so many times?"

"I don't know. The only thing I can figure is that my father is a control freak. In other words, he wants everything to be his decision, and he believes to this day that my mother forced him into marriage. I grew up with them constantly trading insults and blame, and that's something I never want my children to experience."

Selena gave Crystal a sidelong glance. "Do you think you'll ever marry?"

"I don't know." Crystal lifted a crescent to see if the underside was crispy; she added enough water to come about halfway up the sides of each wonton and then covered the wok and waited for the water to evaporate. "Do you have a chip- and dip bowl?"

"Yes." Selena retreated to the pantry, where she stored dishes she used for entertaining. She returned to the kitchen with the large bowl. "Are you marriage-phobic?"

Selena was asking questions Crystal wasn't ready to answer, or to which she didn't have an answer. Not at that moment. She'd always believed she would eventually marry. But it wasn't something that topped her wish list. Her career had become her priority.

When she actually thought about it, Crystal realized she was more like her parents than she would openly admit. She had become a control freak like Raleigh with regard to marriage, and as fixated on interior decorating as Jasmine was with appraising, buying and selling pieces of art.

"I don't believe I am. Right now I don't feel any pressure to marry, because I'm only thirty. I know I'll probably think differently four or five years from now if I want to start a family."

Crystal raised the lid on the wok, smiling. All of the water had evaporated. Pouring the chili-soy dipping sauce into a microwave-safe bowl, she heated it. She plated the warm wontons, arranging them neatly. "I'm not going to fill the dip cup until we're upstairs."

The two women carried platters of herb-infused lamp chops and meat-infused gingered wontons with a chili-soy sauce up the staircase to the expansive theater room. Many of the invited guests had claimed leather reclining seats with cup holders, eating and drinking while watching pregame programming, while the others were serving themselves from the buffet with hot and cold dishes.

Her cousins had spared no expense when it came to renovating the space for entertaining. The contractor had installed a built-in bar with high stools, an efficiency kitchen, a bathroom, four rows of seats, with six in each row, set up theater-style, a crystal-clear mounted flat-screen taking up almost an entire wall. The opposite end of the space contained a game room with skee ball, pool and Ping-Pong tables and several vintage pinball machines. The crisp sound coming from the audio components made Crystal feel as if she were in a modern movie theater.

Crystal reacquainted herself to the guests she'd met when they attended Selena and Xavier's wedding in West Virginia. Most of the men were ex-military, some who'd attended the

Citadel with Xavier and a few who taught at the same military school where her cousin now taught military history.

Within the span of a week she'd interacted with Joseph and Xavier's friends. It was a blatant reminder of how sterile her social life had become. She still kept in touch with some of her friends in New York and the sorority sisters with whom she shared a closer bond, but it had been a while since she saw them in person. Crystal made a mental note to call her former grad school classmates to let them know she planned to spend several months in the Big Apple and looked forward to reconnecting with them.

Crystal smiled as Joseph, carrying a plate, closed the distance between them, her gaze softening when their eyes met. "I thought you could use something to eat before the game began," he said in a quiet voice.

Curbing the urge to kiss him, she lowered her eyes to the plate. "Thank you." However, she was surprised when he dipped his head and kissed her forehead.

"What do you want to drink?"

Crystal glanced up, her eyes making love to his face. "Since it's Super Sunday I'll have a beer."

Joseph lifted his eyebrows a fraction. "There're pitchers of margaritas to go along with the guacamole and salsa."

She scrunched up her nose. "I'll hit them up on my second helping."

He gave her a skeptical look. "Are you certain you're going to have room?"

Staring at her plate, Crystal measured the amount of food on her plate. "It's not that much." He'd served what she would normally eat during a cocktail hour at a wedding. It was enough to stave off hunger until the main meal.

Joseph's expression indicated doubt as he returned to the bar to get a beer for Crystal.

He asked Xavier for a beer on tap as he fixed a plate for himself. Everyone rushed to claim a seat for the coin toss, Joseph handing Crystal her glass of beer and then folding his body down next to hers. Crystal hadn't declared a favorite team be-

cause neither a Florida nor a New York team had made it to the
Super Bowl, while he secretly rooted for the Atlanta Falcons.

Those having to go to work early Monday morning left after
the halftime entertainment because of the three-hour time difference between the East and West Coast. Selena had filled
containers with leftovers and gave each invitee a takeaway bag
filled with samples of the delicious dishes.

The game resumed, going into overtime with the Falcons as
Super Bowl champions, and Crystal and Joseph lingered behind to help clean up, overriding Selena's protests when they
said they didn't have to get up early to go to traditional jobs.

Crystal drove Joseph's Range Rover back to the Beaumont
House, parking it in his assigned space. Resting her arm over
the back of his seat, she angled her head. "Your bed or mine?"

Joseph's teeth shone whitely in the diffused light coming
through the windshield. "Mine."

Leaning closer, she touched her mouth to his. "Yours it is."

Chapter 13

Crystal wished she had the power to hold back time. Her heart felt like a stone in her chest when she closed her luggage. She was leaving Charleston and Joseph. Everything they shared since Super Bowl Sunday had become a permanent tattoo, imprinted in her memory for all time.

She had accompanied Joseph to Eagle Island to see the tea garden, totally awed by the ancient trees draped with Spanish moss. The earth over centuries was worn away under the hooves of horses, bare and booted feet, wagon wheels and automobile tires. Some of the houses appeared to be little more than shanties, lacking indoor plumbing, while others had been updated with a fresh coat of paint, new shutters and paved driveways.

Joseph had maneuvered slowly along the main road, waving out the driver's-side window to elderly residents sitting out on their porches.

Crystal convinced him to stop when she spied an elderly woman weaving a sweetgrass basket as her Lowcountry ancestors had done for centuries. Crystal bought a picnic basket with a cross handle, a sewing basket and an exquisite cobra basket she planned to give to her mother from the weaver's modest inventory. She knew Jasmine would exhibit the African-inspired handicrafts in the section of the gallery dedicated to African and Asian art.

If Crystal found herself awed by the untouched, primeval beauty of an island that had mostly been left to grow in wild abandonment, she experienced shock when seeing the carpet of green leaves stretching for as far as her eye could see that would eventually become a much sought after beverage drunk throughout the world.

Crystal was equally proud to give Joseph an up-close and personal view of her decorating talent when she gave him a tour of one of the completed bedrooms in the B and B. An antique reproduction of a four-poster bed with a crocheted canopy, oriental rugs, heirloom-inspired bedding, Queen Anne chairs and an ornately carved armoire with doors matching the designs on the bed's posts beckoned you to come in and stay awhile.

He'd kept his promise to take her to the Ordinary, the popular seafood hall and oyster bar located in an old Charleston bank. She'd just swallowed an oyster when she felt suddenly ill and retreated to the ladies' room. Crystal hadn't wanted to believe the oyster wasn't fresh, because she'd eaten raw oysters and clams without experiencing a reaction. She returned to their table, apologizing to Joseph, who'd ordered an assortment of cooked fish for her.

A feeling of sadness swept over her when she realized her time in Charleston was coming to an end. She'd met with Al earlier that morning for a final walk-through of what would become the Holy City's latest luxury boutique hotels. She would miss going to the hotels whenever a furniture shipment arrived and directing the deliverymen where to position each piece.

She would also miss dropping in on Selena to watch her create beautiful edible works of art and getting down on the floor to have a tea party with Lily and her dolls. Selena had kept her updated with her collaborative enterprise unwritten by ColeDiz International Ltd., which she and Joseph projected would be fully operational in another eighteen months.

Crystal refused to dwell on missing Joseph. They'd alternated sleeping in each other's apartments, making love with each other as if their very existence depended on it. Joseph hadn't mentioned he loved her again since that momentous Sunday, and for that Crystal was more than grateful. Her body spoke for her whenever she experienced unbridled ecstasy in his passionate embrace.

Three days ago when she'd mentioned her departure, she felt his immediate withdrawal. They'd continued to share a bed but did not make love. Crystal knew if they continued to have sex it would make their separating more difficult and, on her part, very emotionally tolling.

The doorbell echoed throughout the apartment, startling Crystal and shattering her musings. Leaving the bedroom, she went downstairs to answer the door. Peering through the security eye, she saw the face that would haunt her dreams for a long time.

Forcing a smile, she opened the door. "Hey," she said cheerfully. She dropped her gaze to the small shopping bag in his left hand, knowing he'd bought her a gift. They'd celebrated Valentine's Day with a promise not to exchange gifts.

Joseph stared into the face of the woman whose very presence took him to highs and, with her imminent departure, to a low he never could've imagined. His impassive expression did not change or reveal what he was feeling at that moment. "May I come in?"

Crystal opened the door wider. "Of course. Please."

He walked in, waited for Crystal to close the door and then followed her into the living room. She sat on the edge of the cushion on the love seat, while he sat inches away.

Joseph felt her tension as surely as if it were his own. He knew saying goodbye wasn't going to be easy, but he'd given himself a pep talk before coming to her apartment. Crystal had been more than forthcoming with the terms of their short-lived liaison, so he knew he should've been prepared for this day. He'd told her indirectly that he loved her, and then waited for her to acknowledge what were the three most difficult words for him to say to a woman.

He handed Crystal the bag. "I got you a little something to remember your time in the Lowcountry."

Crystal hands were trembling slightly when she reached into the bag and took out a gaily wrapped square box. Carefully she removed the shiny black-and-white-embossed paper. Biting down on her lip, she opened a black velvet box and gasped.

Joseph had given her a Cartier bracelet. The elegant eighteen-karat, oval-shaped bracelet was studded with ten round

brilliant-cut diamonds. She barely reacted to the iconic bracelet when he picked it up and snapped it around her left wrist.
Her body's heat had barely warmed the precious metal when he
picked up an ergonomic screwdriver and tightened the catch.
She looked at him as if he'd taken leave of his senses when he
put the screwdriver in the back pocket of his jeans.

Cupping the back of her head with one hand, he kissed
her hair. "I wanted to give you this for Valentine's Day, but
I changed my mind when you reminded me you didn't want
to exchange gifts. Call me whenever you want to take it off."

"I…" The protest died on Crystal's tongue as she watched
Joseph stand up and walk out of the living door, through the
door and out of her life.

She lost track of time as she stared at the love bracelet on
her wrist; the light coming in through the window shimmered
off the blue-white diamonds. Reaching into the gift bag, she
removed a small dust bag with which to store the bracelet and
an authenticity card for appraisal. What good was the dust bag
when she couldn't remove the bracelet without the screwdriver?

"Call me whenever you want to take it off." His parting
words assaulted her like invisible missiles, eliciting a foreign
emotion Crystal recognized as resentment. The arrogance Joseph had managed to repress had surfaced when he used the
little screwdriver to link them together without a promise of a
commitment, which he claimed he didn't want.

She walked into the office, picked up her cell phone and
tapped Joseph's programmed number. It rang four times before going straight to voice mail. It was obvious he'd turned off
his phone. She repeated the action, dialing his room number,
and again she heard the automated voice asking her to leave
a message.

Replacing the receiver in its cradle, she clamped her jaw
tightly. If he thought her wearing his bracelet signified they
were somehow connected, then he was wrong. The only connection was that as consenting adults, they'd had a brief sexual
encounter. Crystal knew one day if their paths were to cross

again she would not be the same person who'd come to Charleston to decorate two boutique hotels.

She picked up the phone again, asking for a bellhop to come to PH2. A quarter of an hour later, Crystal slipped behind the wheel of her SUV, turned on the engine and maneuvered out of the parking lot. The warm air coming in through the passenger-side window signaled an early spring. Tapping a button on the steering wheel, she searched the satellite radio until she found a station featuring smooth jazz.

Crystal stopped in Savannah to refuel and eat lunch and then drove nonstop to Fort Lauderdale. A smile parted her lips as she drove past the gatehouse and maneuvered down the tree-lined street leading to her town house. It felt good to be home.

A buildup of heat assailed Crystal when she walked inside. Moving quickly, she turned on the central air-conditioning to dispel the stagnant air.

Crystal mentally went through what she had to do: take a bath, check her voice mail and call and check on her mother. Hopefully Jasmine wouldn't be in drama-queen mode. Unpacking her luggage would wait for another day. She was exhausted—physically and mentally, needing at least ten hours of uninterrupted sleep.

Crystal sat in bed, her back supported by a mound of pillows. She checked her messages on her landline phone. There was a call from her father, who'd forgotten she would be in Charleston. There were a few other messages from telemarketers, and one from a sorority sister wishing her a happy New Year. She erased the messages, then dialed her mother's number.

"Hi, darling," sighed Jasmine. "I know you're back because your house number came up on the caller ID."

Crystal smiled. "I got in less than an hour ago."

"When am I going to see you?"

"It'll be either Sunday or Monday." The gallery rarely opened on those days. And besides, Crystal needed a few days to herself to adjust to being at home before taking off again. She needed time to unpack, air out the house and dust. But most of all, she wanted to spend time alone to try and sort out how she'd fallen in love with a man who made her crave him—in and out of bed.

"Please come Sunday. I have a private showing with a client on Monday."

"What time Sunday, Mother?"

"Meet me at Reynaldo's at eleven-thirty. Their brunch is exceptional."

"Don't you want me to pick you up?" Crystal asked Jasmine.

"You know I don't like riding in your car."

"Okay, Mother. I'll meet you at the restaurant."

"I have some good news to tell you."

Crystal shook her head. "You're getting married?"

"Oh, heavens no! There's no way I'm going to give up your father's alimony payments. I'll tell you about it when I see you."

She knew Jasmine wouldn't tell her no matter how much she pleaded. "Okay, Mother. I'll see you Sunday."

Adjusting the pillows under her head, Crystal reached over and turned off the lamp on the bedside table. Her mother always talked about not wanting to cut off her ex-husband's alimony payments when Crystal suspected it was the intangible connection to Raleigh that Jasmine didn't want to give up. And whenever she saw her father he would invariably ask how her mother was doing. He had to know Jasmine was doing quite well because they both lived in Miami and had on more than one occasion run into each other at social events. But because they'd come with dates they refused to acknowledge each other, and no one could be more supercilious than Jasmine Eaton.

Crystal followed the hostess to Jasmine's table, and her mother rose to greet her. She'd always thought her mother beautiful, but as Jasmine aged she'd become even more stunning. Tall and slender with stylishly coiffed prematurely gray hair, a flawless nut-brown complexion and delicate, even features caused heads to turn whenever she walked into a room. For men it was her face and body, and for women it was to see what the art dealer was wearing.

This morning Jasmine had selected a lime-green silk blouse she'd paired with a linen gabardine suit in a becoming aubergine.

"You look beautiful, Mother," Crystal admitted truthfully, pressing her cheek to Jasmine's. And she did. Her mother eschewed fillers and plastic surgery, unlike many of her fifty-something contemporaries, feared needles and going under the knife.

"So do you, darling. Please sit down."

Jasmine stared intently at Crystal. "You've put on weight. Your face is fuller."

"I got used to eating three meals a day." She loved cooking with Joseph.

Leaning back in her chair, the older woman nodded. "You look better carrying a little more weight."

Crystal stared at the uncut emerald studs in Jasmine's ears. "Not too much, otherwise we'll have to go shopping."

Jasmine raised her water goblet in a toast. "It's been a while since we've embarked on a mother–daughter shopping spree."

"It will have to wait until I get back from New York."

"When are you leaving?"

"Next week," Crystal confirmed.

A slight frown appeared between Jasmine's eyes as she sat straight. "Didn't you tell me you weren't—"

"I thought so, too," Crystal interrupted, her voice lowering and softening. "I got a call last night from my client that he'd gotten verbal approval for his liquor license, and that means the project is a definite go."

Crystal had believed she would have at least three weeks to a month before beginning her next project. She'd planned to spend a couple of weeks in Florida and another in New York reconnecting with friends before transforming the town house basement into an updated speakeasy.

"Now tell me your good news," she said, shifting the conversation away from her.

A mysterious smile played at the corners of Jasmine's mouth. "I've stopped smoking."

The three words rendered Crystal temporarily mute. "Why?"

She silently prayed her mother's decision to give up smoking wasn't health-related.

"Between smelling bad and having to bleach my teeth every six months, I decided enough is enough. But what I think really made me stop is the letter from you that was stuck under a drawer in my desk for almost twenty years. You wrote that I would never get to hold my grandbaby because I smoked."

Crystal lowered her eyes. She remembered writing the letter when she was angry with her mother for smoking in her bedroom. The stench of tobacco had lingered for days. "You're not sick, are you?"

Jasmine rested a manicured hand over her throat. "Thankfully no."

"How did you do it?"

"Hypnosis, and I'm now wearing a patch."

Crystal hated seeing her mother chain-smoking and even more inhaling the stale odor of tobacco whenever she hugged her. "Good for you." She paused. "Somehow I can't see you as a grandmother."

"Why not?" Several diners at a nearby table turned to look at Jasmine when she raised her voice. She gave them what Crystal deemed the death stare and they quickly averted their eyes. "Why wouldn't I want to become a grandmother?"

Crystal lifted her shoulders under the navy blue blazer she'd pulled on over an ice-blue silk blouse and gray slacks. When she'd selected her clothes earlier that morning, she'd made certain to wear long sleeves to conceal the bracelet circling her left wrist. The last thing she wanted was for her mother to interrogate her about it.

"It's just that I never heard you speak about wanting grandchildren."

Jasmine smiled and tiny lines fanned out around her large dark eyes. "I'm going to be fifty-four this year, and I think it's time I acknowledge that I'm not too young to be called Grandma."

"I can't imagine you allowing an infant, even if it is your grandbaby, to spit up on your clothes."

The older woman sobered. "You really don't know me, do you, Crystal? I may not have been the mother you needed when you were younger, and I'll carry that guilt to my grave. But I will never pressure you into getting married and having children just to give me a second chance to make it right with my grandbabies."

Reaching over, Crystal covered her mother's hand with her own. "None of us are born knowing how to parent, but thankfully we're given a second chance when it comes to grandbabies." She sighed. "The only thing I'm going to say is *if* or when I do make you a grandmother, you're not allowed to spoil them rotten, or they're going to have to live with you full-time."

Jasmine grinned like the Cheshire cat. "Now I know why I haven't sold the house—because there's plenty of room for them to run amok." Her four-thousand-square-foot home, set on an acre of manicured land overlooking a man-made lake, had four bedrooms and five bathrooms—more than enough room for several grandchildren to frolic in wild abandon.

"And what if they break one of your priceless artifacts?"

"It won't matter, because everything's insured."

This Jasmine Cornelia Eaton was someone Crystal truly did not know. She'd lost track of the number of times she'd begged her to stop smoking, but to no avail. And in the past she had always professed she didn't want to become a grandmother until she was at least sixty-five. What or who, Crystal mused, had been instrumental in changing her mother into someone who'd become a stranger?

"I wonder how Daddy would react to becoming a grandfather."

Jasmine rolled her eyes upward. "Maybe he'd realize he's getting much too old to continue marrying women young enough to be his daughters."

"He doesn't seem to be in a hurry to marry his latest girlfriend. Maybe he'll come to the realization that he can wine, dine and take them away on vacation without being obligated to marry them. I did call him, hoping to see him before I leave, but his assistant told me a group of homeowners and farmers in North Dakota asked to meet with him before they lease their land to oil companies for fracking and drilling."

"And knowing Raleigh, he'll look out for their interests as if they were his own."

Crystal had to agree with her mother. Raleigh Eaton had acquired a sixth sense when it came to investing and financial planning, and those who relied on his business acumen were never disappointed.

She picked up the menu, studying the selections. "What do you recommend?"

Reaching into her handbag, Jasmine took out a pair of reading glasses, perching them on the end of her nose. "The cherry-cheese blintzes are wonderful if you like something sweet, but right now I'm sort of partial to focaccia with smoked salmon and crème fraîche."

Crystal continued to scan the menu. "I think I'll start with a melon salad with a yogurt-honey dressing and a slice of mushroom quiche."

"After we order I want you to tell me about Charleston."

May first—May Day. It was a day Crystal would never forget, nor the doctor's diagnosis: *Miss Eaton, you don't have a stomach virus. We ran a few tests and you're pregnant.*

She remembered screaming without making a sound, and when she did recover her voice she couldn't stop crying. The doctor waited for her to settle down, then called in the ob-gyn to examine her.

When she revealed she hadn't missed a period, the doctor quietly explained there were women who had their period throughout their entire pregnancy, and it was only when they went into labor that it became apparent they'd been carrying a child.

A sonogram revealed she was in her second trimester and she was having a girl. How could she call Joseph and tell him she now was pregnant when they'd been apart for three months? He'd think her either crazy or a fraud—someone who wanted to trick him into marrying her. There was no way she would relive the insanity of her parents.

She instructed her father to sell her Fort Lauderdale property, then called Levi in Kentucky and asked whether she could live in his Mamaroneck, New York, condo until his return.

Initially she refused to tell her parents why she'd decided to relocate to New York, but as her condition became more apparent she set up a videoconference, informing them they were to become grandparents. What she refused to reveal was the name of her baby's father. The exception was Selena and Xavier, whom she swore to secrecy. Xavier protested, saying Joseph had a right to know he'd fathered a child until Crystal reminded him of her parents' volatile marriage.

Everything for Crystal changed when Levi fell in love with Angela Chase and accepted a position as head of pediatrics at a small hospital ten miles from Louisville. And for the second time within a decade, she would claim New York as her permanent home state.

Her pregnancy was uneventful. She delivered a healthy six-pound, two-ounce baby girl on a rainy October night. Jasmine had flown up a week before she was to give birth.

Jasmine and Raleigh alternated coming to New York to visit their granddaughter, while Crystal put her career on hold until Meredith was old enough to attend school.

She'd become her mother, but without the bitterness that had plagued Jasmine for years.

She enjoyed running while pushing her daughter along a jogging path, befriended other young mothers she met in a local park and was only reminded of the man with whom she'd fallen in love whenever someone mentioned the bracelet.

Being a new mother had its drawbacks. She'd become sleep-deprived when she had to get up every four hours to breast-feed, or when she would sleep on the floor next to the crib to feel the tiny hands or feet to check to see if Meredith's fever had spiked.

Being a new mother also had its rewards when Meredith learned to sit up, roll over, learned to say Dada, Mama, bottle, and demand more to eat when it was something she liked. The first time she stood up and took three steps before landing on her bottom Crystal cried happy tears. Her baby was now a toddler.

Crystal had just finished taking a load of wash from the dryer when her phone rang. Anchoring the wicker basket on her hip, she raced into the kitchen to answer it before it woke Meredith. "Hello."

"Is this Ms. Crystal Eaton?"

She went still. "Who's asking?"

"Are you Ms. Eaton?"

Setting down the basket, Crystal flopped down on the chair in the breakfast nook. "Yes."

"Raleigh Eaton has listed you as his emergency contact." She listened, chills washing over her body when the woman informed her that her father had come to the E.R. complaining of chest pain. An EKG indicated several blocked arteries and the attending cardiologist recommended surgery.

"Is he…?" She couldn't complete the question.

"He's stabilized, but the doctor wants to wait until you get here to explain the procedure."

"When's the surgery?"

"Tomorrow morning."

Her fear and anxiety vanished, replaced by a surge of determination. Crystal knew she had to be strong, not for herself but for her father.

Chapter 14

Sweet Silver Bells

Joseph stopped for a red light at a four-way intersection. He'd almost forgotten how heavy Miami rush-hour traffic could be. He stared into the rearview mirror unable to believe the woman who'd haunted his dreams sat a few feet behind him.

When he'd walked into the terminal and had seen Crystal, Joseph believed he'd conjured her up.

He'd been in an emotional tailspin, placing his social life on hold, while waiting for her to call him, not for him to remove the bracelet but to tell her how much he loved her and wanted to share his life with her. And Joseph had been willing to wait, wait another eighteen months or eighteen years.

If he'd changed inwardly, it had been the reverse with Crystal. Her face was fuller, her body lush, and a chin-length, layered haircut had replaced the short coif.

He had given her time, and after ColeDiz Tea's first successful harvest, Joseph checked out of the Beaumont House and found himself constantly checking his phone for her call. He'd scroll through his telephone contacts for her name, but a sense of pride—stubborn pride—wouldn't let him tap her number.

A smile tilted the corners of his mouth upward, the gesture reaching his eyes when they lingered on the angelic face of the child he and Crystal had created. Joseph quickly did the math in his head. If Merry was born in October, then he'd probably gotten Crystal pregnant the first and only time they'd had unprotected sex. His smile vanished.

Why, he thought, had she told him she wasn't pregnant when she had been?

He wanted and needed answers, answers that could wait until after her family crisis.

Crystal quickened her pace when her mother rose slowly from where she'd sat in the lobby of the small private hospital specializing in the heart. "Mama," she whispered, choking back a sob. "How is he?"

Pulling back, Jasmine cradled her face and kissed her cheek. "He's resting." She glanced over Crystal's shoulder at the tall man holding her granddaughter. "He found you."

Turning around, Crystal stared at a babbling Merry, who was pointing to the button on the collar of Joseph's shirt. "I'll explain everything to you later," she said through clenched teeth. She beckoned him closer. "Joseph, I'd like you to meet my mother."

Merry, recognizing her grandmother's familiar face, leaned over for Jasmine to take her.

"Mum, Mum," she repeated over and over. She hadn't learned to say Grandma.

Jasmine took the child from Joseph's arms. "Come here, baby girl." She gave her granddaughter a noisy kiss on the cheek. "Grandma loves you."

Joseph extended his hand to Jasmine. Now he knew where Crystal had gotten her beauty. Her mother was stunning. "I'm sorry we have to meet under these circumstances, Mrs. Eaton." He inclined his head. "I'm Joseph Cole-Wilson. Meredith's father."

Jasmine gave him a long stare. "Only someone with impaired vision would miss the resemblance, Mr. Cole-Wilson."

His mouth tightened in frustration. "Please call me Joseph, Mrs. Eaton."

There was a barely perceptible lifting of an eyebrow. It was apparent her mother wasn't going to make it easy for her granddaughter's father. When she'd finally revealed the identity of her baby's father, Jasmine feared Joseph would sue Crystal for full custody, charging her with deception.

"I haven't decided yet whether I'll allow you to call me Jasmine."

"Mother!" Crystal chastised. Her mother might have been called a lot of things, but never rude. In fact, Jasmine prided herself on having impeccable manners.

Joseph held up a hand. "It's okay, sweetie." He could've bitten off his tongue when Crystal glared at him. The endearment had slipped out unconsciously. He'd found himself in the presence of three generations of beautiful Eaton women, and two of them were giving him the stink-eye. He took a step backward. "I'll wait here, Crystal, while you go and check on your father."

Jasmine handed Crystal her visitor's badge. "He's in room 218." She held Merry at arm's length. "You need changing. And she also needs to change out of these heavy clothes." She rubbed noses with Merry. "Grandma will take you shopping and buy some pretty dresses for you."

Crystal attached the badge to the collar of her jacket. "Her diaper bag is in Joseph's car."

"I'll go and get it," he volunteered.

Waiting until Joseph walked out, Crystal shifted her attention to Jasmine. "Mama, please don't make this more complicated than it is."

"What do you intend to do, Crystal? Roll over and let him take your child?"

She shook her head. "It's not going to be like that."

"Are you sure?"

Crystal nodded. "Very sure. Joseph knows Merry and I are a package deal. He can't have one without the other."

"Have you talked about it?" Jasmine questioned.

"We don't have to talk about it," Crystal countered. *Don't you believe a child needs both parents?* She recalled Joseph's query as if he'd just spoken it. He'd grown up with both of his parents, and he wanted the same for his child or children.

The seconds ticked as Jasmine met her eyes. "Do you love him?"

She paused, wondering why her mother was bringing up something to which she knew the answer. Crystal had admitted to Jasmine that she'd fallen in love with Joseph. "Yes, Mother. I love him." She ruffled Merry's mussed curls, knowing she had to shampoo her hair, which always resulted in a test of wills. Merry didn't like water on her face. Turning on the heels of her running shoes, she headed for the elevator.

Crystal stopped in the doorway to Raleigh's private room. The handsome, elegant man who had women from eighteen to eighty flirting shamelessly to catch his attention appeared to be a shadow of his former self. The rich color in his khaki-brown complexion was missing and his wavy gray hair appeared lifeless, brittle. How, she wondered, had he aged that much since she last saw him at the Eaton family reunion the last weekend in May?

He hadn't brought his fiancée, and Crystal wondered if he'd come to his senses and decided he didn't have to have a woman in his life in order to feel complete.

She walked in, smiling when he turned to stare at her. He was hooked up to a machine monitoring his vitals. "Hi, Daddy."

Raleigh waved her closer. "Hi, baby. How did you get here so fast?"

Crystal pulled up chair next to the bed and took his hand, examining the large, slender, professionally groomed fingers. Her parents were two of a kind. Both had standing appointments for hair and nails. "I flew down, Daddy."

He smiled. "I just had the attack this morning. You managed to get a flight that fast?"

"I paid for a first-class seat."

Raleigh's smile vanished. "I'll reimburse you."

"Don't you dare talk about money when you should be thinking about getting better so you can leave this place."

"But you're not working, baby."

"Have you forgotten I have money from when you bought my condo?" Her father had purchased the condo from her, claiming he wanted to hold on to it for investment purposes.

Raleigh's eyelids fluttered. "Yeah. I forgot about that."

Crystal wondered if her father had been given something to

make him sleep. "What were you doing before you had chest pains?"

"Golfing."

She closed her eyes while shaking her head. "Daddy, you can't golf in ninety-degree weather even if it is October."

"I found that out the hard way. You know that they call a heart attack the widow maker." His eyes opened, meeting his daughter's tender gaze. "If I wasn't golfing, then I never would've known I had a couple of blocked arteries."

"That may be true," Crystal retorted, "but you're going to have to modify your diet." Even though Raleigh didn't have a problem with his weight, she knew he occasionally ate the wrong foods for a middle-aged man.

"I know. No fried, fat, or fast foods." He exhaled an audible sigh. "After surgery I'll be in ICU for a couple of days."

"You know you can't go home once you're discharged."

"Why not?"

"You need around-the-clock monitoring, Daddy. I'll have Mother set up a room for you."

"No, no and no. I'm not going to put your mother out. Besides, Tonya can take care of me."

"Who's Tonya?"

"She's my fiancée."

"The one you didn't bring to the family reunion?"

"We had words, so she decided not to come."

Crystal released his hand. "You had words? What if you have words and she walks out and you end up on the floor? You appointed me to be your medical proxy, and that means I have the final say where it concerns your health, not some stranger who'll bail on you if things aren't going her way."

"What about your mother?" Raleigh asked. "Won't she have the final say when it comes to me staying in her house?"

"I'll talk to her, Daddy." Crystal wanted to remind Raleigh that Jasmine had come to see him round the clock, and that should've been proof enough of her concern for his physical well-being.

"If she says it's okay, then I'll stay."

She noticed he was slurring his words. Rising, Crystal leaned over and kissed Raleigh's forehead. "Get some rest, Daddy. I'll come back tomorrow to see you once you're out of recovery."

Raleigh smiled. "How's my grandbaby girl?"

"All sugar and a little spice." Merry was all sweetness until it came time to wash her hair.

"That's my baby."

She kissed him again. "I love you, Daddy."

"Love you back," he slurred, his chest rising and falling in a slow, even rhythm.

She took the elevator down to the lobby, handing in the visitor's pass. Joseph sat next to Jasmine, who'd removed Merry's outer clothing, leaving her in an undershirt and a disposable diaper.

It appeared as if her mother and Joseph were engaged in a serious conversation. Crystal froze when Jasmine leaned over and pressed her mouth to Joseph's cheek at the same time his arm went around the shoulders of his daughter's grandmother. It was apparent they'd reached a compromise. Now all Crystal had to do was convince her mother to let her ex-husband recuperate under her roof.

Joseph noticed her first, coming to his feet and closing the distance between them. "How's your dad?"

Tilting her head, Crystal studied Joseph's face, trying to catch a glimpse of the man with whom she'd spent the most marvelous two months of her life. She'd gone to bed and woken up in his strong embrace. She enjoyed cooking with him, occasionally teasing him as to who could concoct the best dessert. With Joseph there were few surprises. He was even-tempered, quick to smile—attributes he'd unknowingly passed on to his daughter.

Once it was confirmed that she was carrying a girl, Crystal had come up with a number of names before settling on three. It would be Merry, Hope or Joy. But when she saw her daughter for the first time, she knew which name to choose.

Upon closer inspection, Crystal noticed the hot Florida sun had darkened Joseph's face to a deep mahogany. "He's resting.

He's scheduled for surgery tomorrow, and once he's out of recovery he'll be in ICU for a few days."

"I told your mother that I'm going to take a couple of weeks off and hang out down here. I'll help look after Merry while you visit your father. A hospital is no place for a baby."

"Thanks for the offer, but my mother and I will take turns visiting Daddy."

"Jasmine and I have already talked about it."

Crystal's eyebrows shot up. "So now it's Jasmine instead of Mrs. Eaton?"

He smiled. "You betcha. We're now Jasmine and Joseph."

She tried not to smile but failed. "Thank you for driving us down."

Without warning, Joseph's face suddenly went grim. "I don't need your thanks, Crystal. If I'd known you had my baby, you and Merry would've come down on the company jet, because there's a Cole family mandate that has been in effect for almost fifty years that anyone with Cole blood is forbidden to fly on a commercial carrier."

Crystal suddenly felt as if she'd been threatened. "There's no way you can enforce that."

"Do you want to challenge me?"

"I thought we'd decided not to challenge or compete with each other?"

"That was then, and this is now," he countered. The lines bracketing Joseph's mouth eased. "I don't want to fight with you, Crystal. We share a child and what we want no longer matters. We have to keep in mind that anything and everything we say or do will affect our daughter. You admit to growing up with dueling parents, while if my parents argued, which I'm certain they did, they didn't do it around their children."

Crystal didn't drop her eyes. "You have to understand that I haven't had to share Merry with anyone. It's always been the two of us from the moment she was born."

Moving closer, Joseph cradled her face between his palms. "That's because you believed you didn't have a choice. That has to change, because there's no way I'm *not* going to be a part of my daughter's life."

"Do you think that's possible with you living here in Florida and me in New York?"

"Any- and everything is possible. If your father didn't have a heart attack, or if I hadn't offered to pick up a friend from the airport, who knows when we would've met again?"

Crystal placed her hands over his. "So you believed we would meet again."

Joseph nodded. "We were destined to meet again."

"You believe in destiny." Her question was a statement.

"Yes."

Crystal had no comeback. Her connection with Joseph was something she wouldn't be able to explain if her life depended upon it. When talking to Selena at the family reunion, the pastry chef had updated her as to her enterprise with ColeDiz, but not once did she divulge that Joseph had asked about her.

"I have to go. Merry needs to eat dinner and get her hair washed, and we always have a knock-down, drag-out battle royal when that occurs."

Joseph lowered his hands. "Why don't you let me wash her hair?"

"You don't know what you're in for."

He lifted his shoulders. "Well, there's only one way to find out."

They left the hospital, Crystal riding back to the house where she'd grown up with Jasmine driving, and Joseph following closely behind with Merry in her car seat.

During the ride, she scrolled through her smart phone directory, sending an email to family members about Raleigh's upcoming surgery. "I just sent every Eaton an email blast about Daddy."

Jasmine gave her a quick glance. "You know they're going to descend on Florida like college kids on spring break."

"You should be able to put up some of them. Two of your bedrooms have king-size beds and the other two queen. All of the love seats in the sitting rooms convert into beds, and so do the sofa and love seats in the living and family rooms. Those you can't accommodate can stay with Uncle Solomon and Aunt Holly."

"Why would they want to stay with me? I'm an Eaton in name only."

"Mother, stop it. You're just as much an Eaton as Selena or the others who married into the family. Even though she married Xavier, Selena thinks of herself as an Eaton because of Lily."

"Is it the same with Merry being a Cole?"

Crystal stared out the passenger-side window. Joseph had stated in no uncertain terms that Merry was a Cole, and subject to all of the edicts, mandates and decrees the name epitomized.

"Yes, Mama. The same way Merry is a Cole."

Running her hand through her hair, Jasmine pushed it off her forehead. "It used to work my last nerve when you called me Mama. But now I kind of like the sound of it."

"That's because you're a grandmama."

"I love being a grandmama."

Jasmine signaled, turning off onto a private road with a Sands Point Residents Only sign pointing the way to the gated community. She activated the eight-foot wrought-iron gate and drove through, Joseph following closely behind her late-model Jaguar sedan.

"I like Joseph," Jasmine said softly as she touched another button on the remote, the door to a two-car garage rising smoothly, quietly.

"So do I," Crystal said, as she lowered her window and waved for Joseph to pull into the garage and park beside Jasmine's car. "I told Daddy he could stay here with us once he's discharged from the hospital."

Jasmine cut off the engine. "Now you tell me."

Shifting slightly, Crystal turned to meet her mother's eyes. "Would you prefer I go to his house, Mother, where I'd run into his THOT?"

"What the heck is a THOT?"

"It's slang for ho or That Ho Over There."

It took several seconds before Jasmine caught her meaning. "No. I don't need you getting into it with your father's *lady* friend. We'll talk about this later. Let's go inside where it's cool." She pressed the back of her hand to her forehead. "I don't know why I'm so bothered by the heat."

"It's called hot flashes, Mother." Crystal gave her a saccharine smile when Jasmine rolled her eyes. "I'll be in as soon as I get my bags out of Joseph's truck."

She watched as Joseph unbuckled Merry from her car seat and gently picked her up as if she were fragile bone china. They shared a smile as Merry dropped her head to his shoulder. She knew her baby was hot and tired.

Joseph felt as if he'd entered a high-end furniture showroom with meticulously decorated spaces utilizing light, color and fabrics when walking into the living room. The result was an esthetic assault on his senses. "Who decorated the house?" he asked Crystal as held out her arms for their daughter.

Joseph's expression was similar to many who'd come to her mother's home for the first time. "Mother."

"Don't believe her," Jasmine called out as she headed for the curving staircase. "My daughter is very modest when it comes to taking credit for her incredible talent. Joseph, please come upstairs. I'll show you where you can put Crystal's luggage."

Picking up the bags off the carpeted floor, he followed Jasmine up the stark-white limestone stairs with mahogany banisters and newel posts.

"And my mother can take credit for every piece of art," Crystal said to his retreating back.

It hadn't really mattered to Joseph if the design of the interior was a singular or collaborative effort. The result was sophisticated elegance. He felt like a kid in a candy shop, not knowing where to look or what he wanted.

Craning his neck, Joseph peered in through the open doors of bedrooms on the second story. "How many bedrooms do you have?"

Jasmine smiled at him over her shoulder. "Four. Two with eastern exposure and the other two with southern to take advantage of light throughout the day. Crystal wants her father to convalesce here, which means we're going to be kept busy entertaining Eatons." She stopped at a bedroom on the east end of the hallway. "This is Crystal's room. There's a portable crib in one of the closets."

Joseph entered the bedroom suite, trying to imagine Crystal as a little girl growing up in the house with lush gardens and beautiful water views. "Do you know why she decided to live in New York?"

"That's something you'll have to ask her because I've made it a practice not to interfere when it comes to Crystal's relationships. I will tell her if she asks for my opinion, but that's where it begins and ends." Jasmine touched his arm. "I'll see you downstairs."

Begins and ends. Joseph found the two words profound. His love affair had begun when he saw her checking into her penthouse apartment, and he hadn't wanted to believe it would end when he placed the love bracelet on her wrist. He didn't know if she planned to return to New York to live once her father received medical clearance to resume his former lifestyle.

It no longer mattered if she lived in Florida or New York, because Joseph intended to be an integral part of his daughter's life with or without Crystal's consent. He hoped they would be able to resolve whatever differences they had before forcing a legal determination. Once a family court judge intervened, there would be no winners, but losers.

He set the bags at the foot of the bed before crossing the bedroom suite and opening the closet. Most of the shelves and racks were empty. Joseph found the box with the crib on a shelf with plastic storage containers filled with crib sheets and blankets wrapped in tissue paper.

Removing the crib from the box, he found the enclosed tools needed to assemble it, then slipped the fitted sheet over the mattress.

"You look as if you've done this before."

Joseph glanced to find Crystal sitting on the tapestry-covered bench at the foot of the bed. Merry sat on the carpet floor. "This is my first time putting a crib together." He stood up, watching his daughter pull herself up, using the bench for support before taking four wobbly steps. She fell on her bottom, rolled over and crawled back to the bench.

"Don't help her," Crystal said quickly when Joseph took a step. "She can do it by herself."

He stared, mesmerized by the chubby legs and feet of his daughter, who squealed in delight as she managed to take at least ten steps before collapsing on the carpet. "When did she start walking?"

Crystal saw the rapt expression on Joseph's face as he stared at Merry. "She's been walking around holding on for more than a month. It was only a couple of days ago that she decided to strike out on her own. Now that she's walking I have to child-proof the apartment."

"Your mother needs to put a gate at the top and bottom of the staircase." Going to his knees, Joseph clapped his hands. "Merry. Come to Daddy."

Merry hesitated, then let go of her grip on the bench. Arms upraised in order to maintain her balance, she walked toward Joseph laughing hysterically. She ran into his arms, squealing uncontrollably when he tossed her in the air.

Crystal pushed off the bench. "I'm going to run the water for her bath. And if you're going to wash her hair, then I recommend you take off your shirt because you're going to be drenched."

Joseph pulled Merry close to his chest, kissing her hair. "Why does her hair smell like applesauce?" he asked, walking into the bathroom.

Sitting on the edge of the garden tub, Crystal tested the temperature of the water flowing into the tub. "She's learning to feed herself and most times there's more food in her hair or on her face than what goes into her mouth."

"Is she getting enough nutrition?"

Crystal gave him a quick look and then turned off the water. "She's not underweight."

"Just checking," he said under his breath.

"After I brush her teeth, you can put her in the tub. And

please don't take your eyes off her." Crystal opened a drawer under the vanity and took out a cellophane-wrapped toothbrush. Picking up a sample tube of toothpaste, she squeezed out a minute drop and brushed the tiny white teeth, followed by holding the toothbrush under water, then running the wet bristles over Merry's teeth. She undressed her, then handed her to Joseph. "She's all yours."

Joseph knelt near the tub, his hand covering Merry's back as she splashed water; droplets of water dotted the front of his shirt. Now he knew why Crystal had warned him to take it off. She returned with a towel, face cloth and plastic bottles filled with baby wash and shampoo.

"Should I give her a bath first?"

Crystal knelt beside him. "I'll bathe her and then you can wash her hair." She took over, quickly washing the toddler, then using the retractable nozzle, rinsed the soap off the chubby body. She smiled at Joseph. "She's all yours."

Picking up the bottle of shampoo, he poured a small amount on his palm, pausing when Merry stared at him with wide, dark eyes as if she knew what was coming next.

Joseph disarmed her when he began singing a song in Spanish his grandmother had sung to him as a child. It was a nursery rhyme about the *coquí,* a tiny frog native to Puerto Rico, which spied a bug twice its size and had to figure out how to trap it for its dinner.

Merry was so engrossed in the strange words coming from him that she didn't react to his washing her hair. He repeated the ditty over and over while making the whistling sound of the *coquí,* as Merry sang along in her childish babble.

He motioned for Crystal to give him the retractable nozzle. Leaning his daughter backward, he managed to rinse the shampoo from her hair without water going onto her face and into her eyes.

Joseph lifted Merry out of the tub, handing her to her mother. "Mission accomplished."

Crystal narrowed her eyes at her daughter. "You little traitor. You give me grief every time I wash your hair."

"She wouldn't give you grief if you sing to her in Spanish and make funny sounds."

"I can make funny sounds, but I can't speak or sing in Spanish."

"Don't worry about Merry learning Spanish. My mother and grandmother will definitely teach her."

Crystal concentrated on drying Merry. How could she forget that her daughter had another set of grandparents? "When do you plan to tell them about her?"

Joseph shook his head. "I'll tell them tomorrow."

"I know it's going to be a little crazy around here after Daddy comes here to convalescence, but if they want to see Merry, then let them know they're welcome to come."

Joseph met her eyes, nodding. "I'll be certain to let them know." A beat passed. "I'd like you to answer one question for me."

Crystal blinked. "What is it?"

"Why didn't you contact me when you found out you were pregnant?"

Rocking Merry back and forth, Crystal closed her eyes. "Would you have believed I was carrying your child three months after our separation? I'm certain your first thought would've been that I'd slept with another man and was attempting to pass it off as yours." She opened her eyes, seeing an expression of indecision flit over Joseph's features. "I got my period every month for the first six months, so I'd assumed I *wasn't* pregnant. I'd gained a few pounds, but it wasn't enough to make me believe I was carrying a child.

"I knew something wasn't quite right when certain foods I used to eat gave me heartburn, so I stopped eating spicy dishes. Then I knew something was wrong when I started throwing up. A doctor's visit confirmed I didn't have a stomach virus but that I was pregnant. The doctor didn't know how far along I was until a sonogram indicated I was in my second trimester and I was having a girl. It took a while even before I told my parents and even longer to tell them who the baby's father was."

"So you decided to have the baby and raise it by yourself."

"What other option did I have, Joseph?"

Rubbing his thumb over her cheekbone, Joseph leaned in closer and kissed her. "You could've called me even if you were carrying another man's baby. I would've claimed it as my own because I love you. I love you and anything that is a part of you."

A single tear found its way down Crystal's cheek as she cried without making a sound. What had she done? She'd cheated Joseph out of the first year of his daughter's life and Merry did not have her father in her life.

"What are we going to do, Joseph?"

He caught the tear on his tongue, tasting the saltiness. "We're not going to do anything until your father is better. I don't want to put any pressure on you about what I want for us and our daughter's future."

Crystal looped her free arm around Joseph's neck. She pressed her forehead to his. "Thank you." She wanted to tell him that she loved him, had always loved him, yet the words were lodged in her throat. "I think it's time we put *our* daughter to bed."

Joseph stared at Merry, blissfully asleep in her mother's arms. "Do you give her a bottle before she goes to sleep?"

"No, because I don't want food on her teeth overnight. She's learned to drink from a sippy cup and I only use a bottle when traveling. I told *your* daughter the next time she bites the top off the nipple it will be her last bottle."

"So, she's *my* daughter when she does something naughty, and I assume she's *your* daughter when she's a good girl."

A warm smile spread across Crystal's face like the rising sun. "You learn fast, don't you?"

Joseph stood, cupping a hand under Crystal's elbow to assist her in standing. "I need to learn one more thing."

"What's that?"

"How to put on a diaper."

Crystal blew him a kiss. "Let's go, Daddy. Class is in session."

Chapter 15

"Is this some kind of sick joke?"

Joseph knew he'd shocked his mother when she stared at him as if he'd lost his mind. He slowly shook his head. "No, Mom, it's not a joke. I just found out today that I have a daughter."

Raquel Cole-Wilson buried her face in her hands, her shoulders shaking as she tried not to break down. "Why? How?"

Moving closer to his mother on the love seat in the family room, Joseph draped an arm around her shoulders. He told her what Crystal had revealed about her atypical pregnancy. "If I hadn't walked into that terminal, I would've spent the rest of my life not knowing that I had a daughter."

Sniffling, Raquel pressed her fingertips to her eyes. "Thank goodness you did. Now, when are we going to meet your little Merry?"

"Who are we going to meet?"

Joseph stood up when his father walked into the room, giving him a rough embrace. "My daughter."

"Your what!"

Whenever he looked at his father, Joseph knew what he would look like in another thirty years. Those who saw them together claimed he was Joseph Sr.'s younger clone.

Raquel patted the cushion beside her. "Sit down, Joseph," she said in Spanish, "and let our son explain to you what he discovered earlier today."

Joseph watched his father's expression change from shock to amusement. "I know you guys have been bitchin' about wanting grandchildren, so you've got your wish. It didn't happen the way any of us would've liked or wanted, but what's important is that she's here."

Joseph Sr. grunted. "I can't believe you got involved with Judge Eaton's niece. When are you getting married?"

"Please, Dad. Don't get ahead of yourself."

"You're not going to marry her?"

"Don't put words in my mouth, Dad!"

Raquel placed a hand on her husband's fisted one. "*M'ijo,* please. You have to let your children handle their own affairs."

"And don't forget, *m'ija,* that we didn't raise our sons to be baby daddies."

Joseph pushed to his feet. "Crystal and I have yet to discuss our future, but in the meantime if you want to meet your granddaughter, then please let me know."

Raquel stood. "What about tomorrow?" She looked at her husband, then her son. "I'll get Eduardo to cover for me," she said quickly.

An inner voice told Joseph his mother would not wait until Monday. It was the only day in the week when Marimba closed for business. "I'll call Crystal to let her know you're coming. What about you, Dad?"

"I'm coming, too."

"Good. I'll let you know what time I'll pick you up." He kissed his mother and then rested a hand on his father's head. *"Buenas noches."*

He left the house through a side door and to his truck parked in the circular driveway. As soon as he stared the engine, Joseph activated the Bluetooth feature, tapping the screen for Diego's cell. "Yo, *primo.* I'm calling to tell you that I'm taking the next two weeks off."

"What's wrong?"

Joseph smiled. "Nothing's wrong. In fact, everything is wonderful."

"Is this about a woman?"

His smile faded. "How did you know?"

"Come on, José. You've been moping around, working twice as hard and putting longer hours than necessary for more than a year. At first I thought it was because you wanted to take over as CEO now rather than later, but when I asked you about it you said you were in no hurry to run ColeDiz. That's when I figured it had to be a woman. Am I right or am I wrong?"

His smile was back. "You're right." Joseph had no intention of telling Diego about Crystal, because once his parents met her, the entire Cole grapevine would explode.

Diego's laugh filled the truck. "Take all the time you need, *primo.*"

"How about six weeks?" Joseph's query was followed by a swollen silence. "Diego?"

"I don't have a problem with six weeks. Six weeks brings us to the end of the year. Are you trying to say we should plan on a New Year's Eve wedding celebration?"

"No, I'm not." Joseph wanted nothing more than to exchange vows with Crystal with friends and family members in attendance, yet even if he proposed, he wasn't certain she would accept. The only thing that was a certainty was his love for her.

Joseph stared through the windshield, driving along streets he navigated without concentrating. He decelerated and then maneuvered onto the road where his new home was nearing completion.

Construction had been delayed several times when either the materials the contractor ordered from Europe were unavailable or the inventory wasn't enough to complete a floor or the tiles for the swimming pool. Joseph hadn't put his condo on the market, wanting to do so just before he was scheduled to move into the house to list it with a Realtor.

He stopped and stared at the house's subtle Mediterranean-styled architecture with ocean views. His landscape architect cousin, Regina Spencer, and her daughter, Eden, had drawn up the plans to design the grounds with tropical landscaping and formal hedges. The roof, made up of French clay tiles with a foam setting, made it more resistant to hurricane-force wind.

Putting the truck in gear, Joseph drove the short distance to the apartment in a high-rise he'd called home for the past decade. He wasn't superstitious by nature, yet he could dismiss the fact that the completion of his home coincided with his reuniting with Crystal. Call it coincidence, serendipity, chance, providence or good karma. It was all good.

Crystal exchanged a smile with Joseph when Raquel sat Merry on her knee and sang the "Itsy-Bitsy Spider," while at the same simulating a spider crawling up her arm. It had taken the toddler a while to warm up to her paternal grandmother until Raquel launched into the *coquí* song Joseph had distracted her with the night before.

Dr. Joseph Cole-Wilson appeared visibly stunned by the existence of the little girl, and had spent the past half hour staring at her.

Rising to her feet, Crystal nodded to Joseph. "Joseph, will you please help in the kitchen?"

She now felt comfortable enough to leave Merry alone to bond with her grandparents. She'd felt apprehensive meeting Joseph's parents for the first time, while at the same time she welcomed their presence because it helped her not dwell on her father's surgical procedure.

The hospital had promised to call her once he was transferred to ICU. She wanted to see him even if sedated to reassure herself he had survived hours of surgery.

Joseph took her hand, pulling her into the kitchen, and covered her mouth with his in a passionate kiss that stole her breath. "You don't know how long I've wanted to do that," he explained, staring deeply into her startled gaze.

Crystal's curved her arms under his shoulders, holding on to him like a drowning swimmer. "It's my fault for not trusting—"

"Don't you dare apologize," he warned, cutting her off and kissing the end of her nose. "You did what you believed you had to do, so the issue is moot. Your only concern should be making certain your father regains his health."

She rose on tiptoe, burying her face against his warm throat. "I spent the night tossing and turning because I couldn't stop thinking about Daddy. I…" Her words trailed off when the phone rang. Pulling out of Joseph's embrace, she picked up the receiver on the wall phone. Crystal went completely still when she listened to the woman asking that she come to the hospital to straighten out a familial conflict. Her father's fiancée was making a scene because it was against hospital policy to give someone other than family the status on a patient. "I'll be there as soon as possible." She hung up and shook her head.

"What's the matter?" Joseph asked, seeing the distress on her face.

"I have to go to the hospital. My father's fiancée is acting up because they won't give her any information on him. I need to use your truck. Wait. Who's going to look after Merry?" Jasmine had gone into the gallery to meet with a client.

"Calm down, sweetie. I'll drive you to the hospital while my parents take care of Merry."

She shook her head. "I can't dump her on them."

"It has nothing to do with dumping. They're her grandparents, Crystal."

Pressing her fingertips to her temples, Crystal attempted to massage away the tension tightening around her forehead. She'd found herself between a rock and a hard place. She had enough to worry about without having to deal with a woman who thought nothing of going off on strangers.

"Okay. Please let's go so I can get this over with."

Crystal didn't know what to expect from her father's fiancée, but it wasn't the tiny woman wearing body-hugging designer jeans while teetering in five-inch, seven-hundred-dollar pumps. A thick fringe of fake lashes obscured her vision so much she had to tilt her chin to see. The size of the diamond solitaire on her left hand screamed *six figures*.

However, Crystal could see why Raleigh had been attracted to her. Her smooth tawny brown complexion, doll-like features and short, coiffed black hair made her a standout.

"Ms. Davis, only Raleigh's immediate family members are allowed to see him while he's in ICU. Once he's out you'll be able to see him."

Tonya gave Crystal a once-over look and then wrinkled her

nose as if smelling something malodorous. "I am family. Leigh and I are going to be married on Christmas Eve."

"It's not Christmas Eve and you're not his wife."

"Look, bitch!" Tonya screamed, garnering the attention of those sitting at the visitors' desk. "No one in this hospital is going to stop me from seeing my fiancé. Leigh told me all about you. How you were always jealous of his wives, and that you wouldn't have anything to do with them. Well, let me school you about Tonya Davis. I always get my way, so I want you to put my name on the damn list before I sue you and this hospital."

Crystal struggled to control her temper. "If you don't get out of my face, this bitch will forget her home training and make you regret waking up this morning."

Tonya fluttered her lashes. "Don't you dare threaten me."

"And don't you dare try to intimidate me," Crystal countered. "Now please leave this hospital before I have security escort you out."

"Hey, baby. Are you all right?"

Crystal turned around to find Joseph standing a few feet away. She didn't know how much he'd overheard. "My father's fiancée was just leaving. She was under the impression that she's immediate family, but I think we've cleared up her misunderstanding. Right, Ms. Davis?"

"Wrong, bitch!" Tonya pointed an air-brushed nail at Joseph. "And who the hell are you?"

Joseph gave her a feral grin. "You don't want to know. Now, if you continue to insult my client I'll be forced to sue you for defamation of character."

Tonya pushed out her lips. "You don't scare me, slick."

Joseph signaled to a security guard who'd come to check out the commotion. "My client's father is currently undergoing heart surgery, and this woman isn't on the list of authorized visitors. Could you please escort her off the premises?"

The guard crooked a finger at Tonya. "Let's go, miss." Tonya wasn't given a choice when she strutted across the lobby and through the sliding doors.

Curving an arm around Crystal's waist, Joseph led her out

of the hospital to the nearby parking lot. "I can't believe your father left your mother for *that*."

Crystal grunted under her breath. "She looks good compared to some of the others. However, what she has is less class than his other wives, excluding my mother, of course. I talked Mother into agreeing to let Daddy convalesce at her house, but there's no way she's going to let Tonya Davis cross her threshold."

"The fact that your mother lives in a private, gated community will definitely keep her at a distance."

Crystal wanted to agree with Joseph, yet she knew Tonya wasn't going to sit around and wait for Raleigh Eaton to come back to her. "I have to rent a car because I don't want to rely on you and Mother to chauffer me around."

"I can arrange for you use one of ColeDiz's company cars."

"I don't work for ColeDiz."

Opening the passenger-side door, Joseph waited for Crystal to sit before rounding the vehicle to sit beside her. "I'll drive the company car and you can use this tank."

She gave him a smile. "That sounds like a plan."

Crystal pressed her nose to the oval window of the sleek corporate jet, watching the snowy New York State landscape come closer with the aircraft's descent. She was returning to New York after five weeks, not as a resident but a vacationer.

The days and nights had passed so quickly Crystal had to check the calendar to verify the date. Her father appeared quite content living and recuperating under the roof of his first wife. He cooperated with his therapist and dietitian and slowly resumed many of the activities he'd enjoyed before the heart attack. Raleigh enjoyed reading to his granddaughter, swimming in the in-ground pool, while keeping in contact with his many clients via the internet.

After several volatile telephone conversations with Tonya, he called off their engagement and Crystal celebrated in private because the toxic relationship had begun to adversely affect his convalescence.

Every weekend, she and Jasmine entertained Eatons, whether

from New Jersey, Pennsylvania, West Virginia, Washington, D.C., Kentucky, South Carolina or Texas, who'd come to visit with Raleigh.

And as promised Joseph took a leave of absence from ColeDiz, spending every spare moment with Merry, who reveled in her new mode of independent locomotion. Crystal noticed she was getting taller and slimmer and adding words to her ever-increasing vocabulary. She followed Joseph around as if he were the Pied Piper, and a few times Crystal felt as if she were losing her baby to a man she'd come to love beyond description.

Joseph had surprised her one day when he suggested going for an afternoon drive. She knew when he maneuvered up an unpaved path to a newly constructed house that he wanted her to see the inside of his home. He hadn't asked her to decorate the mansion again, yet she knew it was what he wanted. Their relationship had changed from former lovers to friends and parents of a little girl.

Crystal didn't know what she would've done if Joseph hadn't been there to see to Merry's needs, because there were times when she'd experienced emotional overload. The home health aide saw to Raleigh's basic physical demands until he was able to shower and dress himself. A cleaning service came in twice a week to do housework, leaving Crysal the jobs of making beds, putting up loads of laundry and cooking. Even with Jasmine taking time off and occasionally closing the gallery when her assistant wasn't available, Crystal had assumed the full responsibility of running a household.

In the past it had only been herself, and then as a stay-at-home mother with Merry. Her days were very structured because she was able to accomplish many of her tasks around her daughter's nap time, but all that had changed since returning to Florida.

Two nights ago, Joseph had come into her bedroom and announced he was taking her away for a week. He'd made arrangements with Jasmine and hired a housekeeper to take care of everything during their absence.

When asked about Merry, he said Raquel would share in babysitting their granddaughter. Both grandmothers soothed her fear of leaving her child for the first time, and Crystal reluctantly agreed to get away and relax.

Now her ears popped from the loss of cabin pressure as the pilot brought the jet down smoothly on a private runway, taxiing until it came to a complete stop.

When she'd boarded the jet, a flight attendant informed her an onboard chef would offer breakfast as soon as they were airborne. Crystal got to see firsthand the exquisite service afforded anyone flying in the ColeDiz Gulfstream G650 business jet.

Joseph unbuckled his seat belt, stood up and extended his hand. "Let's go, sweetie."

Crystal slipped her arms into her ski jacket.

"Where are we going?" It seemed like the umpteenth time she'd asked Joseph that question, and his answer was always the same: *You'll see.*

"We're going to a cabin in the woods."

She stared at his broad shoulders under a heavy fisherman's knit sweater. "I'm not an outdoorsy girl, Joseph. I've never been one to rough it in the wilderness."

"You won't have to rough it. You'll have all of the conveniences of home."

Joseph shook the hand of the pilot. The flight attendant lowered the steps as the copilot gathered their luggage.

He descended the stairs, holding tightly on to Crystal as snowflakes swirled around them. The meteorologists had predicted snow, and thankfully they'd landed as it had begun.

Joseph had just thanked the remaining members of the flight crew when the door and trunk to a car parked on the tarmac opened. The driver opened the rear door and in under a minute Joseph and Crystal were seated in the rear of the heated sedan and their bags stored in the trunk.

She stared out the side window. The snow was coming down faster. "How far is the cabin in the woods?"

"Not too far."

Crystal watched the passing landscape through a curtain

of falling snow as the driver maneuvered up a winding road, coming to a stop in front of a cabin surrounded by towering pine trees.

Joseph helped her out and they sprinted to the front door, leaving the driver to follow with their bags. He unlocked the door, and a blast of warmth forced Crystal to take a backward step. "Nice!" The single word slipped out unbidden.

She flipped a wall switch, and light from table lamps illuminated the space with a wood-burning stove, a leather sofa group, a love seat and club chairs with footstools. Rugs made of animal skin and fur covered the rustic wooden floor. She untied her snow boots, leaving them on the mat inside the door, then took off her jacket and hung it on a wall hook.

Crystal took a quick tour of the cabin. She found a kitchen with a fully stocked refrigerator/freezer. It was rustic with the modern convenience of indoor plumbing. A king-size bed took up most of the space in the small bedroom. It'd been a long time since she'd shared a bed with Joseph, and she looked forward to falling asleep and waking up in his embrace. She'd been too overwhelmed caring for her father and her daughter to think about making love.

Most nights when she went to bed she fell asleep within minutes of her head touching the pillow. Whenever Joseph's body would innocently brush against hers, the urges she'd repressed surfaced. And once he told her he was taking her away, Crystal wasn't certain whether he wanted to use the occasion for them to sleep together again, but this time she was prepared. She'd purchased a supply of condoms.

Opening another door, she discovered a miniscule bathroom with a shower stall, vanity and commode.

The last door at the rear of the cabin doubled as a woodshed, mudroom and laundry room. Heat, running water and electricity.

Crystal had returned to the living/dining area when Joseph shouldered the door closed and set the bags down. He met her eyes. "Is it too primitive for you?"

"It's perfect. How did you find this place?"

"It belongs to my parents." Joseph didn't see her jaw drop with his disclosure. "Dad pays someone to look after it when he's not here. That's why the fridge is full. My dad went to college and medical school in New England, where he'd learned to ski. One winter he came up here to ski and discovered he couldn't get lodging because everything was booked up. So the next spring he bought this place. My mother doesn't like cold-weather sports, so she hangs out here in the cabin while Dad's on the slopes."

Crystal sat on a club chair, resting her sock-covered feet on the footstool. "Do you ski?"

"No. And I have no interest in learning. What about you?"

Crystal shook her head. "I don't like being cold."

Sitting opposite her, Joseph gave Crystal a long, penetrating stare. "I don't want you to think I brought you here because I want to seduce you."

"What should I think, Joseph?"

"That I love you and I care what happens to you. I saw you wearing yourself down taking care of your father and our daughter. Maybe I'm selfish, but I need you and Merry needs you."

She lowered her eyes, staring at her clasped fingers. "What do you want, Joseph?"

Joseph's gaze lingered on the hair framing her lovely face. "I want you to learn to trust me. I'm no longer a stranger to you, so you should know that I'll never deliberately break your heart."

"I've always trusted you."

"Did you really, Crystal? You were the one who said I wouldn't believe that you were carrying my baby because we'd been separated for months."

"I suppose I underestimated you."

"Yes, you did."

She glared at him. "You don't have to sound so smug."

"Smug or arrogant?" he teased.

"Both," she said, smiling. "But I wouldn't have you any other way." Crystal paused, knowing what she was going to tell Joseph would change her forever. "I love you, José Ibrahim Cole-Wilson. I love your subtle arrogance, your insufferable sense of entitlement, your generosity, your patience and the way you make me feel whenever we make love."

"I have a laundry list of why I love you, Crystal Riesa Eaton."

"How do you know my middle name?" She rarely used her middle name or even initial except on official documents.

Joseph's smile was as intimate as a kiss. "Your uncle told me."

"Which one?"

"Solomon." He had reunited with his mentor when Solomon came to visit his brother. Joseph and the jurist spent hours together discussing law. Solomon admitted he knew who'd fathered Merry the instant he saw her, but he respected his niece's decision not to identify her daughter's father.

"Why would Uncle Solomon tell you my middle name?"

"He alluded to our names on a marriage license, and when we do decide to marry, he wants the honor of officiating. He's aware of the Cole family tradition of marrying on New Year's Eve."

Crystal slumped back in the chair. "You want to marry?"

Joseph shook his head. "No, Crystal. I don't want to marry. I want to marry *you*."

Her eyelids fluttered. "You're ready for marriage?"

His whole face spread into a smile. "I was ready the first night you came to Club José for dinner." He sobered. "I don't know what there was about you that tied me up in knots, and I regretted ever giving you a choice as to where our relationship would lead. And I knew that what happens in Charleston stays in Charleston was nothing more than a boatload of BS, yet I went along with it because I didn't want to do to you what my ex had done to me, and that is pressure you into doing something you didn't or couldn't do."

Crystal knew it was time to stop fooling herself into believing she didn't want Joseph as a part of her life and future. She gave the man sitting across from her with his hands sandwiched between his denim-covered knees a direct stare. "Ask me, Joseph."

He blinked once. "Ask you what?"

"Ask me to marry you."

His hands moved to his knees. "Don't play with my head."

"I'm not playing. If you don't ask me now, then the topic is moot, counselor."

Coming off the chair, Joseph went to his knees in front of Crystal. His eyes came up to meet hers. He held her hands in a gentle grip. "Crystal Riesa Eaton, will you do me the honor of becoming my wife?"

Crystal smiled tentatively, knowing her response would change both of them forever. "Yes, José Ibrahim Cole-Wilson. I will marry you."

She didn't have time to react when she found herself in Joseph's arms, his mouth covering hers in an explosive kiss.

They would marry New Year's Eve in West Palm Beach like Coles in the past. However, this wedding was certain to attract a lot of attention because it would join two of Florida's most prominent families—the Eatons and the Coles.

Epilogue

Crystal, staring at her reflection in the full-length mirror on the closet door, didn't believe she was about to become Mrs. Joseph Cole-Wilson. When she and Joseph informed their families they would marry on New Year's Eve at the Cole family compound, Jasmine called a preeminent Miami wedding planner to coordinate what was to become the wedding of the season.

Invitations were mailed to every Cole and Eaton, and as the acceptances were received, the quandary as where to house their out-of-town guests became an exercise in logistics.

All of the Coles had arrived on Christmas Eve in time for their annual weeklong family reunion, while the Eatons who'd reserved blocks of rooms in various West Palm Beach hotels arrived throughout the holiday week. They joined the many Coles the night before for a rehearsal dinner in the mansion's grand ballroom.

Two other images appeared in the mirror, and Crystal turned to find her mother and father dressed in their wedding finery as father and mother of the bride. Jasmine was stunning in a black-and-white-striped satin gown with long sleeves and a squared neckline. Raleigh looked very handsome in a black tuxedo, a white dress shirt and a black-and-white-striped silk tie.

Crystal held her arms out at her sides. "How do I look?" She'd selected a platinum A-line Melissa Sweet silk duchesse satin gown with a sweep train and cap sleeves. Five-inch Christian Louboutin white satin pumps and a tulle cathedral-length veil secured in the chignon on the nape of her neck completed her wedding dress.

Jasmine crossed her hands over her chest as she blinked back tears before they fell and ruined her makeup. She exhaled a soft gasp. "You look like an angel. Doesn't she, Raleigh?"

Raleigh crossed the room and took his daughter's hands, bringing them to his mouth and kissing her fingers. "Yes, she does." He checked his watch. "It's time we head downstairs because we don't want everyone to think you're going to be a runaway bride."

Crystal smiled up at her father. He'd regained the healthy color in his face and his once dull hair was lustrously silver. A network of fine lines around his shiny dark eyes added rather than detracted from his middle-aged attractiveness. She'd thought herself blessed to have two parents that complemented each other in so many ways they'd sought to deny or ignore.

She pressed her cheek to Raleigh's clean-shaven one. "The only place I'm running tonight is into the arms of my husband."

Smiling, Raleigh winked at his daughter. "It's hard to put into words, but I…I'm so proud of you, Crystal. I'm sure you learned from your parents how not to make the same mistakes we did. You and Joseph are marrying because you love each other, but it's taken more than thirty years for your mother and me to face the truth that we belong together."

Crystal's jaw dropped as she tried processing what she'd just heard. "You and Mother?"

Jasmine crossed the room, her arms going around the waist of her daughter and ex-husband. "Your father says he likes living with me and we've decided to give it a trial run for a little while. And if we find out we like the arrangement, then maybe we'll think about making it permanent."

Crystal's hands and knees were shaking so much she feared she would collapse where she stood. If someone had told her having Raleigh convalescence at his ex-wife's house would lead to reconciliation, she would've said they were liars.

"This is the best wedding gift anyone could ever give me," she said tearfully.

"Come, darling," Jasmine crooned. "I heard someone say Joseph has been pacing nonstop, wearing a hole in one of the rugs."

Looping her arms over her mother's and father's, Crystal walked out of the bedroom and down a hallway in the twenty-four-room mansion Samuel Claridge Cole had built for his Cuban-born wife and their children in 1928.

Crystal walked into the sitting room amid the excited chatter of her bridesmaids. And in keeping with the holiday-themed colors of black and silver, six of the Eaton women wore black gowns in styles that flattered their bodies. The exception was Selena. As matron of honor her gown was shimmering silver. All wore feathered headpieces, which made them look like graceful black-and-gray swans. Their groomsmen counterparts were huddled together taking bets as to which college football teams would win the various bowl games taking place on New Year's Day.

Initially she only wanted one bridal attendant, but when Joseph revealed he'd chosen his former college roommate as his best man and also his brothers and three male cousins as groomsmen, Crystal knew she had to step up her game and solicit the participation of every thirtysomething Eaton woman, of whom two had married into the family. Angela Chase, of the Louisville, Kentucky, Chases, had become the latest Eaton woman when she married Dr. Levi Eaton in June.

Raleigh cleared his throat, garnering everyone's attention. There was a chorus of gasps and murmurs of approval from the assembly. "I told you she'd look like a model," Selena crowed proudly. As the matron of honor, she'd assumed the responsibility of helping Crystal into her wedding attire.

Raleigh stood straight. "It's time we move into position. I want my daughter married before midnight. That way her husband can claim her as a dependent on this year's tax return." Those familiar with Raleigh Eaton's gift for investing in profitable companies, which paid off handsomely for himself and his clients, laughed.

Jasmine shook her head. "Spoken like a true financial planner."

The bridal party lined up as couples to process out of the house and through a door leading to the Japanese garden. Crystal was given the choice of exchanging vows in the Coles' Japanese or English garden, and she'd chosen the former. And as promised, her uncle Solomon would do the officiating.

From where she stood with her father, Crystal could hear the music of a string quartet coming through the many speakers set up around the twelve-acre property surrounded by tropical foliage, exotic gardens and the reflection of light sparkling off lake waters.

Her knees began to shake and it must have been noticeable because Raleigh tightened his hold around her waist. "It's all right, baby girl. It will be over before you know it."

Closing her eyes, Crystal relaxed as the music changed, segueing into the familiar strains of the "Wedding March."

Raleigh kissed his daughter's hair. "That's our cue."

Crystal felt as if she were a spectator instead of the center attraction when she proceeded over the stone path to where Joseph stood with Frank Lynch.

Joseph, like all of the Cole men, had continued another tradition: they all sported white neckpieces. She smiled at Merry, who'd fallen asleep in Raquel's arms. It was well past her bedtime and only the children over the age of sixteen were permitted to stay up beyond the mandated one o'clock curfew. Joseph had explained that the in-ground pool was covered because the younger children had a habit of jumping into the pool—fully clothed.

The weather was perfect for an outdoor nighttime gathering. Daytime temperatures, topping out close to ninety, had dropped to a balmy seventy-eight with a light breeze coming off the water. A full moon and a clear sky littered with millions of stars silvered the landscape with light.

Joseph stared numbly at the woman moving closer and closer like a vision in a dream. He'd felt himself in suspended animation from the time he slipped the engagement ring on Crystal's finger once they'd returned from New York until less than an hour ago when he began dressing for his wedding. Whenever he woke to find her beside him, he realized the woman in his bed was one he'd willingly give up his life to protect.

"Who gives this woman in marriage?" asked Solomon, his sonorous voice carrying easily in the still of the night.

Raleigh smiled at his brother. "I do." He placed Crystal's hand in Joseph's and then stepped back to sit beside Jasmine.

Judge Solomon Eaton nodded to his former clerk. "Do you, José, take Crystal to be your wife, to love, honor and cherish from this day forth?"

Joseph stared into Crystal's eyes. "I do."

Solomon turned to his niece. "Do you, Crystal, take José, to be your husband, to love, honor and cherish from this day forth?"

She smiled. "I do."

Solomon placed his hands over their clasped hands after they'd exchanged rings. "As you've pledged yourselves each to the other, I do now, by the virtue of the authority vested in me by the state of Florida, pronounce your husband and wife for as long as you both shall live. José, you may kiss your bride."

Joseph dipped Crystal low, kissing her passionately to thunderous applause and wolf whistles. "That's how we Coles do it, baby," he whispered against her lips, easing her upright.

A warming heat filled her chest and face. "You'll pay for that, *mi amor*," she teased with a wide grin. Seconds later fireworks lit up the sky in brilliant color, signaling the beginning of a new year.

Amid a shower of rice, birdseed and flower petals, Joseph and his wife traversed the stone path to a footbridge, where they posed with attendants and family members for wedding pictures and then stood in a receiving line greeting everyone who'd come to celebrate their new life together.

It seemed like an eternity before Crystal was seated at the bridal table with the rest of the wedding party. Guests who were served hors d'oeuvres during the cocktail hour took their seats for the champagne toast offered by Frank Lynch. Raleigh and Selena also offered passionate toasts.

The live Latin band alternated with the DJ for nonstop music throughout the night. Joseph and Crystal shared their first dance as husband and wife, dancing to the Flamingos doo-wop classic "I Only Have Eyes for You."

Crystal danced with her father while Joseph spun Raquel over the dance floor in a spirited salsa. The pulsing Latin rhythms set the stage for a night of unrestrained merriment. Members of the waitstaff and a dozen bartenders circulated efficiently, serving and mixing drinks for nearly three hundred guests. Those of questionable age requesting alcoholic beverages were carded to ascertain whether they were of legal age to drink.

At exactly one o'clock, all those under sixteen were ushered into the house, but not without them protesting loudly.

It was close to four in the morning when Joseph's teenage female cousins crowded around the DJ. The year before, their male cousins had put on an impromptu show during Jason and Greer Cole's reception, stripping down to their boxer-briefs and gyrating à la Channing Tatum's *Magic Mike* to Rihanna's "We Found Love."

Joseph pressed his shoulder to Crystal's. "Watch this, sweetie." He quickly explained what the eight young women had planned to do. "Last year it was the boys, and this year it's their turn."

Crystal laughed until her sides hurt when the young women in matching costumes revealing a prudent amount of skin twerked to Beyoncé's "Crazy In Love." Everyone laughed, gyrated and sang along while their mothers shook their heads in exasperation. The DJ segued into hits made popular by Florida-based artists Flo Rida, Pitbull and Jason Derulo.

Shedding her veil and stilettos, Crystal danced continuously until it came time for her to cut the cake. Instead of tossing her bouquet, she handed it to landscape architect Eden Spencer. "You're next," she whispered, pressing her cheek to the tall, pretty woman with the dimpled smile.

Joseph tapped her arm to get her attention. "It's time we go in and change. We have to board the jet in an hour." They'd planned to honeymoon at one of the family's vacation resorts in the Caribbean. It would be the second time in two months

Crystal would leave her daughter with her overly indulgent grandparents.

The past year had become one she would remember forever. She'd reunited with the love of her life, her parents had reconciled, Merry had met her paternal grandparents and she and Joseph had shared a momentous Christmas and New Year's with their extended family and friends. And she looked forward to the coming months during which she would be kept busy decorating her new home.

Crystal never could've imagined, when checking into the Beaumont House, that the man occupying the neighboring penthouse suite would make her his wife and the mother of his child, but not necessarily in that order.

Reaching for her husband's hand and standing on tiptoe in her bare feet, she touched her lips to his. *"Te amo,"* she whispered in Spanish. Joseph had begun teaching her Spanish, beginning with words of love.

Joseph made love to his wife with his eyes. *"Y yo a ti, mi amor y mi corazón."*

They managed to slip into the house through a side door undetected, to change, and when they reemerged they were ready to begin the year anew as husband, wife, father and mother.

* * * * *

LET'S TALK
Romance

For exclusive extracts, competitions
and special offers, find us online:

- facebook.com/millsandboon
- @MillsandBoon
- @MillsandBoonUK

Get in touch on 01413 063232

For all the latest titles coming soon, visit
millsandboon.co.uk/nextmonth